"This compelling and courageous novel has moved me not only to tears but almost beyond words. . . . I rarely use the world 'brilliant.' I use it now, with respect, about this novel." – Margaret Laurence

"A chilling portrait of how some turn into brutes and others into angels." – *The Financial Post*

"A drama at once moral, illuminating and absorbing." – *The Ottawa Citizen*

"**Berlin Solstice** is a work of the moral imagination, terrifying, fascinating, frighteningly contemporary. It would be unbearable if it were not as compassionate as it is unforgiving." – Sheila Watson

"A searing depiction of greed and corruption, cowardice and hedonism in the period of German history dominated by the Nazi Party . . . **Berlin Solstice** is powerfully written, believably acted out and intelligently plotted." – *The London Free Press*

"Fraser is more than an historical novelist; she is an epic singer for our time." – *The Gazette*

". . . Sylvia Fraser has written a political Grimm's tale so contemporary and compelling it puts her alongside the best of today's fictionists." – Irving Layton

"A novel of operatic scope . . . [Fraser] writes with a moral urgency that makes her story compelling." – *Maclean's*

"Sylvia Fraser has had the guts and the inspired humility to take the true artist's route through the most mind-boggling events of our age. . . . [**Berlin Solstice**] is a remarkably moving and believable reconstruction." – Adele Wiseman

BY SYLVIA FRASER

FICTION
Pandora (1972)
The Candy Factory (1975)
A Casual Affair (1978)
The Emperor's Virgin (1980)
Berlin Solstice (1984)
My Father's House (1987)

SYLVIA FRASER

BERLIN SOLSTICE

M&S

An M&S Paperback from
McClelland & Stewart Inc.
The Canadian Publishers

An M&S Paperback from McClelland & Stewart Inc.

First printing June 1989
Cloth edition printed 1984

Canadian Cataloguing in Publication Data

Fraser, Sylvia
Berlin solstice

(M&S paperback)
ISBN 0-7710-3222-6

1. Germany – History – 1918–1933 – Fiction.
2. Germany – History – 1933–1945 – Fiction.
I. Title.

PS8561.R37B47 1989   C813'.54   C89-093663-3
PR9199.3.F723B47 1989

Cover design by T. M. Craan
Cover photograph by Johnnie Eisen

Typesetting by Pickwick
Printed and bound in Canada

McClelland & Stewart Inc.
The Canadian Publishers
481 University Avenue
Toronto, Ontario
M5G 2E9

To my mother, my sister and Eric

Acknowledgments

Of the hundreds of books which I have read for the preparation of this manuscript, I owe the greatest debt to the following authors and their works:

Anonymous, *A Woman in Berlin*, New York, 1954.
Arendt, Hannah, *Eichmann in Jerusalem: A report on the Banality of Evil*, New York, 1963.
Bailey, George, *Germans*, Cleveland, 1972.
Deschner, Günther, *Reinhard Heydrich*, New York, 1981.
Dodd, Martha, *My Years in Germany*, London, 1939.
Everett, Susan, *Lost Berlin*, London and Chicago, 1979.
Fest, Joachim C., *The Face of the Third Reich*, London, 1970.
Friedländer, Saul, *Counterfeit Nazi*, London and New York, 1969.
Gross, Leonard, *The Last Jews in Berlin*, New York, 1982.
Grunberger, Richard, *The 12-Year Reich*, New York, 1971.
Hillel, Marc; Henry, Clarissa, *Of Pure Blood*, New York, 1976.
Jonge, Alex de, *The Weimar Chronicle*, London, 1978.
O'Donnell, James, *The Bunker*, Boston, 1978.
Pryce-Jones, David, *Unity Mitford: A Quest*, London, 1976.

Reider, Frederick, *The Order of the SS*, London, 1981.
Russell, William, *Berlin Embassy*, New York, 1941.
Shirer, William L., *Berlin Diary*, New York, 1941.
Smith, Howard K., *Last Train from Berlin*, New York, 1942.
Speer, Albert, *Spandau: The Secret Diaries*, London, 1976.
Studnitz, Hans-Georg von, *While Berlin Burns*, New York, 1964.
Waite, Robert G.L., *The Psychopathic God: Adolf Hitler*, New York, 1977

I wish to thank the Canada Council and the Ontario Arts Council for their valuable support in the researching and writing of this manuscript. I also wish to express my appreciation to my editor, Lily Poritz Miller, for her irritating ability to ferret out the flaws of the novel-in-progress.

PART I

"Coming events cast their shadow before."
                                    – J.W. von Goethe

ONE

Berlin

August 1923

I T WAS EXPECTATION that lured Kurt Schmidt back night after night to the Kurfürstendamm, a spine of hot neon cutting a crude yet magical swath through the dark, mean city. Expectation that could be heard in the lick of saxophones from the moist black mouths of cellars and the hum of the crowd drawn out like high notes of a violin. Expectation you could smell in the acrid blend of cabbage-leaf cigars soaked in nicotine, of stale beer, of cheap perfume, of sweat, of sex. It was a giddy feeling that advertised itself in the pelvic thrust of whores in slit skirts and cellophane blouses who twirled lime umbrellas in the doorways of cabarets; in the randy tilt of young boys' caps, their wan faces tipped in lipstick and rouge as they strutted like tomcats on a fence; even in the glint of marquees in the eyes of legless veterans, their uniforms held together by medals as they begged for beer money. It was all around you, sizzling just under the Kurfürstendamm's electric skin – an itchiness that relieved itself in craziness, in violence, in the foolish and the bizarre.

Kurt shoved his way past the display cases that were part of the street's exclusive daytime ambience, sharp nose thrust forward, nostrils dilated. A mongrel dog was dancing on a tightrope at the urgings of its trainer in a clown suit. As bystanders applauded in the sticky August heat, Kurt watched a man, neck bulging like bread dough over his celluloid collar, munch on a Bratwurst in a cardboard trough. Even while Kurt sniffed the succulent sausage, the man discarded the paper and offered the meat to the dog. Resisting the desire to snap at it with his own jaws, Kurt swallowed saliva, tightened the grip on his shopping bags and forged on. His last meal had been a free bowl of horses' entrails ladled out by a woman who had pressed her face so close he could count the hairs of her mustache, smell the reek of her armpits. "With your youth and looks you should be turnin' tricks on the Kurfürstendamm," she chided. "It isn't fair to the others who have nothin' to sell, now is it?"

In Kurt's shopping bags he carried ten million marks, which, given the country's hysterical inflation rate of 20 percent a day, should be enough to buy a beer provided he didn't wait too long. Since defeat in the Great War, followed by strikes, Red Terror, White Terror, a putsch against the shaky Social Democratic republic, unemployment, street fighting, depression and French invasion of the Ruhr, Germany had fallen into economic anarchy in which a postcard that had taken ten pfennigs to send three years ago now cost five million marks; in which businesses and cities had begun to print their own currency secured by food stocks; in which notes were issued on leather, on porcelain, on lace, with the objects themselves guaranteeing their value. Given the government's only solution – to manufacture more and more money so that it now cost more to print a note than its face value – Germany had reverted into a barter society in which wealthier housewives carried dishes of butter instead of purses. Workers insisted on being paid several times a day so they could run out with their suitcases of marks and spend them while they were still worth something. Children played with brown 1,000-mark notes, once the highest denomination the Reichsbank had ever printed. Disgusted shoppers threw away more money than they had expected to make in a lifetime because it was too heavy to carry.

With yearnings honed by the gnawing in his belly and the sour taste in his mouth, Kurt stared over tidy green hedges at women with silver eyeshadow and marcelled hair, sipping Berliner Weisse made of white beer and raspberry syrup, their bare thighs pressed against the shiny black ones of burghers with fists wrapped around Löwenbräus, Spatenbräus, Pilseners, their mouths rimmed with foam. Some drinkers were being serenaded by Bavarians in lederhosen, with mouth organs and accordions, others by gypsies with violins. Some were singing lighthearted drinking songs:

> "When I rise in the morning I'm a man with a barrel,
> When I go to bed I'm a barrel of beer."

At least one group, more in touch with the gritty cynicism of the times, was singing a ditty made fashionable by inflation:

> "We are drinking away our grandma's little cottage
> And her first and second mortgage too!"

Kurt weighed his thirst against the potential humiliation. Last time he had attempted to use marks in one of these West End beer gardens, the waiter had sneered: "We don't take that junk here. Only foreign currency, butter, eggs and cigarettes. That's not worth the paper it's written on."

"It was worth a beer this afternoon," Kurt had protested.

Signaling for the bouncer, the waiter had grunted: "But what will it get me tomorrow?"

Kurt felt something hard then soft bump and rub against him: a whore in short gold skirt with violet boots. Flicking her whip like an abrasive tongue against his thigh, she crooned: "Wanna be my slave? Only ten million and a cigarette." In the yellow gaslight of the Kurfürstendamm's candelabra, filtered through the heart-shaped linden leaves, her face seemed painfully young, even innocent, despite its mask of makeup hardened by truculence. Longing to reach out, to touch the glowing outline of her cheek, Kurt clamped his jaws and yanked back his shopping bags. Her price in marks was negotiable, but the cigarette – that was hard currency, like asking for a piece of the moon. Pushing his hand into the girl's breasts, feeling her nipple sear his palm like the burning tip of the cigarette she had demanded, he growled in a phlegmy voice: "Go home to your father. Go home and clean yourself up."

"Freeloader!" she spat, showing her tongue like a raw pink clam. "Big spender."

Forcing his way between two men in lilac sack suits who refused to unlink arms, Kurt slumped against a kiosk stinking of urine. Already Violet Boots was sizing up another customer, a youth no older than himself, as glossy as a ripe olive, with a Balkan cigarette dangling from his lips, its oversweet scent wrapping them in yellow fog. As she preened, advertising her crude magic, Herr Olive Oil dug deep into his chocolate suede satchel and hauled out a string of sausages. Face coarsened by greed, Violet Boots snatched at the sausages which Herr Olive Oil looped around her neck like a leash. Pulling it tight, he brought Violet Boots to her knees, urged her forward on all fours with a smart whip-crack across the buttocks. Guffawing, the crowd parted for them – another piece of street theater, not much different from the mongrel who danced or the gypsy with Tarot cards and a green parrot that squawked: "The future foretold! The future foretold!"

Kurt struck his hand against the kiosk. "Schieber! War profiteer." His palm stuck to the breast of a nude advertising the Winter Garten. Yanking it away as if from a hot stove, he plunged into the human flow.

Ahead he could see the Gloria Palast cinema ablaze like a neon wedding cake; and beyond that, the Tiergarten, separating the fashionable West from the political, déclassé East – a dark and clammy refuge for the city's bolder and more desperate lovers, for criminals and the homeless, made even more sinister by the coughs and cries of the four thousand exotic animals that inhabited its famous zoo. Clasping his money, Kurt sprinted toward it, sending pedestrians fluttering like starlings. As he neared the cinema, his clog caught on something pulpy, pitching him forward. He found himself groveling at the feet of a one-legged lieutenant propped against a lime tree, his field-gray uniform mended but immaculate, his mustache neatly trimmed, his brass polished as if awaiting review. For a few seconds Kurt stared mesmerized into the fierce and haunted black eyes, like coal pits gouged in an illuminated skull. When the war is over, your father will come home and there will be meat in the soup. You'll have a coat and real boots. *When the war is over . . . When the war is over . . .*

Resisting the impulse to dump his shopping bags in dumb sacrifice on the lap of this proud yet suffering man, Kurt lurched off once more toward the Tiergarten. Ahead he could see tramps collecting for the night like powdery gray moths under the ornate iron gas lamps. He could hear the silky rustle of thousands of birds that nested in the linden trees, and smell the dark wet scent of animal refuse and decay.

When the war is over . . . When the war is over . . . That had been the expectation running like a golden thread through his childhood – the magic refrain that had made the present bearable, even noble. Today's cold, hunger, bad smells, humiliations, were merely a sacrifice for the real life that would begin when the war is over . . . when . . . when . . . when . . . With such hopes Kurt's mother had made the sepia picture of the sad-faced soldier with drooping mustache awkwardly carrying a rifle come alive then grow in dignity and power. One day in November 1918, when Kurt was almost twelve, that future had begun to take concrete shape, like a dim silhouette on the horizon of someone you think you might know. Everyone was talking at once and everyone was saying the same thing: The war is over! The men are coming home. Back from the battlefields of Ypres and Flanders. Back to Germany. Back to Kurt's village, clinging like a burr to the smoky skirt of the city of Dortmund. Suddenly everyone was scrubbing and fixing and sweeping. His mother was mending his father's blue serge suit. Kurt and the other boys were given a holiday to build a triumphal arch of pine boughs while the girls sewed a banner with silver letters: YOUR FATHERLAND SALUTES YOU. The old veterans of other wars had put on their uniforms smelling of mothballs to flank the triumphal arch – an honor guard ushering in the real future.

Kurt stood stiffly by his mother, who was holding the hand of his sister Gretchen, his head held high, wearing a medal he had won for running faster than anyone else. Would his father notice? Would he recognize Kurt? Would Kurt recognize his father?

A shout went up from the crowd. The village's retired policeman came pumping over the hill on his bicycle, the sunlight striking his brass-trimmed helmet. "They're coming! They're at the Old Mill." Kurt stretched even taller and was embarrassed for his manhood when his mother clasped his hand.

Another shout. As the band struck up "Deutschland, Deutschland Uber Alles" and girls threw paper flowers, human shapes appeared on the horizon, grew darker, larger, firmer, but now Kurt had to clamp his jaws so as not to cry out in dismay. Who were these ragged transparent men, many without guns, some carrying red flags, quite a few with bandaged heads, some without shoes and arms, with lumps of coke for eyes? He could make no connection between them and the schoolroom photos of the spike-helmeted Kaiser and his generals, their chests cascading with gold. By comparison even the old veterans, sucking in their stomachs and chewing aniseed drops to sweeten their beer breath, seemed resplendent.

Faces were recognized. Names were called. "Fritz!" "Karl!" "Wilhelm!" Now his mother was shouting: "Ernst! Ernst!" She flung herself into the arms of one of the stickmen – the picture hanging on their wall but deepened and darkened, as if Kurt were looking at the negative. While they hugged, wept, laughed, Kurt stood even more stiffly, waiting till his father at last drew back, looked at his son, revealing the haunted black eyes of the one-legged lieutenant. Reaching out a skeletal hand, he ran it through Kurt's hair . . . just that, an old gesture barely remembered. Then scooping up Gretchen, the daughter he had never seen, he kissed her tenderly and rocked her in his arms.

Kurt looked around him. Everything seemed the same. The houses were as bleak, the sky as bloated with smoke, the cobbles as gritty. What had he expected?

Again his mother and father were hugging, with Gretchen between them. Taking Kurt's hand, Hedda Schmidt drew her son into the family circle, with Kurt stealing glances at his classmates to see how well they had done in the human lottery.

For at least a week the village retained its high pitch of celebration. At the potato shop the women's cheeks glowed as they talked with pride of their husbands' appetites. In the beer gardens the new veterans drowned their memories in schnapps and song while their children compared their trophies – medals and enemy insignia that had emerged from the packets and pockets of the coke-eyed stickpeople. Nothing had come out of Ernst Schmidt's pockets but a book of silly poems. No heroic story of the enemy vanquished fell from his thin sad lips, though Kurt hovered by his side day after day, waiting. When he ventured questions of that strange man now growing less real to him than the portrait on the wall, Ernst Schmidt had merely turned those black, bottomless, fathomless eyes and run his hand through Kurt's hair – that same weary gesture now grown irritating – while his mother intervened: "Hush, hush! That's all done with. We must think of other things."

Later Kurt discovered there had been medals, including the Iron Cross, but by then it was too late. The future was now, and instead of more food the family had less. At first Kurt blamed his father – one more mouth to feed from the same crate of turnips – but it was that way in every house in the village. Children's faces grew as blue as the milk. No matter how humble or desperate, the men could not find work. Rib cages protruded, bellies bloated, everyone coughed and his sister spat blood.

The words "abdication," "blockade" and "reparation" were on everyone's lips. Kaiser Wilhelm II had abdicated, then hot-footed it to Holland. The English and French were still starving the Germans with a blockade, though the war was over. At the same time they were demanding billions of gold marks in reparation. Every day mile-long trains rattled by Kurt's house carrying coal and timber to France while he and his family shivered around a cold stove. Gretchen died of pneumonia that winter. Kurt's mother, pregnant with her third child, died early in the spring. It was then Kurt began to believe that ugly rumor which had been circulating like a putrid smell ever since the men had returned. Unbelievably, Germany had lost the war!

Now on the other side of the Tiergarten, Kurt Schmidt arrived at his Saturday-night destination: The Red Fox, a cellar club up an alley slippery with fish scales among tenements northeast of Alexanderplatz. Outlined in hissing red neon, it held out the promise of girls in skimpy red tights to workers from Berlin's factories and iron foundries. Eight months ago, when Kurt had arrived in Berlin, his nostrils clogged with coal dust from the Nibelungen mines of the Ruhr, he had reached out to the bright lights of the Kurfürstendamm only to discover they produced fire that did not heat. At The Red Fox he had found tolerance. Before the life-sized portrait of Kara Kohl, The Red Fox's star, lit up like an altar, he smoothed his spiky white-blond hair while staring into her rouged and parted lips. Even in the West End he had never seen anyone more beautiful.

The smoky red brick cellar was hung with red velvet curtains and flooded with undulating red light, creating the illusion of life at the bottom of a warm red sea. Frau Hildebrand Fuchs, the statuesque owner, stood in the doorway in red satin gown and feather boa, her outrageously peroxided hair precariously piled, her false eyelashes scraping her rouged cheeks, a hearts-and-flowers tattoo on her left bicep. Nonchalantly accepting Kurt's bags of money, she dropped them on a giant weigh scale and, when the pan did not dip far enough to register the price of a beer, added a generous thumb. Tossing them into a bin, she sighed: "Most of my customers brought cabbages tonight. This crazy government that won't stop printing money is turning me into a grocer. Who needs a cash register? Better an icebox!"

Seating himself at a rough table, back against the wall, Kurt grabbed a beer from a midget named Fritz, who communicated only with hand gestures. Sticking his tongue deep into the foamy amber liquid, he lapped it like a dog, letting it trickle down his parched throat till his stomach gurgled and churned. Only then did he lift his head.

At center stage stood The General. An old man with tobacco-stained white mustache, dressed in a pastiche of uniforms from Bismarck's wars, he played an accordian with his hands, a mouth organ wired to his jaw, a drum with one foot, bells with the other and cymbals attached to his backside. As middle-aged clerks and foundry workers in threadbare three-piece suits and boiled collars yearned, a dozen girls in red satin girdles did bumps and grinds behind a gauzy curtain. While the men who could afford the luxury chose partners by number, the rest asked each other to dance, shaved cheek to shaved cheek, bodies turned sideways to accommodate bellies that swayed moodily to a foxtrot or jiggled to a polka.

Kurt had arrived in time for the last floor show. Wiping sweat from under his Pickelhaube, The General cleared the stage while red spotlights ricocheted. Materializing at center stage and twitching her boa like a tail, Frau Fuchs launched a slow but lusty striptease, pausing to tell risqué jokes or to mouth lascivious lyrics with just enough self-mockery to make them funny:

> "As long as my panties are hanging on your chandelier,
>   You'll know I still love you."

Last to be shed were bra, panties and blond wig, to reveal a bald-headed male wearing a gold jockstrap.

As the audience cheered, the spotlight careered dizzily, catching the heads of two men being seated by Fritz at a front-row table marked RESERVED. In pearl-gray suit and plum cravat with a diamond stickpin, the older one had a massive head and shoulders, prematurely gray hair and bushy brows that clung to his grainy skin like lichen to rock. He eased himself into the ringside seat, wearing elemental power as if it were a well-cut cloak, then laid his large hands on the table like the paws of the Sphinx.

In an ivory silk suit so exquisitely molded it glowed like a second skin, his younger companion wore a white fedora and monogrammed scarf which coiled once around his throat before dissipating itself in a fringe. His black hair was slicked from elegant features perfect but for a dueling scar across his soft cheek – a self-conscious flaw making the rest more beautiful. His lips had been darkened and moistened, his cheeks hollowed and rouged, his brows plucked into Gothic arches which, along with his slim mustache, completed the Trinity. Though only about twenty, his expression of bored insouciance and the drumming of his long fingers like ivory chopsticks on the rough table suggested several lifetimes of jaded weariness.

A gigolo from one of the expensive West End bars with his wealthy prey, assessed Kurt. A profiteer who got rich while other men fought wars.

As Herr Diamond Stud ordered champagne, paying for it with foreign currency, his Glowworm Lover slid a Balkan cigarette into an ivory holder and cocked his head, waiting for a light. Looking from Glowworm's daintily manicured hand lying on his lover's wrist to his own broken fingernails grimy with soot, Kurt knew hate. Parasite, he cursed inwardly. A jackal and his lice.

A sudden roll of The General's drums drew Kurt's attention back to the stage and caused him to purge his mind of unclean thoughts. *She* was about to materialize, Kara Kohl, the She of his dreams. Already Kurt could see the outline of her body through the gauzy curtain – a femme fatale no more than sixteen in red satin girdle. Pausing briefly in the diaphanous doorway while The General played something slinky, she glided toward a red stool at center stage and, drawing up her red net legs like the tail of a mermaid, sang in a pewter voice that seemed far too large, too deep for her slender frame, becoming for Kurt the embodiment of all women, ageless and eternal.

> "Love was just a game to me,
> But oh so nice
> And full of ecstasy."

Flushed in red light, her face was both mysterious and erotic: high flat cheeks curving like a wishbone to a cleft chin, nose slightly flattened and flared, deep-set slanted eyes, a full sensuous mouth soaked in red. But what had sealed Kurt's amorous fate was her glorious red hair. As the spotlight teased and tossed it the way firelight had flickered through his own mother's red hair, he involuntarily reached out his hands, a man half in ecstasy and half in despair.

> "A woman is only beautiful when she is in love.
> Only through love.
> Oh, if it only could be so forever,
> Because love alone makes beautiful."

Though Kara was as mesmerizing as always, Kurt's concentration was marred by the presence of Herr Diamond Stud and the Glowworm. Not only did the spotlights cast their shadows in intimate brackets on either side of his beloved, but at the end of each song Diamond Stud drowned everyone with the thunder of his applause while Glowworm, tilting on his chair and blowing smoke rings, stared in silent, insolent appraisal. Leaning back in his chair, Kurt narrowed his eyes, assessing Kara through the disdainful slot of Glowworm's phony sophistication, seeing now the mend in her stocking, the mascara smudge on her cheek, the sweat stain under her arms. "Reptile!" he cursed aloud. "War profiteers!"

> "We steal as birds do,
> In spite of the fact
> We are rich.
> We do it for sexual kicks."

Uncoiling from her stool, Kara swaggered away from the audience, hands on hips, legs spread. Pausing at the slit in the curtain, she glanced saucily back over her shoulder – her trademark exit. Simultaneously, Diamond Stud launched a paper dart that hovered in the spotlight before settling. Stunned, Kurt saw it was a $20 U.S. bill – enough to buy a house! For a second Kara – gripped by the same greed that had coarsened Violet Boots – seemed about to pounce. Regaining her composure, she sauntered to the front of the stage and down the steps till she could reach the bill without looking at it or stooping. Stuffing it into her bodice, she taunted in that remarkable bluesmoke voice: "That's fine for starters, mate, but don't I get champagne too?"

Laughing, Diamond Stud proclaimed: "Champagne for everyone!"

While the patrons of The Red Fox cheered, Kurt felt rage thrust up from his loins, expand through his chest then explode in the sinews of his arms. With a snarl, he grabbed Diamond Stud by the lapels, yanking him upright. "Swine! You pick pfennigs from Germany's misery." As he drew back his right fist to smash the craggy face, the startled fingers of his left hand discovered a familiar shape under the silky jacket – an Iron Cross. Paralyzed by this talisman of authority, Kurt stared into Diamond Stud's face, unable to advance or retreat.

"Take your hands off me, you goon," growled Diamond Stud. "If I had two good legs instead of the hunk of shrapnel the French left me, I'd lay you flat." Snatching up a walking stick with a steel knob, he struck the seat beside him. "Sit!"

Kurt did.

As Diamond Stud glared eyeball to eyeball, the anger drained from his face so his gravelly voice sounded almost fatherly. "Fortunately for you, young man, I know the bad temper hunger can give."

Before Kurt could stammer a reply, Diamond Stud turned his attention back to Kara. "The night is young, my little star. Do go and get changed so Count Wolfgang and I can take you to dinner."

Never before had Kurt seen Kara offstage among mortals. Never before had he smelled her musky perfume with its slight underpinning of sweat or been close enough to touch the mole on her left shoulder, to caress her hair crackling like fire. As she strode off to change, Kurt gazed after her and then at the empty space where she had been.

Diamond Stud sized him up with bemusement.

"Well, why not, my boy? She's beautiful. Let's all go to the Adlon. By the look of your rib cage you could use a square meal."

Summoning Fritz, he tapped the waiter's cardboard shirtfront with his walking stick. "Get my friend one of those and a jacket. Some pants, too, if Frau Fuchs can spare them."

Berlin's premier hotel, the Adlon stood at the corner of Unter den Linden and Wilhelm Strasse, a classical gray-stone guarded by a gold-braided doorman under a striped awning. Inside it was grander than Kurt had imagined: gilt mirrors, plush carpets, crystal chandeliers. A waiter in formal coat and starched collar pulled out Kurt's chair while he tugged at his false shirtfront and hid his clogs under the tablecloth. The linen napkin snagged on his callused palms. Nervously he rubbed them as if they might come clean.

After ordering pink gins and caviar, Axel Berg studied the gold-crested leather menu while his dandy – Count Wolfgang von Friedrich – perused the wine list through a gold-rimmed monocle. Senses overloaded by the sight and smell of food, Kurt examined the tablecloth, so starchy it seemed to stand at attention with its silverware spread like a row of medals. He wondered how easy it might be to steal a few pieces. Would he be searched at the door? As he sized up the Oberkellner he was startled to feel a warm leg rub against his own. Dressed in clingy red jersey and smiling through the veil of her matching hat, Kara Kohl was pressing something hard and cold against his thigh – a spoon bearing the Adlon eagle! With nimble fingers she poked it into Frau Fuchs' tuxedo pocket, humming under her breath: "We steal as birds do in spite of the fact we are rich. We do it for sexual kicks!" As Kurt glanced like a naughty child from the waiter to Axel Berg, he felt her push a salad fork in with the spoon, and a bubble of hysterical laughter forced its way into his throat.

Setting aside his menu, Berg ordered for the whole table: "Smoked salmon with capers, lobster with beer sauce, wild rice, asparagus hollandaise, green salad."

In the flat clipped accents of the native Berliner, Count Glowworm added: "A bottle of Louis Roederer" – the first time he had deigned to speak since Kurt had joined the party.

A full orchestra in tails was playing "My Man." With an arm drooped languidly over his host's chair, the count identified various people around the dance floor, casually dropping names in his caustic, nasal voice. "The stylish woman in silver – that's Frau Louis Adlon. She won Berlin's first motoring beauty contest – 28 Royal Pekinese in a white Mercedes. Her fat puffing partner is of utterly no consequence, though he thinks he is – Willis Bliss, the theater critic for *Berliner Tageblatt*. His last column was filled with ecstasy over the goings-on at Eve's Apple.

According to Bliss, it was so hot and crowded on Friday night that the bouncer dumped a basket of white mice on the floor to clear it." The count heaved a dolorous sigh. "How outré. During the revolution I was at Eve's Apple when the orchestra was drowned out by machine-gun fire. Though blood was dripping over the musicians from exploding glass, the leader merely apologized: 'Meine Damen und Herren, please excuse the competition. Don't let it ruin your enjoyment.' I can assure you it did not. Then being a Berliner meant something."

Kurt had been watching the waiters dip and dive like fireflies with their silver trays. When one arrived with the pink gin and caviar, he was waiting. Even as the waiter fussily weighed out the caviar, his white butterfly gloves dancing over the little brass scale, Kurt snatched a roll and stuffed it into his mouth – the first solid food he'd had in three days.

"That's right, my boy," approved Axel Berg. "Eat up. Eat up. Who in this room has more right? A native German with the empty belly to prove it." Ignoring the waiter, he heaped caviar on Kurt's plate. "I've known in my time what it's like to make a meal out of a pickled herring. Now I'm one of the lucky few – a German who can afford a few trillion for a meal. This is Berlin's finest restaurant. But look around you. Who in our population of four and a half million can afford to be here? The Prominenz, as the count has pointed out – that's to be expected. But who are all these others? Take a look at that plain little woman reading a guidebook by the pillar. Probably an English school marm who found the halfpenny she used to tip *The Times* newsboy would be worth billions of marks in Germany. Then there's the French couple – he's probably a bank clerk. The four young men by the orchestra, each with his own bottle of champagne, are American students. People of no account in their own countries who can flash their dollars and francs and pounds all over Germany like true conquerors. That's to be expected – the hard cost of losing a war, no matter how unfairly. But who else is here, many of them born in Germany?" Raising his voice, attracting other diners, Axel Berg rudely jabbed the air with his butter knife. "See that one in his orange sack suit with his woman in flashy jewels? Or how about that bunch by the orchestra? Look at their hooked noses dipping like oil rigs into their caviar. See their hands like grappling hooks with the fingerpads worn smooth from counting their money. Hear their voices dripping with olive oil. They love inflation, and why shouldn't they? They invented it. You find them in all our banks and boardrooms and infesting our Weimar government, but I know from experience where you don't find them. You don't find them toiling down mines or working the soil, and I never came across one in the trenches."

Leaning closer, becoming confidential, Axel Berg piled all the food he could find on Kurt's plate – bread, celery, caviar, black olives. "Listen, my friend, and I'll tell you why I'm so rich and you're so poor. For four generations my family owned a hardware store in Düsseldorf – just a simple place with nails in a barrel. While I was fighting in France, my wife had to take out a second mortgage at usurious rates from a man she thought was a friend. After I returned, we had the Red revolution and that French trouble in the Ruhr, and then this crazy inflation when the mark grew in five years like a poisoned puffball from 184.8 to the pound to well over eighteen trillion. Like the rest of Germany's middle class I was wiped out while my 'friend,' who had shrewdly protected himself with an anti-inflation clause, took over. At first I was grateful when he allowed me to run my own business for a pittance. Then it dawned on me what he and all the other 'Germans' who were prospering had in common. It was so obvious to anyone with a pair of eyes and the sense to use them. To be fair, there's no law against what these swarthy gentlemen were doing – no law, except for the moral law. And there's no law against what I did in return. I buttered up my employer the way our friends over there are buttering their rolls, and I became his shabbas goy who looked after his business on his Sabbath when he wasn't supposed to show his face at the store, and I went over all his books and learned all his dirty tricks. Then I used them against him till I had my own business back and a couple of his. So you see . . ." Axel thumped the table in triumph. "I have not profited from Germany's humiliation. I have gobbled up the lice that feed on the German carcass and I'm not ashamed to say that I've grown very rich."

While Kurt digested this bitter moral tale along with the food he had bolted, the Oberkellner arrived with the smoked salmon, the salad and wine. As Count Wolfgang smelt the cork of the Louis Roederer, tested the temperature, savored the bouquet, Axel shifted from Kurt to Kara as abruptly as a spotlight. "To Berlin's next cabaret star," he toasted. "I'm tired of investing all my money in ball bearings. I look forward to a very interesting year." He challenged Count Glowworm: "You've seen her perform. Did I deceive you? Isn't she spectacular?"

Examining Kara through his monocle as if she were a bowl of soup he expected to contain a fly, the count admitted: "The bones are good, and the mouth. Of course the packaging is all wrong. These clothes are impossible, and that makeup – it's atrocious. I'd have to develop a new style for her. Even the name must be changed." Concentrating on Kara's eyes, like liquid honey, he came close to delivering a compliment. "Something warm but with more depth than fire . . . Karmel. Yes, that might do. Spelled with a C for mystery. Carmel."

"But the voice. You haven't mentioned the voice – that wonderful throaty rumble."

The count nodded. "That's the big surprise. It's very, very good." He reverted to type. "Of course the presentation and her material are all wrong. She'll have to expand her range or learn tricks." Nostrils flared, he delivered the cruelest cut: "For the West End the sex appeal must be upgraded. Even to be satirical."

"How long would it take?" demanded Axel.

Removing a Balkan cigarette from his pocket, the count

waited while his host lit it with his gold lighter bearing a swastika crest. "To build an entire production around her? Songs, costumes, promotion . . . we're talking two years. At a minimum. If it's possible."

Rolling up a giant silver salver, the Oberkellner unveiled four steaming lobsters, which he dissected as deftly and impersonally as the count had Kara. Kurt looked from the glowing pink crustacean, with its dismaying array of surgical tools, to Kara, hoping to restore their earlier conspiracy. Lost to him, she was ogling Count Glowworm, holding her lobster in her left hand just as he, reaching for the silver crackers with her right just as he. Seizing his lobster in both hands, Kurt tore it down the middle, then fell to stuffing flesh into his mouth, startled by the peculiar flavor, unwilling to temper his manners and unable to control his appetite, his eye on the gold cigarette lighter with the swastika, wondering when he might steal it.

Delicately wiping his mouth, the count directed his haut-monde monologue exclusively at Axel Berg: "Josephine Baker is planning to dance at Chez Vollmoeller wearing bananas. After the Winter Garten's nude ice show, clothes had to make a comeback. Next we'll hear that Anita Berber has decided – for the sake of sensation – to go back to wearing a G-string . . .

"Max Reinhardt is selling his Grosses Schauspielhaus. The acoustics were wonderful – a 5,000-seat auditorium and you could hear a whisper – but even with Max's genius for the spectacular, it was like entertaining in a cave of stalactites . . .

"Duke Ellington's *Chocolate Kiddies* will change the future of the musical in the same way Arnold Schönberg's 12-tone lunacies have transformed serious music. That's the good thing about republicanism – the door that lets in idiocy is the same one that occasionally welcomes genius."

Hanging on the count's words, Kara mimicked every elegant gesture with just a touch of satire – a too-crooked finger, a more precise wiping of the mouth, even chewing in rhythm with his fine white teeth as they delivered their irrefutable pronouncements while that same superior example perversely drove Kurt to lower his own homey manners down to the level of the dosshaus. At last as Axel Berg paid his bill – 548,600,000,000 marks, or $30.00 U.S. – Kurt stuffed an extra two rolls into his pockets, still coveting the gold cigarette lighter.

Never lifting his eyes from the bill, Berg shoved the lighter toward the count then remarked amiably: "You might as well take another fork, Schmidt. They've already charged me for it."

After the Adlon they went to the Sports Palast on Potsdamer Strasse where socialites and cabaret stars in beaded gowns and diamonds, along with officers wearing dress swords and riding boots, mingled with gangsters packing guns, with ditchdiggers in overalls, with shop girls in caps and baggy sweaters, to hoarsely cheer contestants in the six-day bicycle race as they whirled around the tilted wood track, a blur of T-shirts, of pumping legs and of hypnotically spinning wheels as they sweated it out to sprightly tunes played on an organ. Then it was on to Eve's Apple to applaud an all-girl jazz band in striped bathing suits – the latest rage.

Hit of the evening was Resi's – an eccentric dance hall with glass roof painted in birds and flowers, revolving mirrors, gushing fountains and telephones at numbered tables for patrons to invite each other to dance. So successful were Berlin's transvestites at creating sexual confusion that it was customary for gentlemen to insist their pickup dates prove their sexual identity by showing their breasts before escorting them home. At Kara's bold insistence, she and Count Wolfgang exchanged clothes in a cubicle in the women's washroom, with her red scarf becoming his turban while she sported his fedora and false mustache. Two drunks fell for their ruse, while Axel laughed in hilarity and Kurt, arms crossed, projected a mixture of envy and revulsion.

More sensibly, they breakfasted at a square marble

table on the terrace of the Romanische Café, a squat and
turreted hangout for journalists and artists to gossip and
read newspapers on rollers. Later they greeted dawn with
a stroll through the Tiergarten where thousands of spar-
rows, nightingales, grebes, thrushes and magpies were
turning the tops of chestnuts and lindens and limes into
twittering umbrellas.

Haggard in the watery morning light, and leaning on
his walking stick, Axel Berg gulped fresh air. "Berliner
Luft – best tonic in the world for a hangover. I should
bottle and sell it."

Pensive, perhaps even sincere, the Glowworm murmured: "We people come and go. The birds are the true
inhabitants of Berlin."

Rifling Kurt's pockets, Kara produced one of the rolls
he had squirreled away, and ripping it into tiny pieces,
hurled it into the sky. With head flung back, the first
fingers of sunlight caressing her red hair, she warbled like
one of the thrushes she had summoned:

> "It happens only once,
> It will not come again.
> It is too beautiful to be true."

Now there was no artifice in her voice, no touch of
coyness or brash sexuality, just the notes, clear and sweet
and vulnerable as they slid like drops of dew down the
long line of her throat. Kurt felt something fragile and
precious burst inside, sending sharp, cruel shards into his
throat. Helpless, he walked away. Axel called after him,
and then Kara, but he continued to walk and then to run,
head pulled down into his borrowed clothes, scuttling
back to his own life – to the slums and soup kitchens and
dosshauses of the East End.

The tramps were lying like dead moths at the base of
the gas lamps where they had gathered for mutual protection. Against one post, ramrod straight, sat the lieutenant
with polished brass and only one leg, already engaged in
his morning toilet. Without altering his pace, Kurt pulled

the Adlon's silverware from his pocket and flung it onto the lieutenant's lap. Tearing off his false shirtfront and jacket, he hurled those to the ducks in Neuer See.

When the war is over . . . when the war is over . . . when the war is over . . . All that bitter winter young Kurt had watched the pine boughs of the triumphal arch he had helped build turn brown, while the silver letters of the FATHERLAND banner fell like teeth from rotting gums. One night while everyone was asleep, he soaked that arch with cooking oil and burnt it to the ground.

TWO

Berlin

December 1925

CARMEL KOHL'S lips were lushly curved and fluted like a siren's lyre. Wolfgang von Friedrich filled his lens with them. Silent films concentrated on a woman's eyes, mute with mystery, sucking the observer into a dizzying inner vortex. Wolf quixotically focussed on the mouth as the most alluring erogenous zone – a bold and extroverted advertisement for the new age of expressionism.

Wearing black turtleneck and slacks, Wolfgang moved in and out from his camera curtain, adjusting lights and shifting the tripod. A year ago he had floated Carmel Kohl's lips on billboards throughout the West End, adding the rest of her face bit by bit as he had redesigned it – the eyebrows plucked, the cheeks sculptured, the amber eyes blacked with kohl, the thick curls tamed in a burnished copper cap. When everyone had become curious about this haunting, nameless beauty, he had introduced her at the brightest theater openings, the smartest clubs and sporting events, playing on the theme they had explored during their first encounter: sexual ambiguity. Just as Wolfgang had banished all that was blatant from Carmel's face, so he – like an artist mixing colors – had broken down her scarlets and fuchsias into dark burgundies and coppers that highlighted her hair. Then, as a final touch of promotional genius, he had appeared with her identically dressed in white monks' hoods with copper crosses; in backless burgundy gowns with fishtail trains; in white tuxedos with black lipstick, canes and monocles. When this "double-exposure" gag wore thin, he had reverted to photographer, ensuring each picture circulated in the trendier magazines projected the right balance of cool and hot sex, of remoteness and availability, of putdown and promise, thus controlling Carmel Kohl's public image as he controlled her professional life.

Again adjusting his lights, Wolf pushed back his tripod to encompass all of Carmel perched on a stool in white Grecian gown and draped with the red fox furs which were her trademark. He demonstrated the pose he wanted – a deliberately stressful one which would cause her guard to slip, allowing her confused and painful past to seep through, knowing that was when he captured his most sensitive pictures. Understanding this tactic, Carmel held the pain for him, put a frame around it, at the same time she resented his exploitation.

With a snap of his fingers, Wolf directed her to move spontaneously. While she shook out her red hair and arched her neck, he cast aside the classical search for perfection that informed his work to pursue her at crazy angles, through happenstance lighting, marveling at her inventiveness and grace while he pushed himself and his craft as far as it would go, creating stunning photos he had never wanted to show anyone else. As a boy ill-at-ease with his body, Wolf had trained in front of mirrors to excel at fencing, tennis, dancing, developing through will-power the "natural" elegance for which he was now noted. Carmel Kohl was the real animal.

Hands on hips, Carmel glared.

Snapping that one last picture, Wolf spoke his first words of the afternoon. "Yes, you can go but I'll need you back at eight sharp. I want to take apart your closing number. With luck, we may get this damned show together by opening night."

Turning up his Persian lamb collar, Wolfgang left the Pariser Platz townhouse where Carmel lived with Axel Berg and where he had his studio. The nippy air with its peppery taste pleased him. Winter was his favorite season. He liked the chasteness of it, the discipline, the whiteness apiece with the classical serenity of the Karl Schinkel architecture gracing the square. Even the squat and grandiose Romanesque buildings which were the Hohenzollerns' heavy-handed mark upon the city looked lighter and more attractive when rimmed with snow, their statuary transformed by icicles into monsters of abstraction sure to have excited the wrath of the literal-minded Kaiser Wilhelm.

Several cars had stalled in the new fall of snow, clogging traffic through the Brandenburger Tor. Despairing of a taxi, Wolf started on foot across the Tiergarten.

Children were skating on Landwehr Kanal. Pausing to watch them throw snowballs, play tag, push sleds, he imagined photographing them – the flash of red and yellow scarves against the blue sky, the flush of plump cheeks. As always, their impact on him was visual. For him childhood had been a time of discipline and observation. With their shouts and laughter he could make no connection beyond a vague, echoing melancholy.

As a little girl with freckles stuck out her tongue at a boy who had been bullying her, he though of his last shot of Carmel Kohl. At first Carmel had interested him only as a project Axel Berg was willing to fund. Then her special talents had imposed themselves on him. The quality of her voice – that had been obvious, a gift of genes. What had surprised him was her knack for musical comedy. After a night at the theater, she would recreate the lead roles, improving dialogue, adding bits more inventive than the stars. Wolf especially remembered her rendition of Pearl, the street girl from the smash-hit *Broadway*, with its colorful cast of bootleggers, jazz musicians, gangsters. Handling Axel's walking stick like a machine gun, she had stalked Wolf with convincing venom through the potted palms of the Eden's roofbar. "Turn around, Rat. I don't want to give it to you like you gave it to him – in the back. The last thing you're gonna see before you go straight to hell is Joe Edward's woman who swore she'd get you."

When Wolf heard the comic Brooklyn accent and the laughter of the other Eden patrons, he knew he had a product worth developing and canceled a pending move to London.

Now as Wolf emerged from the Tiergarten, he saw a young man in a naval greatcoat charging head down from Zoo station. Something about the way his arm shot up to hail a cab while his gangly legs slid from under him on an unseen patch of ice caused Wolf to shout: "Reinhard!" As the young man turned, a habitual look of suspicion cleared from his hooded blue eyes and he galloped forward, grinning. "What luck. I hoped I'd see you here."

Shaking his gray-gloved hand, Wolf demanded: "What brings you to Berlin?"

"My first leave in six months. Hamburg wouldn't do – you did hear I joined the navy?" His unfashionable Saxon accent grew arrogant. "I've been doing some special work with Commander Canaris."

"Join me for weck, wurst and wein. I'm meeting friends at Café des Westens – Café Megalomania to the initiated. Artists who argue about all the great questions like where their next meal is coming from and how many pigeons can sit on the head of a Kaiser Wilhelm statue."

Reinhard Heydrich's dour hesitation made Wolf regret the invitation. An outsider who covered an inferiority complex by excelling in the activities of a loner, Heydrich had given Wolf his dueling scar in a vicious match that almost cost an eye. Yet it was because his former classmate pushed to excess the darker things Wolf felt in himself that he found him fascinating.

Without actually accepting the invitation, Reinhard fell into step with Wolfgang.

"How's your father?" inquired Wolf, referring to Bruno Heydrich, the founder of the conservatoire in Halle where

Wolf had studied piano to Reinhard's violin. "I heard one of his études at a concert in Dresden just last week."

Reinhard shrugged. "How is anyone who tries to live by music in a world of war, inflation and revolution? Always on the edge of bankruptcy, and doesn't Mother let him know it!" A bitter smile shivered across the bony, asymmetrical features. "I'm the family's Great White Hope."

As they crossed Hardenberg Strasse, a broad artery spoking out from Zoo station, the shriek of a schalmei wiped out the ordinary sounds of traffic. Created out of car horns, it was the preferred parade instrument of revolutionaries of both the right and left. A gang of men in brown uniforms – perhaps two hundred, ten abreast – marched past bellowing and singing:

> "Why should we cry when a putsch goes wrong?
> There's another one coming before very long."

"By the pricking of my thumbs," mocked Wolf. "Usually these guys stick to the East End."

"Who are they?"

"Who knows? All their uniforms look alike." He glimpsed red-and-black swastika armbands. "Ahh, the National Socialists. A Bavarian gang. The ones who staged the 1923 Munich putsch."

Reinhard shrugged in disdain. "Who remembers? There were so many."

"This one was special – as farce. My Aunt Gertrude from Munich had the whole story. A runt in a badly cut morning coat who thought he was Napoleon jumped on a table in a beer cellar and fired his little revolver. The street fighting lasted less than a minute. Four government men were killed and fourteen revolutionaries. The police captured the 'leader' two days later hiding in his girlfriend's closet. If laughter could kill, that would have been the end of it, but the trial was a farce of another sort. The little leader – Adolf Hitler – proved quite an orator. Gave a ringing speech claiming he was obeying nature's law against the 'November criminals' who shamed Germany by signing the Versailles treaty – not bad given all the anti-republican, anti-parliamentary feeling. He was rewarded with a sentence so light it was a pat on the back and released in a year for good behavior. Since then his followers have celebrated the putsch as a great victory. How's that for the alchemist's dream of spinning dross into gold?"

The rowdy parade blocked the street. Some marchers were drunk, others brandished brass knuckles and truncheons. Few attempted to keep in step. Wolf remembered the military parades of his childhood with thousands in their Sunday best jamming the sidewalk of Unter den Linden, cheering as the cavalry galloped by, his father in the lead – the nodding plumes, the burnished helmets, the rattling swords and clattering hooves. Afterward when he strode beside his father, smelling of horse's sweat and leather, every man and boy had saluted.

This gang was screeching:

> "When Jewish blood spurts from the knife
> Things go twice as well."

And another old favorite referring to the murder of the Communist activist Rosa Luxemburg:

> "A corpse there is a-swimming
> In the Landwehr Kanal.
> Please give her to me
> But do not pet her too much."

"They're disgusting," snorted Reinhard, his hand on a pistol inside his naval tunic. "Where are the police?"

"Directing traffic," laughed Wolf. "These revolutionaries of the right are supposed to beat up the ones of the left. That's democracy under the Weimar Republic, December '25."

The two men turned into Café des Westens at the corner of Joachimstaler Strasse and Kurfürstendamm – a cozy, unprepossessing tavern charmingly lit by gaslight.

While Reinhard combed his flaxen hair from elongated features and an enlarged, twice-broken nose, Wolf inspected the art that a sympathetic proprietor had hung. Today's show was very good indeed – portraits of gypsies, bold, vibrant and original. As Wolf inserted his monocle to study the brushwork, a plump, middle-aged man hailed him from a corner table. "Come and meet the artist!"

Professor Max Stein, a cherub with gray-blond curls and pale-blue eyes enlarged by thick glasses, introduced Wolf to a sinewy gypsy with mustache so long it drooped on the table. "This is Raymon Arno." He gestured toward a vivid brunette, the subject of several portraits. "And this is Raymon's twin sister Renate, a novelist."

Wolfgang presented Reinhard Heydrich – "a superb violinist now playing at being admiral" – then continued around the table: "Max Stein, our revered linguistics professor and chief peace-keeper; Christian Jürgens, our matinee idol-in-waiting; peoples' director Leo Warner, son of a robber baron who has seen the Marxist light – meaning he wears a poisonous green workman's cap and overalls while still smoking the finest black Brazilian cigars."

Ordering a bottle of Rüdesheimer wine for himself and Heydrich, Wolf easily found his way into the exuberant conversation. "Clearly, I've arrived just in time to prevent the political perversion of the freshest talent to land in Berlin in a year." Raising his goblet of golden wine to Raymon Arno, he toasted: "The eroticism of your nudes reminds me of Lucas Cranach while your draftsmanship has markings of the early Dürer. Of course none of that will mean anything to my dear friend Leo, who thinks the finest piece of art is the Red flag. He doesn't understand what poor bedfellows art and politics make. By definition politics deals in black and white: 'Because I am right, you are wrong' or, in Leo's case, 'Because I am left, everyone else is wrong.' Art must be free to celebrate life in its full spectrum of colors."

Puffing his cigar clenched between bad teeth, Warner retorted: "For Wolfgang it all ended with the Acropolis.

He doesn't see that art to be vital must not only spring from its own time but also take responsibility for it. Art is revolutionary. It opposes power."

"Why should art be anything more than itself?" queried actor Christian Jürgens. "Some artists are visionary, some build on the past, some react to their times."

"You don't have to lead a revolution to be part of it," offered novelist Renate Arno. "Politics creates art by changing the times we live in – it creates something new to reflect, protest, applaud, evaluate and absorb. But art can also explode out of private pain."

"Bah – expressionism with the world in flames," jeered Leo Warner. "Fiddling while Rome burns. You pee in a pot, frame it, then present it to the world. 'This is art. Why? Because I did it.'"

Jürgens chuckled. "If the artist's aim is true, he may pee into the flames and help put them out. Last year when Laszlo Moholy-Nagy presented his collage The Bankruptcy Vultures made from banknotes, that was a political statement."

"But it wasn't art, just a pamphlet," insisted Wolf. "Yesterday's pamphlet now that the government has stabilized the mark by pegging it to land values. Art that doesn't seek to be universal is nothing. I'm sick of collages of bus tickets and races between typewriters and sewing machines. I'm sick of artists who display themselves instead of their work – the sort who read their bad poems in public, slice them up, glue them where they land and claim a masterpiece." He grimaced in exaggerated pain. "I'm especially sick of donating money to save George Grosz from yet another obscenity charge. Next time he bares his bottom in public as part of his artistic expression, I wish someone would tell him Anita Berber does it better."

Interrupting the hoots of laughter, Leo Warner protested: "Grosz can be an ass, but his merciless portraits of our robber barons are pure genius."

"That's because he patterns them on your robber-baron father," mocked Wolf. "Scratch a zealot and you'll find a boy who's mad at his dad."

"Perhaps in your nihilistic world," sniffed Leo Warner. "I stand for something more than posturing in cafés. What do you stand for, Wolfgang?"

"Nothing. For posturing in cafés. But I do appreciate beauty and I've never understood why art to be 'truthful' has to be ugly like the portraits of Grosz and the other so-called popular realists."

"Ahh yes, your damnable intellectual search for the perfect brushstroke, the perfect bar of music, the perfect statue – Keats' Grecian urn as Holy Grail. You're the sort of critic who smothers art that takes chances."

"If you want sensation, you'd better be prepared to forgive silliness and the inconsequential, which are the by-products – like peeing in pots and framing it."

"I'm talking about risk-taking that has some point, that comes from a value system," protested Leo Warner. "Not just Dadaism. Infantilism."

Turning to Reinhard Heydrich, who had maintained a superior silence, Wolf remarked: "You'll notice our Leo has an 'ism' for everything. If you showed him a child playing in the sand, he would call it 'sandism.'"

"Now, now," soothed Professor Max Stein, laying a fatherly hand on both Wolf and Leo. "I'm glad you mentioned the child, for isn't that where everything starts? Art begins as play, and play is indiscriminate, thus allowing for growth. When German artists play, there's likely to be a more serious element than the Swiss artists who invented Dadaism since we Germans have been through a war and a revolution."

"All this is rubbish," exploded Raymon Arno. "When Laszlo Moholy-Nagy used marks for his collage, it was the cheapest material in Germany. Far cheaper than paints and canvas – that's what an artist understands."

"A statement from his hungry gut that was political but not necessarily ideological," agreed the professor. "That's the point I'm making." He sighed. "In the end I suppose only an artist can say what art is, though his critics have a right to disagree."

"Art as democracy! Art as politics! What depressing thoughts," chided Wolf.

"Anything is better than art perpetrated by the rich and powerful," jeered Leo Warner. "The Kaiser gave us his 'gut feelings' about architecture, and what did we get? The Kaiser Wilhelm Memorial Church – constipation in stone."

"I agree, I agree, so why not art purely as entertainment?" Drawing a dozen tickets from his pocket, Wolf announced: "These are for *The Rhinegold Maiden*, with Carmel Kohl, opening in two weeks at The Glass Slipper." He spread them across the table. "With my compliments. They're the last I have."

As his friends scooped up the tickets, the peaceful atmosphere of the café was shattered by breaking glass. "A fight!" yelled Christian Jürgens as all but Professor Stein rushed to the window.

"More like a beating," snapped Wolf.

Four Brownshirts were punching a little man on the terrace of Café des Westens where they had already smashed one of the globular light clusters. As they pummeled him against the iron railing, Christian, Wolf, Leo, Reinhard and Raymon rushed to the terrace. Finding themselves outnumbered, the Stormtroopers took off with Reinhard Heydrich chasing them, while the others carried in the bleeding victim.

"It's Otto Heines," observed Christian. "He does Charlie Chaplin imitations at the Katakombe. Why would anyone want to hurt him?"

"The mustache," snorted Wolf. "They probably thought he was mocking their silly-looking leader."

As Renate bathes Heines' face, Professor Stein rocked back and forth in his chair in self-rebuke. "They were murdering that man and I couldn't move."

"Where's Reinhard?" asked Wolf.

As all looked toward the door, it burst open with a blast

of snowy air. Heydrich stood before them, waving his smoking pistol, half his face frozen in horror, the other twisted in a smile. "I might have got one," he squealed in the startling falsetto that inspired the nickname White Billygoat. "I think I shot him through the chest."

THREE

MOUNTED on a twenty-foot pink neon podium, The Glass Slipper radiated light like the Star of Bethlehem onto the Christmas shoppers of the Kurfürstendamm. As Axel's chauffeur Rudolf nudged the white Mercedes up a side alley through garbage cans to a rusty fire escape, Carmel consoled herself that this stage door was no better than the one at The Red Fox. It was as if these pleasure palaces with their fantastical fronts needed a harsh dose of reality to even the score.

Once inside she strode directly to the stage. Its set, designed by Wolf, was spectacular – a crystalline underwater grotto later to be struck for a forest fire and then the mountains of Valhalla. Standing center stage, Carmel gazed over the orchestra pit at two rings of royal-blue seats and a massive crystal chandelier which would be raised to clear the view. She would have preferred to make her West End debut more modestly in a cabaret, backed by a quartet, where she had to compete for attention with the waiters. Never before had she played to a captive audience with nothing to do but stare at her, coughing and rattling their programs, demanding she fill an hour of their lives till intermission set them free. A wave of dizziness swept over Carmel, lasting two, three seconds in which she ceased to exist – the same feeling she had experienced the day Wolf had changed her name then made up her face so that when she peered into the mirror she saw a

43

stranger. That had triggered a recurring nightmare which she had most vividly last night:

Carmel Kohl returns to The Red Fox to find Kara Kohl still performing her old numbers. Terrified, she shouts to Kara from the mirror in which she is trapped, begging her to look, but Kara dances on and on in a frenzy, as unable to stop as Carmel is to free herself from the mirror in which she is suffocating.

Pulling off her shoes and stockings, Carmel forced herself to pace the stage, even to strut a little, dragging her fox fur as a seductive prop, familiarizing herself with the nooks and crannies of the set, its pockets of light and shadow, feeling the boards, cold and hard like stones under her bare feet, remembering how she, as a child, used to rehearse with her mother at The Red Fox, learning all her routines, including the broad-hipped swagger and the sardonic glance over the left shoulder. Later she had mimicked her mother's male "guests," satirizing their vanity and eccentricity as she wielded their hats and gloves and canes – to her mother's amusement if not to theirs. She had even invented a pantomime in which she played neighborhood characters – the fat woman who sold cabbages, the blacksmith who quoted Goethe. When her mother had been too drunk to work The Red Fox, Kara had pleaded to go on.

Cutting off that line of thought, Carmel fled to her dressing room, already a bower of flowers. Though most were roses from Axel, there was a gardenia corsage from Frau Hildebrand Fuchs, The General and Fritz; pink carnations from Professor Max Stein, who had been helping Carmel purge her speech of mannerisms; a red-rose nosegay on a lacy heart from actor Christian Jürgens and his fiancée Renate Arno; even a basket of white mums from Willi Bliss, the critic for the *Berliner Tageblatt*, requesting an interview after the show. Nothing from Wolf, of course. Though she had expected nothing, she felt disappointed. During two years he had changed her name, her vocal range and her singing style; taught her how to sit, to walk, to use her hands; forced her to lose ten pounds; designed her hairstyle and her clothes; told her what to say to interviewers; plundered her mind and body for anything that might be of use to him in the creation of Carmel Kohl, even inventing an impossibly romantic Sturm and Drang past for her without bothering to inquire about the one she had. All that without her ever learning anything of the slightest consequence about him – where he lived, where he came from, what he did when they weren't together. Even now he scarcely looked at her except through his monocle or his camera lens. After a photographic session with Wolf, she understood why primitives believed the camera stole their souls.

Sitting at her dressing table, Carmel cleansed her face with cold cream then applied her makeup as precisely as Wolf had instructed her, trying to fix in her mind her own features as they disappeared under hollowed cheeks, blacked-out eyes, a copper lipstick impregnated with gold dust. As she powdered and painted, she heard the buildup of pre-curtain noises – the technicians calling for more lights; someone complaining about a missing prop; the tuning of a harp, an oboe, a violin and the sound of Wolf's nasal voice controlling, ordering, directing. By the time she was affixing her last false eyelash, she was humming her opening number, feeling it purr through her body, revving her motor.

Fifteen minutes before curtain, Wolf entered Carmel's dressing room. She was in full costume – a gold fishtail coat fastened with one button to produce a deep décolletage; gold mesh tights, gold sandals, a mermaid's long golden wig. Squinting at her through fingers squared like a viewfinder, Wolf complained: "Your left brow is too high. It looks like the center arch of Der Dom. Fix it, please . . . no wait, I'll do it." As he bent over her with dark pencil, Carmel realized Wolf's face was without makeup or artifice of any kind. His eyebrows had grown in; his hair, without pomade, was thick and wiry. For a panicky second she realized: He has transferred his mask onto me.

Already Carmel could hear the orchestra begin Wolf's overture – slow and sluggish, each note slurring into the next, swelling to suggest the powerful rise and fall of water. Hugging Axel, who had come backstage to wish her luck, Carmel sucked strength from his brawny chest then took up her solitary place in the wings. Through a hole in the curtain she could see the restless first-night audience. Thanks to Axel's money and Wolfgang's press-agentry, the show was a sellout. All the theater greats had been invited, and many had accepted: directors Max Reinhardt and Leo Warner, actors Pola Negri and Emil Jannings.

Taking a deep breath, Carmel propelled herself to the golden rock at center stage, then sat with back to the audience, her coat trailing like a mermaid's tail. Now she heard the whir of the opening curtain, exposing her. She felt the warm ripple of lights, like water. In mid-note the orchestra stopped playing. Silence stretched as long as the audience could bear. An instant before the first embarrassed coughs, she pushed the button that rotated her golden rock, then announced in her foggiest voice: "Hello, I'm Carmel Kohl." Opening wide her gold-mesh legs, she inserted a golden saw between her thighs and began to stroke it with a heavily resined bow, producing a weird and wailing vibrato, kinky, primal and unreal, soaring higher the more she bent the saw. As the audience listened dumbfounded, she crooned a song Wolfgang had based on Wagner's haunting chorus of the Rhinegold maidens:

> "The waves have whispered your desire
> For happiness beyond all dreams.
> You know that my heart is listening.
> You know to whom it belongs.
> You know for whom it beats.
> I bring you love and wealth

> My arms to you unfolding.
> Rhinegold, Rhinegold! Come . . . come."

Carmel's throaty voice, undercut by the bizarre mockery of the musical saw, produced the kind of elemental ambiguity that Wolf had always sought to project through her. Electrified, the audience listened till the last strange note had died away, then exploded in laughter and applause. Carmel felt the warmth of their approval sweep over her, seep into her pores, reverberating through her as the music had done, healing the split which self-doubt had created. After two years she was back on stage, only this time no drunk dropped his bottle or demanded a refill or shuffled noisily to the washroom. Feeling a surge of power, she abandoned her musical saw, stretched her arms toward the audience and belted with full orchestration:

> "I have known love that was bittersweet,
> I have known passion, I have known retreat.
> I have explored all the channels of bliss.
> And I have tasted, never wasted, one kiss."

The rest of Wolf's production, inspired by Wagner's *Ring of the Nibelung*, ingeniously ran the tightrope between mocking the original and mining it for its primordial depths, with Carmel playing not only a comic Brynhilde but also a heroic Siegfried. A dozen curtain calls and shouts of "Bravo!" summoned her again and again. When at last it was time for her to swagger to the back of the stage then wink sardonically over her left shoulder, she impulsively threw out the famous last line of Goethe's *Faust*: "The eternal feminine draws us on."

Besieged backstage, Carmel was elbowing her way to her dressing room when the critic Willi Bliss seized her by the wrist and forced her inside a prop room. "Five minutes, please, Fräulein," he begged. "I need to know your past – how this large and glorious talent came to be."

Trying to press past him, she gasped: "My biography has been sent to all the papers."

"Nein, nein. I can't use that. I need an exclusive. The sausage demands it."

Bliss waved a fan of yellowed newspaper clippings in her face. "Your mother was the tragic Rosa Kohl. The voice, the gestures, the name – I couldn't be mistaken. What do you remember of the . . . accident?"

Banging her fists against his chest, Carmel screamed: "Let me out! I can't breathe."

FOUR

K URT SCHMIDT waited at the stage door of The Glass Slipper in a baggy overcoat along with two dozen other fans. Though the wet snow penetrated his mismatched overshoes, he scarcely noticed as he stared up the fire escape from which Carmel Kohl would emerge. In his left hand, protected by cellophane, he held a program for *The Rhinegold Maiden*, while in his right he carried a pencil left at Zoo station by a man who fell asleep over a crossword. For two years he had tracked the rise of Carmel Kohl in magazines left in washrooms and in newspapers crumpled in garbage cans. His was a sacred love which he pursued with the dedication of a Parsifal – the one thing that kept him above the derelicts he met in soup kitchens and dosshouses. His love was the reason he tried to keep clean, like the one-legged lieutenant with his chest of medals, though no one he met ever believed he had once dined with Carmel Kohl on caviar and lobster at the Adlon.

Three months ago when Carmel's debut at The Glass Slipper was advertised, Kurt had painfully saved until he had two marks for Standing Room Only – not the old marks good for nothing but bum-wipe but the new Rentenmark that stabilized the economy without doing anything about unemployment. Now as Kurt waited amidst the broken wine bottles with a gregarious theater crowd sheltered under black umbrellas, he imagined his first sight of Carmel – how their eyes would meet, how the look of recognition would transform her face. Taking his program in her hand, she would write a message to him alone – something that would legitimize his claim on her forever.

That last was important. Already Kurt had foolishly confided his relationship with Carmel to the only other person at the stage door who was not in evening dress – a toothless old hag named Gerda who had bragged about knowing Carmel when she was a scrub lady at The Red Fox. She had taunted him by calling him the Addled Adlon Lover.

At last the stage door clanked open. Waving his arms self-importantly, the watchman cleared a path to the white Mercedes. "Back, everybody, back. Give Fräulein Kohl room." Next to appear was a jovial Axel Berg, physically impressive as always despite his handicap, and brandishing his steel-headed walking stick like a magic wand.

The iron door clanked open for the third time. Carmel Kohl appeared on the rusty fire escape, shimmering in white fox furs and diamond tiara. Lighting up the drizzly alley with a radiant smile, she descended on the arm of Count Wolfgang von Friedrich to shouts of "Bravo!" As the other fans rushed forward with their programs, Kurt pressed against the clammy brick wall, paralyzed by shyness yet memorizing each gesture – the tilt of her head, the deep-throated laughter: *We steal as birds do in spite of the fact we are rich . . .*

The shivering crowd thinned out. Kurt saw Carmel flex her stiffening fingers as Axel Berg signaled to the chauffeur of the white Mercedes. He lunged forward, elbowing out Gerda who had also been holding back. As the scrub lady flew at Kurt in a rage, Carmel reach for his program. Propping it against her beaded purse, she smiled into his eyes, her floral perfume melting the frosty air between them. "Hello. Thanks for coming. What's your name, please?" As he waited for recognition, Kurt felt his tongue turn to a toad.

Frowning, Carmel repeated: "Do you want me to sign

your name?" When he still couldn't answer, she scrawled her signature then turned to Gerda who was shoving from behind. Now she unleashed her transforming smile. "Gerda. How wonderful to see you. If I'd known I'd have sent tickets."

Kurt gaped in disbelief. So intensely had he remembered each detail of their night at the Adlon, it had never occurred to him that she might forget. As Gerda the scrub lady flashed a triumphant, toothless grin, Carmel nodded to Axel, impatiently waiting by the Mercedes.

Unable to abandon his dream, Kurt grabbed Carmel's arms. "You must remember me! The Red Fox. The Adlon. We stole spoons." As recognition finally dawned, Axel strode forward while Count Wolfgang materialized from the shadows. He twisted Kurt's arm so he fell to his knees before the pyramid of wine bottles. With an aggressive growl, the Mercedes drew up to the fire escape, received its three passengers, then shot like a white arrow from the alley.

Kurt gave chase, heard the cackle of Gerda the scrub lady, and kept running around the corner onto the Kurfürstendamm. It had begun to snow – fat wet flakes that melted against Kurt's cheeks. Fir trees shone with red and silver balls; carolers under a lamp post sang "O Tannenbaum," but Kurt felt only humiliation, remembering the supercilious face of Count Wolfgang von Friedrich as he glanced out the back of the speeding Mercedes like an overlord peering at the peasant who has fallen under the wheels of his coach. He remembered some of his father's stories about the war – not heroic tales of men in battle but bitter ones about those who had ordered the battles. How Crown Prince Willi waved his father's regiment off to Flanders from his balcony in a blue silk dressing gown with two naked mistresses clinging to his arms. How the rich and titled had danced to cabaret tunes with their French whores while his father had bled in the trenches. How the November criminals had handed the Fatherland over to her enemies on that silver platter called the Treaty of Versailles, stripping the German nation of her land and forcing thousands of loyal Germans to become Polish, French and Czechoslovakian.

Like every Ruhr schoolboy, Kurt could recite the rules of the Rhineland's wretched period of occupation by heart: No telephones for the conquered Germans. No postal service. No radios. Censored newspapers. No travel or public meetings without a permit. A curfew with infractors to be shot. All German citizens to list their names on their doors. Greenwich time instead of Central European time so Germans might experience their defeat every minute of the day. Signs on all the better restaurants, swimming pools and first-class train compartments: "No Germans Allowed." Signs on public buildings: "Germans use the back door." Even worse, German males were required to doff their hats to the victorious enemy and to pass them in the gutter.

Body trembling as if he had a fever, his hands in fists, Kurt suddenly remembered whom the count reminded him of and why he hated him – an incident from the winter of 1919, deeply repressed in guilt and shame.

He and his father, unable to get work. All day they trudge along the railway tracks, picking up lumps of coal that have fallen from the cars on their way to France. As they stumble home carrying their sacks, their hands and faces grimy, they are confronted by an immaculately dressed French lieutenant with a beautiful German girl on his arm, la gloire de France written all over his silky face – a duplicate of Count Wolfgang's. After ordering Kurt's father into the gutter, the lieutenant insists he remove his cap. When Ernst Schmidt refuses, the Frenchman flicks it off with his riding crop, then slashes the whip across his face. As the elder Schmidt stands capless in the gutter, the ugly crop mark across his cheek, unwilling to drop the precious bags of coal to retaliate, Kurt curses: "I wish you had been killed in the war! I wish you had died for Germany."

That night Ernst Schmidt – a passivist – joined the

Revolutionaries. Eight months later he was dead, shot
with his back against the wall for sabotage.

As Kurt turned the corner, the shriek of a schalmei
galvanized him – a call to revolution. About thirty men
flailed at each other in the slushy yellow light of a gas
lamp, their fallen Red standards like pools of blood. He
heard the soft, sickening thwack of wood and rubber
against flesh and bone, the snarls of rage and grunts of
pain, the crack of skull against concrete. He smelt the reek
of blood and vomit and sweat. With a cry, Kurt snatched
up the truncheon at his feet. Hurling himself into the
chaos, he fell into rhythm beside a putty-faced blond giant
who laughed as he bashed, choosing the aggressors, needing their confident pursuit of victory to right the balance
of too many defeats, reveling in the feel of the rubber, the
surge of power as he cracked one skull and then another,
working in tandem with the blond giant as he once
chopped illicit wood with his father, the ax head now
biting into flesh, splashing hot sap, laughing with the
blond giant.

Kurt heard a warning squeal: "Police!" As his head
swiveled, a brass knuckle caught him under the chin,
clamping his jaws, while a knee jarred up through his
groin, pitching him forward, making him retch blood.
As his face struck snow, he heard the pound of hooves
and saw the police in their coal-scuttle helmets as they
closed in.

FIVE

K URT SANK into the snow, drifts of it, soft like clouds. Yet he felt warm. How could that be? He tried to move his arms, to feel his body, but he was too tired, too lacking in will. Again he let himself sink into the whiteness, the softness, the warmth, imagining he was a baby lying in a hamper of clothes smelling of the wind, feeling the sun beat down while his mother pegged white sheets to the line – sheets she washed in exchange for flour, for eggs, seeing her large, competent hands peg the flapping white cotton, her forehead puckered as she fought the wind.

Now the heat was more intense. The hamper had been brought inside and placed on a chair by a porcelain stove while his mother, the same shape as the stove, stirred soup in a cauldron, her forehead matted with copper curls like tendrils of flame.

Kurt reached out his hand to the flame – not a child's hand but the rough square hand of a man with callused palms and broken nails from chipping coal, from breaking stone. He used that hand to explore his environment, the milky comforter, the downy pillow.

He was in a low-ceilinged room with rough-hewn timbers lit by a gas lamp and smelling of pine boughs. A porcelain stove with its fire framed by an open door. A woman stirring something sweet and succulent in a cauldron – not his mother, a girl his own age in Bavarian dress, bosomy white blouse, blue-and-white print apron over a voluminous skirt, her body thick and firmly rooted. She turned her face, solemn in its wreath of steam, her features child-like and unformed, with snub nose, round blue eyes and thick plaits of blond hair wound in earmuffs.

"My name is Ilse. I'm a nurse." She corrected herself: "A student nurse."

Ladling broth into a blue bowl with precise gestures, she brought it to him. "For your strength. You've been sick." As she sat on the bed, he felt it sag, saw her dip a wooden spoon into the liquid then blow on it as his mother used to – a ritual of such intimacy it almost broke his heart. Now the spoon with its maddeningly sweet burden was sliding into his mouth, the flavor bubbles bursting against his swollen tongue – real chicken broth, not juice squeezed from the gnarled yellow feet. Greedily he gulped more and then more till his belly was a soft warm circle expanding like bread dough.

"That's enough for now. There'll be more later." She tucked him into the down comforter, her breasts brushing his cheek. "I'll be here beside you."

As she sat in a pine chair, she reached for a ball of blue wool. A vase of pine boughs mixed with bittersweet stood on the table between them. The whole room was decorated with pine boughs, the rafters entwined with them. Closing his eyes, he smelled the forest, remembered a winter's morning very long ago, before the war, when he and his father had gone to cut a tree for Christmas. His mother had made gingerbread men to hang on the branches and at the top they had placed a star lit with a candle.

Kurt opened his eyes. He could see Ilse, screened in pine boughs, knitting a blue scarf, her body moving rhythmically with the thick wooden needles so she seemed to be knitting the scarf from her own substance, back and forth, *click-click-click*. Her hands were like his mother's, large and capable, willing to absorb themselves in small tasks – stirring soup, kneading bread, rooting through soil for potatoes – yet leaving her spirit free to dream, to soar with the birds. Instinctively Kurt reached out his own hand, lay it on the one she was using to loop her wool.

Ilse stopped knitting. She looked at him, face smooth, sucking on her lower lip. Without words, she put down her knitting, began to undo the lacings of her belt, the ties of her blue-print apron. She was wearing thick white cotton pants and heavy stockings with lace-up boots, all of which she removed, piece by piece, folding each and laying it in a neat pile. Sitting on the edge of his bed, her flesh so white it looked as if the slightest touch would bruise it, she unbound then unbraided her hair, her fingers moving among the plaits with the same matter-of-fact absorption that had guided them through the strands of wool, Rapunzel letting down her golden hair.

Kurt opened the coverlet, inviting her into his dark nest smelling of flesh, of desire. She slid inside, her body hot like a stove, her skin yeasty and moist like bread dough. Gently kneading her breasts with his fists, he hungrily filled his mouth with her nipples, feeling tears of gratitude, of longing, squeeze like gritty rain from under his dry lids. Never before had a woman freely given herself to him. Always there had been some wrangle over a cigarette or a beer. Now she lay, legs parted, waiting for him, a cavern into which he could bury himself, thrust and pulse and burst. He climaxed almost before he had begun, spilling over her in a copious white stream like a bullrush bursting with its pent-up immortality.

He buried his face between her thighs, tasting her juices mixed with his own, lapping like a thirsty animal, a lifetime of needs unleashed, a greediness and generosity, and yes, at last, there was an end, there was enough.

When Kurt awoke, Ilse was again sitting beside him, almost prim in her pine chair, her hair so tightly replaited it pulled her eyes, the *click-click-click* of her wooden needles sounding almost metallic. If it hadn't been for the contented curve of her lower lip and the blood which rushed up from her chest into her cheeks when he spoke her name, he would have thought he had dreamed the whole incident. As she fluttered to life under the intensity of his gaze, tucking imaginary bits of hair into the braids coiled over each ear, he remembered how his mother had emerged from the "master bedroom" created by hanging a faded khaki curtain across one end of their cottage, avoiding his accusing eyes, tying and retying her apron, straightening pieces of furniture, disassociating herself from the playful slaps, the laughter and groans that had emanated from behind the curtain, yet humming to herself, her eyes over-bright and catching fire as his father emerged, moments later, to wash himself with the water on the stove, to groom his mustache, re-part his hair. Then Kurt had resented his father, this man who cast his shadow between himself and his mother, so that he no longer dared to lay his head on her lap while she combed his hair or to offer her his àrm when they crossed the street. Now, too late, he understood.

Breaking off a piece of pine bough from the vase, Kurt smelled the sticky resin, thought of the Christmas tree he and his father had cut, then dropped it on Ilse's lap. She sniffed the resin and smiled, aware she was sharing in some deeper memory, some secret exchange. "You'll be wanting more soup. When my brother comes again, there'll be bread."

Again Kurt lay back while Ilse spooned warm broth into his mouth, becoming aware of the subtleties of the room – the cuckoo clock over the kitchen table, the crucifix and intricately carved Christmas crèche, the swastika banner and the poster of Adolf Hitler trimmed in pine boughs.

As Ilse put away the blue bowl, he heard someone stamp snow from his boots. Seconds later the door burst open to reveal the blond giant with the pink putty face at whose side Kurt had fought. Far too big for the room, he offered a hand, misshapen from having been broken many times. "Bruno Schultz. Welcome," he exclaimed in a voice with the rough texture of wood shavings. "You bashed six Bolsheviks before they bashed you." He growled the National Socialist motto: "Strike first – you or me!"

Kurt shuddered, remembering the violence into which he had thrown himself. As a boy who had gained his height too late to help him against neighborhood bullies, he was not used to seeking out situations in which to prove manhood. He remembered something else. "The police?"

Bruno grinned through lips thickened with scar tissue. "They always come in on our side after the fun is over. They want us to wipe up the streets. That way they don't get blood on their nice clean uniforms or their artsy-fartsy constitution. They think we'll get rid of the Commies so they can get rid of us." Pointing to the poster of the National Socialist chieftain, decorated with pine boughs, he snorted: "They don't know Adolf Hitler."

Bringing both Bruno and Kurt a beer, Ilse boasted: "My brother was one of our Führer's first followers. He took part in the revolution."

Bruno removed a rubber truncheon from his brown breeches and ran it lovingly across his palm. "Even against pistols I'll take my 'eraser.' I've used this baby since Munich – it's had its share of blood. Our Führer – he's a miracle worker, that man! My friends and I have the muscle. He has the silver tongue. First time I heard him speak I was drunk in the Hofbräuhaus. A man in a greasy trench coat stood on a table and shook his fist. I thought: 'Silly clown.' Then I listened. 'Struggle is in our blood. It's not with softness that a man preserves himself. It's with brute strength.' Even the prison guards learned to address him with his own salute." Putting an arm around Ilse, Bruno teased: "Little sister came to fetch me home to the mountains. Then she became a believer. When the big revolution comes, our nurses will be with us on the front lines. Then the blood will run!"

Turning up her small nose, Ilse spoke with a firmness that demonstrated a mind of her own: "Since our Führer was released from prison, he speaks of a peaceful solution, of winning our ends through legal means. Already he has a shadow government."

Bruno gave Kurt a comradely wink. "Don't let my sister's womanly talk put you off. There's still lots of fun to be had bashing heads. Brutality is respected. After our beerhall battles, who rushed to join up? Those with the broken heads." Waggling his truncheon at Kurt, he chuckled. "My unit is the Dance Band. Now I know how you use one of these, I'll put in a good word for you."

"My father died as a revolutionary," boasted Kurt. "When the French demanded more and more coal, he helped blow up the trains. After they occupied the Ruhr, they caught him after curfew with explosives. They lined him up against the wall with a half dozen others, then rounded up our village to come and look. You could see the bullet holes in the limestone and the splotches of blood stuck with bits of brain. They shot low so the suffering would be longer."

Bruno slapped Kurt on the shoulder. "You must come with us Christmas Eve. What luck you found us now!"

"He's still too sick," protested Ilse. "He's been feverish twenty-four hours."

"Nonsense, Little Sister. Any man who can't recover from a fight in a day is a dead man. He'll go if I have to carry him." Clasping Kurt's hand, he stared into his eyes in blood-brother intimacy. "We're preparing a field for him in the Grünewald. You'll see – he's one of the masses and yet he is a God above us. He will give Germany back to us. He will restore our honor."

SIX

$\mathbf{A}$ S THE BLACK Daimler sped down the Kurfürstendamm with Kurt holding Ilse's hand, he couldn't
remember being happier. No longer did Berlin's street of
pleasure torment him with false lures. As he saw the red-
gold-green-blue shimmer of bar and cabaret lights in the
snow, he knew it for what it was: a neon rainbow with a
pot of dross.

In the front, Bruno sat by his friend Felix Krell, a
flinty-faced Stormtrooper with a fishhook smile and
unnaturally golden hair. Kurt and Ilse shared the back
with a good-humored dumpling named Hermann Humm,
who served as lookout for the Dance Band. As soon as
Kurt heard his voice, high and thin as a whistle, he recognized it as the one that had squealed: "Police!"

All evening this group had been celebrating in the
Shultz's little house in the working-class district of Neukölln. The transfer of the party to Felix's car had in no
way deadened it. Passing around flasks of schnapps as
Felix careered around corners, they drowned out Christmas Eve carolers with songs of their own:

> "Swastika on helmet,
> Black-white-red brassard,
> Hitler's Stormtroopers
> Are what we are called."

It was only when Felix attempted to run down an old

Jew in spats, then took aim at a traffic policeman in his white cage, that Ilse assumed a prim authority over the group. "Stop it! Do you want to risk jail tonight of all nights?"

More soberly they passed over Halensee bridge to suburban Berlin, then into the pine trees of the Grünewald. Becoming secretive, as if traveling to the heart of a mystery, they extinguished their lights and navigated by moonlight, though dozens of cars were sliding down the same back roads on the same well-advertised quest.

Their destination was a meadow on which a stage had been constructed, backed by a thirty-foot gold eagle and a dozen National Socialist banners that snapped in the wind. Though warmly dressed in fleece jacket and boots borrowed from Bruno, teamed with blue scarf and mittens knit by Ilse, Kurt felt reluctant to tear himself from the womblike coziness of the car, to share his friends and his new-found sense of belonging with this larger event.

The night was clear and brittle. A dozen searchlights, marking an improvised landing strip, swept the starry sky. "What if anyone tries to break up the meeting?" asked Hermann, echoing Kurt's fear.

Bruno and Felix laughed contemptuously. "Just let 'em!"

Yet the mood of most Stormtroopers and their friends seemed merry as they drifted over the meadow carrying beer and blankets. Along with other women wearing swastika armbands, Ilse ladled soup from one of the pots over the fires that dotted the site. As Kurt smelled the tantalizing odor and felt the cup warm his mittened hands, he knew a week ago he would have killed for such a feast.

The band to the right of the stage played carols as frequently as party songs. No functionary attempted to meld or control the crowd. All that was confidently being left to The Great Man for whom everyone seemed content to wait. The unemployed had nothing else to do, while the party faithful were enjoying the drama of the vigil. As the hours drifted by, each drone of a plane caused necks to crane and arms to point until the moving light veered off, grew smaller, became lost in the maze of stars. Despite the spiraling excitement, Kurt held stubbornly to a mood of cautious optimism, like a man who has heard too many good things about the wife his relatives have picked for him and insists on making up his own mind.

Just after eleven o'clock a pinpoint of light approached from the southeast and, instead of banking over Tempelhof airport, waxed brighter. More and more people stopped carousing to follow its stately progress while the band played:

> "They looked up
> And saw a star
> Shining in the East
> Beyond them far.
> And to the earth
> It gave great light
> And so it continued
> Both day and night.
> Star of wonder, star of light,
> Star with royal beauty bright,
> Westward leading, still proceeding,
> Guide us with thy perfect light."

Now the churn of the motor could be distinctly heard as the plane circled – once, twice, three times. After catching it like a luminous bird, the searchlights turned the landing strip into a golden carpet.

As soon as the wheels touched, informality gave way to precision. While four Stormtroopers unrolled a red carpet from plane to stage, others – including Felix and Bruno – formed an honor guard. A small figure emerged dressed in brown and hatless. Flipping back his right hand, he accepted the salutes of the crowd while the band struck up Wagner's stirring overture to *Die Meistersinger*. At first the brown stranger's steps were short and dainty, punctuated by a nervous cock of his right shoulder like a matron crooking her finger to drink tea. The closer he came to the stage, the more assured he grew so that by the time he hit the illuminated platform backed with National Socialist banners, he was striding.

Kurt managed to see his face – the greasy forelock of dark hair cutting the broad forehead, the black mustache like a doormat under the misshapen nose, the pouched and glittering eyes. Without introduction, the little man raised his hand for silence then began to speak. Slowly at first, as if fumbling for the exact word and yet with every syllable clear, he spoke of the world's primordial past, as if invoking the gods: "Long ago there was no forest here, only the unbroken earth worked smooth by primal tides as they ebbed and flowed over the world. Then the fires burst up from the core of the earth. The ice marched down from the poles. After long cycles of cataclysmic change, some titanic force, elemental yet governed by supreme laws, shaped the contours of our land. Who knows what set that force in motion? We believe these things are ruled by law but that law eludes us. This cataclysmic process has its counterpart within mankind, creating surging growth through titanic struggle and upheaval. Struggle is as old as life itself. In struggle the strongest wins while the weakest loses. It is not by softness that man has preserved himself above the animals but by brutal struggle."

Building slowly, he recounts his own triumphant fight against poverty in Vienna. "When the Goddess of Suffering took me in her arms, my will to resistance grew, and this will was victorious."

While the crowd breaks in more frequently to clap and cheer, he recalls the glorious history of the German people, their tragic struggle and greatness. "The war of 1914 was not forced on this country – no, by the living God! Two million men and boys, of which I was lucky to be one, thronged to the colors, eager to prove the right of the German nation to exist. The romance of battle was soon replaced by horror, enthusiasm by duty. After three years of struggle without flinching, Russia collapsed and for the first time victory seemed within our reach. As we prepared for the final attack – at the very moment when we were receiving our last orders – we were told there would be no more ammunition because the Bolsheviks back home were staging strikes. Think of that! A soldier is preparing to give his life and he hears of this disgraceful situation. Then, when he is still reeling deep in his soul, he is told that the Kaiser, to whom he has been taught since a baby to give all his duty, has abdicated. Morale is decimated. With no guns and no leader, these men who thought themselves on the brink of victory after four ugly years – what could these men do but march home? Through the terrible devastations of France we traveled like thieves in the night but without looting or shooting. After crossing the Rhine, we are greeted with flags and flowers and triumphal arches. Here the land is untouched – not a twig is out of place. It is then we felt the true bitterness of the victory that had been snatched from us by betrayal, by treacherous politics, by a stab in the back!" Shrieking, he demands: "And whose fault is this? Whose? Whose?" He answers himself rhythmically: "It's all the fault of the Bolsheviks!"

Eager to release pent-up emotions, the crowd takes up the chant: "It's all the fault of the Bolsheviks! It's all the fault of the Bolsheviks!"

Hitler raises his hand while dropping his tone, speaking slowly now, in full control, the voice of reason: "But who allowed the Bolsheviks to come into our country? Who allowed them access to our workers? Who encouraged them?

"When I was a boy growing up in Linz, I scarcely remember hearing the word 'Jew,' and yet in Vienna they were all around me. You could tell by the smell of their caftans that these people were no lovers of water. Through a thousand years of incest the Jew has preserved his race and his characteristics more sharply than most of the people among whom he lives. Though he has never founded any civilization, he has destroyed hundreds because he lives as a drone, making other men work for him. He can't form a state of his own because he lacks the most essential ingredient – an idealistic attitude. For a Jew the will to self-sacrifice doesn't go beyond naked self-preservation, so he is forever a parasite protecting himself under the flag of 'religion.' Then he becomes active in economic life, but never as a producer, exclusively as a middleman. With thousands of years of mercantile skill behind him, he begins by lending money, at a usurious rate, to the helplessly honest Aryan. His power is the power of money, which multiplies in his hands effortlessly and endlessly in the form of interest. Everything which makes the Aryan strive for higher things is to him a means of satisfying his lust for money and power. Finance and commerce become his complete monopoly. To advertise himself to the fullest advantage, he takes over the press. While we German troops were marching through the mud and blood of Flanders, a certain segment of the German press supported the Bolsheviks by pouring wormwood on the general enthusiasm and by encouraging strikes. And who was it who controlled the press? Who? Who?"

This time, as his voice peaks shrilly, the crowd is lying in wait. With fanaticism born of relief, they shout: "The Jews, the Jews, the Jews. It's all the fault of the Jews!"

"Yes!" he shrieks, his voice hysterical. "It's the Jew, the Jew!" Flinging out sentences, phrases and paragraphs ringing with sarcasm, drenched in venom, he demands: "Who filled the offices at home, though you could never find one at the front? The Jew! Every Jew was a clerk and every clerk a Jew. In economic life the Jew became "indispensable." In the war all production was controlled by Jewish finance. When we had inflation, when our savings and homes and the very bread was taken from our mouths, whose fault? Whose fault?"

"The Jews, the Jews! It's all the fault of the Jews!"

"Then, with the defeat of his Aryan host, the Jew begins to reveal his true and most disgraceful qualities. With his money and repulsive flattery, he worms his way into the heart of government. Who controls the Weimar Republic?"

"The Jews!"

"Who is responsible for unemployment and poverty?"

"The Jews, the Jews! It's all the fault of the Jews!"

The words spewing forth like lava from a volcano, he speaks with the freedom of fire, cataloging abuses, citing crimes, melding the huge crowd into a single entity despite the challenge of outdoor oratory, not so much by his words but by his fanaticism, his repetitions, the hypnotic rhythms like a primitive drumbeat, the swaying of his body and the emphatic gestures of his hands as they carry on a monologue of their own.

"The fact that nine-tenths of all literary filth, artistic trash and theatrical idiocy can be ascribed to this people, constituting one-hundredth of the country's inhabitants, speaks for itself. The relationship of the Jew to prostitution and the white slave trade has always been there for the world to see. Was there any form of filth or profligacy without at least one Jew? If you cut into such an abscess, you found – like a maggot in a rotting body – a kike, often dazzled by the sudden light. In order to lull his victims – to wipe out his own inferiority while purging pride from the soul of the Aryan – he talks of the equality of all men without regard to race and color. Yet all the things that we admire on the earth today – science, art, technology – all are the creative product of only one race, the Aryan race.

"Race is the core of all that is valuable. Race and our struggle to keep it pure. The Folk philosophy, reflecting the inner will of nature, demands the victory of the superior race over the weaker one. The Folk State must wipe out class and set race at the center of all life. It must declare the child to be its most precious treasure. The prime concern of all education must be to burn racial pride into the instinct and the intellect, the heart and the brain of the youth entrusted to it.

"German boy, never forget you are German! Little girl, remember some day you will become a German mother!

Yet it is here where our Jewish 'guests' are the most insidious. The black-haired Jewish youth lies in wait for hours satanically spying on the unsuspecting Aryan girl he plans to seduce, thus adulterating her blood and removing her from her own people. Who can be called to account for this? Who will shout 'Enough'? Certainly not our Jewish parliament!

"What luck for any one person to be able to hide behind the skirt of 'the majority' in all decisions. One hundred empty heads will never make one wise man, nor will a heroic decision arise from a hundred cowards. The true character of German democracy, without Jewish or Bolshevik impurities, is for the free election of a leader who is obliged to assume all responsibility for his own actions and omissions – one who must answer with his fortune and his life. When I speak to you today, I have more right than anyone else. I have grown out of you. In my youth I was a worker like you. I dragged my way up by industry, by study, and by starving like you. I was among you in the war for four years, so that now I speak to you to whom I belong, with whom I feel myself to be bound, for whom I have been in prison. When I hear you calling to me, cheering me, my heart beats faster and I think to myself: This is our Germany. This is our people, our glorious German people! The man who is born to be dictator has no right to say, 'If you want me, summon me.' It is his duty to step forward. Surrender yourself to me! Surrender your powerlessness, and receive as your benediction the full power of the mass.

"The army we have formed is growing from day to day. I nourish the proud hope that the hour will come when these rough companies will grow into battalions, the battalions to regiments, the regiments to divisions, that the old cockade will be taken from the mud, that the old flag will wave again, that German honor will be avenged. I know your enemies! I know your suffering! I know those lice who seek to feed on you, to seduce you, to bleed you with your own money, to poison your precious German blood. Who are these people? Who? Who? Name me their names."

By now everyone around Ilse and Kurt is on his feet, shaking fists and screeching: "Ja, ja! The Jews! The Jews!" Women are sobbing, beating their breasts. Many rush the stage and have to be restrained.

Kurt has long since ceased hearing words. Carried on waves of adrenalin, his response as he crushes Ilse's body to him is the grateful, helpless and unreasoning one of someone drowning inside an intoxicating and unfamiliar piece of music. At last someone understands! At last someone cares! At last after nineteen years of fruitless wandering, his life has purpose. At last there is something larger than himself to which he can aspire, to which he belongs.

As the Führer builds to another climax, invoking Germany's pagan spirit with myths and oaths, his eyes like liquid fire, his face radiating an eerie glow, Kurt is a part of the collective rapture, with the need to shout, to cry, to stamp, to hiss.

"We are strong now, but we will get stronger. Germany will be ours! The government will be ours! I go the way Providence dictates with all the assurance of a sleep-walker. Together we will celebrate the proud resurrection of Germany. From the order which I am founding, the final stage of human mutation will emerge – the Man-God! In the future it will be better to be a street cleaner and a citizen of this Reich than a king in a foreign state."

The response was fated: "Sieg Heil! Sieg Heil! Sieg Heil! Sieg Heil! Sieg Heil! Sieg Heil! Sieg Heil! Sieg Heil! Sieg Heil!" It lasted forty-seven minutes.

PART II

"The German nation is sick of principles and doctrines. . . . What it wants is power, power, power! And whoever gives it power, to him it will give honor, more honor than he can imagine."

–Julius Froebel, a disappointed liberal, 1848

"All who feel Germany's need deep within their hearts await a Savior. With the greatest longing thousands upon thousands of minds imagine him; millions of voices call unto him; one single German soul seeks him."

– Kurt Hesse, 1922

"That is the miracle of our time, that you have found me – that among so many million you have found me! And that I have found you! That is Germany's good fortune."

– Adolf Hitler, 1932

ONE

Berlin

June 1932

CARMEL KOHL fought her way up through sticky mounds of feathers that clogged her mouth, her ears, her nostrils while her arms and legs felt bound in a silken web. Though she was sure it was daylight, everything was black. In panic, she grabbed Axel by the chest hairs. "I can't see. I can't breathe!"

Awaking with a snort, Axel yanked the sleep mask from her face. Sunlight exploded like a flashbulb. She was twisted in pillows and pink satin sheets with Axel leaning over her, his gray hair ruffled like a lion's mane, his bloodshot eyes clouded in concern. With a gasp of relief, Carmel buried her face in his armpit, warm, slightly moist, smelling of talcum powder.

"Bad dreams?" whispered Axel, gently stroking her hair.

She nodded into his armpit, no longer remembering what she had dreamed, but retaining a vivid sense of smothering, of being blinded. "Pink champagne," she murmured.

Kissing her wet eyelids, her cheeks, her lips, Axel made love to her as if she were something precious entrusted to him, something that might break in his rough hands. Opening to him in trust, she felt his vulnerability, the body which at fifty was no longer so young, the twisted left leg with its throbbing core of shrapnel causing him to drink too much, take too many pills. At first she had been repelled by his mutilation and the violence such a wound suggested. Violence had been too much a part of her childhood, with her own healthy urchin's body her first line of defense. Gradually she had realized Axel's handicap was also his strength – the humbling doorway through which a ruthless man had learned all he could of love and humanity. Such thoughts released another flood of tears, this time for both of them.

"That's no way for 'Germany's brightest gift to international cinema' to behave," teased Axel, quoting from Willi Bliss's review of her first movie, *Lorelei*, premiered the night before. "Are you just feeling blue because I'm going away?"

It was the path of least resistance. "Yes."

Next time Carmel awoke sunlight was streaming through the french doors onto the pink bed. Idly reaching out a friendly hand, she found only a cold indentation where Axel's body had been. Jolting upright, she found Axel on an ivory seat, in three-piece pinstriped suit, sipping tea and laughing at her. Knowing he had enjoyed the dismay his imagined departure had caused, she felt the resentment of a trusting child tricked by a game of hide-and-seek that has become too real. Axel liked to catch her unawares, to study and possess her with his eyes, the way Wolf did with his camera. Between the two she sometimes felt like an intricately painted Easter egg with the yolk sucked out.

"Tea, darling?" asked Axel solicitously, seeing a shadow cross her face without precisely knowing its cause. Pouring from a handsome Meissen pot, he brought a cup to her without using his walking stick. Knowing what a proud and difficult effort this balancing trick was for him, her heart went out to him, understanding that he – unlike Wolf – used his eyes in compensation. Waiting till he set down the cup, she mischievously stuck her finger up his vest into his belly button.

"Now behave," he admonished, retreating to the love seat, retrieving his corporate dignity while secretly pleased to have lost it. Lifting his teacup, he announced: "I may be gone a month this time."

It was something they had already discussed. "I understand."

"You don't mind?"

"I'll miss you, but I know your past is part of you."

His smile was wistful. "I wish sometimes you'd make a fuss." To cover up such a naked statement, he collected his briefcase and pulled out architects' sketches. "I'll have to deal with the housing project first off. It's for four hundred families. For the first time many of these kids will have fresh air, a park, even a swimming pool. It used to be a swamp." He grinned. "We caught bullfrogs when I was a boy. Now it's a dump." His voice grew uncertain. "Wolf thinks the whole setup is too regimented. What do you think?"

Impatient at his – and her – dependence on Wolf's opinion, she retorted: "Wolf is comparing it to the romantic charms of the sort of village his family used to rule. Not to a city slum. I'd love to have grown up in a place like that."

"Exactly. For a certain trade-off in freedom and privacy, my tenants will get a healthy, well-ordered life." Rolling up the sketches, he smiled. "I'm calling it after you. Carmel Park. What better way to get rid of some of my money? Everything I touch turns to gold – including you, my Rhinegold Maiden."

Before she could respond, he picked up his bowler, walking stick and briefcase, as if he intended to leave. Thinking better of it, he merely rearranged them on the love seat. Locking his hands around his good knee, he tilted back – a nervous gesture that meant he was going to discuss his Other Life. "Of course there's more than just business to attend to this time in Düsseldorf. With my daughter getting married I'll have family duties – nothing I'm looking forward to, I can assure you. A hot day in

July, speeches and toasts – I'll probably have to change my shirt three times, the same as when I was married." His voice took on the self-righteous tone Carmel detested. "I know you understand that Hilde will never give me a divorce, that we can never marry. Though she and I never talk to each other unless it's about the children, it's a contract like any other. One I feel obliged to honor." A long exhalation. "It's strange. There's no love between us – probably never was. Nothing like the way I feel about you. At a certain age I was supposed to marry, have children, take over the family business. There seemed no choice, no thought, no alternatives, and Hilde was the daughter of my mother's best friend. Now our marriage is just habit. Form. Ritual. We sit together like two weathered tombstones waiting for the last line to be engraved, each hoping to outlive the other. She's relieved, I think, when I leave. I hope you never feel that way – relieved to see me go?"

Though he was seeking reassurance, Carmel felt like throwing down her teacup and pulling the pillow over her ears. Never once in nine years had she mentioned they should marry, yet he had taken to lecturing her in this increasingly priggish way, justifying himself to himself as if she had raised the issue. When she refused to respond, he rumbled on like a mechanical doll that hasn't quite run down. "No doubt with Hilde it's the security. Her position in the community. She resents change."

The same as you, Carmel thought. Aloud, she snapped: "It's probably her age," instantly regretting both her words and tone.

"But I'm three years older than Hilde," lamented Axel. "Twice as old as you. What about my age?"

"But look at you," soothed Carmel. "You're ready for work after a premiere, a nightclub and two cafés where you drank everyone under the table. Here I am, a rag doll. We women wear out faster."

Moving to the bed, Axel clasped Carmel's hands. "When we first met, I was afraid life was slipping away and I had to do everything fast. Now I know it is, but I'm more content to enjoy myself and to encourage my friends to do the same. I often think that if it weren't for me, you and Wolf–"

Putting a hand over Axel's mouth, Carmel delivered a devastating imitation of Wolf's clipped Berliner argot: "You were three seconds over on your first number. Didn't you hear the orchestra slow down for you? The pianist was snoring so loudly I thought it was the bass horn."

Chuckling, Axel squeezed her hand. As if his pinstriped suit were a steel corset, he leaned over to kiss her chastely on the cheek. Impulsively she locked her arms around his neck and pulled him on top of her, rubbing herself against him like a cat, filling his nostrils with her scent and insisting on something more lingering, knowing that despite his protestations he would not call her while he was away, that he would concentrate all of himself on that Other World of wife and family and slum clearance and ball bearings just as he concentrated on her now, returning to her wrapped in other smells – of Düsseldorf, not Berlin. That was the mystery of men, that they could compartmentalize themselves so completely, disappear so thoroughly into another world, like dissolving into a different dimension.

Straightening his blue cravat, Axel cleared his throat as if embarrassed to be seen making love by his board of directors, then scooped up walking stick, bowler and briefcase. Hand on the door, he winked over his shoulder – her trademark exit. "Now don't forget me."

The click of the lock plunged Carmel into depression, as if a safety net had been yanked from under her. Holding firmly to the bed, she closed her eyes, recalling the premiere of her first movie, the thrill of seeing herself blown up so many times her normal size, a night of celebration capped by rave reviews at the Romanische and a plunge into the pool at Luna Park where everyone frolicked in evening clothes till the machine that made real waves triggered their hangovers. Stretching across her bed she also reminded herself of the obverse of loneliness: freedom.

Though the tea was cold, Carmel poured more, not wishing to summon Axel's snooty housekeeper Lotte. She glimpsed Axel's latest gift to her – a cat's-eye ring which he insisted captured the yellow light in her eyes. Switching it to her engagement finger, she perversely fantasized herself in all those settings Axel had denied to her – as his bride in white gown and veil; as his chatelaine, graciously receiving the rich, respectable and wellborn. A vision of Frau Fuchs crashing her soiree in full regalia caused her to giggle, breaking the spell.

Removing the ring, Carmel tried to guess what it would fetch in a pawnshop. That too was a joke, one inspired by a mother who had rushed every expensive gift from its fancy wrappings to Tauber's Pawnshop, then set about – in increasingly elaborate terms – to explain to the donor why she never wore it: The necklace had been stolen by a bandit with a red scarf. The earring had been flushed down the toilet. The fur coat had been set down by the stove and accidentally burned. . . .

So touched had some gentlemen been by her sorrow that they had replaced the necklace/earrings/fur coat, only to have it disappear once more.

Restored to good humor, Carmel padded out into the June sunlight. No matter how often she admired fashionable Pariser Platz from the balcony of Axel's mansion, she never lost her sense of privilege. Eager to throw in her lot with this remarkable day, she ransacked her walk-in closet for something cheerful: yards of copper dresses, of white, burgundy, black, silver, gold, in every possible fabric and style; with feathers, beads and sequins; draped, cut on the bias, long, short, backless, frontless. Crushed against the wall she found a yellow organdy with puff sleeves, full skirt and sash that she had bought with her first check from The Glass Slipper. Wolf had laughed when he saw it, calling her Alice in Wonderland, then had forbidden her to wear it in public. "We want men to dream of buying you diamonds, not lollipops." Slipping it on, she examined herself in the mirror, liked the sunny effect and decided, Wolf be damned, she would wear it.

Now seated at her dressing table, Carmel cleansed her face to begin the elaborate makeup Wolf had prescribed for her. As she touched her eyelid with her stick of kohl, she froze, feeling an uncanny chill sweep over her, vividly conjuring up last night's dream:

The premiere of her new movie. Kara Kohl stamps up the aisle of the theater, leaps onto the stage and viciously attacks Carmel Kohl's celluloid image with a high-heeled shoe. Snarling, she drags Carmel Kohl, naked except for her red fox stole, through the hole in the screen. The two fight over the stole till it rips in two, spurting blood over both. With her talons Carmel claws out Kara's eyes, only to discover both are now blind, both are bleeding to death . . . .

Shuddering, Carmel dropped her eyeliner, deciding to do without makeup. At the same time she asked herself why Wolf had left so abruptly after last night's premiere. Was he disappointed with the picture or had he simply become bored with being Carmel Kohl's director? Lorelei was the same as every other woman she had played in the past seven years under different names – the Rhinegold Maiden, Delilah, Eve, Cleopatra, Helen of Troy. Whenever she had suggested other challenges, Wolf had become high-handed and rigid. The public liked Carmel Kohl exactly as he had invented her, and no one – including Carmel – was going to tamper with her. Yet even in the congratulations of old friends and between the lines of rave reviews, she had sensed something that made her uneasy: Carmel Kohl was becoming an anachronism.

In flight from such depressing thoughts, Carmel scooped up the picture hat and white gloves that went with her organdy dress, then raced down the front stairs. Today she would do something she hadn't done for half a dozen years – meander through the Tiergarten.

Down loamy green tunnels thick with the scent of

linden blossoms she found portly gentlemen exercising
their dogs; families spreading picnic lunches of Bismarck
herring and potato salad; lovers in rowboats languidly
trailing their hands through the opaque green lagoons;
children working paddleboats, playing tag, throwing
balls. Here was respectable Berlin out for a Sunday excur-
sion, its citizens more exotic to her than the pickpockets
of the Kurfürstendamm or the whores of the East End.

Strolling toward her, Carmel saw four little girls in
organdy dresses like her own, with sunhats, white stockings and patent leather shoes, flanked by Mama and Papa,
each carrying a Bible. She remembered suddenly where
she had seen something like this before, where she perhaps
had stolen the idea for her own dress. In Axel Berg's
photograph album – his wife and children a dozen years
ago. Peering under Mama's prim straw hat, she tried to
imagine what it would be like to be Frau Axel Berg of
Düsseldorf and whether she would like to change places
with her. An involuntary spasm convinced her she would
not. It was the little girls safely in the middle that she
envied, as her dress and sunhat betrayed. But did the one
necessarily grow up to be the other?

Hands on hips, "Frau Berg" halted on the cinder path
and scowled so scornfully at Carmel that she dropped her
eyes and flushed. Then Carmel realized the poor woman
was only returning her own rude stare. She also realized
with delight that she had been wandering in the park for
over an hour in "disguise" without one person recognizing
her.

Looping back toward Pariser Platz, Carmel came to
the Reichstag, Germany's House of Parliament since
1894, with its spiked domes like Prussian helmets and
Corinithian portico inscribed "Dem Deutschen Volke."
Long before she reached the formal gardens and reflecting
pools she could hear the competing bands, the shouts and
songs of demonstrators. A few days ago, Field Marshal
Paul von Hindenburg, a hero of the eastern front and
president of the republic since 1925, had dissolved the

Reichstag at the request of Chancellor Franz von Papen.
With almost one-third of Germans on the dole, voters
were furiously flocking to radical parties of the left and
right, ensuring the July 31 election would be a hot one.
Already papers were reporting atrocities, and with the ban
lifted on the wearing of partisan uniforms, the poorer
sections of town resembled armed camps tyrannized by
strutting, brawling "war" parties.

As Carmel drew close enough to read opposing placards and banners, she felt tension swirl around her as if
she were being sucked into a whirlpool. The National
Socialists, who had surged from 12 to 107 seats in 1930 to
emerge as the second-largest party, were offering bread,
the leadership of Adolf Hitler and pride in being German.
The Communists were offering bread, international fel-
lowship and pride in being a worker. The Social Demo-
crats, having failed in the past to deliver on the bread,
were offering continuity and protection under the reassuring umbrella of Hindenburg's mustache.

Like many industrialists, Axel was supporting Hitler's
National Socialists as a check on the Communists, but
when Carmel tried to talk to him about the aims of the
thirty-odd splinter parties, he either dismissed her with an
airy wave or snapped: "Go ask the Jews. They know
everything." Ironically, Carmel decided to follow Axel's
advice – she would ask Max Stein, her linguistics professor, to tutor her. Her mother had been destroyed by a life
of thoughtless passion. To Carmel, knowledge was a
safety preserver.

Now as she wandered from speaker to speaker, she felt a
strange and dangerous electrical current sizzling through
the air. Not just here. Everywhere in Berlin. The old world
was dead or dying. Anger, that was obvious and everywhere. More disturbing was the fear. Even in the faces of
the respectably dressed. Fear and hunger – a combination
she knew from her days at The Red Fox where men
crawled in to get warm. For seven years she had been so
busy performing for the rich behind a mask of lacquer

that she had stopped noticing the beggars shivering in
doorways or – an ingenious sop of the Weimar Republic –
receiving mass chess instruction in the Tiergarten. The
country yearned for powerful leadership. No wonder the
favorite slogan of university students, hardest hit by unemployment, was: "We shit on freedom!"

Deciding she had absorbed enough hostility for one
day, Carmel hiked toward Brandenburger Tor, with its
dumpy Doric columns. Though rival gangs also challenged each other here, their impact was watered down by
the presence of Sunday crowds basking in the fine
weather. A vendor sold roasted chestnuts. Women hawked
flowers. A clown teetered on stilts. An organ grinder
played for his dancing monkey. Carmel joined a group
knotted around a boy who seemed about to perform.
Nudging closer, she realized: Not a boy. A girl with shaved
head, a look of abject misery on her face. Accompanied
by two Stormtroopers, she was wearing a placard: SPIT ON
ME. I HAVE GIVEN MYSELF TO A JEW!

Carmel recoiled, as did most other onlookers. Seeing a
policeman directing traffic through the Tor, she ran
toward him, then stopped. What could he do? From the
broken look on the girl's face, she had submitted herself
to such a penance. Paralyzed, not knowing whether to run
toward authority as her head told her, or back to protest
as her heart instructed, Carmel chose the path of least
resistance. She hailed a cab. "Alexanderplatz, please."

Once the station at Alexanderplatz had seemed the most
thrilling building in the world – a curved glass dome shimmering in the sun like a crystal palace, filled with silhouettes of people who had somewhere to go. Now as
Carmel poked alongside the elevated tracks, its red-brick
Roman arches crowded with shops, she was seeing the
neighborhood as it used to be: Herr Zweig, in blood-
streaked apron, who tried to slip fish heads onto the scale
when you weren't looking. Frau Kraus, her gimpy leg

resting on a hamper of cabbages, who gave Carmel apples. Herr Pechstein, who would sell you coal by the scuttleful. Herr Engel, with corncob teeth, who could sole shoes that had scarcely any tops left. With all these delicate negotiations having to compete with the rattle and rumble and whine of the trains. "What's that, Frau Kraus? Three pfennigs each, or thirty by the kilo?"

Yet as Carmel followed the gleaming trolley tracks north and east, past the Backhaus Bar where her mother had spent too much time, even nostalgia could not drown the stench of beer, urine and fly-blown heaps of excrement, of rotten potato peels and vomit. On either side teetered grimy stucco buildings, six stories high, looking onto sunless courtyards without a tree, filled instead with rotting mattresses, broken pottery, blown-out tires; crisscrossed with gray laundry that never seemed to dry; noisy with young crusaders jousting with sticks and garbage lids, with girls skipping over butchers' twine, with scuttling rats.

Regretting the yellow organdy dress, Carmel slanted the picture hat over her eyes to escape detection, embarrassed by her good fortune as she made her way to the tenement where she was born. Nothing had changed except for the Communist and Nazi banners dangling from many windows, the slogans slashed across walls. As she stood in the archway of a building that to judge by the stink was still a pickling plant, she stared at a grubby door reached by six iron stairs, with a fist-sized hole where the knob should be. She imagined climbing those steps, inserting her hand through the hole, slipping the bolt that stuck in cold weather. She imagined mounting three inner flights covered in brown linoleum – sixty-three steps through mud-colored halls clamorous with flushing toilets, blaring radios, yowling babies, brawling drunks and one canary belonging to Widow Mathers. She imagined standing outside flat No. 9, with the door her mother had whimsically painted a shocking pink. She imagined extending her hand, grasping the brass knob . . .

Darting from the slimy pickle plant, trying to put space between herself and this evil place, Carmel found her way blocked by a skinny girl with tight red curls and freckled face who gazed at her in awe. Without a word, Carmel yanked off the picture hat, white gloves and ruffled dress. She handed them to the astonished little girl. Dressed in a beige silk shift, she fled the alley.

In the six months since Carmel had seen it, the outside of The Red Fox had been stripped of its neon and the word Fox altered to Forum. Finding the door unlocked, Carmel slipped into the darkened theater. Here, too, the tinsel had been peeled away, leaving red brick walls and exposed pipes. The stage had been extended with a walkway into the audience and the red velvet curtains replaced with black-and-white banners that read: JUSTICE EXISTS ONLY ON THE STAGE. BREAD BEFORE CIRCUSES. WE ARE A LIVING NEWSPAPER. WHAT CAN BE FANTASIZED CAN BE DONE. THEATER IS PARLIAMENT, THE AUDIENCE IS THE LEGISLATURE.

Several actors and actresses in black leotards lounged about the stage while an artist with drooping mustache, whom Carmel recognized as Raymon Arno, painted a slum backdrop like the one she had just left. As she seated herself, a swarthy little man in green workman's cap, a cigar clenched in his jaws, stormed onto the stage, arms flapping like seal flippers from his blue overalls.

"No no *no*!" shrieked Leo Warner. "This set is so pretty it makes me puke. What are you trying to do to my reputation? A slum beside a railway track doesn't look like a bloody Renoir. Where's the soot? The gutters floating with dead rats? I want the audience to smell the stench of smoke like acid eating through their nostrils, to feel the grit of sand scratching their eyeballs. Is this really how poverty looks to you, Raymon? Then I despair for your social conscience. You must change your rose-colored spectacles. That's it! You've given me the spectacle of poverty rather than the fact of it. If it's spectacle you want to paint, then work for Max Reinhardt, the master of waving flags and flaring trumpets. What I want is reality. When my audience looks at the stage, I want them to feel depressed. I want them to make honest contact with the dark side of themselves." Sticking his hand into brown paint, Warner smeared it across Raymon's tenement wall. "I want *shit*!"

As the argument continued, with the artist in spirited but low-decibel defense, Carmel heard the sandpaper rub of thighs encased in net stockings, smelled a distinctive blend of musk with grease paint.

"Mein Liebling," greeted Frau Fuchs, outrageous as always in peroxide wig and red Chinese kimono with flapping pink mules.

Crushed in tattooed biceps, Carmel bemoaned: "I'd heard about your innovations but it's still a shock. Like a desecration."

"Well, one must change. Whether with the times or behind them, I haven't quite decided. Our Wunderkind announced cabaret was out while People's Theater was in. Since nearly half Berlin's cabarets have been closed by depression, who could guarantee we wouldn't be next? The man's a blazing Marxist but he swore he could pack 'em in by offering our customers 'relevance' along with their beer at only a few pfennigs extra. I'm sure most would prefer pretzels but so far curiosity and the next election have worked their magic, so who's to argue?"

"Don't you miss performing?"

A barky laugh. "Who says I don't perform? Warner believes in Total Theater. One night when the audience was slow to respond, I stood up and spoke my heart out to the smelly s.o.b., telling him what I thought about the sillier parts of his production. The audience loved it, so now I'm a regular. You wouldn't believe the stuff that pours out of my mouth – I've never improvised before. Everything was craft craft craft, each gesture divided into a dozen pieces like the frames of a cartoon. It's a sweet arrangement for me. Not only can I –"

"Shut up down there!" bellowed Leo Warner, leaning from the stage at a precarious angle. "You sound like moose in the rafters. I can't hear myself shout."

Unfazed, Frau Fuchs roared back: "We have a guest. A Red Fox graduate – Carmel Kohl."

Hand to greasy cap like a visor, Warner leaned even farther into the darkened theater. "Ahhcht, yes. I've seen her humble herself in the West End – Figleaf Theater."

Advancing on Warner, paintbrush in hand, Raymon Arno exploded: "There we have it – the Kaiser of Communist theater! Like any dictator, you claim to be for 'the little people,' but let one of them become a star, and you turn nasty because you can't patronize her anymore."

"Do you think I'm impressed by someone who knows 159 ways to wear sequins?" croaked Warner, exuding cigar smoke like an engine about to blow. "Whatever natural charms she might have had she's ruined."

Jabbing his paintbrush in Warner's face, Raymon raged: "The only people who like wallowing in poverty are those who've never known it. You come here in workman's cap and overalls then leave in a taxi. If I didn't know poverty, I wouldn't be painting your shitty sets!"

"But that's it. You see poverty with the stylish eye of the artist down on his luck. You don't see it with the despair of the permanently dispossessed."

"Next you'll say it's only the bourgeoisie who understand poverty because they've never been ruined by it."

"Enough, enough!" screeched Warner, pulling his cap over his ears. "I'm a fair man. I'll give her her chance. Bring her up here, let her do her worst. Let's get it over with." Yanking a crumpled page from his overalls, he beckoned to Carmel. "Here's Gretchen's prayer to Our Lady of Sorrows from *Faust*. Read it with some innocence and I'll agree to overlook your past indiscretions and foolish mannerisms."

"I didn't come here to audition," protested Carmel. "I came to visit Frau Fuchs."

"Unprepared? So much the better your chance of pleasing me. I thought every would-be thespian of the feminine gender lisped this out at her mothers's breast." Leaping from the stage, he strode down the aisle, grabbed Carmel's wrist and dragged her back. "I'll give you ten minutes of my time – not a second more."

Trapped by her sense of the ridiculous, Carmel accepted the well-chewed script which she *had* recited to her mirror. While Warner climbed a stepladder, the better to see the part in her hair, she sank to her knees before a hypothetical altar to the Holy Virgin, feeling her heart thump and uttering a genuine prayer of gratitude that she had been spared the humiliation of her organdy dress.

> "You who have suffered so, mistress of suffering,
> Turn your face to me and be kind.
> Wherever I go, this anguish goes with me.
> No sooner am I alone than I weep and weep.
> My heart is breaking.
> This morning I plucked these flowers for you
> And watered them with my tears.
> Help me! Save me from shame. Save me from –"

"Help *me*! Save *me*! Deliver *me*!" wailed Leo Warner. "Deliver Goethe, O Lady of Sorrows, I think we've all suffered enough."

Carmel had not endured ten years pitted against tough Red Fox audiences and the relentless Count von Friedrich without developing a thick hide. Sauntering to the back of the stage with the broad-hipped gait she had perfected in this very place, she glanced scornfully over her shoulder. "Thank you for your time, Herr Warner. I suppose to you it must have some value."

As she swiveled to complete her exit, Warner dove from his perch like a flying mouse. "Perfect. Perfect!" he applauded. "The hair, the face, the style, everything is perfect for my prostitute."

At the word "prostitute," Carmel froze. "Impossible, Herr Warner. As you've already explained, I prostitute myself nightly in the West End. Why would I turn tricks here for the little you could scrape up?"

"I've heard enough. You *will* do it. You must! I implore you! I command it!" Falling on his knees, he plastered Carmel's hands with wet kisses. "How could I have been so blind? You must forgive me. Tell her, Frau Fuchs. Beg her for me. Tell her she must do it!"

Carmel withdrew her hand. "Send your manuscript to my manager, Herr Warner, if you must. Perhaps in five years you'll hear from him."

Interpreting this as serious capitulation, Warner wailed: "But the script isn't written. We do that on the stage, all of us together. We start by interviewing the workers in the neighborhood. From that reality we create our drama, we build our sets. We arrive at the truth." Fumbling through his overalls, he produced another crumpled paper. "Here – read. This is the beginning."

Against her better judgment, Carmel smoothed the paper. "A three-floor walkup. A parlor with a lumpy couch where the child sometimes sleeps, and a small 'guest' room. Instead of wallpaper, poster of old movies. A kitchen with icebox, wood table, three chairs and a gas stove. The flat has one unusual feature – a shocking pink door."

Carmel dropped the page. "I can't do this. This *is* real."

In a well-modulated, even fatherly voice, Leo Warner insisted: "You will do it. Your coming here is fate. You have to do it as a tribute to your mother, like putting flowers on her grave. You must open that shocking-pink door to the past. You will be magnificent!"

TWO

Bavarian Alps

August 1932

KURT SCHMIDT awoke slowly, his body light and full of air, as if every pore were a pocket of sunlight:

He is standing by a dusty road with his mother, or perhaps it is Ilse. The day is warm and the smell of pine so powerful it's like a drug. They hear music. A troop of soldiers crests the hill, their tattered uniforms snowy white, piping flutes instead of toting guns. Kurt's father, or perhaps it is Adolf Hitler, leads the parade, his hair and mustache a glowing white, and every note he trills is like a crystal bubble that hangs translucent, collecting all the rays of the sun before it bursts.

"It's the Pied Piper!" claps Ilse. "See how the children follows him." As Kurt kneels, his father, who is also the Führer, runs his fingers through his hair. "Rise, my son."

For several minutes Kurt held his eyes closed despite the efforts of a flock of birds to pry them open with joyful song, remembering how often as a child he had been awakened from a dream of milk and honey only to find his belly gnawing with hunger and the fire out in the stove.

Now a cock was crowing with more than the usual persistence. Kurt remembered in a burst of clarity what day this was. Leaping from his cot in a room smelling of beeswax, he pushed open the shutters and sucked in a lungful of wine-sweet alpine air. Below him stretched a meadow with grass so green it startled his eyes, each blade outlined in dew. The air was silver with the tinkle of

87

cowbells, the sunlight thick with the syrupy hum of bees. And above him – against an ice-blue sky – a crown of sunstruck mountains. Could anything be that white? In Dortmund the snow turned to grit before it touched the ground; the clouds were like sooty lambs, but here . . . no wonder the cocks crowed with such pride!

Below in the valley, a family in local dress worked a hayfield – father and son scything in parallel rows while mother and daughter forked grass onto fir crossbars, with two toddlers scooping up the leavings. Watching their slow rhythmic progress under swallows that wheeled in graceful arabesques, Kurt felt a profound sense of peace. How had life brought him to such perfection? He thought of the winter he and his father had spent down a coal mine in the Ruhr – the perpetual choke of dust, the stink of gas, the soot that seeped through his pores, blackened his hair, lined his hands, etched permanent half moons under his nails so no matter how he scrubbed he never felt clean.

Taking another draft of fresh air, Kurt imagined he was drawing in everything he could see and smell and hear, making it a part of himself. This was how it should be. This was what the Führer meant when he talked of the Folk State and of Germany's heroic destiny. His words, delivered in the crisp purity of that Christmas Eve a half dozen years ago, still reverberated through Kurt's soul: "Race is the core of all that is valuable. Race and our struggle to keep it pure. . . . German boy, never forget you are German! Little girl, remember some day you will become a German mother! The Folk State must wipe out class and set race at the center of all life."

Kurt glimpsed Marthe Schultz, his future mother-in-law, and young Heidi, thick blond braids coiled around their ears, unpegging starched sheets from the line. As Frau Schultz tossed pins into Heidi's red apron, the wind lifted their skirts, revealing thick wool stockings and heavy lace-up boots, while the family goat tugged at the little girl's apron, sending her into fits of giggles. Seeing the hamper overflowing with snowy sheets crisp with wind and sunshine, Kurt thought of how often his mother had had to redo a line of laundry because a shift in the breeze had showered soot upon her morning's work.

Glancing up, Frau Schultz caught Kurt's eye and nodded without smiling. Though a jolly woman with a mouth organ and a pint of beer, she still found her future son-in-law too Prussian for her taste, a lapsed Lutheran instead of a Catholic. Like many Bavarians, she held the Prussians, with their severe military tradition, in grave suspicion, well aware that the Prussians returned the disfavor by patronizing Bavarians as self-indulgent bumpkins. As Bruno mockingly summed up the difference: "The favorite sidearm of a Bavarian is the beer mug!"

Kurt's SS uniform had been neatly laid out by Ilse on a trunk at the foot of his bed. After two years of part-time service in The Black Order, he was now a lance corporal, entitled to wear a collar badge with one stripe. Though the uniform had cost forty marks – more than Kurt had earned in a week as a road worker – Ilse had urged him to join the more recently formed Black Guard, owing loyalty directly to Adolf Hitler rather than the Brownshirts organized by Ernst Röhm to protect party meetings. Despite her love for Bruno, she shrewdly guessed that the closer the Führer came to being elected head of state, the more the unruly Brownshirts with their unsavory reputation would become an embarrassment to him.

The July 31 election a couple of weeks ago had proved Ilse prophetic. Though the Führer had been maneuvered out of the chancellorship by another coalition, the National Socialists had won 230 seats to become Germany's most powerful party, and already influential members were dismissing the Stormtroopers as "Brown Trash." By contrast, even the unaligned public regarded the highly disciplined Black Guards, armed only with ceremonial daggers, with relief bordering on respect.

After scrubbing in a wooden tub, enjoying the bite of cold water on a body toughened by military training, Kurt put on his SS uniform, making a ritual of it like a knight donning his armor. As he reached for his shirt, he intoned the SS motto: "*My Honor Is Loyalty.*" Then he asked himself: "Why do you believe in Germany and the Führer?" He answered: "Because we believe in the Germany He created in His world and in the Führer, Adolf Hitler, whom He sent us." By the time Kurt was tugging on his glossy black boots, he was repeating the oath: "I swear loyalty and courage to you, Adolf Hitler, as Führer. I vow obedience to the death to you and my superiors appointed by you. So help me God."

In a mirror under a crucifix, Kurt adjusted his black cap, with its aluminum eagle and silver Death's Head borrowed from the famous Black Hussars of the Imperial Cavalry and symbolizing his readiness to give his life for duty. Though he took great care angling it on his sleek blond head, he felt more pride than vanity. To become No. 33754 in the Black Guard, recruited by Reichsführer Heinrich Himmler, Kurt had had to prove his Aryan ancestry back to 1750 and to be six feet tall with a coordinated body of specific dimensions. Then Reichsführer SS Himmler had scrutinized closeups to ensure he conformed to strict racial type: long narrow face and head, well-defined chin, thin nose with high root, silky golden-blond hair, deep-set light-blue eyes, pink-white skin. Only fifteen of every hundred who applied for the 50,000-member honor guard were selected. A filled tooth would have disqualified him!

As Kurt affixed his dagger, Bruno kicked open the door. His rumpled blond hair, flushed face and messy SA uniform suggested he had not been to bed since last night's stag party. He was carrying a brimming glass of schnapps in each hand. Disappointed at his friend's appearance, Kurt accepted the schnapps.

"To all the Führer's new children beginning tonight,"

toasted Bruno, adding with a malicious wink: "And, to a dozen more saints for Himmler's 'Nigger' Guard."

As best man, Bruno was to drive Kurt to the church in the family ox cart, which the children had decorated with flowers and bells. As they sat in front, they were joined by a drunken Felix Krell, his Stormtrooper's cap at a rakish angle over his too-gold hair, while a half dozen younger brothers and cousins, wearing deerskin shorts with embroidered braces, jumped in back, all vying to sit where they could examine Kurt's wonderful black uniform.

As the two cream-colored oxen made their easy, sonorous way down a grassy path, Kurt forgot his irritation with Bruno and Felix in his enjoyment of the magnificent panorama of mountain, forest and stream. Overwhelmed by his own good fortune, he began to sing a folk song expressing Germany's defiant response to centuries of invasion and partition:

> "What is the Fatherland of the Germans?
> Is it Prussia? Is it Swabia?
> Is it where the grape ripens near the Rhine?"

His young companions trumpeted their response:

> "Oh no! no! no!
> His Fatherland is larger still."

Kurt sang:

> "What is a German's Fatherland?
> Name me then the great land."

A stirring chorus:

> "As far as the German tongue is heard
> And God in heaven is singing songs,
> So far shall it stretch.
> So much, brave German, call your own."

Awash in sentimentality, anxious to heal the rift

between himself and Bruno, Kurt clasped the big man's
right hand and gazed deeply into his eyes – the traditional
way in which German youths established brotherhood.
Deliberately misunderstanding, Bruno grounded their
elbows on the seat, turning a handshake into an arm wrestle. For ten seconds the two men stared each other down,
their strength evenly matched, sweat oozing from their
armpits, while the young boys cheered and Felix beat the
oxen, causing them to buck and veer. Though Kurt had
always been intimidated by Bruno, he saw weakness in his
eyes caused by too much boozing. As he slowly broke
down the big man's strength, Kurt remembered his Black
Order training: that he should only fight by duel with
another SS member and never sully his honor with an
inferior. Reluctantly Kurt withdrew from competition,
allowing Bruno to press his knuckles against the seat of
the ox cart to partisan shouts behind.

"So much for chicken-shit farmers!" jeered Bruno, a
mocking reference to Reichsführer Himmler's former
occupation as a chicken breeder. Jaw clenched, Kurt
refrained from mention of the dirty stories attached to SA
Chief Röhm's name, to rumors of the homosexuality said
to be rife throughout the rank and file.

While Ilse's second-oldest brother Erich calmed the
oxen, the two drunken Stormtroopers fell, arms around
each other, into the back of the ox cart. Producing a flask
of schnapps, they bellowed the Brownshirt anthem:

"The banner raised, the ranks firmly closed,
 SA marches with calm and steady pace.
 Comrades the Red Front and Reaction have gunned down,
 March in spirit with us in our ranks."

By now the dirt path had turned into a cobbled road,
with other carts and carriages headed in the same direction. A welcoming crowd awaited in front of the onion-
domed Catholic church, the men wearing leather shorts
with bright silk braces and green hats trimmed with

brushes, the women in black dresses with brilliantly colored aprons and black bonnets piled with satin ribbons,
flowers and semi-precious jewels. As the groom debarked,
the band of lutes, zithers, accordions, cymbals and mouth
organs broke into a lively folk song.

Kurt stood stiffly in the sunlight, aware of the scrutiny
of this close-knit clan, grateful for the approach of a pony
cart carrying Ilse's three younger sisters in long white
dresses and veils. Clambering down in a self-important
flurry, they just had time to get into mischief with the
choirboys in red cassocks when the church bells pealed. A
black gig covered in marigolds, driven by Ilse's grandfather smoking his pipe, trotted into the churchyard.
After a surprisingly sober Bruno had helped down his
plump mother, wheezing a little from the heat and excitement, the two youngest sisters sprang into action, casting
white rose petals in a carpet.

With a smile for everyone, Ilse stepped from the gig,
dressed in black like the other women but with a white
apron and diadem of pearls over her plaited hair. Curtsy-
ing, the eldest bridesmaid tripped forward with an armload of lilies, and recited in a rush: "This-is-the-happiest-
day-of-your-life. Take-care-of-the-children-God-gives you."
Growing red-faced and tongue-tied, she shifted from one
foot to another. When Ilse whispered the next words, she
rushed on: "Remember-to-be-faithful. Remember-to-be-
good." Emboldened, she glanced sideways at her mother,
twisting a rosary, then at her brother Bruno. Raising her
arm, she blurted: "Heil Hitler!" Which she offset with:
"God Bless." Pushing the lilies into Ilse's arms, she
retreated in a fit of giggles.

To another peal of church bells, the procession filed
through a cedar arch into a cemetery, with the petal
droppers leading the way. Kneeling at a large marble
tombstone, Ilse laid a lily on the grave of her father,
Bruno Schultz, killed in 1924 by an avalanche while rescuing two students trapped on the mountain. As Kurt

glanced around, he noticed most of the other gravestones in the small cemetery were equally impressive, many engraved in gold. A disproportionate number of deaths had occurred between 1914 and 1918, with the names marked by an Iron Cross or other military decoration, thus proving patriotism had not, as some Prussians maintained, stopped at the mountains.

As Marthe Schultz knelt beside her daughter to strew flowers on her husband's grave, Kurt thought of his own dead parents, and especially his mother – of the procreative process which had made one woman bloom while sending another to an early grave. He remembered how Hedda Schmidt had coaxed flowers out of their cinder patch and how the fall after she was buried a giant sunflower had sprouted from the acidic soil.

Kurt adjusted his eyes to the interior of the wood church lit by candles, its walls frescoed by local artists, its carved pews decorated with flowers. After the men seated themselves on the right, the women on the left, he and Ilse strolled up the aisle, then knelt on the stone before the altar. While the priest – a jovial, melon-faced man whose belly threatened to burst his robes – prayed over them, hands theatrically raised, Kurt peeked at his bride, saw her stolid form, plain face and child's turned-up nose, the laced boots with thick soles protruding from her plain black skirt, and envisioned the form of another woman superimposed on hers, white and shimmering, with red hair and honey eyes, the girl of his dreams, part real, part fantasy. As he shifted on the cold floor with stirrings of panic, Ilse opened her eyes and smiled in adoration, reminding him of the day she had fed him broth and unplaited her silky hair and raised her homespun skirt to reveal thick wool socks and sturdy shoes more erotic to him than silk stockings and a glass slipper.

"Do you take this man to be your husband?"

"Ja!"

"Do you take this woman to be your wife?"

His response was just as firm: "Ja!"

"Wives submit yourselves unto your husbands as it is fit in the Lord."

For several days Kurt and Ilse jogged in the black gig through Bavarian villages with their gabled pink, blue, green and yellow chalets, looking as if they were molded of marzipan, clinging to mountain slopes. Most villages centered on a cobbled square with a fountain, a Catholic church and a statue of the town's saint, often purchasable in maple sugar along with the carved toys and Christmas ornaments for which the region was noted. Ilse could not resist a crèche while Kurt bought a flute, remembering how his father used to play in the dark to save precious oil, with the sad silver notes sliding through the long winter's night like falling stars.

Everywhere they visited they found flowers – in windowboxes, stuck in hats, entwined in the manes of horses, sprouting from rocks as if struck by the wand of God, even in the mouths of fresh trout ordered for lunch. Everywhere they galloped they were pursued by music – the jangle of cowbells, the chime of clocks, the echo of church bells, the fluting of birds, the song of the lute or accordion or zither or mouth organ that every Bavarian seemed to play, the gurgle of streams as they swirled around gorges like champagne in a glass or dripped down glaciers to spatter into millions of dewdrops. Looking at Ilse, her hair plaited in a halo, her cheeks aglow like apples, Kurt couldn't imagine thinking of her as anything but beautiful. By contrast, the faces of fashionable Berliners seemed masks of chalk.

The swastika banners draped around many public squares reminded Kurt that this was Führer country, the cradle of the National Socialist movement, imported to Berlin. How wonderful to have participated in those early times with Ilse and Bruno, and how easy in this alpine setting to understand Aryan pride. It was reflected in the faces of the white-haired couples, arms entwined like the branches of oaks, as they hiked up mountains in the sunrise, just as it shone in the eyes of the Hitler Youth, who seemed to be everywhere – singing around campfires and holding military maneuvers in which they "killed" a comrade by ripping off his red swastika armband, a symbolic enactment of their pledge to fight to the death for their Führer. A few Bavarian towns had already renamed their squares Adolf Hitler Platz. Race, that was the answer. Though Kurt knew little of the Jews, he accepted the rightness of the yellow banners that boldly marked the gates of some villages: JEWS NOT WELCOME HERE.

The newlyweds spent their last day in the town of Kufstein, just over the Austrian border. Cut by the Inn River, it was dominated by a fist of gray rock crowned by a gloomy medieval schloss, once a prison. Buried in the stone were the pipes of a powerful organ which sent the Pilgrim's March from Wagner's *Tannhaüser* or the lyrical notes of Mendelssohn's *Spring Song* pouring through the seams and crevices in throaty waves that vibrated in the faces of the inhabitants before swishing down the valley.

As Kurt and Ilse sprawled on the white pebbles at the edge of the silty green water, they felt the notes pulsing through them, causing their flesh and bones to vibrate. Picking up his flute, Kurt managed a simple, plaintive tune, one his father used to play. For the first time he found himself able to speak freely of Ernst Schmidt, who had set out before the war with hundreds of other idealistic young men to found a society based on values beyond material ones. Calling themselves Wandervögelers, many of them had, like Himmler's Black Order, tried to restore the Teutonic code of honor from the Middle Ages. Like adherents of the Folk State, they had shunned cities for the forests and the farm.

"My father and mother built a log cabin to raise their own food and even spin their own clothes," Kurt confided. "My father was too soft-hearted. The turkeys got old and scrawny because he wouldn't kill them. They gobbled up the corn. He was studying to be a schoolteacher when war broke out. In his knapsack he carried the poetry of Schiller and Goethe instead of food, the legends of Parsifal and the knights of the Grail instead of an extra pair of boots. They gave this man who could not wring the neck of an old turkey a gun and told him to kill."

"Didn't you say your father was a revolutionary?" Ilse gently reminded him.

"He was. A war hero and a revolutionary." Staring into the clouds, Kurt confessed his secret. "My father fought for the Reds. After the war everyone was fighting everyone else. There was no leadership, as we have today. My father didn't fight other Germans. He knew the true enemy – he fought the French as if we were still at war, and that's how he died, in battle." Defiantly he insisted: "If my father were alive today, he would have been a believer. The insignia he wore on his Wandervögeler's cap was the same as ours – a swastika. Their greeting was the same – Heil!"

"If only he could have known the Führer," agreed Ilse. "The first time I saw him he walked into the Ratskeller where I had gone to fetch Bruno. Without speaking to anyone else, he gazed into my eyes as if piercing my soul. 'You will become one of us. I see in you the future of Germany.'"

Leaning over her new husband, Ilse admired the shock of baby-fine blond hair over closely set eyes and sharp nose, the muscular well-tanned torso and long limbs, feeling a fierce sense of possession. Always she had been intimidated by the birdlike women of Munich and Berlin who bobbed their hair, wore Paris fashions and wielded flirtatious powers over men. War had killed so many German youths, she had resigned herself to spinsterhood, devoting herself to others as nurse and National Socialist. Now there had been some miraculous shift in the universe. To marry a Black Guard she had gone through an equally stringent test of her Aryan ancestry and had been awarded the highest rating. Suddenly the way was open for her to play an even more glorious role in the forging of the New Germany. Untying her white drawstring blouse, she urged Kurt: "I want to become pregnant. Now, here, before we go back to Berlin."

They made love against the hard white pebbles of the Inn River with the music of Wagner's "Pilgrim's March" still pulsing through them. As Kurt slowly blended his rhythm with Ilse's, his mind drifted back to the day his father told him about this mystery that occurs between man and woman – the official explanation as to why his mother's belly waxed like a cold moon under her faded dress while her limbs and face grew thinner, verified by the man who had unwisely planted his seed in such a frail container, so that she died in agony between two blood-red sheets. Now, as Kurt's groin tightened then released, he understood the elemental force so impossible to refuse, and felt purged of his resentment toward the haunted man who had fathered him. He forgave him the bowls of steamy blood which might have been a brother unceremoniously dumped by the midwives in the last of the snow, forgave even Kurt's own careless banishment to the empty woodshed. He remembered only how they labored side by side with shovels to turn a patch of cinders into a grave.

Ilse could not understand why the act that gave her such uncomplicated joy frequently left her husband in tears. Sensing his birth in a darker womb, she simply offered her breast – the unthinking answer, in her peasant's world, to fears without a name.

Berlin

November 1932

CARMEL KOHL and Axel Berg were married November 1 at the villa of Count Wolfgang von Friedrich in fashionable Hansa-viertel bordering the Tiergarten. The wedding took Berlin by surprise, but none more than the bride. Cutting short his Düsseldorf trip, Axel casually announced to Carmel he had arranged a divorce and now wanted to get married.

The ceremony was conducted by a Lutheran minister in the Friedrich library – a hexagon lined with leather-bound military histories. Subdued in high-necked mauve chiffon with matching gloves, Frau Hildebrand Fuchs functioned as both mother and father to the bride. It was also she who cured Carmel's eleventh hour jitters.

"What's all this crap about freedom?" she chided, mouth bristling with pins as she tucked the lace bridal gown she had designed. "Axel has never taken your freedom. He's given you the confidence and the dough to do things you couldn't manage without him. Too much freedom destroyed your mama. She had far more of the bourgeoisie in her than she cared to admit. Just like you. Oh don't we all! Get that out of your system first, then grow old and foolish like me. When I was your age, I was married to the elderly widow of an undertaker. Her first husband staked me to The Red Fox, though he would have turned in his silk-lined mahogany Beauty Rest to know it. He never smoked, drank, danced or fornicated –

died in the best of health. I'm sure." Draping Carmel's train over her tattooed bicep, she concluded: "As for Axel's age – it's Germany's young men who have the habit of kicking the bucket first."

Wolfgang von Friedrich was the natural choice for best man. To Carmel's relief and secret sorrow he took both the news of her marriage and her defection to work for his arch-rival Leo Warner with aplomb bordering on indifference. Now as he produced the ring from his vest pocket, his eyes were as enigmatic as poker chips.

". . . till death do us part."

Axel embraced Carmel. As their kiss blossomed into something more passionate than formality required, she glimpsed his two daughters, stolid as boiled potatoes, scowling at her and she grieved for them, that they had never known their father's adoration. She also grieved for their mother, in her over-polished, over-furnished mansion in Düsseldorf – the woman who had been abandoned, bought off, outmaneuvered as her reward for always doing what she was told she should.

The reception was held in the Friedrich ballroom – a two-story, ice-blue oval with baroque dome painted in plump cupids and lightly clad Italian Renaissance maidens. While the bridal party received in the burgundy hallway marked with stern portraits of Friedrich forebears, chauffeur-driven Mercedeses and Daimlers, Rolls-Royces and Fiats swept through the crested iron gate to disgorge their occupants: princes and pretenders with almost as much gold braid as the doorman; generals with complexions as waxy as their mustaches; glittering names from stage and screen with glittering gowns to match; diplomats as stiff as their starched shirts; industrialists as fat as their cigars; financiers trying to get the hang of their new monocles. And scattered about like ominous Black and Brown shadows, ranking members of the National Socialist party to which Axel Berg generously donated.

As soon as Carmel broke from the receiving line, she sensed, with a performer's canny instinct for crowds, that the party was in trouble. Voices were too shrill, gestures too animated. Though no one had touched the sumptuous banquet, the bodies were four deep at all the bars despite blue-liveried waiters with silver trays. Instead of buzzing from group to group, gossiping and showing off their feathers, guests were knotted in fists from which the adrenalin rose higher than the cigar smoke. When one waiter dropped a champagne bottle, the room exploded.

It had been folly to mix so many high-powered and hostile people at this juncture in German politics. Less than three months after the last election, on July 31, the Reichstag had again been dissolved. Though the National Socialists had won a stunning 230 seats, the Communists had also gained at the expense of the moderates. Since no party had an overall majority, President Hindenburg had refused to make Adolf Hitler chancellor, and Hitler had refused to support Chancellor von Papen's cabinet of barons sympathetic to restoring the monarchy. Germany's fourth election of the year was to take place in less than a week. The country teetered on anarchy.

One person in the room seemed oblivious to the tension. The groom. As Axel moved from group to group, he was like a headwaiter with nothing more pressing on his mind than whether the sauce on the roast duck had enough brandy. He observed to deposed Crown Prince Friedrich Wilhelm – a waspish, gray-blond man with face pinched as if squinting through a pince-nez: "A few months of the House of Hitler to wipe out the Communists, then it's back with huzzahs to the House of Hohenzollern."

The prince sniffed. "Perhaps a little longer, Herr Berg, but who can take seriously a man who doesn't know how to eat artichokes?" Angling his head toward SA Chief Ernst Röhm, he scoffed: "You see his gang of Brownshirts strutting in those overcut children's breeches and Devil's dinner jackets and you long to press upon them the card of a good tailor. Surely we Germans have far too much sense of history to let ourselves be governed by street bums playing soldier."

With scar-faced Ernst Röhm, known unaffectionately as the Bavarian Brawler, Axel sympathized. "It's refreshing after decades of decadence to feel the country on the move again."

"I look after the streets, while the Führer bashes heads in that gentlemen's sewing circle called the Reichstag," boasted Röhm. "We're just beginning. My men like making revolution better than celebrating it." Jerking his thumb toward Field Marshal Werner von Blomberg, resplendent in his gray Wehrmacht uniform covered with medals, he threatened: "Very pretty, but soon the Brown flood will rise like shit to the level of that delicate nose."

Shifting to Blomberg, Axel reassured him: "Since Hitler and his gang have so little sense of legality, they're our chance to rearm in spite of the Versailles treaty. Then you and Hindenburg can incorporate the Brownshirts into the army. Once again Germany will be a world power to reckon with."

Sucking on his champagne glass, Blomberg glowered. "It takes more than an army uniform to breed honor in a man, Herr Berg. The Wehrmacht has never put up recruitment posters in prisons, urinals and dosshauses."

With fellow industrialists, Axel had no trouble finding common ground. To Gustav Krupp, he winked. "Rearmament under Adolf Hitler isn't going to hurt you and it isn't going to hurt me. Like Faust, I'd make my deal with the devil for that."

Dr. Josef Goebbels, boss of Berlin's Nazis since 1926, was served a dose of flattery. "Let me congratulate the man who has done more than any other to turn politics into religion. Your publication *Der Angriff* makes inspirational reading."

The unprepossessing little doctor revealed: "I once considered becoming a priest. A lot can be learned from the Catholic church about manipulation." Unctuously, he added: "Of course it isn't I who chose the Führer. It was God."

As Carmel listened to Axel deliver contradictory opinions with both enthusiasm and conviction, she reminded herself it was her husband's ability to reshape reality to his own desires that had enabled him to rise above pain and adversity to become an industrialist instead of just another crippled veteran begging in doorways. She remembered how nervously she had confessed to Axel she was working for Leo Warner's Red Forum only to have him laugh. "If you like the role, so what? We'll need a token Communist at the wedding to keep the Jews happy." Perhaps it was the flexibility of influential men like Axel that would keep Germany stable in the treacherous months ahead, Carmel rationalized.

A flawless host, Wolfgang glided through the room as gracefully as if on roller skates, offering the balm of wit, charm, even truthful observation. Yet there was only one person he was eager to draw out: his school chum Reinhard Heydrich, typically off by himself, pretending to study a nineteenth-century landscape by Caspar David Friedrich. Of greater fascination was the fact Reinhard was wearing an SS colonel's black uniform with a silver SD on the sleeve, meaning espionage and security service.

Approaching from the rear, Wolf teased: "Since that landscape painting mesmerizes you, perhaps you'd better take it. It's by my great-great-uncle, and my late mother's favorite. Since she forced me to reproduce it so often in the vain hope the family talent would blossom like orchids from my fingers, I'd still see it on that wall even if I burned it."

As he spun around, Reinhard almost upset a waiter with two brandies. Catching them as they slid, Wolf offered one to Reinhard. "Congratulations on *your* wedding. Sorry I couldn't make it. I was up to my knickers in

Lorelei. I hear you've done very well for yourself. Danish nobility. Lina . . . ?"

"Von Ostend, from the Baltic Islands. Danish, yes, but committed German nationalists."

"Then that explains the National Socialist uniform."

"Certainly Lina was all for it."

"And the Security Service badge?"

"How did you spot that?"

"You forget. I was brought up on badges, epaulettes, insignia. My father, the General. I read them the way some youths identify cars by their headlights."

"My new career is based on a misunderstanding," confessed Heydrich. "When Reichsführer SS Heinrich Himmler interviewed me, I told him I was an experienced Nachrichtenoffizier, meaning wireless officer. He though I said Nachrichtendienst-Offizier, or intelligence officer. Handing me a couple of cigar boxes stuffed with notes, he announced I was in charge of the Security Service. That, a chair and a kitchen table made up my empire. The office and typewriter I had to share with an SS major. When we moved to a two-room flat so my wife could join me, we still had to fetch the same typewriter by tram. Now we're almost grand in a suburban villa, with seven assistants and our own typewriter. Still, I admit my pay doesn't always arrive on time and once my telephone was cut off."

Since it wasn't like Reinhard to boast about poverty, Wolf concluded he must be caught up in something so engrossing it transcended his need to show off and he experienced envy. "When you called this morning, you said you had something to ask me."

Reinhard nodded. "I want you to sponsor me for the Imperial Dueling Club."

"After the butcher's scar you slashed across my face? Never!"

Refusing the comic bait, Reinhard confessed: "I should warn you that I've already been turned down. I was accused of being Jewish."

"Ahh, the old trouble. I thought your SS uniform would make that a contradiction in terms."

"Your imperial club is harder to convince than the SS racial committee or the law courts," complained Reinhard.

Wolf knew the story: Reinhard's father, Bruno, had delighted in malicious Jewish imitations that earned him the nickname "Isadore." Ironically, Reinhard's peers had taken that name seriously and dubbed him White Moses. Confusing the issue, his paternal grandmother had taken a second husband with the Jewish surname Süss, although he denied being Jewish.

"You know, my brother won his slander case when he was refused membership in a student's organization," reminded Reinhard.

"Yes, I remember, but frankly I'd have more fun sponsoring you if you *were* Jewish. I'll send a letter tomorrow to Old Bony, the president - if he lasts the night. I'm always surprised to see my father's cronies still doddering around. I would have thought he'd have fallen on his sword a decade ago."

Reinhard pumped his hand, his voice rising to the high pitch that had also made him a butt of jokes. "No doubt I'll soon be in a position to repay you. I want the SD to be an elite force like the British Secret Service – lawyers, academics, chemists, engineers, aristocrats, technocrats. Not blockheads from the SA. Even now ten percent of the SS section leaders are of noble birth – many of your old friends. Count von der Schulenburg is interested, the Duke of Mecklenburg, the Prince of Waldeck-Pyrmont. I'll be in touch."

"You forget. I'm allergic to uniforms. The General again."

"Think about it."

"I'm mildly intrigued. But first I'm going to London and Paris for a few months to buy art. I may even go to America. I've had some flattering offers since *Lorelei*. Right now I'd better revert to host! I see one of your

Brown blockheads bearing down on you. Do you want to be introduced fast to someone else?"

Glancing over his shoulder, Reinhard saw Ernst Röhm, head of four and a half million Brownshirts. "I don't mind Röhm. He's courageous, well organized and powerful. It's the party peacocks that raise my gorge and –" he shifted his eyes toward Josef Goebbels – "the demigods-in-waiting."

They touched brandy snifters. "Auf Wiedersehen."

By now waiters were clearing the banquet tables from the dance floor. Hypertension had given way to gloom, the screech of voices to a drunken slur that made traversing the room like wading through a swamp. Wolf perceived only one piece of drollery: The General from The Red Fox was receiving sodden salutes from those who were the real thing.

Not surprisingly, the Café des Westens irregulars had congregated at the bar. Joining them, Wolf heard Christian Jürgens – Carmel's co-star in *Lorelei* – challenge the rest: "Can you guess the major cause of death among my friends this past year?" He held his finger to his head. "Suicide, and the last one was only twenty-three."

"I'll lay odds half the bullets were in the back," insisted Leo Warner, puffing his Brazilian cigar. "Since the Reichstag was dissolved, I can verify five bomb attacks and a dozen beatings. In Frankfurt, Brownshirts forced a comrade's aged mother to watch while they poked out his eyes and carved swastikas on his back. He died of stab wounds – twenty-nine in the chest alone."

"You café Communists must take some blame," interjected Wolf. "You take simpletons from farms and factories, flatter them into thinking their ignorance is healthy common sense, and next thing they're out on the streets with their pitchforks and monkey wrenches. When I see Nazi truncheons fight the Red hammer, I'm looking at cobras and mongoose. What is communism but international fascism? The one subordinates race to class, the other class to race."

"Ahhh, a blueblood who hides behind Hindenburg's mustache," taunted Leo. "The Old Gentleman will save us all."

"Hindenburg? What foolishness! Why would I put my faith in an old geezer who brags the only two books he has read are the Bible and the army manual? I'm no different from every other German. I yearn for the Great Man who'll save us, but I don't see him wearing a long gray mustache or a little black one or a Red one. The Old Guard is bankrupt – I admit it. Just look at them with their noses in their brandies. Have you ever seen as many medals in one room? Not a gewgaw won in junior fencing but what it's on display. What's it all for? A prayer to ward off evil!"

"Last month the Norn Players were putting on *A Midsummer Night's Dream* in Hamburg," informed Christian. "A nice safe choice, wouldn't you think? At dress rehearsal our director got an anonymous call forbidding him to use Mendelssohn's music for the wedding march. Why? Because it was Jewish music! Very well. He decided to use none at all. We would walk in rhythm with the music in our heads. It drove the audience crazy. We received a standing ovation, and for two nights played to full houses. Then the Brownshirts came with their stink bombs. Who wants to live in a country where music is not free, like air and sunlight?"

Frau Sara Stein, as dark and angular as her husband, Max, was pink and plump, emphatically agreed. "Ja. Ask my husband. All our friends and relatives are leaving, mostly for Palestine. For a Jew it's the brick through Herr Steinberg's groceteria window last week, and the money he must pay so it doesn't happen again. It's the inspector who altered our butcher's weight scale when he was at the cash register, then accused him of cheating Aryans. It's the Adolf Hitler brats who chase my eighty-year-old mother home from the bus stop, cursing her with the swastika *and* the cross. It isn't enough that my husband is fired from the university, but we also get anonymous calls saying my sister is dead, and packages of excrement through the mail!"

The group spun toward the distinguished professor. "You were fired?"

He shrugged. "An occupational hazard, given my specialty."

"Since when? For what?"

Adjusting his thick glasses as if they might help him see the truth, he confided: "It's been brewing a long time. Especially since my last paper – a dull and scholarly effort in which I explored how languages reflect the people who invent them. As Nietzsche said, German is a language shaped by military commands, but the soldier and child are alike both in their literal-mindedness and in their need for authority, don't you think? One way I demonstrated this was by pointing out how German names for unfamiliar things are created by joining the words for things already known, like a child shunting the cars of a toy train: Speisekarte, which would be food list or menu in English. Fernspecher, meaning far-talker or telephone. Magenschleimhautenzündung, which is stomach-mucous-membrane-inflammation – a diagnosis where the English just use the word gastritis. What I find most revealing are words considered taboo. The French most often curse with religious words, the English with sexual words, but we Germans regress to the anal, like Scheisskopf for shithead."

"Is that why you were fired, for shitting on German pride?" asked Leo Warner.

"That and a little worse," confessed the professor. "My true crime was in tracing many German words back to their Semitic roots. For that I was branded a dangerous heretic."

"Didn't your colleagues protect you?" demanded Christian.

"Who do you think petitioned for his dismissal?" fumed Frau Stein. "Who arranged the boycott of his classes? His colleagues who took over his department!"

With a heavy sigh the professor admitted: "In deciding to get rid of me, the university senate had more inside pressure than outside. What can you do? Radicalism in our colleges has traditionally been right wing. Many students and professors were demanding Aryan-only enrollment clauses long before the general population warmed up to the idea."

"Didn't any of your colleagues defend intellectual freedom?" persisted Christian. "Couldn't they see they were cutting off their noses to spite their faces?"

"Not their nose but the Jewish nose, always deemed a little too long for comfort," reminded the professor. "When Jews and Communists lose teaching posts, the joy of those who profit through advancement is at least easy to understand. What is harder is the craziness of those professors who are now denouncing Einstein's theories as 'Jewish physics' – as if the stars themselves care about a man's race!"

"I'm told by friend at Heidelberg University that the gallop of sycophantic professors to join the Nazis has made even old-line party members indignant," informed Wolf. "It's becoming such a scandal, Hitler himself is considering putting a stop to it." Without his usual flippancy, he added: "At times like this it's impossible for me to eat as much as I'd like to throw up."

"Yet we stay in this terrible place!" wailed Frau Stein, wringing her hands. "Thank God all my relatives have the sense to leave."

"Now Mutti, Mutti," soothed the professor. "Others have children or wealth or talent to protect. What excuse do we old fogies have beside one aging dog? Always Jews have been forced to wander. My family has lived in Berlin for six generations. It's our duty to stay put, not to run away as if being a Jew were a crime. We must not desert our posts."

Tightening his arm around his gypsy wife, endangered by the same Aryan prejudices, Christian mourned: "As an actor, it's folly for me to learn another language and start over somewhere else, but if thought I was jeopardizing my dear Renate, I'd want to kill myself. Can things get worse? If the Nazis win the election, will they be content to gorge on the plums like that fat one, Göring?"

"Anything can happen in a country without a powerful ruling class or a liberal tradition," warned Wolf. "We're experiencing in politics the same force we experienced in art – the impatient turning away from the rational to the miraculous. Sturm und Drang."

"The rest of Europe should pity us rather than hate us," defended the professor. He launched into a lecture as if trying to convince himself. "Here we sit on the fault line between East and West, with few natural boundaries to protect us. Because our princes were too jealous to unite, they allied themselves with foreign nations who invaded and partitioned us. Bismarck almost united us with Berlin as capital, but the hatred of Prussia was too strong. Germany's alliance with Rome, creating the Holy Roman Empire, gave the illusion of unification while delaying the reality. Then Luther's Reformation split us again, with Protestants in the north and Catholics in the south. We Germans passionately love our Fatherland, but where is it? When a country can't define itself by land and the need is strong, it will do so by ideas, such as language and race."

"Talk, talk, talk. Who needs fancy explanations when a rock is being tossed at you?" demanded the exasperated Sara Stein. "How convenient for the Bavarians and Prussians to decide to love each other and to hate the Jews instead!"

"But we Jews also have this other problem," the professor reminded the group. "Because of a wanderer's familiarity with international customs, some of us were better prepared for the Weimar Republic, Germany's one experiment with democracy, and rose too high too fast. Others were better able to weather inflation so the theory grew we created it to profit from it. Now to overcome a sense of inferiority for losing both the military war and the economic one, some Germans are falling in love with themselves as the blue-eyed, blond-haired master race, and everyone who doesn't fit is forced to pay the price."

"Oh it's a joke, but I can't laugh," exclaimed Raymon Arno. "Who is the ugliest person in the room? Is it that swine-faced Röhm, said to be a homosexual, or the rat-faced Goebbels, a notorious seducer of women? Yet when each looks into his Führer's mirror, he sees Superman. I've even heard a man who claimed to be a racial specialist refer to Hitler as blond-haired in a room of people who managed to keep straight faces. As an artist I must trust my eyes. How can I survive in a world where people look at black and insist they see white?"

"Ja! For you the greatest murder is that of images, for me it's words," exclaimed the professor. "*Volk* used to mean peasant until Adolf Hitler perverted it to mean untainted by Jewish blood. In his rag *Der Angriff*, Herr Doktor Goebbels uses *fanatic* as if it were something good, like heroic, and *wild fanatic* as something better. That man even talks of *simple pomp*. When you distort a language, you distort the people who speak that language. The twisting of truth, like a baboon playing with a coat hanger – now that I can't forgive."

Wiping sweat from his brow with a mended handkerchief, the professor calmed himself. "Sanity will return, it must. Aren't we Germans the people who gave the world Bach and Handel, Beethoven and Brahms, Goethe and Schiller, Kafka and Kant and Einstein and Mann? Though sometimes we pursue our romantic excesses with a streak of barbarism, we also have an equal love of order. When revolutionaries stormed the Reichstag after the Great War, they not only obeyed signs forbidding them to step on the grass, but also signed the guest book and put cloths under their machine guns so as not to scratch the marble floors. I trust we Germans have rushed far enough in one direction and will soon come to our senses – with good luck, in time for the election."

"Can you believe this man?" asked Frau Stein with an

exasperated sigh. "For thirty-five years we've shared the same bed, and the only quarrel we've ever had is about immigrating to Palestine. What can I do with such a husband? Even now he insists he's as much a German as a Jew!"

Clasping his wife's hand, the professor mocked, "Always there is prejudice, but what can I do with this woman, my wife, who thinks she is without a drop of it while being as proud as a cat with a mouse of belonging to the Sephardic Jews from Spain, the oldest aristocracy in the world, with the poor Galician Jews from Polish Galicia at the bottom. Always she talked talked talked of moving to Palestine, but remember, mein Liebling, what happened the time we bought our tickets? When it came to go, my Sara, who told me she was willing to leave with only the clothes on her back, insisted on packing every stick of furniture from a twelve-room house, every piece of mended underwear, every chipped cup. To Palestine with half of Germany? Easier for a rich man to squeeze through the eye of a needle!"

Together they laughed, suggesting this was an old and familiar quarrel. As Sara Stein puffed herself in indignation, the orchestra struck up "The Blue Danube." Turning to the dance floor, her husband joked: "What is an Austrian but a German in three-quarter time? Where is the bride? We're not being fair, talking this way. We must forget our troubles. This is a wedding."

As he spoke, Axel Berg, distinguished in formal dress with medals and decorations, escorted Carmel onto the floor and, sliding his arm around her waist, began to waltz. After a few gallant turns, during which he strove to conceal his limp, Count Wolfgang von Friedrich tapped him on the shoulder. Bowing, Axel retired with dignity to a Louis XIV settee while the best man swept off with the bride.

Other couples moved onto the floor, transforming it into a swirl of gowns like water lilies on a pond. For the first time, Frau Axel Berg relaxed, feeling the happiness that tension had bottled up inside her. She watched the Steins glide by, saw Sara laugh flirtatiously at her husband, easing the frown lines from her brow, becoming the carefree young girl she once had been.

Carmel closed her eyes, feeling pretty pink bubbles of champagne burst in a fizzy spatter in her head, spinning around and around. . . . She felt Wolf stiffen then stop. She opened her eyes. He was frowning over her shoulder. A dozen yards away the Steins were dancing, eyes closed, encircled by Brownshirts.

"Oh my God!" Carmel remembered the girl with shaved head at Brandenburger Tor: SPIT ON ME, I HAVE GIVEN MYSELF TO A JEW. As she watched, one of Ernst Röhms Stormtroopers lurched to the orchestra leader, then bullied him into playing the Brownshirts' anthem:

"The banner raised, the ranks firmly closed . . ."

While the Brownshirts snapped to attention, the Steins opened their eyes in bewilderment.

Without a word, Wolf whisked Carmel across the floor and, clicking his heels, bowed before Frau Stein. Before she could protest, he had her by the waist and was twirling her in three-quarter time. Carmel grabbed the bewildered Max Stein. Humming "The Blue Danube" over competing strains of the Brownshirt anthem, she waltzed him around the room.

Now all eyes were on Axel Berg, seated on the Louis XIV settee. After only a brief hesitation, he limped toward the conductor, gaining momentum. Waving his steel-headed walking stick in what was intended as waltz time, he guided the orchestra back from revolution to Strauss. A pause. The guests surged onto the floor. Soon every square inch was filled with waltzing couples, some singing gaily if drunkenly. Röhm, his arms folded across his chest, his face like the blood on the Nazi banner, stared as if fixing every face in his memory. With a snap of his head he signaled his Brownshirts toward the door. In less than three minutes all had filed out, as if the stopper had been yanked from a bottle of whiskey.

FOUR

Berlin

January 1933

FOR A MONTH Ilse Schmidt had had January 30 circled on her calendar. That was the day she and Kurt were to move from the cottage they shared with her brother Bruno to a two-room flat several blocks away but still in the cozy working-class district of Neukölln. Though they could barely afford it, neither could they resist it. As a nurse at the Berlin Prenatal Clinic run by Dr. Alfred Zuckmayer, Ilse earned 130 marks a month. Through party connections Kurt had wangled a job at the Northstar Tool and Dye Works, coincidentally owned by Axel Berg, where he earned 160 marks a month with opportunity to acquire engineering papers. The rent on the flat was 100 marks a month, but who could balk at that when optimism was in the air they breathed? Admittedly, the National Socialists had lost ground to the Communists during the November 6 election, but it was still the most popular party, and President Hindenburg's stubborn attempt to create yet another conservative government under Chancellor Kurt von Schleicher had collapsed after only fifty-eight days. Despite the Old Man's vow that he would never appoint that "upstart Bohemian corporal," he had run out of options. Adolf Hitler waited in a suite in the Kaiserhof Hotel for the summons to the palace expected daily. His star was rising. The Schmidts were moving up with him.

All through the Christmas season Ilse and Kurt had

scoured secondhand stores for furniture, while shopping
in Wertheim's department store for smaller items such as
dishes and linens. Never before had Kurt owned more
than he could carry in two shopping bags. Never before
had he entered this ritzy Jewish temple of consumerism
except as a prowling dog trying to get warm. Then one
sniff had brought the white-gloved floorwalkers. Now
clerks in neat serge suits with detachable white collars
solicitously demonstrated to him the advantages of one
can opener over another. He was especially enchanted by
the appliance department with electric irons many times
lighter than the one his mother had heated on their stove,
not to mention electric toasters to ease the labor of
browning bread with a fork. While Ilse compared bolts of
material, deciding on yellow sheers for the kitchen, lace
for the living room and blue cotton for the bedroom, Kurt
watched the clerk roll off yard after yard of the slippery
colorful fabric, so dazzled he thought he must have
rubbed Aladdin's lamp.

Later, when the Schmidts arranged then re-arranged
their chesterfield and one chair, Kurt was dismayed to see
how little impression their store of treasures made on the
two modest rooms. Secretly he yearned for the timbered
cottage which Bruno now shared with his friend Felix. A
burrowing animal, Kurt felt safest close to the ground, but
Ilse had declared she could never feel like a Berliner until
she lived in a flat.

Sensing his disappointment, she soothed: "You'll see,
accessories make all the difference" – a sentiment she had
gleaned from decorating ads. "Right now we're a Christmas tree without decorations."

Over the mantel they arranged a framed poster of the
Führer flanked by photos of Ilse in her nurse's uniform;
Kurt in his SS uniform shaking hands with Reichsführer
Himmler; wedding pictures taken by Ilse's brother Erich.
In an alcove of pine tables and chairs made by Ilse's
grandfather they hung Kurt's chalk drawing of Kufstein,
which they had visited on their honeymoon. Over the

secondhand bed purchased for only six marks, with its patchwork quilt painstakingly sewed by Ilse's sisters, they nailed Marthe Schultz's gift of a crucifix.

As they relaxed on their chintz chesterfield before the fireplace, sharing a bottle of Riesling, Ilse gave Kurt his housewarming gift – an electric toaster. Laughing, he presented her with a silky pink nightgown and a wooden cradle. Rocking it with her bare toe, she sighed. "Five months and I'm not pregnant. I do everything Dr. Zuckmayer suggests. Do you think there's something wrong with me?"

Kurt grinned. "Do you think there's something wrong with me? Maybe I've been marching in too many parades, handing out too many leaflets, studying too many engineering textbooks." Laying his hand on Ilse's lap, feeling the fullness of her thigh through her peasant skirt, he gazed into her face, framed by shoulder-length braids shiny with firelight, remembering how the Teutonic hero Siegfried had claimed his Valkyrie bride from a bed of flames. "My Brynhilde, isn't it time we tried out our new bed?" Attempting to carry her like Siegfried, he grunted under his burden, then settled for walking, arms entwined.

They were lying in bed enjoying the lazy aftermath of love, with Kurt improvising on his flute, when they heard a thump on the door.

"It's me. Open up," bellowed Bruno.

Groaning, Kurt pressed his hand over Ilse's mouth.

"I know you're in there," brayed Bruno, banging all the louder. "And I know what you're doing. Come on out, little lovebirds, or we'll smash the door."

Disgruntled, Kurt yanked on his pants while Ilse fumbled for a skirt. Before he had even opened the door, Bruno and Felix burst in, stamping off snow. "I knew we'd catch you at it," leered Bruno. "Making little babies for the Führer!"

"Where were you when we had furniture to move?" grumbled Kurt.

"Watching history being made."

"What?" Seizing his brother-in-law's arm, he demanded: "You mean the chancellorship? It's happened?"

Backing down, Bruno admitted: "Not officially, but the crowds are ten deep around the Kaiserhof and the palace and the chancellery. We've left Hermann to bring us the news as soon as it happens."

Though still sulky, Kurt's pride at being master of his house resurfaced. While Bruno and Felix flopped onto the chesterfield, he fetched a round of Pilseners, then took the armchair, leaving Ilse to drag in a kitchen chair. Ignoring the bottle opener, Bruno fit two beers together and snapped his wrists, shooting off the caps in a spray of foam, again forcing Kurt to swallow his annoyance at seeing his newly painted floor so casually desecrated.

"Here's to the shit-end of the Weimar Republic!" toasted Bruno.

"We hope," cautioned Ilse.

"It's in the bag," assured Felix, who specialized in the latest rumor from the highest source. "Röhm told me himself that we've got something on Hindenburg's son Oskar. Now Papa Hindenburg has to pay by giving us the chancellery or risk scandal."

"But it was a free election and the Führer won," protested Ilse. "We don't need blackmail."

"Leave politics to me, Little Sister," growled Bruno.

"What I'm hoping is that shithead Schleicher will try to get his power back by using the Potsdam garrison for a coup," gloated Felix.

Patting his "eraser" as if it were a dog, Bruno confided: "I'd love the Commies to call a general strike. Wouldn't that be fun! They'd find more than fish in the Landwehr Kanal."

Opening four more bottles of beer, Bruno cheered: "To the revolution!" Since Radio Berlin was filling in time by playing a Liszt prelude, Bruno put a record of the Brownshirt anthem on the gramophone he had given Ilse and

Kurt for their wedding, turning up the volume. Still unsat-
isfied with the pace of history, he flung open the living-
room window, despite the blast of January air, and bellowed to passersby: "Long live Adolf Hitler, our new
chancellor!"

Carmel Kohl sat at her old dressing table in the new Red
Forum applying her makeup. A man of obsessions, Leo
Warner insisted his company have an afternoon dress
rehearsal for *Our Motherland*, despite the fact it premiered this evening.

The last few months had been extraordinarily vivid
ones for Carmel – a time when all paradoxes seemed true.
Though never stronger, she feared she would fly into a
thousand pieces; though never clearer of vision, she suspected she was insane; though never closer to the edge, she
felt centered and serene; though never more self-absorbed,
she had never worked with such selfless dedication.

The focus had been her struggle to get inside the skin of
her own mother Rosa for her role in *Our Motherland* – a
heartbreaking and exhilarating experience, like a fetus
crawling back into the womb. But first the past had had to
be faced, memories released, especially the torturing ones
from the night of July 7, 1921, almost twelve years
ago. . . .

Awakening, age thirteen, on the lumpy sofa in the parlor, gagging on gas. Stumbling to the pink door. Struggling to open it but finding the cracks jammed with rags.
Staggering to the window. Smashing it with both fists.
Retching and vomiting even while she swallowed fresh air.

Mother! Lurching to the bedroom, tears burning her
eyes. A lump in the bed. Reaching out. Not her mother.
The body of a man, a butcher knife plunged into his
heart! Panicking. Unable to catch her breath, even to
scream. Groping her way back to the window. More gulps
of air. Dizzy. Vomiting. Frantically searching for her
mother. Finding her. Her head in the oven. Dead.

Again the window. Sobbing. Finding the bloody butcher knife in her hands. Using it to unjam the rags from the pink door. Hysterical now. Racing down three flights of stairs into the street. Not stopping till she had collapsed into the arms of Frau Hildebrand Fuchs.

Twelve years later, Frau Fuchs comforted Carmel Kohl, age twenty-five, as she had the child. "Your mother loved you but she couldn't protect you. She couldn't love or save herself. That was her real tragedy. Not her death."

The day after that shocking-pink door had unlocked inside her, Carmel read all the yellowing newspaper accounts of the sensational murder-suicide in which Rosa Kohl had played the star role she craved. Afterward, she spoke to dozens of people who had known her mother – neighbors, regulars at The Red Fox and the bars where she drank, even a couple of clients. At last she came to understand with compassion this unfortunate woman who was all vital force without a container strong enough to hold it. At last she could forgive her, and herself.

Now – January 30, 1933 – Carmel was finishing her makeup when a clanging bell caused her to smear her mascara. Damn. The alarm meant either fire or all hands on stage. Smelling no smoke, she decided "all hands" was more likely.

Leo Warner was pacing across Raymon Arno's stark black-and-white set, hands knotted behind his back, green cap pulled over his ears, puffing so incessantly on his Brazilian cigar that smoke seemed to stream from his pores. Occasionally he would stop, fling out his arms and cry: "This is all done. It's the end. Kaput!"

When someone found the courage to ask if he meant the play, Leo turned on him. "The play? No! I mean everything. It's the end of civilization in Germany." Blowing his nose on a soiled handkerchief, he announced: "An hour ago that slimy little dosshaus graduate who flunked art school was named chancellor of Germany. The oath has already been taken. It's irreversible. He's moved into the chancellery vowing no one will ever get him out alive.

Last month Nazi thugs closed down *All Quiet on the Western Front* and the Communist Volksbühne. If we open tonight, it will be a provocative political act. While I'm a tyrant on the stage, I believe in every man's conscience off the stage. If we are to open, we must agree unanimously. Otherwise . . ."

Without waiting for the alternative, cast and crew chorused: "Ja! We must go on. Ja! We open tonight." For them all, the play was something that couldn't be stopped any more than you could forbid a woman in labor to give birth.

Confronting Frau Fuchs, sitting alone in the darkened theater, Leo demanded: "And you, madame?"

Grandly tossing her feather boa, she delivered the most famous line in showbiz: "The show must go on."

Black top hat beside him, Count Wolfgang von Friedrich maneuvered his car through the crowds blocking Unter den Linden. As he skidded to a halt on glare ice, a dozen hornblowers surrounded him while two jumped on his hood, waving swastika flags in the windshield. Calmly he lit a gold-tipped Balkan cigarette, grateful he had chosen his father's old BMW, built like a tank, though it was almost a family heirloom.

Just as his merrymakers tired of their game, a band of Stormtroopers marched past, playing the Nazi anthem, thus obliging those who didn't want their heads bashed to stand at attention – again in front of his car. Admittedly the music was stirring, if one chose to forget it was a turn-of-the-century Viennese cabaret song with abominable lyrics written by Stormtrooper Horst Wessel. Though revered by the National Socialists as a martyr killed by Communists, Wolf knew Wessel was a pimp murdered in a battle over a prostitute. The man responsible for that moral inversion was Dr. Josef Goebbels, one of the few top-ranking Nazis whom you could accuse of having a brain, no matter how Mephistophelian.

Seeing a break in the crowd, Wolf dove for it, was stopped again by half a dozen Stormtroopers out to prove the myth they were Supermen by hefting his BMW by the bumper. Wolf didn't begrudge them their celebration, though not on his time and definitely not on his car. At least this was more fun than strikes, poverty and unemployment. During times like these he envied the zealots their simple faith in their Bavarian Pied Piper.

All day he had watched in fascination as the drama unfolded. At dawn the streets had been as quiet as a still photo. By eleven rumors were spreading; by late afternoon the oath had been taken; and now this – an extravaganza like the ones Max Reinhardt used to mount with thousands of Berliners waving swastika banners, carried away by the euphoria. What happened in the harsh light of tomorrow – well, that would be a different production.

It was 7:45 when Wolfgang parked behind The Red Fox. "You're just in time. We held the curtain," assured Frau Fuchs, delightfully decadent in red satin with ruby tiara. Then she spoiled it by adding: "Herr Wunderkind has just begun his overture."

Wolf groaned. Leo's overtures were notorious – fifteen minutes of silence and darkness in which the audience was to purge itself of bourgeois thought as a prelude to receiving The Message.

To Berlin's credit, the theater was full, though the palpable gloom made Wolf suspect most wished they were somewhere else – either out on the street where the real action was or safe at home with the doors locked. As little as six weeks ago, the air would have crackled as aficionados pressed forward on their seats, anticipating the mating of the radical, unwashed Leo Warner with the incandescent Carmel Kohl. Now, he imagined, most would prefer to see Carmel burst forth in copper sequins as Lorelei or the Rhinegold Maiden – a reassuring reprise of the past.

From the red glow cast by two exit lights, Wolf identified the profiles of Axel Berg and Leo Warner, slouched low under a thunderhead of cigar smoke. He also recognized Max and Sara Stein, Renate Jürgens, critic Willi Bliss, and a couple of dozen others, signifying this was a loyal West End audience, though subdued in their plumage. He doubted many were in the mood for proletariat experimentation, while the working classes, whom this was intended to dignify, had stayed away in droves. No group was more conventional than the poor in their lust for escape and, given the wretchedness of their lives, who could blame them? Why should they seek out "entertainment" ponderously designed for their own good when they could have for free the magical illusions played out tonight on the streets of Berlin?

Since he couldn't read his program, Wolf attempted to study the set. Leo Warner had, of course, done away with the curtain, the conventional barrier separating the audience from the elect. That was something Wolf loathed even more than proletariat theater's determined ugliness – its hypocritical democracy, as if an artist's years of dedication counted for nothing. Nevertheless, when the stage lights did come up, he was jogged out of his snobbery by the brilliance of Raymon Arno's design – a brilliance that lay in its geometric simplicity. A black fire escape zigzagged up a gray tenement wall to a shocking-pink door, with everything at a rickety angle suggesting precarious living, like a woman teetering on high-heeled pink shoes. At various windows, silhouettes of the inhabitants conveyed despair, anger, fear, by the subtle slump of a shoulder or the jut of a jaw. Taking the political banners, which Leo habitually draped over his sets like washing on the line, Arno had quite sensibly turned them into washing strung on lines between tenements.

Wolf was less entranced by the clutter of garbage cans down a ramp into the audience, smelling of real garbage – a Leo Warner signature. It was no help when the lids popped open to reveal urchins who swung about the fire escape to atonal music. When Arnold Schönberg had introduced his dodecaphonic technique to Berlin ten years ago, it had caused a riot. *Then* it had been revolutionary.

Minutes later Carmel Kohl entered in low-cut red jersey dress, veiled red hat, red net stockings and shocking-pink high heels. Despite a half dozen lines of impossible dialogue, moralizing on the hard life of a street girl, she soon seized the part then came at the audience with the impact of a red express train.

The plot was pure melodrama: Rosa, a cabaret singer of innocent passions, is wooed by a wastrel count who jilts her when she becomes pregnant. After he's killed in a duel with a man who claims the count seduced his wife, Rosa fantasizes The Great Love as it should have been. Now easy prey, she becomes the mistress of a war profiteer in hopes of saving her daughter from the life she's led. When she discovers her lover makes his money by exploiting her former neighbors in his sweatshops, she lures him to her flat, stabs him with a butcher knife, then commits suicide by climbing into the gas oven.

Predictably, the count – as played by Christian Jürgens but created by Leo Warner – was based on Wolfgang during his Kurfürstendamm phase. The accent, the affected use of the hands in adjusting a monocle, the cut of the clothes, the fondness for capes – all were his and all were there. More intriguingly, the industrialist, played with heavy Nazi overtones, was patterned on Axel Berg, suggesting to Wolf that Leo Warner was in love with Carmel Kohl.

Overriding such gossipy considerations was the performance of Carmel. Always Wolf had recognized her genius for invention. Often she had taken a scene beyond his material. What he had never guessed was he depth of grief and compassion. As she conjured up the doomed prostitute, each gesture was pared to a terrible purity, each word was a pebble dropped into a still pond. In less subtle hands the murder-suicide would have been mawkish, but Carmel overwhelmed the script with such a sense of tragic waste that jaded theatergoers sobbed openly.

If Wolf had been capable of shedding tears, he would have. As it was, he cried a little inside, and some of those tears were for himself. As Carmel's director, he had taught her everything about surfaces, slicking her over with so many layers of varnish that the natural grain had been all but lost. Leo Warner, in spite of his ideological puffery – perhaps because of it – had scraped her down to flesh and bone so what shone through was her womanhood.

The play should have ended with Rosa-Carmel's death. If this stage had had a curtain instead of a clothesline, Wolf would have yanked it down. Instead, Warner, the Peoples' Pedagogue, had someone in black rags stand over the dead body, trying heroically not to breathe, and deliver a Shakespearean soliloquy on the pathos of this prostitute, hence of all prostitutes and poverty in general.

As the official Voice of the Author majestically rose and fell, underscoring and undermining, Wolf escaped into the lobby ablaze with light. Here, at least, familiar values of the West End held sway: Champagne glasses in a glittery pyramid. White linen tables spread with smoked salmon, oysters, caviar, pâté de foie gras. A celebration paid for by that well-known proletariat sympathizer – Axel Berg.

Though Wolf yearned to steal off, sparing himself the ignominy of Carmel aglow on the unkempt arm of Leo Warner, her accomplishment deserved his homage. Accepting champagne from Fritz, he loitered in the lobby, idly wondering what was happening on that other stage set – Berlin – and how much of the city would be left after the Nazis had finished congratulating themselves.

His eyes caught a new oil of Carmel Kohl by Raymon Arno, hanging near the canapés. Vivid, powerful, compassionate, it was the Carmel Kohl who had just illuminated the stage like a 1,000-candle birthday cake. Inserting his monocle he studied the eyes, the mouth. Remarkable. For the second time that evening he was confronted with another artist's version of material he thought bore his exclusive copyright, only to discover a vision that beggared his own. The political surrealism that had overwhelmed Germany had produced a powerful artistic reaction, caustic, laid bare, stripped of illusion. While fancying himself a trendsetter, Wolf had missed both the artistic and the political bandwagons. He wondered what SS Colonel Reinhard Heydrich would be doing tonight. Not celebrating, he was sure. In an office somewhere, scrutinizing the SD files that had once fit into a couple of shoeboxes, preparing for the takeover of government. Awaiting the main chance.

9:05 p.m. A cavalcade of three cars, traveling with lights out, parks under the frosty girders of Alexander station. From the lead Daimler stumble Bruno, Felix, Hermann and Kurt, while eight Brownshirts pour from the other two. Giddy from carousing, they goosestep single file, *tramp-tramp-tramp*, up one alley and down another, occasionally retrieving a comrade who sprawls giggling in the snow. All carry truncheons. All but Kurt wear brass knuckles.

As they zero in on their target, the crispness of the air sobers Kurt sufficiently to arouse misgivings. Anxiously his left hand caresses his SS dagger engraved *My Honor Is Loyalty*. Honor, he knows, means distancing himself from the hooliganism Bruno and Felix have fixed on for this evening. Sweat trickles from the armpits of a dirty overcoat concealing his SS uniform. Stolen from a drunk rolled by Bruno and Felix, it stinks of beer and urine, increasing Kurt's self-disgust. Even Bruno's earlier goad of "chicken farmer's chickenshit" now seems insufficient for SS Corporal Kurt Schmidt to jeopardize a promotion to sergeant by engaging in a brawl.

"Shhhhhhh!" The line halts at a familiar corner. It's then Kurt realizes The Red Forum – high on the hate list of SA Chief Ernst Röhm – is the refurbished Red Fox. Now he would bolt if he weren't jammed between Bruno and Felix. Whooping, they carry him forward to ram the red door of the cabaret. It collapses, shooting them inward in a muddy sprawl.

To business. While Bruno cracks the skull of the old doorman dressed as a general, Felix brass-knuckles the face of a midget. Then they and the other Stormtroopers rush the theater.

Holding back, warming up, Kurt slashes his truncheon through a pyramid of goblets, enjoying the spectacular explosion, then kicks over a table of canapés. Just as he feels the murderous rise of adrenalin, his eyes focus on something poignant and familiar: a portrait of Carmel Kohl as beautiful as he remembers her. Impulsively, he reaches out to touch her cheek.

"Drop your hand, you goon!" A caped figure materializes between Kurt and the portrait. "Don't touch *her*. Don't touch that picture. Both are masterworks."

As Kurt draws back his truncheon to strike, he smells the stink of his old man's coat – the vomit, the beer, the urine – and the dignity he acquired since last meeting the disdainful Count von Friedrich falls away. Retreating in humiliation, he throws off the foul coat, then plunges through the darkened door into the theater.

Here all is chaos. Women scream while portly men try to protect them with their programs and canes. Frau Fuchs, minus her blond wig, is strangling a Stormtrooper with one of Leo Warner's ART-IS-POLITICS banners. Other cast members wield railings ripped from Arno's fire escape along with garbage lids to fight as Teutonic knights. Bruno is bashing a fat Bavarian who pleads for mercy on the grounds he's just a reporter, while Felix has a Jew by the throat. As Kurt falls in beside Bruno as of old, now relishing his work, Axel Berg mounts the stage. Waving his steel-headed walking stick like King Canute battling the tides of history, he roars: "Stop! Don't you know who I am?"

With a snarl, Kurt hurtles onto the stage. Grabbing Berg by the silky throat, he crashed his truncheon on the grizzled head: "Schieber! Profiteer!"

Hermann squeals: "Police!" This time his comrades defiantly refuse to disperse. When officers in their coal-scuttle helmets salute them, "Heil Hitler!" SS Corporal Kurt Schmidt understands the true power of his Führer's victory. Piling into the Daimler, Bruno's gang return to Brandenburger Tor, where hundreds of thousands of torches illuminate the Tiergarten so that it seems to have caught fire.

Kurt, Bruno, Felix and Hermann fall in behind one of dozens of bands. Torches high, they flow like lava through Brandenburger Tor. As they cross Pariser Platz, marching twenty abreast past the French embassy, cheering and singing, their band stops in midchord to produce an ominous roll of drums. Then it strikes up the battle song: "Victorious We Will Crush the French." Snapping their heads left to glower at the French ambassador visible in the window, Kurt and the rest switch to the goosestep.

As Kurt jerks out his leg, then slaps down his boot on the cobbles, he regurgitates every childhood humiliation for which he can blame the French: the number of times he was forced to enter German buildings by the rear or take off his cap and grovel in the gutter to a French offer; the blockade during which his sister died of pneumonia and his mother of malnutrition; the invasion of the Ruhr; the execution of his father against a limestone wall. And such is the carpet of hate that Kurt and his comrades lay in front of the French embassy that for the rest of that night every band passing that spot plays the same roll of drums and the same battle song as if compelled.

When the column turns into Wilhelm Strasse, traditionally banned to political demonstrations, the mood dramatically changes. They march past the palace, where President Paul von Hindenburg, a rheumy-eyed man of eighty-six preserved behind glass, nods to the beat of a rocking chair. Casting eyes right, the column dutifully salutes while Bruno sneers: "Tomorrow we'll sweep the streets with that old man's mustache!"

The real hero – young, dynamic and alive – stands in an

illuminated window in a newer building down the street. Hatless, radiating light, he leans into the chilly night, as if to embrace the marchers as they shout, returning their salute with vigor: "*Sieg Heil! Sieg Heil! Sieg Heil!*"

Against all the odds, Kurt finds Ilse in the crowd milling around the Angel of Victory, where she's been distributing party armbands. Embracing with tears, they keep watch for another four hours, while the columns march, while the bands play, while stranger clasps stranger.

"Now someone is going to look after us."

"Now the uncertainty and rottenness will end."

"Now there'll be jobs and bread."

"Now there is honor."

"Now he has come. Now we are safe. Now he will save us. *He will save us!*"

PART III

"As Jesus freed men from sin and hell, so Hitler freed the German people from destruction. Jesus and Hitler were persecuted, but while Jesus was crucified, Hitler was raised to the chancellorship. Jesus strove for heaven, Hitler for the German earth."

– School dictation, 1934

"I must admit that I was glad to see the Nazis come into power because at that time I felt that Hitler, as a Catholic, was a God-fearing individual who could battle Communism for the church. . . . The anti-Semitism of the Nazis, as well as their anti-Marxism, appealed to the church . . . as a counterpoise to the paganism which had developed after 1920."

– Father Falkan, a Catholic parish priest

ONE

Munich

October 1938

T HE FALL of '38 was a mellow and lingering one with the
flame of beeches, the copper of oaks, the wines of
maples blending with the rosy old stones of Munich in an
amber haze that made the city look brushed with maple
syrup. As Carmel dawdled over tea in Marien Platz, an
artist chalked an ersatz Rembrandt on the sidewalk. A
clown with a squirting flower teased a handful of children.
The knights on the famous city hall Glockenspiel performed their elaborate joust as the clock struck eleven. It
felt good to be back among people, if only for the day.

Three years ago the Bergs had quit Berlin to live as
virtual recluses on an estate outside Munich. Though the
immediate cause was the stroke Axel suffered the night
the Brownshirts closed *Our Motherland*, Carmel had
been glad to escape. Berlin, as she knew it, was gone –
kaput. With the nationalization of the arts under Joseph
Goebbels as Minister of Propaganda and Enlightenment,
the persecution of the Jews and anyone politically suspect,
the brash genius that had characterized the city, had been
outlawed. Kurt Weill and Lotte Lenya had escaped to
Paris. Wolf von Friedrich to London. Leo Warner, Josef
von Sternberg and Ernst Lubitsch to the United States.

Despite the patient efforts of Professor Max Stein to
explain these things to Carmel in terms of German history, she could not grasp why her country would devour
its most creative people. Why the Jews? Why the gypsies?

Why did race matter? Why didn't talent or intelligence or character?

While Axel ruled his empire through the magic of the telephone, Carmel Kohl had transmogrified from an extrovert who craved applause into one of those edible and defenseless creatures of nature who curl up under leaves, flatten themselves against the bark of trees, cling to rocks, fold their petals, lock their shells, assume the color of the environment and lie very still hoping no one will notice them.

During the harrowing days of September, when Hitler had brought the world to the brink of war by demanding that the Czechs return Sudetenland to the German empire, Carmel had wandered through the forests around their estate, soaking up the pungent scent of resin and rotting wood, of fungus and leaf mold – a sensuous brown smell, thick and rutty, recalling her childhood when she had fled the crowded slums to pay by the ponds of the Tiergarten. Then she had admired the gentlemen as they exercised their sleek mounts. Now she had her own horse, which she had quixotically named Kara. Riding bareback and full out kept her sane while the Czechs mobilised and Britain's Neville Chamberlain flew to Munich to appease Hitler.

It was 11:15. Paying her bill, Carmel wandered north from Marien Platz up Theatiner Strasse toward the Glyptothek, which maintained a permanent exhibition of Greek sculpture. Munich, with its jumble of baroque, rococo, classical and renaissance architecture, its gay trams painted in the white-and-blue colors of the old Wittelsbach monarchy, was a city rich in tradition. It was also a jolly, unpretentious place for fun-loving people. Now that world war had so recently been averted, even Hitler's Brown and Black Guards, Wehrmacht soldiers in forest-green, Luftwaffe pilots in sky blue, only added to the Bavarian capital's vitality on this golden day.

Carmel came to Königs Platz. Before her was the Denkmal, a Nazi shrine to the martyrs of Hitler's 1923 putsch, which everyone was obliged to salute. Even as she watched, a dozen Hitler Youth in brown shirts and short black pants solemnly raised their arms, bodies rigid, eyes glazed, as mechanized as the jousters on the Glockenspiel. Lowering their arms, they sang:

> "We follow not Christ but Horst Wessel.
> We are children of Hitler.
> The swastika brings salvation on earth . . ."

Though saluting was something Carmel did as little as possible, now she had no choice. Positioning herself before the pillared shrine, she tried to raise her right hand, but found it clenched in her pocket. Just as she began to attract the attention of several young zealots, a cab drew up beside her. Panicking, she yanked open the door. "To Englischer Garten, please."

Sitting amidst the willows edging the icy emerald Isar, Carmel pondered her disturbing case of stage fright. Her defiance of the Nazi boycott of Jewish stores while still in Berlin had had some meaning. So had her public indignation against the burning and banning of books by such authors as Freud, Mann, Proust and Remarque, now deemed by the Nazis to be subversive trash. But what would have been the point of being arrested today by a pack of howling Hitler Youth? She would have embarrassed Axel and drawn upon herself the publicity she shunned.

Like so many other Germans, Carmel was trapped with a foot in both camps. Across stately Prinzregenten Strasse she could see Adolf Hitler's Munich apartment where she and Axel had attended receptions. To her right was Paul Ludwig Troost's grandiose House of German Art, opened last year with a six-mile parade for which Axel had donated thousands of telegraph poles bearing sixty-foot flags and heraldic banners. Celebrating two thousand years of Aryan culture, it had featured floats from

Valhalla, a sixty-foot map of Germany, Teutonic warriors dragging a giant tinfoil sun, columns of wimpled chatelaines, hundreds of bronzed plaster gods and goddesses – all presented with such solemnity that Carmel had fled the official reviewing stand in a fit of laughter. Was she demonstrating good taste or having a breakdown?

Carmel checked her watch. Rudolf wasn't due to pick her up with the Mercedes for another two hours. On impulse she decided to fill in time with a tour of the House of German Art, the temple of officially approved painting which had been irreverently dubbed Palazzo Kitschi, the Munich Art Terminal, the Temple of Terminal Art and the House of German Tarts. Strolling down an austere block-long colonnade bearing the legend ART IS A NOBLE MISSION DEMANDING FANATIC DEVOTION, Carmel purchased a catalog, then visited the first gallery, determined to withhold judgment until she had seen a fair sampling.

After an hour, she knew with some certainty what ART DEMANDING FANATIC DEVOTION meant in the Third Reich: war as glory; size equated with power; power equated with rightness; Germany's folk past idealized as the font of all virtue; nudity celebrated as innocence; men prized for their military use, women for their fecundity; all innovation and foreign influence denounced as decadent – meaning Jewish or Bolshevik.

As she shifted from room to room, becoming more outraged, Carmel consulted the catalog notes, at first to learn something of the artists and then in a spirit of comic relief. Whether unintentionally or by design, the descriptions of each exhibit seemed more humorous than informative. A broad-hipped nude by realist Adolf Ziegler was praised as "an eloquent testimony to the *what-is* – each cheek gleaming with opalescent flesh tints, every hair in place." A sculpture by Josef Thorak of a massive nude holding a wreath and leaning at a precarious angle with heels pressed against a pedestal was described as "massive nude, holding wreath, leans forward at a precarious angle with heels pressed against pedestal." Thorak's drawing for a gargantuan motorway monument, consisting of a horse and three Herculean nudes with pea-sized heads and contorted torsos pushing boulders up an incline, was described as "a gargantuan with every gasp and grunt faithfully depicted. In execution, Professor Thorax [sic!] has now made it up to the horse's rear." A poster of a pregnant Gretchen suckling a child in a cornfield was described as "Germania with her bursting corn harvest." Another canvas, entitled "Clear the Streets," depicting Stormtroopers clubbing Jews, was captioned: "National Socialism Speaks for Itself."

Suspecting the bold cataloger was satirizing the art with literal-minded hyperbole, Carmel flipped to the name – Wolfgang von Friedrich. When had Wolf returned from London? Why had he come to Munich? Was he here now? Rushing to the stout attendant in party uniform who had sold her the catalog, she pleaded: "Fraülein, do you have the address of Wolfgang von Friedrich who wrote your notes?"

The woman frowned. "The count? Oh, he drops in from time to time."

"Please give him a message from me."

Across one of Axel's business cards, Carmel scrawled: "Why didn't you tell us you were back? Please call soonest!"

TWO

W OLF PARKED his red upholstered Alfa Romeo carelessly and illegally outside Munich's Four Seasons Hotel. The fines he did or did not receive when driving such a dashing car had little to do with his own actions and everything to do with the other guy's feelings about privilege. Besides, he was fifteen minutes late and he considered punctuality one of his few virtues. On balance, it would amuse him to be arrested while dining with the man who was head of both the criminal and political police, including the Gestapo. In seven years, Reinhard Heydrich had quietly drawn into his hands more reins of power than anyone else in the Third Reich other than the Führer.

Acknowledging the porter's salute, Wolf strode through the discreet Four Seasons lobby to the restaurant where British Prime Minister Neville Chamberlain and French Prime Minister Edouard Daladier had carved up Czechoslovakia and served it to Adolf Hitler along with the venison. Circular with a glass dome, it was decorated with screens bearing eighteenth-century Bavarian paintings of mountains and inns – voguishly folk as well as pretty.

"The Lieutenant-General is waiting for you," announced the Oberkellner, bowing. Like all clever headwaiters, this one was quick to sniff shifts of power. A year ago he might have said: "Your guest is here." Now there was almost reproach for Wolf's tardiness.

Typically, Reinhard Heydrich had taken the extra time to read a report, continuing to make marginal notes for several seconds before looking up. Power agreed with his old student friend. The high forehead, hooded eyes, protruding ears, oversized nose and other asymmetrical features, once producing a gauche, horsy look, seemed sanded, buffed and chiseled to create a strikingly handsome bust of polished stone. Equally impressive was the sleek black SS uniform with its silver encrustation, including a three-leaf oak cluster on each lapel. As they exchanged the appropriate banalities, Wolf noticed Heydrich's voice retained some of its adolescent squeak and his white hands were still those of a man who could draw tears from a violin. Heydrich was drinking blond October beer from last season's hops – a German specialty other Europeans had not yet discovered. Wolf also ordered a mug, the only time he preferred beer to wine.

"Since we're both in Munich, I thought I'd take advantage of the coincidence," greeted Heydrich.

"I was amazed when you called. I was opening my Aunt Gertrude's door when the phone rang. Even she hadn't expected me."

With a superior smile, Heydrich handed Wolf the report he had been marking – a day-by-day breakdown of Wolf's last three weeks in London, ending with his arrival time in Munich and his aunt's address on Leopold Strasse.

"The SD has come a long way since it shared a typewriter and kept its files in cigar boxes," marveled Wolf. "I'd heard you moved to Berlin to take over the Gestapo from Göring. How do Lina and the children like living there?"

Heydrich frowned. "I'm not sure. I scarcely see my family, as Lina is at pains to point out on the few occasions we do meet." He grinned. "Not serious conflicts. Just the usual tension between love and ambition that women have so much trouble understanding, especially since we worked so closely together in the early days when

I was running a kitchen table operation." He switched the conversation away from the domestic. "So far, Wolf, I've let you go your merry way without interference because I've liked the foreign circles you've been traveling in. Your London contacts could prove invaluable to the SD in setting up a foreign espionage network. I told you years ago I wanted you. Now you still have a choice. When . . . if . . . war breaks out, recruitment becomes conscription. Then we'll need you."

"But, my dear Reinhard, have I ever led you to think I was a believer?"

"You always boast you have no ideology. I prefer men of reason to men of faith. Whenever I find a dangerous man in a competing organization or uncover a clever spy in my own, I work hard to convert him on pragmatic grounds. I'm not one to waste human resources. That would be irrational."

Wolfgang dared to ask: "And Ernst Röhm? How did his murder and the purge of the SA fit your philosophy for conversion? I thought you admired Röhm? Wasn't he your eldest son's godfather?"

With a dismissive almost effete wave of his hand, Heydrich bleated: "Ahhh, well. Röhm. He had guts, but he and his Brownshirts couldn't understand the most basic element of politics – the difference between having power and not having it. He couldn't adjust, so I followed the orders for extermination. Even today my greatest fear is that the SS might deteriorate into the rabble the SA became. Of course, such decisions were taken on a higher level, though I willingly carried them out. Even in these unprecedented times, no conversion is possible for stupidity."

Pausing while the Oberkellner served he filet he had recommended, Heydrich continued. "I choose men to work for me whom I'd least like for enemies. Though I've been known to blackmail them through their weaknesses, I prefer to win them. Since you were born too rich, too privileged, too gifted to be ambitious in the usual grubby way, I offer you another lure – adventure."

Wolf laughed. "Remember how jaded I am."

"Yes, but you remember" – and again he used his favorite word – "how unprecedented these times are. Especially regarding state security. In the past criminals were arrested, tried and punished for their crimes. The state reacted. With modern methods, potentially hostile elements can be detected, then converted, isolated or eliminated in advance."

"In other words, the state functions like an insurance company with risk tables showing who is likely to have accidents so they can raise their premiums and repair their cars before the accidents happen."

"A better metaphor is that of the doctor," responded Heydrich coolly. "Through modern diagnosis, he prevents disease, thus protecting the state as a healthy organism. Let me be specific. While I don't share Reichsführer Himmler's racial fanaticism, I do perceive the Jews as a hotbed of potential criminality because of their alien traditions. Since the problem is a hereditary one, they're irredeemable as converts. Therefore, I'm a Zionist. I dislike the assimilated Jew as much as racists of both sides. Immigration to Palestine seems the logical solution. Since the Führer's takeover of Austria last March, Adolf Eichmann, our agent there, has arranged forty-five thousand emigrations. Obviously that situation is well in hand – a matter of logistics, like a troop movement. Soon it will be time to turn our attention to more challenging security problems."

Stabbing a piece of filet, Heydrich shook it at Wolf like a bloody finger. "What group, subtler and more dangerous, operates like the Jews as a state within a state? What organization, tolerated and even revered, undermines the unified political will of the German people?"

"Revered? I suppose you mean the Catholic church."

"Right. Again I'm not talking about faith. The eyeglasses through which a man sees God are of no concern

to me. I'm talking about power. The power of the politicized church. Unlike Communism, which has been
destroyed as a political force in Germany, the Catholic
church hides its earthly powers behind the shield of religion. However, it's more difficult to expose and cure than
Jewry since any good German can convert to Catholi-
cism." He interrupted himself with a braying laugh. "As I
can prove from my own family – a Catholic mother and
converted father, even more pious, as the born-again often
are. Being a son of that unfortunate combination, I can
guarantee such conversions are not hereditary. The irra-
tionality of the Immaculate Conception disgusts me as
much as the church's organization excites my admiration – and envy."

"I thought the Vatican went out of its way to be friendly
with the signing of the Concordat five years ago," mused
Wolf. "Newly appointed bishops to swear allegiance to the
National Socialist state. Prayers for the government at
every service. What was left for the Pope except to make
Hitler a cardinal?"

"Oh, for now," admitted Heydrich. "As a sop, and on
the surface. They hide their real power under their skirts. I
assure you, the church and National Socialism are in irrev-
ocable conflict because both make claims on the total
man. The Führer and Himmler were quite frank about
modeling the SS on Jesuit principles – an initiation of the
elect, offering loyalty, comradeship and discipline under
authoritarian leadership. They're also frank about breaking the church's insidious influence by such things as
changing the calendar to celebrate state anniversaries
instead of religious ones. It's my own ambition to break
the church from within as well. Since priests are forbidden
by the Vatican to join the party, we must seed their semi-
naries with minds as subtle and cunning as their own, to
learn their slyer tricks and strategies. That may be where
you come in."

Wolf laughed in disbelief. "You're joking! You know
I'm allergic to uniforms – even ones with skirts."

"But you've always been a defrocked priest."

"I?"

"Ever since the Kaiser's abdication when the world for which you were so well trained collapsed. You love to be at the centre of things if only to mock them. Now you're so far outside, it's impossible for you to show either your talent or the scorn which is so much a part of your personality." Offering Wolf a cigar, Heydrich observed: "You used to let me beat you at fencing so you could feel superior to me. Your version of noblesse oblige. In the end, you let me win when I could have taken you. Are you afraid to fight to win because you don't like to get beaten, or are you afraid you might like winning too well?"

As Wolf recalled those adolescent matches, he had sometimes thrown one because the young Reinhard staged a tantrum when he lost. For Heydrich then or now, the only consideration was winning. Wolf let that pass – more noblesse oblige – and lit both cigars with the gold swastika lighter Axel Berg had once given him.

"That brings me to my next temptation," continued Heydrich, exhaling smoke in a luxuriant plume. "Power."

Noticing the lieutenant-general's face light up as if a bulb had switched on inside his skull when he said that word, Wolf acknowledged: "Power interests me – as a concept. How did you get so much so fast?"

"Because I wanted it. And because I'm good at it. Unlike Göring or Goebbels, I don't let gluttony or lust deflect me. I also confess to an odd piece of luck. Himmler. Since he was in the movement from the first, he has the prestige I lack, but he's only interested in his hobbies – herbalism, Aryanism, reincarnation. Though he slows me down like a cowcatcher on an express train, he also conceals me." Reinhard chuckled. "When Heinrich Himmler became Reichsführer SS, the state lost an excellent teacup reader!"

The sound of his own laughter acted as a brake on Heydrich. Checking his watch, he frowned. "I have to leave. There are a couple of men in the Bavarian police force I have to see. Converts. I'll be in touch. For now I just want you to know what's open to you. How many roles you can play, how many masks you can wear. What unique opportunities for your energy and ingenuity, and what unique rewards. Power, that's the only game. Especially now. When the war begins –" Again, he corrected himself: "If war begins, the future will be –"

"– unprecedented," finished Wolf.

Speeding from the restaurant in his Alfa Romeo, for which he had not received a ticket, Wolf found himself as fascinated by his old friend as he was repelled – a response he had often had during student days. Even in the restaurant, Heydrich – with his slit-eyed stares and frequent glances over his shoulder – had created a pool of distrust around them so palpable that the Oberkellner had deferred to Wolf by presenting him with the bill. It was Heydrich's absence of a sense of right and wrong that gave him his inhuman air, all the more sinister since he didn't seem to know he lacked these things. Wolf remembered a statement Hermann Göring had once made: "Himmler's brain is called Heydrich. After a tough session talking with Reinhard, he looks as if he's been raped."

On a whim Wolf could not later explain, he stopped at the House of German Art. He was given Carmel's note. Though he hadn't seen the Bergs since they moved to Munich, he found thoughts of Carmel often bubbled up in his mind. In years of working together, he had grown used to playing his intellectual responses against her more instinctual ones. It was that collaboration he missed more than the professional one.

THREE

THE BERG residence was constructed of white concrete coiling in upon itself like a giant seashell – a perfect Bauhaus marriage of art and technology. As Wolf reached out his hand to the circular portal, it opened electronically, revealing Axel's butler Rudolf wearing a party badge along with the arrogance that labeled him a 110 percenter – the sort who slept with right arm raised.

"Wolf!" Carmel flew to embrace him, then both stepped back, looked at each other and laughed. By coincidence they had dressed identically, as they used to – the same three-piece copper suede suit with ivory cravats pricked by gold monograms Axel had given them for the premiere of *Lorelei*.

Cupping Carmel's face, Wolf studied the angles as if to photograph it. "You look beautiful. Your bones are coming out."

She sucked in her cheeks. "You mean I'm aging."

"I mean you've never looked better."

Axel's voice boomed: "That you, Wolf?" As he slid through another round portal in a silver wheelchair, he crunched Wolf's hand in a thick paw, exuding vitality from the waist up, using volume to cover up the tragic contrast between his well-muscled torso and spindly legs. "Come! See our dreamhouse." He led Wolf into a glass-and-mirror room furnished with suede sofas and tubular

steel Beuer chairs, turquoise cushions, nubbly wall hang-
ings, white fur rugs and dozens of long-stem white roses.

"Your taste, Axel?" teased Wolf. "Exactly what I
would have expected from a man who learned aesthetics
in a hardware store."

Laughing heartily, Axel admitted: "You're right. I did.
My father's hardware store, and I'm proud of it. If a tool
was of high quality and well shaped for its task, it was
beautiful, but if a workman had shown off by adding a
gewgaw, he upset the balance. Turned the damn thing into
a gadget."

Axel picked up the model of an experimental train
shaped like a torpedo with a propeller. "I helped finance
this. Look – a darting fish. The very shape of speed."

"A fish with a bow tie," observed Wolf. "The Zeppelin
of train transportation."

Again Axel laughed. "I suppose you prefer one of those
creaking gold coaches we keep in museums. Take a ride in
this and you'll know the difference between round wheels
and square. Form shaped by function – that's beauty."

As Wolf sprawled by Carmel on a suede sofa, he continued to spar with Axel, aware of his need for attention and
Carmel's smiling approval. "That depends on how
broadly one defines function. When Wren designed the
Gothic spire, its function was to fly the spirit up to heaven.
Of course, the pure aim of all art is to open the eyes to
new possibilities."

Pivoting, Axel announced: "Today I'm half machine,
and frankly, it's my most efficient, most beautiful part."

Rudolf brought in a shaker of martinis, which Axel
served. "Dammit, Wolf. I haven't seen you three minutes
after three years, and already we're quarreling. It's great."
Raising his drink, he toasted. "To reunion." He savored
the icy liquid, then plunked down his glass with a sound
like an exclamation mark. "Now, then, what the hell have
you been up to?"

"To no good. Mostly in art, between Berlin, London
and Paris. It's a booming business these days." Referring

to Hitler's four-man tribunal appointed to purge non-Aryan art, Wolf fumed: "When our Four Apocalyptic Norsemen began counting pubic hairs on nudes and checking landscapes against photographs to ensure they were clichéd enough, outdated enough, sentimental enough, patriotic enough, realistic enough, folkish enough, to be acclaimed as art by the Third Reich, I gleaned their rejects. I'm talking here about masterworks by Picasso, van Gogh, Cézanne, Matisse, some already scorched by flame. I smuggled them out to London and Paris where they found a grateful and profitable reception."

Noticing Rudolf hovering with ears pricked, Wolf pitched the rest to him. "Lately I've done an even brisker business selling confiscated art to the greedier members of the party, like Fat Hermann Göring and that club-footed Beelzebub who presided over our book-burnings. Hypocrisy is the growth industry in the Third Reich. Art is just a modest offshoot."

"Ahhh, so you've managed to remain uncommitted."

"Let's just say that I don't hold our Führer's appalling taste in art against him as a leader. In fact, it's the most encouraging sign yet. Good art and good politics seldom go together."

"What you're saying is that so far you've managed to avoid reality by refusing to join the party."

"Not exactly. I may have joined. I'm not sure. The Potsdam Riding Club, which my family founded generations ago, was absorbed into the Nazi party so Foreign Minister Ribbentrop would have a place to show off the phony 'von' he purchased at vast expense. I went to bed one night unaffiliated and awoke next morning engorged. But despite such twists of fate, my loyalties remain what they always were – to my class and the tasteful world privilege can create. To genius wherever I find it. To my friends. To myself."

"But why do we never see you? Where do you live when you're here in Germany?" prodded Carmel.

"On planes and trains. Occasionally sleeping at the wheel of my car. Hamburg, Frankfurt, Berlin. I had dinner with Christian and Renate three months ago. We drank a toast to you. Renate's pregnant again. Since her novels are too Bolshevik for this regime, she's turned to poetry."

"Christian must be doing well. I've seen exactly nine films since Axel and I moved to Munich, and he's been in five of them."

"He's very adaptable. Those historical epics, showing what heroic folk we Germans are, have worked well for him. Especially since he bleached his hair. He's everyone's Siegfried."

"But he's also a wonderful actor."

"Sometimes. When they give him a chance. He's studying French, but rather half-heartedly, I think. Part of him tells him he should go to Paris for the sake of Renate and the children. The other part resents giving up the excitement here. And the adulation."

"He's earned it. Poor Christian."

"No – lucky Christian. He still has a choice. But the person I want to hear about is you. What are you doing?"

"Nothing. Nothing at all."

"That can't be for want of asking. Even these days."

"They're always sending her scripts," confirmed Axel. "She fires them back by the truckload. I tell her, if she wants to go to Berlin for a while –"

"Oh, I couldn't!" protested Carmel. She grinned: "You should see the scripts. All those ridiculous Blut und Boden movies UFA churns out about nobly suffering wives called Gretchen. Can you imagine me in braids, and where would I get a milkmaid's figure? The stories are all the same. The husband goes off to do something noble, like fight a war, and Gretchen gets raped by a fiend who looks Russian."

"As good as at all that?" teased Wolf. "You're lucky Goebbels hasn't conscripted you for one of his Thingspiele."

"Oh he's tried. It was called *Struggle Has Been the German's Eternal Destiny*, with a cast of thousands doing morris dances and marching. The grande finale was a ballet of nutritious vegetables representing the one-pot meals all we sacrificial German housewives are supposed to prepare. I think I was supposed to be a rutabaga."

"Where is Bertolt Brecht now that we need him?" lamented Wolf, rolling his eyes heavenward. "Where is Leo Warner? Where Fritz Lang?"

"Where is Wolfgang von Friedrich?" thundered Axel. "Just say the word. I still have the marks."

"That's generous, Axel. I don't have the stomach." A taut smile. "But maybe it's my duty to the arts. A very expensive production. So you'll have less money to give to the party. I see by the papers that you continue to pour largesse into Hitler's pocket."

"And why not? I consider every pfennig an investment. Since our Führer banned trade unions and scrapped the Versailles treaty by reclaiming the Rhineland and rearming, my profits have multiplied five times in as many years. Our Führer found me a wealthy hardware man and turned me into an industrialist."

"It's not hard to create full employment when you have three shifts in every munitions plant and all the country's youth in uniform. Hitler has merely found the usual military solution to a vexing economic problem. 'Guns before butter,' as my friend Göring likes to boast. Now that we have those guns, I'm afraid we're going to want to use them."

"Why? Admit it. Our Führer has performed brilliantly. First reclaiming the Rhineland, then the annexation of both Austria and the Czechs' Sudetenland – a diplomatic coup providing the thrill of seeing two world leaders beg us to take back what they stole at Versailles. It's having the guns – and the nerve – that means you don't have to use them." Slapping his wasted thigh, he guffawed. "Chamberlain takes a weekend in the country, and Hitler takes a country in a weekend – my man Rudolf told me that one."

"I was in London when Chamberlain returned with the Munich Agreement," mused Wolf. "As he stood on his balcony, the British sang, 'For He's a Jolly Good Fellow.' As a German, I could only laugh. But the British didn't get their empire by staying home. Poland may not be so easy."

"Poland? Who said anything about that?"

"It's between the lines of everything in the newspapers. Even Goebbels can't help occasionally telling the truth. As a general's son brought up on lead soldiers, I can say for sure that Hitler will not tolerate a military power on our eastern frontier. On my way here, I was stopped twice by convoys of tanks and guns and soldiers in full war gear headed east. The return of the city of Danzig to the German empire will be the lever. We'll hear how the Poles are abusing the Germans living there and how they're begging us to save them. Then we'll hear the Poles have viciously sneak-attacked us and we have no choice but to declare war. Hitler has a nice little formula worked out. I've seen it now from both the British and the French viewpoint."

Stroking his right leg scarred with shrapnel, Axel defended: "That's where you generals' sons misjudge our man. The Führer wasn't fooling around with maps behind the lines in the Great War. He was one of us. He knew the trenches. He's no warmonger. That's one place we know we can trust him."

With a pitying look, Wolf remarked: "You still see Hitler as an ordinary politician, a little cleverer than most, don't you? A seal that's learned to spin balls on its nose, so let's all applaud till the next act."

"How else am I supposed to see him? Your father's gang with their officers' caste system was too inflexible, so they lost out. This new gang has unified us. It's not only the business community that supports Hitler, but the little guy at the machines, along with all the snobs. I heard last month that Prince August Wilhelm is working at the

Brown House and Prince Alexander is a Stormtrooper. Remember the plebiscite when Hindenburg died – ninety percent wanted Hitler as president. He'll do, till a better one comes along."

"How's that going to happen? He's dismantled the whole democratic process. For hundreds of years Germans have yearned for a dictator. Now they have one." Wolf sighed, sick of the whole topic. "I have the sinking feeling you money-makers are so used to trading off political rights for profits that you scarcely notice. In my worst dreams I see Germany as a train racing downhill while you go up the aisle collecting tickets."

"So be it!" Axel exclaimed cheerfully as he shook another batch of martinis. "Your initial resistance to change always amuses me, my friend, since no one is more capable of it once you decide on it, as you proved when you gave up your ancestral trappings to become the very style of the Weimar Republic. In another year at most you'll be one of the National Socialist elite. I guarantee it. To change one's spots to suit the situation as I do is a simple thing. You seem able to change yourself organically – to become that new thing."

"Perhaps. But for now the best news I've heard out of Berlin is that Frau Fuchs has reopened The Red Fox for satiric revue. She's packing them in."

"It worries me sick," admitted Carmel. "How can she be so courageous after –" Glancing sideways at Axel, she finished weakly ". . . what happened before?"

"Goebbels knows it's smart to leave a few places where people can let off steam. She's too hot to touch for now."

Leaning forward and twisting her wedding ring, Carmel confided: "The person I'm really concerned about is Professor Stein. I haven't heard from him in over three months. He's been sending me reading lists and lecture notes. My last letter came back yesterday stamped ADDRESS UNKNOWN."

"Maybe he emigrated. Sara Stein was becoming frantic – I can't say I blame her. I got a letter from Christian today that I didn't have time to read. My aunt handed it to me as I was running out the door. I must have left it in my raincoat in the car. I'll get it. Perhaps–"

"Jews, Jews, Jews!" exploded Axel, cutting off Wolf with his wheelchair. "We're not going to talk about the goddamned Jews." Swiveling on Carmel, he stormed: "Your Jew professor and his Jew wife are probably in Palestine right now eating pigs' knuckles under a palm tree. Let's hope so – that's two less to worry about."

"Please, Axel," begged Carmel. "Please –"

"No! Let me speak. I'm tired of being patronized in my own house. Don't you think I know the kind of money you've been sending to that professor?

"He's my tutor."

"He's your ward! That's the trouble with us Germans. We were too tolerant so now we're infested with all of Europe's Jews." Including Wolf in his tirade, he roared: "Did it ever occur to you bleeding hearts that it was the Chosen People themselves who introduced racial superiority to the world? Our Nuremberg Laws are based on their Mosiac Laws, denouncing the foulness of mixing blood. We turned them around and put some teeth in them."

"Please, Axel. Wolf doesn't want to hear –"

"Let me have my say!" exploded Axel, his face red and sweaty, waving his walking stick. "Do you think I'm crazy? All sensible Europeans distrust the Jews. Are we all mistaken but you? Martin Luther made it clear what he thought about Jews way back in the First Reich." Shooting his wheelchair over to the bookcase, Axel hauled down a well-thumbed volume. Pointing to the gold lettering, *Anti-Semitic Works of Martin Luther*, he flipped to a chapter entitled "On the Jews and their Lies – Pamphlet, 1543," and read in a sonorous voice:

"First, set fire to their synagogues or schools . . .

"Second, I advise that their houses also be razed and destroyed . . .

"Third, I advise that all their prayer books and Talmudic writing, in which such adultery, lies, cursing and blasphemy are taught, be taken from them . . .

"Fourth, I advise that their rabbis be forbidden to teach henceforth on pain of loss of life and limb . . .

"Fifth, I advise that safe conduct on the highways be abolished completely for Jews . . .

"Sixth, I advise that all cash and treasures of silver and gold be taken from them . . .

"Seventh, whosoever can throw brimstone and pitch upon them so much the better, and if this not be enough, let them be driven like mad dogs out of the land."

Axel snapped the book shut. "Luther was one of the first to discover the international Jewish conspiracy, but those were more primitive times. As a reasonable man, I say let's just encourage them to leave. For the past two years that's where my charity has been going – packing off the Jews to Palestine." He lowered his voice confidentially. "I have to do it clandestinely with the World Zionist Organization because the bloody British try to stop us. They think it upsets the Arabs too much, but then they don't have our problem." Winking, he downed his martini: "Now what do you think of that?"

"I think," pronounced Wolf, "that the Jews have some peculiar friends these days."

The Berg Pool was a freeform turquoise with a channel leading into a sculpture garden of boulders startlingly balanced amidst white roses. With the sky sparkling through the glass dome and the poolside heaped with pneumatic sculptures, it seemed like a crystal spaceship floating through fleecy clouds.

Restored to good humor, Axel was under no physical disadvantage here. Plunging naked into water heated to body temperature, all three splashed like children, throwing inflated balls and diving under a glass partition into the frosty November air, trying to wipe out former unpleasantness, perhaps even to recapture the spirit of Berlin of the twenties as they now remembered it.

Gripping two metal rings, Axel swung into his wheelchair and reached for a terrycloth robe. Carmel slid down a water chute into pneumatic sculptures that scattered like bubbles, while Wolf playfully pulled her under by the foot. Admiring the two beautiful bodies almost untouched by age, Axel murmured with tears in his eyes: "Of all the great works of art, the human body is the most magnificent . . . especially when it's doing what its parts are ideally shaped for." Turning up the music, he waved from his wheelchair. "I'm going to have a nap. See you upstairs. Take your time."

The invitation so painfully delivered broke the mood of innocent joy between Carmel and Wolf. Simultaneously both swam to opposite sides of the pool and donned their bathrobes.

A husky female voice crooned:

> "Only one hour, I belonged to you
> And for this hour, I'm thanking you.
> You talked of love and happiness
> And we both believed in fate
> But this hour was to be our last."

Carmel snapped off the music, while Wolf reached for his cigarettes. The click of his gold lighter echoed through the glass dome.

"I'm sorry about what happened upstairs," said Carmel. "Axel tries so hard to be cheerful for my sake, and then he has relapses. It's the drugs for the pain. It makes him . . . unreasonable. Then I was stupid enough to mention that last night at The Red Fox . . . the night of his beating. That triggered him."

Nodding, Wolf refrained from noting that Axel had always been unreasonable on the subject of the Jews.

The silence lengthened. Though earlier Wolf had wanted a chance to talk with Carmel, now he felt as tongue-tied as an adolescent. The intense physical activity had stripped his intellectual veneer, leaving him acutely conscious of the desires of his body and the grace of hers. As he watched her shake the water from her red hair, he realized how much he yearned to make love to her.

Stubbing his cigarette, he stood. "It's chilly here. Let's go upstairs."

It was sundown when Wolf left the Berg estate for Munich. A cold, violent shower had drenched the forest, leaving crystal beads in the palms of the pines and slickering the coppery oak leaves. Staring at the fragile, luminous beauty, he shifted uneasily in his Alfa Romeo, wishing it were winter with everything encased in snow and ice, clean and pure and dead. He feared these transitional seasons with their sadness, conjuring up a deep and treacherous vulnerability in him.

The aristocracy for which he had been trained had collapsed, followed by the outré theatre world for which he had trained himself. He had tried Paris and London, but here he was home again more dissatisfied than before. Perhaps he should consider Reinhard's offer to cast his lot with the SS. Both Reinhard and Axel, each shrewd in his own way, had sized him up and seen the same man: an actor skilled at playing parts but needing a lead role. Though many of the disapproving old junkers held back from the new regime, the younger aristocracy had indeed rushed to the SS, attracted by its elitism and the continuation of the Prussian military tradition. Yet he clung to the past like one of those dying yellow leaves holding tightly to its dead branch, waiting for a gust of wind to blow it in one direction or the other.

Wolf had to admit he felt pride in the rebirth of the German empire, though he had no illusions about the Führer's peace-loving nature. When he heard Wagner's "Ride of the Valkyrie," his pulse raced. When the Führer offered to lead him like the Pied Piper, his heart yearned to obey. Only his head held out, reminding him of the follies of romanticism over reason, forcing him to see the dark side of the Aryan dream. Yet his mind was also a deceiver. When he was with Axel Berg, it argued silver-tongued for democracy and the Weimar Republic. With Leo Warner, it converted him into a royalist; whereas five minutes with former Crown Prince Friedrich Wilhelm, and he was an ardent Communist.

He did have absolutes. He hated violence and stupidity – the category under which he would file racism. As for that unsavory part of the regime, every story had two sides, every deed a potential for good or evil. Though the Nuremberg Laws deprived the Jews of political rights, they seemed to imply a guarantee of their civil rights as second-class citizens – an improvement on their status in many other European countries, as even Professor Stein was quick to point out. Since the regime had vitality, youth and animal spirits – things tragically lacking in a demoralized Europe – why not capture, bridle and civilize the beast? Become a part of the system, transform it from within, purge it, cultivate it, turn it into the ordinary. Overwhelm it with its own success. Life has only one constant: nothing stays the same.

Again changing gears, Wolf turned from the soggy forest onto Hitler's autobahn. As he accelerated with relief, he heard something low and predatory behind him, like a growl caught deep in the throat, intensifying into a roar. Twenty SS men on motorcycles, wrapped in black leather, helmets and goggles, swooped over the hill, forcing him off the road. Swerving, he skidded into a shaggy stump.

Something was wrong in Munich. Ever since he had left the Bergs, he had been vaguely aware of the twilight sky brightening instead of darkening – a crimson glow reflected on low-lying clouds that could be smoke. What was happening? Fire was a National Socialist rite: the Reichstag arson of February 1933 blamed on the Communists and used as an excuse to purge "radical" opposition; the book burnings in May of the same year when chanting students and Stormtroopers carbonized thousands of books while Josef Goebbels proclaimed "the end of the age of extreme Jewish intellectualism"; the torching of artwork which Wolf now estimated at about ten thousand pieces. Tightening his grip on the wheel, he jammed his foot to the floorboard in pursuit of the dark riders on their motorcycles.

By the time Wolf reached the suburbs, the acrid stench of smoke was unmistakable. Flame licked the sky in angry snarls across the horizon. Parking his car at the Victory Arch opposite his aunt's decaying mansion on Leopold Strasse, he assured himself that all was in order there, then raced southward past stalled and abandoned cars. At Odeon Platz people were running in every direction like headless chickens, but when he asked what was wrong, no one would answer. Even the Stormtroopers, cordoning off the roads with weapons and dogs, merely pointed to the flames with immobile faces and stated the obvious: "Fire."

Elbowing his way through the surging, strangely silent crowd to Munich's labyrinthine core, Wolf could see flames everywhere but could discern no pattern in what was happening. Now the smoke was steel wool clogging his nostrils while charred paper fluttered like bats' wings against his face. Ducking down a lane lined with shops, he heard a primitive howl and flattened himself against a wall just as a gang with torches charged by. Jumping high, one grabbed the ANTIQUES sign from Otto Cohen's store, swinging on it till the chain broke. Laughing, he flung it through the window, to general applause. Others were dragging clothes and mannequins from Goldberg's secondhand shop, pouring gasoline on them, setting them ablaze. Kaplun's bookstore simultaneously exploded in flames as the youths chanted: "Juda verrecke!" Croak the Jews.

The sound of breaking glass shattered the night as the gang systematically worked its way down the street. Choking and screaming, people stumbled out of doorways, some with towels wrapped around their heads. Wolf saw two faces peeking through the lace curtains over Goldberg's shop and, snatching a torch from one of the hooligans, beat him over the head. "You fool! People are dying in there."

The youths wrestled back the torch. "You're the fool. Those are mannequins. Watch their faces melt. They're dolls. Don't we wish they were Jews!"

Escaping down an alley, Wolf came upon two men under a lamp post kicking something that groaned. Over and over he heard the hollow sound of boot against skull and thought with wonder: They're kicking that poor bastard to death.

He moved in closer, like a photographer angling for a better shot, his air of detachment so impenetrable it was as if his Burberry were an invisible cloak, allowing him to stand beside the assailants while their boots struck flesh.

Farther up the street a man in a nightshirt was having his beard and earlocks shaved while another was being dragged facedown, leaving a warm and oozy trail that stuck to Wolf's shoes. Again he told himself, as if it were a thing necessary to state: People are bleeding to death. They're dying. Yet he remained unable to connect thought to feeling or feeling with action, as if he were watching scenes from a play.

All night long Wolf wandered from disaster to disaster, as others were doing. Whenever he happened upon policemen, they seemed to be standing with their backs to the violence like pickets in a fence, not fighting it but containing it. Firemen trained their hoses away from the flames onto the roofs of buildings next door. Incredibly, at one of the more spectacular blazes a band in lederhosen tried to get the crowd to sing. When they paused between choruses, the silence seemed uncanny, broken only by the steady crunch of boots through the jagged, glittery carpet of glass that lay over the city.

Dawn came slowly – a gray and stingy affair, as if all shades of gold and crimson had been squandered by the night. Now the city bristled with men in uniform – Stormtroopers and SS men, the police and their auxiliaries, soldiers and Hitler Youth – boarding buildings, shoveling glass, sifting ashes. In a smoking pit Wolf stared at the twisted superstructure of what had been a synagogue with three domes, now contorted like the skeleton of a humpbacked monster that had died a hideous death. Already it had been cordoned off and a white-gloved policeman in elevated cage was redirecting traffic as smartly as if he were saluting.

Though some Jews, dragging their belongings in handcarts, were taunted with catcalls, most Aryans wore the air of innocent, even scandalized, bystanders. When two Stormtroopers pushed a Bechstein piano from a third-floor balcony so it smashed on the pavement, an indignant gentleman out walking his dachshund sputtered: "Such waste. Such stupidity! It's not the piano's fault it belonged to a Jew."

Already hawkers were proclaiming November 9, 1938, to be Kristall Nacht, the night of broken glass. To hear the party view, Wolf purchased the *Völkischer Beobachter*, though his hands felt grubby holding the paper. According to Goebbels, the fiery rampage which Wolf had witnessed was the "spontaneous surge of outrage" by the German people for the assassination of German diplomat Ernst vom Rath in the Paris embassy by a Jewish youth named Herschel Grynszpan. From this Wolf deduced that the pogrom had been nationwide, that thousands of Jewish homes and shops and synagogues had been torched and many Jews arrested. November 9 marked a change in National Socialist policy from harassment of the Jews to physical abuse.

Exhausted and covered in soot, Wolf headed for his aunt's house on Leopold Strasse, cutting through a Jewish neighborhood where once-fashionable mansions, encrusted with pilasters and gargoyles and turrets, had been converted into flats, then subdivided into rooms with fire escapes and sheds and porches stuck on like patches of an inner tube. In basement shops, where passersby could usually see a tailor at his machine or a clerk selling buttons, all shutters were locked. No one was on the street – not a child playing ball or a woman with a grocery basket; not a man on a bicycle or a delivery wagon or even a dog. No fires had been set, but windows had been broken, garbage strewn, lawns churned and fences defaced with anti-Semitic slogans scrawled in yellow paint. Twice Wolf stepped around dry brown patches he feared had been red, hearing an echo of the hollow crack of boots on skull and the moan of a man under a lamp light.

In the square beside his aunt's venerable old mansion Wolf encountered the stand where he bought his newspapers, now overturned and partially burned. The owner – Frau Bernstein – an arthritic old widow who always wore black, was perched on her wrecked counter surrounded by students. Her despairing form reminded Wolf of a silhouette in Raymon Arno's backdrop for *Our Motherland*, and in that moment art and life coalesced.

Elbowing his way through the locked circle, Wolf laid his raincoat gently on the old woman's shoulders, then sat beside her. From his vest pocket he removed his handkerchief – one of a succession of white linen squares washed, starched and ironed by a succession of maids over three decades. At first he merely choked into it – a brief return of his childhood asthma. Then he cried, a gush of tears such as he hadn't shed since his favorite horse broke her leg and his father, catching him at his grief, had thrashed him for his weakness.

Blowing his nose and wiping his eyes, Wolf stuffed the crumpled handkerchief into a pocket of his raincoat still resting on Frau Berstein's shoulders. He felt the outline of a letter. Removing it, he saw Christian Jürgens' name in the left-hand corner. With his thumb he tore open the sealed flap.

Dear Wolf,
Sorry to be the bearer of bad news. Two months ago Max Stein was taken into "protective custody" by the Gestapo in a purge of "radical intellectuals." Sara Stein contacted my Renate a month later. Apparently the poor woman had gone into shock and then into hiding. It took another two weeks before we learned Max had been taken to Dachau, outside Munich. While we were awaiting more news through official channels, the enclosed letter was delivered to Sara Stein by a man who had known Max in Dachau. We're all heartsick. Please contact us to see what can be done.

Faithfully,
Christian

Unfolding the second letter, penciled on sheets of toilet paper in Max Stein's precise hand, Wolf read:

I was arrested just after midnight. The loud knock on the door. The terror of my Sara clinging to my arm. Five minutes to dress and pack. I was one of many shoved into a truck that night and driven to an unknown place where we were left standing overnight, jammed together in the dark without sanitary facilities. Next morning, cramped and foul, we were herded into the light along with the inmates of a dozen other trucks and marched between two guardhouses into a wood enclosure. The mocking sign on the gate read: WORK MAKES YOU FREE. Then I knew – Dachau! Ahead of us was a vast square with two rows of barracks. It was divided by a broad road lined in scrub poplars casting their meager shadows as if scratched with a fingernail. Though the air was cold jelly, we were told to strip and then stand naked beside our bundle of clothes. Those who were too slow were struck by whips. We tried to keep up each other's spirits in our little group formed in the truck – some friends and relatives, others strangers like me, melded by the accident of shared terror. Hoses were turned on us as we heard ourselves denounced in obscenities. We were supposed to stand till we dried in the sun. When it rained instead, we were left to dry again while dogs snarled and strained on their leashes as if they wanted to tear our throats. When one man fainted, the pack reduced him to blood and bone in minutes.

We were handed blue-and-white-striped clothes and wood shoes, all the wrong sizes. Some of us were given yellow stars, meaning Jew. The political prisoners received red chevrons, the criminals green, the homosexuals pink and the religious prisoners violet. Our heads were shaved and we were forced to line up again while roll call was taken. I became prisoner No. 5368. Most "new recruits" were assigned bunks, with some being singled out for special attention. Two priests were accused of interfering with the state, and the political prisoners were confronted with such crimes as possessing pamphlets critical of the party. I was denounced for my old sin – writing a book in which I hold the German language up to ridicule. When questioned we tried to answer calmly. After obscene insults about the Virgin Mary, one priest refused to reply. A lighted cigarette was thrown down his throat. When he screamed, a guard knocked him to his knees and urinated into mouth – a favor "to put out the fire."

After the political prisoners were hauled away, the priests were ordered to wear placards stating I LOVE JEWS and to scrub the Jewish latrines. The guards read aloud a paragraph from my book in which I say excremental words are commonly used by Germans as "swear" words. I was told it would be my special privilege to clean out the guards' latrines with my bare hands. When I asked to wash before eating, I was forced to lick my hands. I had no bathroom privileges. When I soiled my clothes, they read me parts of my book in which I said infantile qualities of the German character were reflected in the language. For this they made me stand in a corner. Later they took away my clothes and sewed my gold star to my naked chest. During the night I was awakened every ten minutes by a flashlight in my eyes and forced to perform lewd dances for the amusement of my captors, who spat in my face, burned my chest hair and demanded I answer the question, "What whore shit you out?" For this I was to name my mother. Though I was stupid with fatigue, I was luckier than the political prisoners, for my punishment was only humiliation.

I don't know how many days passed before I was pulled from my private cell, allowed to wash with water and given clothes. Now they fed me food that hadn't been pulverized to mush, including a real apple, and even let me sleep through 3 a.m. reveille. I knew what was happening. I had heard the stories: a bit of good treatment to remind you you're human and to break your heart before they break your body. I was assigned a bunk in No. 3 barracks with bunks for 180 men. Here everything is neat and clean, though it stinks of disinfectant. While I have to get up for roll call and do light domestic chores, my only other job is to check the officers' latrines to see they have soap, towels and paper. That was when I began this letter on stolen tissue.

I've tried to discover what happened to the rest of my truck family. Three Jews have been assigned to the Moor Express, which must be seen to be believed: a five-ton truck is pulled by two men harnessed with wire, while four push from behind, their bare and blistered feet like misshapen hooves as they attempt to gallop. Sometimes only a single oil drum sits on the truck. I've been told the team once ran to the train station with the dogs on them for a package of screws. The political prisoners fared even worse. Three were beaten about the legs with boards containing rusty nails till the flesh cleaved from the bone, then were hung for nearly a day by the arms, with feet dangling. Others have been beaten on the trestle with leather whips soaked in water. When they lost track of the number of strokes, the entire procedure was repeated. The priests were confined in a standing cell for two days, then forced to insult and defile each other in sadistic ways.

I've been informed that the next stage of my "treatment" begins tomorrow. One of my truck family who is to be released promised to deliver this to my friends, to be passed from hand to hand. This is a story that must be told, but not with names as that would endanger too many others. I'm not a brave man. I stand here trembling with my sorrows. I pray I'll not disgrace those I love. Dear, dear Sara, what, my darling, has become of you? I can't say more. It will break me. Go to Palestine if you still can. It is my dearest and only wish. Go! Only that hope makes these last days bearable.

FOUR

Berlin

July 1939

S S LIEUTENANT Kurt Schmidt moved fussily about the living room of his four-room apartment on Fasanen Strasse, tugging the drapes over the venetian blinds, checking for dust on the thirteen volumes of *Animal Life* and the collected works of Goethe and Schiller, which he had learned from his father were worth possessing, though it never occurred to him to read them. In seven years of pooling a double salary, he and Ilse had acquired all the appurtenances of middle-class life, including a down payment on a Volkswagen, the new strength-through-joy car.

As he straightened the photographs over the electric fireplace, Kurt decided to shuffle them so the one of him shaking hands with Reichsführer SS Himmler on the day he swore the Blood Oath was predominant. Since this picture was the same size as the one of Ilse and him on their wedding day, he transferred the Reichsführer's picture into the expensive silver frame. He also moved his engineering certificate beside the Reichsführer's picture so if you noticed one you'd notice the other. With Ilse's encouragement, he had worked day and night for five years for that piece of paper. The SS – unlike the ill-fated SA – preferred even its rank and file to be professionals. As key man in the secret reconversion of Axel Berg's Northstar Tool and Dye Works for munitions work, he was proud of his skills. Kurt thought of the joke circulating among Northstar employees: "Did you hear about the line worker who stole a vacuum cleaner piece by piece? He ended up with an anti-aircraft gun in the middle of his living room."

Though Kurt considered domestic matters women's work, today was special. Not only had Reichsführer Heinrich Himmler agreed to be his firstborn son's godfather, but he was coming here to conduct the naming ceremony. All this was Ilse's doing. When Kurt married her, he thought her a simple girl, loyal and warm-hearted. He had not expected her shrewd political sense.

An altar had been created from a card table covered with white linen, draped with swastika banners then decorated with white candles in silver holders and white carnations. Kurt's eyes shot critically from the portrait of the Führer mounted overhead to one of his deceased brother-in-law Bruno pushed behind a vase of snapdragons. The one time he tried to eliminate that portrait from the room altogether Ilse had had hysterics. Dr. Zuckmayer, her superior at the Klara Hitler Prenatal Clinic, had used the word "trauma." Ilse, he explained, had transferred hero worship of her father to her brother Bruno. When Bruno had been liquidated five years ago in the SA purge, she had found it necessary to pretend he had died a noble death in the service of the Führer, even though a deeply buried part of herself knew otherwise. It was the "protective lie" that she used to keep her personality intact, and since she was sunny and level-headed in every other way, it was wise not to disturb it.

Though none of this made sense to Kurt, he bowed to the doctor's authority. Women, he reasoned, had "moods." His mother had been that way, and now Ilse. Best to leave Bruno's portrait, fortunately a blurred and youthful one, on the mantel in hopes the Reichsführer would not recognize him as one of the perverts shot along with SA Chief Ernst Röhm during the Night of the Long Knives.

As Ilse sat on a rocker in the nursery, her son nestled against her breast, she could hear Kurt roving around the apartment and her sisters, Heidi and Gudrun, squabbling in the kitchen. She knew she should hurry but felt too lazy, too contented. After six months this miracle she held in her arms was still so new she could scarcely believe it, and yet so perfect she could hardly remember a time when it had not been. Bruno Kurt Heinrich Schmidt – as he would officially become that afternoon. Her son. Kurt's son. The tangible, indissoluble bond that joined them in a timeless river of genes and protoplasm.

Ilse laughed at herself. She sounded like the National Socialist pamphlet *Joy through Birth* which she distributed at the prenatal clinic. As the eldest daughter in a Catholic family of nine, she had always taken the annual arrival of babies for granted, had sometimes even resented it, but at thirty-two, after three miscarriages, she had nearly given up hope despite the encouragement of Dr. Zuckmayer. And then . . . Bruno Kurt Heinrich Schmidt.

Ilse smelled the sweet flannelly odor of her son, felt the powerful draw of the wet pink wreath like a suction cup on her left nipple while a tiny fist held her right one. From the first she had known this pregnancy would be different. Even as a fetus he seemed to cling to her, riding higher and more confidently in her body, close to her heart where she could protect him. As her belly and breasts had swelled, she had gloried in the bulk of her body, while Kurt treated her more and more delicately, as if she were a Dresden shepherdess instead of a thick-ankled Bavarian peasant rooted in the soil. Yet in her seventh month, tragedy had struck. While conducting a blood test in the lab, Ilse had gone into premature labor, her baby's head pressing against a uterine opening which, despite her outer girth, was treacherously small. Performing a caesarean, Dr. Zuckmayer had rescued her son with his umbilical cord around his neck, already turning blue from lack of oxygen.

After two months in an incubator, Bruno was still a

small baby but reassuringly greedy, and Ilse did not disappoint him. Her breasts overflowed with milk so that more than one baby at the clinic had reason to be grateful. It amazed her how often young girls wished to put their babies on bottles. As a purveyor of National Socialist policy, she had been quite stern with them. Now she would try to share with them the marvel of this vital connection like none other. Sometimes as she rocked she felt like one giant breast in a warm sea of milk. Again she laughed at her sentimentality. Her mother would call it too much Sächsisches Warmbier – milk and warm beer.

Ilse saw Bruno's face crumple against her with that ridiculous fuzz of red hair like a shaggy ball of yarn, eyes closed, satiated. Though she continued to rock him, her mind began to wander. Could her sisters be trusted to find the good linen, to polish all the silver? Would the swastika cake be sufficient or had she better send Heidi for some pastries?

As Ilse sifted through her list of housewifely duties, she heard the drone of planes drift through the yellow-organdy window along with an innocent breeze. They came over all the time now, flocks of silver birds, usually headed east, the powerful throb of their motors rattling glass, reverberating through the faces of pedestrians as they bent backward in a futile attempt to count them, as if that might lessen their threat. Some people were even talking war. Something to do with Poland and the city of Danzig. Swaddled in her own happiness, Ilse had lost track. Now tightening her grip on Bruno, she felt empathy for the mothers who let it be known they were not thrilled to have their sons parading about in uniforms, practising with daggers and guns, chanting heroic slogans of sacrifice and death. Despite the legitimate claims of the Führer on her son, what Ilse wanted for him was what she had had – mountains and pine forests.

Tears filled Ilse's eyes, tears she had promised herself she wouldn't shed. She had one sorrow on this day of all days, one that cut more deeply than she cared to admit.

Though Heidi and Gudrun had come for the naming ceremony, and her brother Erich was expected later, her grandfather and her mother had chosen to snub her. As a Catholic, Marthe Schultz had refused to accept the SS naming ceremony in place of a church christening, and even Ilse's secret hope of slipping home for a second religious ceremony was not likely to appease her. As for her grandfather, he had pleaded ill health, though he still hiked fifteen miles a day. When pressed, he had pronounced: "That man, who claims to save us all, will bring this family very bad luck, *as he has already done*." Clamping his teeth on his meerschaum pipe, he had refused to say more.

Grandpa Schultz and her mother were simple mountain people. They blamed the Führer and even Kurt for Bruno's death. They couldn't understand that sometimes men had to die, even in peace, for an ideal.

Ilse sought out the small urn she kept on a shelf over Bruno's crib – the ashes of her brother killed five years ago last month, a double tragedy since the shock had caused her first miscarriage in her fifth month. Still feeling the pain as a steady ache through her heart, Ilse buried her lips in her son's fuzzy hair, hugging him close as she christened him with her tears. I want my mother, she repeated as if that were a magical incantation that might conjure her up. I want my mother. . . .

Kurt had expected Ilse to appear an hour ago, serene, prettily dressed, ready to receive guests. Perhaps she had fallen asleep. Should he knock on the nursery door? It seemed to him she spent more and more time in there with the door closed, but a paralysis overcame him where such matters were concerned. Having lost his mother in childbirth, Ilse's difficult confinements had made him feel fearful, impatient, reverent, angry and confused as to what was expected of him.

Giggles from the kitchen assured Kurt feminine help

was at hand. At the least he was grateful for Heidi's and Gudrun's good humor. Would Erich take after their side of the family or the bitter half? On impulse, Kurt had also invited Hermann Humm, who used to pal around with Bruno and Felix but seemed to bear him no malice. Though Kurt had always thought Hermann simple-minded, the push for his engineering papers and his SS duties had left no time to make new friends.

Again Kurt checked the improvised SS altar to see all was in order, then cast a bitter eye on Bruno's portrait. If only Ilse hadn't insisted on naming their son after her dead brother, perhaps he wouldn't find him so disturbing a ghost in this room. Certainly having a brother-in-law who was a homosexual and an insurrectionist had done nothing to advance his own career. Kurt still asked himself: Should I have guessed? Though Bruno and Felix had been as thick as thieves, surely a person's mind would have to be in the gutter to suspect his own brother!

Soberly Kurt recalled those five days in 1934 which had proved to be his blood initiation into the SS.

June 28. Kurt's SS troop leader warns him to stay within earshot of his telephone until otherwise informed.

June 29, 7:00 a.m. As Kurt helps Ilse through her first bout of morning sickness, the phone rings. An unfamiliar voice, deep and low: "Sergeant Kurt Schmidt?"

"Ja."

The code word: "Hummingbird." Then: "Take the 8:15 a.m. train to Munich. Check into the Bayerischer Hof, and do not leave your room." Still no hint of the purpose of the assignment.

June 30, 5:00 a.m. A second call. "Stand in front of your hotel in ten minutes. You'll be picked up by a car and driver identifying himself with the code word."

Pants, shirt, tie, belt, tunic, cap, dagger, gun – the motions swift and automatic. As Kurt steps from the door of the hotel, a Mercedes containing four other Blackshirts slides up to the curb. "Hummingbird," mouths the driver. Kurt climbs in and the car speeds off through the empty predawn streets.

At the Munich airport some two dozen Blackshirts and Göring's green-uniformed special police wait on the tarmac. As the first rays of dawn shoot over the horizon, a small plane circles while necks discreetly crane. It touches down. Stairs are rolled to the door. Adolf Hitler steps out, in brown shirt, brown leather jacket and high black boots, followed by six members of the SS Leibstandarte, his bodyguard.

Kurt is thunderstruck.

The Führer silently shakes hands with everyone, face white and frozen, his forelock so flat it looks painted, his eyes hooded. Still without a word, he strides toward a line of chauffeur-driven Mercedeses and climbs into the lead one. Though Kurt's stomach is in knots, he experiences euphoria. What began as an adventure has become a historic mission.

As the convoy heads south at a steady 80 mph through the dew-fresh air, SS Major Strachwitz, with slit eyes and lips as thin as razor blades, informs his group what Operation Hummingbird is all about:

"Irrefutable evidence has reached the ear of our Führer that SA Chief Ernst Röhm is planning an insurrection. That Bavarian swine must be stopped! Even as I speak the gang leaders are holed up in a hotel a few miles from here. Each movement of our attack has been planned to the second. You will follow orders to the last syllable."

This news is so stunning it is difficult to absorb. For years rumors of sexual perversion have followed Röhm like flies a garbage truck, but never has Kurt heard the faintest rumblings of disloyalty. Röhm is one of the old guard who joined the party even before the Führer.

The faces of Kurt's SS companions remain immobile, as if they have heard nothing unusual. It is the same mask he is wearing. After sixty minutes they arrive at their destination – Hanslbauer Spa Hotel. Hatless, with no weapon, the Führer is first out of the cars. While half the men are deployed around the turreted old Bavarian resort, weapons drawn, Major Strachwitz orders Kurt and two others to fall in behind the Führer and his six-man bodyguard as they approach the front door.

At the sight of the Führer marching through the lobby, the mouth of the sleepy desk clerk gapes, his eyes bulge – a face so comic Kurt almost erupts in laughter. Though he knows shooting is likely to break out and that he's placed to get hit, his only feeling is one of privilege. To give his life for the Führer would be the ultimate glory.

Without pausing, the Führer mounts the stairs, marches through glass doors to a wooden one marked No. 5. He speaks his first word: "Open." Using a duplicate key, Major Strachwitz turns it.

Bodyguards in front and behind, the Führer pushes inside, with Kurt and the major close on their heels. Stinking of stale smoke and sour beer, the room is strewn with bottles, dirty glasses and overflowing ashtrays – the remnants of a party.

A groggy lump moves in the bed. It has the beefy, bullet-scarred face of Ernst Röhm. Simultaneously another man – young, slim and naked – leaps from the bed and grabs for a shirt tossed over a chair. As Kurt and one of the bodyguards restrain him, Hitler yanks Röhm from the bed.

"You pig!" he screeches. "Pig, wretch! You should be whipped and shot." In a towering rage, he rifles through the clothes lying on the floor till he finds Röhm's SA jacket. Tearing off the insignia and throwing it in Röhm's face, he shrieks: "Pig! Pig!"

Never before, in the dosshauses or on the streets of Berlin, has Kurt witnessed so much human fury. Though his bowels turn to liquid, he keeps his jaws clenched and his eyes steady.

Also cursing and swearing, Röhm attacks Himmler, Göring and Goebbels, interspersed with whining pleas to the Führer to remember their long friendship. "Your mind has been poisoned. You've been deceived. What is the charge against me?"

After letting Röhm debase himself, the Führer spits out one word: "Treason."

Up and down the corridors of the hotel, other doors are opened, other rooms raided, other SA officers and their male "companions" arrested, without one shot being fired. Kurt is in the thick of it, seething with moral outrage, driven by his repulsion at the sight of the cringing Röhm with spittle on his lips. In room No. 17 he and Major Strachwitz find Bruno and Felix wrapped in a loving, fearful embrace.

Later that day, at Stadelheim prison in Munich, the arrested Stormtroopers appear before a small tribunal where charges are read and sentences passed without opportunity for defense. All have their insignia ripped off, and those caught in homosexual relations have their heads shaved.

Sergeant Kurt Schmidt is put in charge of an execution squad of ten. Before the condemned are lined up against the wall, he explains that one of their guns contains a blank cartridge.

Most of the Stormtroopers die bravely, some with bravado. Heads shaved, Bruno and Felix are Nos. 20 and 21. When Kurt tries to give the command, it sticks like a bullet in his throat.

Tracing a circle over his heart, Felix taunts: "Fire!"

Bruno raises his hand: "Heil Hitler! Glory to the Fatherland."

As his squad grows twitchy, Kurt reminds himself that these men risked the honor and life of the Führer. Looking into Bruno's bright eyes, he commands: "Fire!"

After it becomes too dark to shoot, Kurt inspects the wall where the Stormtroopers were executed, feeling the bullet gouges sticky with blood, remembering the one against which his father had stood and died. Now he knows it's as hard to shoot a brother as it is to die for one. *Believe, fight, obey*!

July 2. Kurt returns home, red-eyed, unshaven, his SS uniform crushed in his suitcase, along with his dagger engraved *My Honor is Loyalty*. He wants only to bury his face in Ilse's breast, to confess, to purge his soul, but by then she's already heard of her brother's death and is in hospital overwhelmed by her own tragedy.

Kurt pulled his eyes from Bruno's portrait. Was that a knock at the door? Had he missed the downstairs buzzer? Straightening his uniform, he opened the door.

Ilse's brother Erich stood smiling in a reserve air force uniform. At first Kurt felt shock – the resemblance was so striking. A youthful, innocent version of Bruno as he appeared in the mantel photo. Relieved this was neither ghost nor Reichsführer Himmler, Kurt ushered Erich to the couch. "I didn't know you joined the air force."

"Just last week. Flying is the closest I can get to mountains. That's all I've ever wanted. To climb. To ski. My father's life." With charming modesty, Erich apologized: "I guess I'm not very progressive."

The downstairs buzzer. Hermann Humm in the uniform of the Labor Service, as shiny as a new pfennig, carrying a fistful of daisies. While Kurt seated him, Ilse's sisters flew in from the kitchen where they had mounted guard.

"He's here!" gasped Gudrun. "I saw him."

"In a big black car with a chauffeur," corroborated Heidi.

The buzzer confirmed their report.

"Get Ilse," ordered Kurt.

"But I'll miss him!" complained Gudrun, skittering off.

As Ilse glided in from the nursery carrying their son, a third rap sounded on the door. Kurt froze, holding Hermann's pathetic handful of crushed daisies, while Hermann bobbed up like a butler to answer it. In strode Reichsführer SS Heinrich Himmler, accompanied by Dr.

Alfred Zuckmayer. Arms shot up like exclamation marks. "Heil Hitler!"

Kurt stuffed the daisies in with the snapdragons as Gudrun and Heidi, suddenly shy, hid in the kitchen.

A strangely unprepossessing man when you got beyond the uniform, with toothbrush mustache, receding chin, close-cropped head and steel-rimmed glasses, Heinrich Himmler was formal, courteous and prim. Bald with a gold-toothed grin, Dr. Zuckmayer was elfin and cheerful. Both turned to Ilse, radiant in a buttercup dress she had copied from a magazine picture, her blond hair sleeked back in a bun.

"What a wonderful advertisement for all mothers," complimented the Reichsführer. "We should have you pose for one of our folk posters."

Running his hand through young Brunos' red fuzz, Dr. Zuckmayer joked: "You've got more hair than I have, young man."

Out of respect for the Reichführer's schedule, the naming ceremony took place without delay. Cradling Bruno, Ilse stood with Kurt at the SS altar while the others arranged themselves in a semi-circle. As second godfather, Dr. Alfred Zuckmayer offered the child a blue ribbon. "May the blue ribbon of loyalty mark your existence. Whoever is German must be loyal unto death. I wish you to become a true boy and a complete German man." Next he offered a spoon. "May this spoon nourish you until you attain man's estate. May your mother give witness of her love and may she chastise you by depriving you of food if you transgress the laws of God and the Führer." Offering a ring bearing the SS rune, he attested: "This ring will be worn by you when you become a young man and show yourself worthy of the SS and your unit."

Now taking the child in his arms, Reichsführer Himmler recited: "At the desire of your parents, who can trace their Aryan blood back to 1750, I give you the name Bruno Kurt Heinrich. Through your veins courses the warrior spirit of Charles the Great, Otto the Great,

Frederick the Great. Of Bismarck and Siegfried and the
Teutonic Knights of the Round Table. The blood, the
blood, the blood, that is the beginning and the end. It is
the karma of the Germanic people that we must unite
ourselves. It is the karma of the Führer that he is our
destiny. I accept this child of superior blood on behalf of
the Führer and I dedicate him to the use of our Führer
and our Fatherland, ever mindful that this is a fateful time
in our history. Even now the Poles threaten us with armed
invasion because of their refusal to return to us the city of
Danzig, stolen from us during the Great War. Never have
we had more need of the spirit symbolized by such a
child."

Dropping a medallion bearing his own signature
around the neck of Bruno Kurt Heinrich, the Reichsführer confirmed: "I accept this child into my own family
as my godchild. It shall be our responsibility, parents and
godparents, to cultivate in this vessel a true and courageous heart. I wish, my dear child, that you shall show
yourself worthy of the proud names you bear and the
hopes placed upon you. So be it."

Presenting the son to the father, Himmler removed his
glasses and unashamedly wiped away a tear. "When I
held your child I was thinking of his great luck in receiving
life in the same era as our Führer. Oh, what opportunities
for greatness. Did you know the Führer was born on
Easter Day and that he took up his mission when he was
thirty, the same age as Jesus Christ? In centuries to come,
people the world over will hold him in the same reverence
as the Messiah."

Together the group sang the Horst Wessel anthem while
the young Bruno, laden with his booty like a dead Viking,
fussed and fumed and fidgeted in his father's arms.

To everyone's astonishment, the Reichsführer stayed for
coffee and dessert. While Dr. Zuckmayer discussed with
Erich the use of alpine flowers for medicinal purposes,
Heinrich Himmler and Hermann Humm discovered a
mutual interest in stamp collecting.

Though Ilse was relieved that she had found time to bake a swastika cake, that she had hounded Heidi and Gudrun into dusting every corner of the house including under the doilies, that she had scoured the kitchen floor, she was nonetheless shocked to the bottom of her hausfrau's heart when she turned around, after carrying a tray of dirty cups into the kitchen, to find both Dr. Zuckmayer and the Reichsführer had followed her.

Beckoning Kurt to join them, the Reichsführer requested: "May we have a brief word with you and your husband in private, Frau Schmidt?"

Before Ilse had a chance to suggest the guest room, Himmler had seated himself on a chair, from which he had had to brush cake crumbs with his white gloves, while Dr. Zuckmayer had settled opposite. No longer in the state of euphoric self-forgiveness she maintained when holding her son, Ilse noticed there were coffee stains on the oilcloth, that her sisters had dumped the grounds in the sink, that strawberry jam had been smeared on the icebox door. Where were those sillies now that she needed them? They'd had time to primp before the mirror, even to paint swastikas on their fingernails. She'd box their ears when she found them. Blushing, Ilse summed up her inner turmoil with a timid: "I'm sorry this setting isn't a little . . . grander."

"Nonsense!" reassured the Reichsführer. "I prefer the modest to the showy, Frau Schmidt . . . the homey." Yet while he spoke, his long white fingers were working as energetically as a herd of sheepdogs to round up all the cake crumbs inside the largest coffee stain.

Resisting the urge to run for a cloth, Ilse folded her hands in her lap, encouraging herself to enjoy the singular flattery of the occasion: Reichsführer SS Heinrich Himmler wished to talk to her! Kurt, opposite, looked on, handsome and dignified.

Having successfully corralled the last of the cake crumbs, the Reichsführer began: "As you know from your work at the Klara Hitler Prenatal Clinic, one of the tragedies of the Great War has been our plunging birthrate. Because of the decimation of our male ranks, only one woman in four between the ages of twenty-five and thirty-five could afterward find a husband. If we're to correct this abysmal situation, drastic, visionary measures are called for. One solution has been the emancipation of women from distracting male work. Married secretaries, doctors, lawyers and teachers have been alerted to their maternal function, even if that meant removing their jobs. In this way we've begun to reverse the trend."

As Ilse watched the Reichsführer apply himself to the delicate problem of the cake crumbs, releasing them one by one from their coffee lasso, she felt her heart sink. At age thirty-two, with only one child and a difficult gynecological history, she had hoped she might be allowed to continue her work. Concentrating on keeping hurt from her face, she listened to the Reichsführer.

"Another way in which we Germans have attempted to deal with our horrendous birthrate problem has been to expand and purify our stock through applied genetics. After generations of study, our scientists can now reconstruct the perfect Teuton to the exact millimeter. To take advantage of these leaps in racial perceptions, the Führer and I established the SS as a force of biologically superior men who know it's their duty to fight and breed for the Fatherland.

"Even this does not get to the real heart of the problem – what to do with the surplus of women, *amounting to three-quarters of those child-bearing age who will never find husbands*." Eyes magnified by his glasses, Himmler ogled Ilse at close range. "Have you heard of the Lebensborn Movement, Frau Schmidt?"

Ilse stammered: "Dr. Zuckmayer has mentioned it."

The Reichsführer nodded. "Then you understand its basic thrust: to free German males of superior blood from monogamous marriage, which is the Satanic work of the politicized church. In this way we make it possible for German girls to become mothers even if they can't become wives. To the narrow-minded, that may seem sinful, but what could be more humane than providing special homes for German girls dedicated enough to produce Aryan children for the Führer? What could be more logical, for what's the point of having one half of a perfect breeding unit without the other? In the Lebensborn Movement – my lifetime dream – no child will go hungry. All will receive the best medical care and no child whose race is pure will bear the stigma of illegitimacy or class. Through biological marriage we shall, in thirty years, produce six hundred new regiments for our Führer. We shall also have demonstrated our main thesis: that sex and marriage can no longer be a private affair between two people, but is a public matter producing children belonging to the state."

Ilse felt her cheeks burn with shame. In seven years of marriage she had produced only one child, instead of the four required of SS men for advancement. Was she supposed to release Kurt from his marriage vows so he could breed with another more fertile woman?

"Till now the movement has been small and secretive, but I've persuaded Dr. Zuckmayer to oversee its expansion into phase two." The Reichsführer paused, then turned, once again speaking exclusively to Ilse. "Dr. Zuckmayer has asked for you as his head nurse. Will you be willing to serve?"

It took a few seconds for his words to penetrate. Ilse turned to Dr. Zuckmayer, who was beaming, and then to Kurt, who nodded.

"Ja!" she gasped.

"Good. One more consideration, Frau Schmidt. This appointment means you'll have to move to Mullhorig, thirty miles south of Munich." Without a glimmer of a smile, he added: "I'll personally see Lieutenant Schmidt receives ample time to do his conjugal duty, which, I've already made clear, is a vital responsibility of every SS officer."

Kurt and Ilse stared helplessly at each other. Separation was unthinkable but so was refusal.

The Reichsführer sweetened the pot. "I think, Herr Lieutenant, the time has come for you to serve full-time with the SS. Your practical talents could prove invaluable."

Since such an offer was not usual under the rank of major, this involved considerable flattery.

Kurt and Ilse simultaneously replied: "Ja!"

The Reichsführer's departure was swift after that. Sweeping up the cake crumbs into a neat pile like a fastidious hausfrau who would sell her soul for a dustpan, he picked up his gloves and marched into the living room where a blushing Hermann was being teased by Gudrun and Heidi, while Erich looked on in bemusement. Retrieving his hat, the Reichsführer strode to the door with Dr. Zuckmayer, then backtracked. Glancing vaguely about the room as if to remind himself of something he was in danger of forgetting, he focused on the mantel. Passing up the picture of himself shaking hands with Kurt, the engineering certificate, the Schmidts' wedding photo, he brushed aside the snapdragons and Hermann's wilted daisies to stare at the portrait of Bruno. While everyone else held his breath, he turned to Erich. "A very good likeness of you, well-posed. Get the person who took that to photograph Frau Schmidt and your nephew for the Lebensborn recruitment posters." Himmler nodded. "Ja, I think that will do nicely."

Pirouetting, he again saluted – "Heil Hitler!" – and marched out the door.

FIVE

Munich

September 1939

C OLUMNS and columns of tin soldiers are marching in lockstep down Unter den Linden toward Wolf, as he stands inside the Brandenburger Tor. He is supposed to direct them, they are waiting for orders, but all he wants is to stop them, and he can't. Now he hears the slow hypnotic rhythm of the snare drums and he understands: It is his father's funeral – there's the black carriage with the black horses, dragging the black coffin draped in the Kaiser's black-white-red flag with the red stripe dripping blood. There's the riderless horse with boots turned backward. A woman with hair of flame but with no face glides in front of the coffin, strewing white rose petals. She hands Wolf a rose, its petals pulpy like flesh but flecked with ash from her hair, exuding such an exquisite perfume it brings tears to his eyes. As he reaches for his handkerchief, the lid of the coffin opens. The corpse sits up, chest shiny with medals. Grabbing Wolf by the ear, it beats him with a riding crop.

"Father, let me weep for you," pleads Wolf, but when he gazes into the face of the corpse, he sees it is not his father but . . .

Sitting on the edge of his bed, Wolf tried to shake the dream images from his head. Slowly his brain cleared and he opened his eyes.

It was the second day of a September heat wave. Not a breath stirred, as if a bell jar had been clamped on the city. He had been planning to tour the art galleries today in preparation for another trip to London and then perhaps to play tennis. Certainly tennis was out.

In the antique marble bathroom Wolf cleaned his teeth, took a cold shower, ran a comb through his hair and shaved, then put on a white cotton shirt and white slacks. As he padded down the stairs of his aunt's decaying mansion, he was vaguely aware of an unusual silence. With six students on this floor and another six in the subdivided ballroom upstairs, you could usually count on the banging of doors, the rattling of plumbing, the blaring of a radio or phonograph. Maybe it was the heat. Everyone had melted.

He brushed aside the velvet curtains into the parlor, officially called The Maroon Room, overfurnished with antiques and dripping with antimacassars. His Aunt Gertrude was up a stepladder, dressed in a green smock and his tennis shoes, nailing black curtains over one of the windows. Pulling aside earphones clipped over her peppery hair, she announced: "Well, I guess it's happened. We're at war. Hitler attacked the Poles at dawn. He claims it was a counterattack, but –" She pointed to the earphones. "I got it from the BBC."

War. Everyone had been talking about it, predicting it, preparing for it, but still – "What did the BBC say?"

"No details yet. All Berlin Radio does is play Wagner. The British like to play Beethoven. It's fun when both play the same piece at the same time. Why is it all the best war music is German?" As an afterthought she disclosed: "That man is going to speak to the Reichstag at ten and tell us why."

At the sound of *that man*, her old bulldog lifted his drooling mouth and growled.

"I feel sorry for those buggers in the Reichstag," said Aunt Gertrude, showing off the slang she gleaned from her English boarders. "They're like cuckold husbands, always the last to know."

Wolf checked his watch. It was 9:25. He strode to the ladder. "Tante, let me help."

She shrugged him off. "Spare me. You'll only hit your thumb and be the first war casualty. I'm the only one in the family who's any use, and *I* have to work at it. Incapacity is in our genes. If you have any doubt, take a look at that one." With a jerk of her head she indicated her sister Mathilde, stretched out on a sofa in a mauve negligee with an ear trumpet lying beside her gray ringlets. For Aunt Mathilde, who could conjure up the memory of a royal ball to the last curtsy, the abdication still lay like a stone in the center of life. After the falloff of her business teaching court etiquette to the nouveau riche, she had taken to filling time by sewing ruffles on lampshades while Gertrude ran the boarding house. In fact, the only thing the sisters had in common was an enjoyment of their poverty, which Wolf had discovered was a myth.

"I suppose," rationalized Gertrude, "Mattie's problem was being the prettiest in the family. Or perhaps it's because I was educated in England while she was educated in Italy." Gertrude climbed down the ladder. "That's the last curtain. I'll let you do your own room. Would you like iced tea? It's already made."

"I would, Tante. Thank you," murmured Wolf, still stunned by the news.

Despite the size of the room, the quantity of furniture required Wolf and Gertrude to sit knees almost touching, with a crowded tea table between them.

"It's dark as a cave in here with those curtains. If that man" – another growl from the bulldog – "gets his way, we'll all be living like Neanderthals again."

"At least it seems cooler."

"It's the doilies, don't you think? Rather like snowflakes." Pouring hot tea for her sister, too deaf to join in the conversation, Gertrude served the iced tea to Wolf and herself, then slipped a digestive biscuit to the dog, Gustav, whom she had wickedly named after Wolf's father, the general.

"The worst in all this war mess is to be told after all these years of being 'saved' from the Red hordes, that we've climbed into bed with Stalin over that German-Soviet accord thingummy," bristled Gertrude. "How does he dare? Your father was lucky to have kicked the bucket. This would have killed him faster than the abdication. Do you think the British will back down?"

"No, I don't," retorted Wolf, surprised at the conviction in his voice. "I noticed a distinct change in attitude on my last trip. Hitler's demand for Danzig made the British feel hoodwinked over Czechoslovakia. I think they'll honor their agreement to defend Poland."

"That's my feeling," agreed Gertrude, who had worn her earphones almost continuously since Goebbels urged Germans not to listen to foreign news. "There's a man in the British parliament who bears watching – Something Winston or Winston Something." She sighed. "I used tó get my information from the BBC and the Mitford girl, but since she swore as sure as grass was green *that man* would not go to war because he promised her, I've decided to stick to the BBC. The British ambassador got down on his knees a month ago, begging her to leave, but she refused, said her Führer would look after her. . . . You met her, didn't you? Unity Mitford."

"No – you might have mentioned her. She was before my time."

"Lord Redesdale's daughter," specified Gertrude, as if Debrett's was her turf. "*That man* used to call her his 'perfect Aryan.' Of course I don't think there was anything physical between them. Unity is about as sexy as Big Ben. It was just the British aristocratic connection he liked. She claims she and her Hitler used to go over *The Tatler* together picking out the British lords who might come over to Germany."

"I'm pleased he was getting such good advice," joked Wolf. "I was afraid he was consulting Ribbentrop."

"I'll have to remember that," chuckled Gertrude. "The day Ribbie was named our foreign minister, his own mother-in-law rang me up to say, 'I can't understand it. My dumbest son-in-law has gone the furthest.' I rather blame myself. . . ."

"For Ribbentrop?"

"Now don't spoil a good joke by being dim-witted, Wolfgang. I mean Unity, naturally. She was absolutely dotty over *that man* when she first came to Munich. Had pictures of him everywhere – plastered over the walls, on the mirror, a canopy of swastika banners for her bed, even little SS flags in flowerpots. You would have thought he was a movie star. Finally I said: "If you're that daft, why don't you have tea at the Osteria Bavaria? They say he drops in when he's in Munich." She was off like a bolt of lightning and then for months after, all I heard was how 'cute' he looked that day in his 'sweet little mackintosh.'"

"How did they meet?" inquired Wolf.

"Oh she made no bones about that. She just stared goo-goo-eyed till he noticed her. Next thing I knew he was sending his chauffeur. Then she really drove us batty. She claimed it was her destiny to unite Britain and Germany – 'The Ruler of the Seas and the Lord of the Earth.' That's exactly the way she talked. Any time he would speak on the radio, she'd have several of them blaring so loud even Mattie complained, and you know what that takes! Worst of it was the dogs. Her Great Dane and Gustav here. They were at each other's throats. If you want to know who won that war, I'd say Gustav, defending his own German turf, but then he's an English bulldog, so figure that out." Affectionately, Gertrude slipped another digestive biscuit to the dog, who had never failed to growl on cue.

"Tante," prodded Wolfgang. "It's ten."

She waited a few seconds for BBC confirmation. "Bless my socks, so it is! There goes Big Ben." Pulling off her earphones, she switched on Berlin Radio just in time to hear "Deutschland, Deutschland Uber Alles," which she informed Wolf they still sang in the Church of England as "Glorious Things of Thee are Spoken."

"It's going to take a while to get these things sorted out."

Tilting forward, Wolf wiped his mind of his aunt's chatter. Imagining the imposing Corinthian portico of the Reichstag, now protected by anti-aircraft guns, he glowered into the radio, waiting for the Führer to speak. What he heard, after the usual protocol, was not the expected fire of the godhead but a dazed and even addled voice, husky with fatigue. "Yesterday the Polish army invaded German soil by attacking our defenseless radio station at Gleiwitz near the Polish border. Germany has answered this intolerable act of aggression with counteraction. Since 5:45 this morning our armed forces have been moving into Polish territory. We have been shooting back. From now on we will answer bombs with bombs. . . ." A little dutiful raging at the obduracy and insolence of the Polish people, but without the usual gnashing of teeth, snarl of hate, flash of fire, grind of brimstone.

"He's running down," noted Gertrude. "Sounds like his swan song."

Even more surprising was the Führer's announcement that Italy would not be coming into the war despite the Axis military alliance: "Because we are unwilling to call in outside help for this struggle, we will fulfill this task ourselves."

At the same time, he reconfirmed the recently signed German-Soviet accord: "I can only underline every word of Foreign Commissar Molotov's ratification."

Now a little of the old juice: "I have put on the uniform of a soldier. I will not take it off until Germany is victorious. If I should fall on the battlefield, Hermann Göring is to be my successor. If Hermann Göring should fall, Rudolf Hess will be your leader. Deutschland Sieg –"

"Heil!" responded the Reichstag, picking up their cue as neatly as Gustav.

"Sieg –"

"Heil!"

"Sieg –"

Snapping off the radio, Gertrude sighed. "So much for the Ruler of the Seas and the Lord of the Earth curling up together like two old dogs with fleas. Poor old moon-face, moon-struck Unity! One wonders what will happen to a girl like that, split between two worlds at a time like this."

"Perhaps if I knew, I might know what'll happen to me," mused Wolf.

Gertrude handed him some black cloth. "Do stick this up, dear, before you go out. I know you – here for breakfast then gone for a year." Picking up her sister's ear trumpet, Gertrude inserted it like a gasoline funnel, and hollered: "Nothing's different, Mattie. That man said it wasn't our fault."

Relieved to get back to his own thoughts, Wolf did as his aunt commanded. Standing on a ladder, hammering his black curtain, he watched students streaming into the university through Munich's Victory Arch, their shoulders hunched over their books, silenced and sobered by their Master's Voice, remembering the joy with which his countrymen had twenty-five years ago cheered the announcement of the Great War. How proudly he had strutted down the street, wearing two medals pilfered from his father's ample stock, while women ran from house to house, waving flags and shouting the good news. Today's students would sooner bait Jews, celebrate bloodless coups, burn books – set fire to Germany's past. Bullets and ration books, those would be real to them.

Leopold Strasse was filling up fast – nervous, cautious crowds seeking human contact, reassurance, their gloom palpable as poison gas. Like dogs at hydrants, they sniffed at the colored notices they had ignored for several days – how to black out houses and cars, what to take into an air-raid shelter.

Surprisingly no one was buying the papers headlined GERMANY AVENGES VICIOUS POLE ATTACK. A boy of about seven, with a wooden dagger, had folded a copy as a sun helmet – the best use for one of Dr. G's papers, considering the soupçon of truth it contained. Better gear for this

heat than the ton of leather and brass trundled past by
two young army officers. Why did the German military
wear so much leather? Was it nostalgia for their warrior
ancestors draped in pelts?

Wolf chastised himself. He had no right to sneer at
everyone as if he were a spectator. For the past couple of
years he had played cat-and-mouse with Reinhard Heydrich and pattycake with Göring, while grooming his
London connections. He remembered Heydrich's words at
their last meeting: "If war breaks out, recruitment gives
way to conscription. Then we'll need you."

War changed things absolutely. Overnight justifiable
discontent became treason. How long, he wondered,
would it take for Britain and then the rest of Europe to
answer Hitler's challenge? How long before he was wearing one of the uniforms he despised? He recalled his collection of exquisitely crafted toy soldiers, every detail perfect down to the gleam on their boots. How gleefully his
father had moved them around on relief maps, showing
him the strategies of Moltke, all the maneuvers, everything but the corpses. The kind of battles all generals
fought – bloodless ones. Again Wolf heard the echo of
snare drums. Had his dream been a premonition of war?
Though Wolf scoffed at the supernatural, such things happened to him too often to dismiss entirely.

He struck his thumb with the hammer, as his aunt had
prophesied – nothing psychic there, just deduction from
past experience. While he was bathing it, the first sirens of
this war wailed. Practise sirens, shattering the air like glass
and sending everyone running. Loudspeakers on lamp
posts ordered: "Take cover! Everyone must take cover.
When the siren sounds, your air warden becomes supreme
authority." Another supreme authority in a country with
more of them than Olympus. Soon everyone but Wolf
would have police powers, and he'd be the only one left to
arrest.

Shifting around the bathroom for earplugs, Wolf traded
up from toilet paper to wads of cotton and was settling for

his own index fingers when he discovered the sirens had
stopped and his phone was ringing. As he reached for it,
he knew with an uncanny certainty what his dream had
meant, and who was calling, though he hadn't spoken to
her for a year. He also knew what she would say.

"Hello, Wolf?" That unmistakable throaty voice, now
very somber. "This is Carmel. I wanted you to hear it first
from me." A quick intake of breath. "Axel died this
morning. He was listening to the news about Poland when
he had a seizure."

"I'm sorry, Carmel." Though Wolf hated everything
that reminded him of death, even faded flowers, he immediately scrapped his day. "I'll be right over."

Was it just imagination or did the Berg residence already
look like an empty seashell from which the flesh had been
picked? Carmel answered the door, dressed in pale green,
without makeup, her red hair in a curly mop. Wolf handed
her an armload of flowers – mums, roses, delphiniums.
She hugged them to her in surprise, then burst into tears.
Though Wolf's impulse was to put his arms around her, to
comfort her, he waited a shade too long. Already she was
walking from him. "Thanks. Thanks for coming, Wolf."

Unlike the rest of Munich, the shadowy house seemed
cool and serene. "Since spring we've been living in two
rooms. I sent Rudolf and Lotte to Berlin – it was so much
cozier that way." After leading him up a spiral staircase,
she ushered him into her bed-sitting room. In antique blue
with white furniture covered in dainty prints, it was as
feminine and old-fashioned as a cameo in contrast to the
technocratic starkness of the rest of the house.

Wolf slid into an armchair while Carmel arranged the
flowers – each action so seamless and graceful it was as if
the crystal vase, scissors and cut stems were flying about
by themselves without her touching them.

"You said Axel died listening to the news. A stroke?"

She nodded. "That broadcast brought back all the

memories of the trenches and the pain of old wounds. Axel knew what war meant. Just the night before, he had asked me so plaintively: 'You do trust the Führer, don't you?' It was odd. He awoke from a sound sleep, looking grim, and turned on the radio as if he *knew*. I noticed that quite a lot at the end – as his body wasted, his intuition sharpened as if he had found another way of communicating."

It seemed important to Carmel to take Wolf on a tour of Axel's bedroom, to show him the radio still tuned to the BBC. The rumpled sheets. The pillow bearing the indentation of Axel's head. "He had shrunk to nothing – just that large head on the pillow, kept alive by his mighty pumping heart, yet still so gallant. In the last three months all the rancor drained out of him, leaving only the sweetness."

She was making the event of death more real by sharing it, yet at the same time distancing it by turning it into a series of snapshots, the same way Wolf used his camera. "When I held him in my arms to say good-bye, he was so frail it was like holding a freshly hatched bird. Then he spoke in that lusty, booming voice that never deserted him. He had loved life, he said, which was why he had taken so long to die. He apologized to me for that – can you imagine? Though humiliated by illness, he still found it hard to leave."

Pointing to the balcony, Carmel testified: "Just yesterday he asked me to wheel him out there. Maybe he thought it was time to leave. He's suffered so much. . . . All my tears have already been shed."

Below them the swimming pool afloat with white rose petals protruded into the sculpture garden. "I'm afraid this place is badly overgrown. I tried to do the work because I know how proud Axel is . . . was . . . of his home, but it was stealing too much time from us, so I just tended the patch he could see. It was a peaceful time. We grew very close."

Listening to Carmel's compulsive talk, Wolf thought of

the evening the three of them had spent together almost a year ago. Then he had been nostalgic for their frenetic times in Berlin. Now he was nostalgic for the tranquility of that evening. Was that his destiny – to yearn for the past through a rearview mirror? He castigated himself for not having made the effort to see Axel at least one more time. Once or twice he had actually had the phone in his hands, then had become paralyzed with indecision. What was he afraid of? Staring down at the sparkling glass dome where he and Carmel had romped among the white balloons, he thought he knew.

Slipping her arm through Wolf's, Carmel touched him for the first time. "Take me away, please." Again he felt the desire to hold her but drew back, respecting her grief, her fragility and perhaps his own. "Axel is being cremated. He wants his ashes blown by the wind through the roses."

By mid-afternoon they were speeding around the shore of Starnberger See, a boomerang-shaped lake south of Munich. Surrounded by forest and meadows dotted with villas, it was thinly edged in sand and backed by a fold of blue mountains that morbidly reminded Wolf of Axel's crumpled bed sheet.

"King Ludwig II drowned himself here," he asserted, happier dealing with distant deaths. "That proved he was mad. How could he be untouched by such tranquility? I'd give my soul to be able to express this in colors and shapes." He laughed caustically. "Perhaps, like Faust, I have no soul left."

"Have you ever painted?"

"As a child. I had every kind of lesson – riding, dancing, fencing, painting. Trouble was, each time I veered away from an exact replica of the picture I was copying, my mother rapped my knuckles. By the time I was old enough to rebel, it was too late. If ever I did something pleasing to me, I'd hear my mother's blue-veined voice complaining:

'That doesn't look much like a tree,' and my hand would freeze. I might have overcome such an obvious trauma, but by then I was old enough to judge myself in the harsher light of other people's genius. Since I was sure I would never be Matisse or van Gogh, why go on? What point in becoming an artist without a hint of greatness? I was at Heidelberg University, so I dumped my paint pots into the Rhine then settled for photography."

Renting a sailboat at Tutzing, they pushed out from the fairytale, red-roofed town in the hot September sun, with Carmel trailing her fingers while Wolf operated the boom, scanning the water's surface for puckers and glancing in mild concern at the gently luffing sail.

She laughed. "You're so earnest in your pleasures."

"That proves I'm a dilettante. Some people turn work into pleasure. The frivolous make work of pleasure."

As the wind picked up, Carmel talked about Axel. "It's true he was like a father to me. What people might have more trouble understanding is that he was also a mother. A brood hen with one chick. Like Frau Fuchs, he understood most of my bravery was bravado. He nurtured me, swaddled me in love. Nothing I did was insignificant or unwelcome, whether it was putting a flower in my hair or pouting about a pimple on the end of my nose. He was that uncritical – a rare and glorious gift. And I grew to love Axel, though not so unselfishly. He had fewer needs."

"He needed you."

"I suppose." She grinned. "And I needed you. To criticize me, since Axel wouldn't."

"Oh, I'm good at criticizing."

"I wanted to murder you at times, but I knew I needed the discipline. Anyway, you're such a perfectionist, you're much harder on yourself."

Though the words stuck in his throat, he forced himself to confess: "I missed the golden ring with you. All that style without content. Leo Warner got it right . . . *Our Motherland*."

"But I couldn't have done that without the West End

first. I wouldn't have had the confidence or the craft or the maturity. I'm a collaborative effort – you and Axel and Leo and Frau Fuchs and Professor Stein. A whole production. Aren't we all!"

To Wolf's humiliation, he felt his eyes grow misty and seized on the end of Carmel's sentence to change the subject. "Poor Max Stein. I've pulled every string I could to find out what happened to him after he left Dachau – *if* he did. No one knows. Or, no one's saying."

"I still have nightmares thinking there might have been something I could do. At least Sara Stein made it to Paris, thanks to you."

"Thanks to everyone. Another collaborative effort. She wanted Palestine. I told her America."

"There's someone else on my conscience – no, on my heart. Raymon Arno. Would money help?"

"Not at the moment. He'd just drink it. It's tragic. His talent has been dry for three years. Not even a picture postcard. That man has so much ability. He was the second star of *Our Motherland*. The sets and lighting were superb – sinister, unsentimental, with all the shadows falling the wrong way, creating their own craziness. The science of lighting that was the key to our post-war films. I haven't seen anything that touches it for magic in the last ten years – except, I hate to say, Albert Speer's architectural effects for the Führer's speeches at Nuremberg. His cathedral of light – 150 searchlights pointed vertically into the night sky. Magnificent!"

By now the setting sun was spinning the water into circles of sherry gold, apple green, fluorescent purple. Scooping up a glistening handful, Carmel marveled: "Look, this is what happened to all the paints you threw into the Rhine."

Admiring her aglow in the pink light, Wolf admitted: "I wish I could have painted you. You've always been my best subject."

She smiled. "I've always dreamed you'd look at me the

way you're doing now. I've had such a terrible crush on you. Axel used to tease me about it."

"You should have told me!" He had intended to joke but sounded wistful.

"You were so polished and hard. I couldn't imagine that anything I ever said made the slightest difference to you – like trying to write with a fingernail on steel." Still spinning intricately colored circles with her fingers, she inquired: "Why didn't you come to see us this past year? Axel talked about you so often. I ran out of excuses."

"You reminded me of the past."

"That's cruel."

"I'm sorry but I can't help these things. They are."

Distracting himself with an unnecessary tack, Wolf shifted the conversation into safer waters. "What are you going to do now, Carmel? Do you have plans?"

"Leo Warner wants me to go to Hollywood to film *Our Motherland*. He wants to turn it into an allegory of everything that's happening in Germany. What do you think?"

"That you'd better make up your mind quickly. If Britain and France go to war, will America be far behind?"

"Why don't you come too?"

"And do what?"

"What can't you do?"

He didn't smile. "Quite simply, everything."

"But what if there's war with Britain and France?"

"I ask myself that daily. I'll join the SS. No, I'll join the Resistance . . . if I can find it. Because I know there isn't any, I can make such a handsome offer."

"Be serious."

"I thought I was. I haven't the remotest idea what I'll do. Perhaps I'll go to Switzerland and make goat's cheese. I haven't tried that yet. Your career is transportable. You can go anywhere people appreciate talent. I need props."

By the time they returned to Munich the city was in full blackout, though neither Britain nor France had declared war. Since Carmel wasn't prepared to return to an empty house, they did what most others were doing: they took one last fling. Shuffling and groping and stumbling, whispering and giggling like naughty children caught after lights out, would-be merrymakers wound their way through crooked streets, their cigarettes bobbing through air as dense and muggy as oil while unlit streetcars eerily rattled by. Less cheerfully, drivers of cars with blinkered lights guided themselves by the whitewashed curbstones, often colliding with screech of brakes and crunch of metal, then cursing each other in lieu of the undeclared enemy.

Wherever two people stood together, the rumors flew, now on the side of optimism, one impeccable authority competing with another.

"A cousin of mine who's close to Göring says Papen is already in Paris negotiating disarmament for all European nations."

"I have it direct from Admiral Dönitz that if Britain is so impertinent as to declare war, he'll surround her with three hundred subs and starve her out."

"The British ambassador confided to his staff that Chamberlain has already fallen. That leaves only Anthony Eden, and he's a Jew. How can Britain declare war without a government?"

The more dubious the rumor, the more vigorously it was espoused, and always the speaker could invoke one universally revered source: "I heard it on the BBC." There was even a whole category of discussion that had to do with appearances: How can we help Britain and France back out of supporting Poland without losing face?

Determined to be frivolous, Wolf and Carmel visited the Hofbräuhaus, a multi-story beerhall where thousands of celebrants at wooden tables on sawdust floors swayed to an oompah band, arms linked, singing "Trink, Trink, Brüderlein, Trink." Deciding this was harder on their ears than the sirens, Carmel and Wolf pressed on to the Artist House on Lenbach Platz, where voluptuous girls, distributing flowers, lined a staircase leading to a bar with vaulted lapis lazuli ceiling depicting the zodiac.

As they drank a bottle of 1915 Schloss Reinhartshausener, Wolf mocked: "Unbelievably kitschy, of course. Do you know whose taste this represents? Our Führer's. He keeps a suite here – or he used to. This place and Theater Am Gärtner Platz, where they staged nude comic operas, were his favorites. The high point of his evening was when he sat in his box, with high-powered binoculars, while cancan girls in *The Merry Widow* heiled him with their legs."

"You're joking."

"I'm perfectly serious. Herr Hitler has always had a yen for actresses. In the old days his pet was Dorothy von Bruck, whom he spied at Berlin's Winter Garten, though all close to him insist the only woman he ever loved was his niece Geli."

"The girl who committed suicide?"

"That's the official version. A competing one – known only to the gossips of Munich – claims Hitler killed her in a rage over her affair with his chauffeur. A third states Himmler had her murdered because he was jealous of her influence. By all reports, Geli was an unaffected charmer – a little princess whom Adolf worshiped and tyrannized. Eight years ago she was found dead with a pistol in her hand. She had been writing a Viennese friend to say how glad she was her uncle was finally letting her go there to study music. Since she wasn't the hysterical type, her 'suicide' was hard to swallow. Her uncle was so broken up that even now her room in his apartment is sealed off, with one servant allowed in each day to leave fresh chrysanthemums." Wolf took a deep breath. "I know all this is true because my tante told me, and she's never wrong on these matters." He grinned. "She probably heard it on the BBC."

Grateful to Wolf for working so hard to distract her, amazed that he could, Carmel teased: "But what about the rumor that our Hitler is a homosexual?"

"Ahhh, yes, dominant with secretary Rudolf Hess, and passive with the late unlamented Ernst Röhm. . . . No, I think not. I have irrefutable proof. You see, I've met the Führer many times, and he's never made a pass at me."

A cloudless morning in Munich. Sunday, September 3, 1939. The third day of fighting in Poland and still the British and French have not declared war. All the news from the front is good. German troops are advancing. The Polish air force is all but destroyed. A new spirit of hope and even bravado blossoms across the Third Reich: *You see, the Führer was right, as always. It worked. The Polish thing will be over in a couple of weeks and then the others will be happy to see reason. Trust the Führer!*

On a high-tension wire from too much liquor and too little sleep, Wolf and Carmel wind up their two-day wake at Munich's Theresienwiese amusement park. Hawkers sell balloons and taffy apples. Giant canvas beer halls pulse to the rhythm of brass bands eager to outdo each other. Roller coasters. Loop-the-loops. Games of chance. Merry-go-rounds. All shrill with music and slathered in neon like cakes at a kid's birthday party.

After winning a celluloid doll on a ring toss and a ghastly bottle of lilac toilet water in a lucky draw, Carmel and Wolf finish up on the Ferris wheel. As the ground recedes, with the wind billowing Carmel's skirt, Wolf observes: "I've always wanted to shoot a film at a carnival. The British envision freedom as a pleasant day at the seaside; the French, as a picnic in the country with a good wine; the Italians, as any family celebration. For us it's Oktoberfest and the masked balls of Fasching, a carnival with giddy lights, gaudy sights and lots of noise, a few freaks in cages, a chance to try one's luck, barrels of beer, sweet things to eat, anarchy, chaos – fine for a few days but not something you can live with. . . ."

Even as Wolf speaks, everything begins to go wrong, like a giant music box that breaks a spring then grinds down. The roller coaster swoops into a wooden valley and never comes up again. The calliope stops playing, the loop-the-loop ceases to spin. Hawkers put down their megaphones while the band players fold up their accordions. An eerie silence creeps over two hundred thousand merrymakers who shuffle, pause, then stand motionless. The Ferris wheel stops turning.

Loudspeakers on every pole dispense something mournful, like Wagner's "Death March." When everyone is at attention facing them, they squawk, all at once, like a barnyard of metallic chickens. Not sentences, only words, but repeated so insistently their meaning becomes clear. . . . ULTIMATUM . . . WAR . . . BRITISH . . . THEIR GUILT . . . WAR . . . DEMANDS WITHDRAWAL. . . . FÜHRER REFUSES . . . WAR . . . IN A STATE OF . . . WAR . . .

Two children below Carmel and Wolf rock in their seat, as if on a porch swing. Concerned for their safety, Carmel leans forward to warn them, causing her own seat to sway. Ignoring her, they rock harder, while Carmel turns from insistence to hysteria, aware as she begins to scream that it's the precariousness of her own life she fears.

Whether motivated by Carmel's distress or just common sense, the operator reactivates the wheel, releasing his prisoners two by two.

Now it is the Führer who screeches from every lamp post as if with a thousand voices. . . . CAPITALISTIC JEWS . . . BRITISH WARLORDS . . . COWARDLY POLES . . . BRAVE GERMAN FIGHTING FORCES . . . JEWS . . . POLES . . . BRITISH . . . showering venom like poison rain on everyone's back while each stands mute and frozen, as required by law.

Arm wrapped around Carmel, Wolf propels her out of the park. By the time he's starting his car, the Ferris wheel has once more begun to turn, the roller coaster to swoop, the bands to play, but already it is another world.

PART IV

"To have character and be German undoubtedly mean the same. . . . We are the Chosen People. Chosen by God . . . with a moral right to fulfill our destiny by every means of cunning and force."
— Johann Gottlieb Fichte, philosopher, 1762–1814

"To us Germans everything is religion. What we do we do not merely with our hands and our brains, but with our hearts and souls. This has often become a tragic fate for us."
— Baldur von Schirach, leader of the Hitler Youth

"I know my destiny. Some day my name will be associated with the memory of something monstrous."
— Friedrich Nietzsche, 1889, the year Adolf Hitler was born

ONE

Berlin

September 1940

I T HAPPENED as soon as Carmel stepped out of Zoo station into the sunlight – the thrill of coming home. After the drug of the train journey, Berlin's freshly washed fall air tasted like a tart crisp apple, turning her fatigue into joy. Five years. Why had she stayed away so long?

Leaving her luggage, Carmel succumbed to an impulse to walk towards the Kurfürstendamm. At the Gloria Palast a comedy called *Gas Man* was playing. At the UFA Palast it was *Bomber Wing Luetzo*. Kiosks advertised the Winter Garten and the Scala. Flowers were everywhere – in hanging baskets, in window boxes, in swatches of park, encircling the bowls of trees, decking curbside stalls. Even the monstrous Kaiser Wilhelm Memorial Church looked splendid.

During the past year Berlin had slid easily into war. Anti-aircraft guns poked through the brilliant fall foliage. Sandbags were a permanent part of the cityscape. As yet bomb damage from British air raids begun in August had been minimal and were discreetly hidden behind gaudy posters advertising the war as if it were an exciting movie one must not miss. Designed by Propaganda Chief Josef Goebbels, they gloated over Germany's springtime triumphs, when tanks aided by Stukas steamrolled western Europe in a new style of warfare called blitzkrieg. One poster was a collage of headlines from the London

Times – an ironic admission by Goebbels that Germans only believed what they read in foreign papers: DENMARK OVERRUN IN TEN HOURS. BRUSSELS BOMBED. GERMAN WAR MACHINE PULVERIZES BELGIUM. DUTCH ARMY CAPITULATES IN FIVE DAYS. BRITISH ARMY WITHDRAWS.

Another poster showed the swastika flying from the Eiffel tower: THE CANDLE ON THE CAKE. A third featured Churchill's face ground into the mud by Hitler's boot: YOUR TURN NEXT, LYING LORD!

Making good on that boast, a skyful of Reichsmarschall Göring's bombers were on their way to London for the Battle of Britain, while another skyful were on their way back, bent and blackened like spent cartridges. Berlin was in a military trance. Don't think, *feel*. Hitler was invincible. War was a national sport in which things happened so fast yesterday's paper was nostalgia. The cafés along the Kurfürstendamm were jammed with soldiers and their girlfriends, hausfraus carrying babies, stout gentlemen with their dogs, all on a high, like extras in a big-budget movie everyone knows will be a smash.

Not that there hadn't been sacrifices. Only after a bitter winter in which the poorest families had lived without heat, on a diet of potatoes and grease, had imported foods become available from conquered countries. Display cases along the Kurfürstendamm once again advertised luxury goods – Belgian lace, Copenhagen china, Napoleon brandy, Norwegian furs. Since everyone was now employed, secretaries in Paris fashions tottered on high heels where once whores in gold lace-up boots had plied their trade. Cleaning ladies proudly displayed silk stockings off the black market, while every Fritz home from the front was like a one-man magic show as he unpacked a bottle of Courvoisier from a trouser pocket, a Dutch cheese from under his cap. Only a few bereaved women wore black, in defiance of Nazi propaganda celebrating death in the service of Valhalla as a glorious God-given honor.

As Carmel strolled back toward the Tiergarten, even the gritty pavement was transformed into a thing of beauty by puddles that caught patches of blue sky. In front of the Romanische Café, several magpies and a nightingale splashed amidst a golden clog of chestnut leaves. With a bittersweet rush, Carmel remembered that morning when she, Wolf and Axel had breakfasted here, then fed the birds in the Tiergarten, flinging bits of bread like snowflakes into the sun, drunk on impossible dreams.

> "It happens only once.
> It will not come again.
> It is too beautiful to be true."

Funny how memories became embedded in melodies like bits of stained glass in cement.

On claiming her luggage, Carmel hailed a cab, one of a hundred still left in Berlin. Since her three suitcases were impossible to carry, the driver beckoned her in. Otherwise his services were confined to the handicapped, old ladies having seizures, pregnant ones en route to hospital and officials on government business – meaning any party big-wig with a hangover. More than one able-bodied Berliner hobbled on crutches through the "special permissions" loophole.

This driver, like everyone else on the Kurfürstendamm, seemed drunk on the new optimism. Catching Carmel's eye in the mirror, he flashed a gap-toothed grin. "Today I rent this old heap, but after the British plead for peace, all those empty Rolls-Royces will be wanting owners."

With bicycles and horse-drawn carriages competing for space along Berlin's broad boulevards, the cabbie soon reverted to type. Snarling at each red light as if it came as a complete and unreasonable surprise, he slammed on his brakes. On yellow he ground into gear. On green he lurched forward, thumb on horn, working himself into a red-faced sweat. As Bavarians were fond of saying: A good Prussian stops on red and crosses on green even if he knows he'll get hit by a truck. Carmel would add: Yes, but he'll grouse about it.

The Berg townhouse on Pariser Platz seemed larger but not so white as Carmel remembered. In front of the former French embassy, bleachers and a victory arch, built for a review of Germany's conquering army home from France, had been refurbished with the Luftwaffe's golden eagle in anticipation of the triumph of Göring's airmen over the British. By contrast, across the street hysterical crowds besieged the American embassy for U.S. visas, though the waiting list was years long. Here Carmel could smell the panic – the dark side of the bright coin of victory.

Using her own key to avoid Rudolf and Lotte, her party faithfuls on the third floor, Carmel let herself into the home she had shared with Axel for ten years. Steeling herself against the flood of memories, she trod from room to room reacquainting herself with the Biedermeier chesterfield, the porcelain stove from Saxony, the silky mahogany sideboard, the plush Persian rugs, the Dresden music box that played "The Merry Widow," the paperweights with their exploding flower centers. After the sleek functionalism of their Munich house, she felt a shock of delight over this mansion she had once found so imposing, as if it were a discarded photograph of an earlier self.

Opening her alligator purse, Carmel unfolded a letter written on the thinnest, most elegant of papers. Bearing the gold letterhead of the Minister of Propaganda, it was signed with the green pencil that was a prerogative of all Reich ministers.

Dear Frau Berg,
Once again I entreat you! UFA Studios remains in full production under my personal patronage. Many of your esteemed colleagues, such as Emil Jannings and Christian Jürgens, continue to make German films pre-eminent in the

world. One name is missing from our illustrious roster – the most glorious of all. Please inform me by return mail of your intention to grace our cinema screen. Heil Hitler!

> Your devoted fan,
> Dr. Josef Goebbels

Carmel's appointment with the little doctor was for 3:00 the next afternoon. Since he had refused her request for an exit visa for America, she envisioned a tough bargaining session.

Picking up the phone from Axel's desk, Carmel listened for the clicks and buzzes that indicated the Brown snoop assigned to her number was at his post, pencil posed – a task so boring that more than one had succumbed to the temptation to chime in. Dialing the familiar number, she head the phone ring three, four, seven times, imagining the sound spreading outward like circles in a silent pond through the empty Hansa-viertel villa.

Typically, Wolf had vanished again, this time to Switzerland. For six months after Axel's death, he had hovered by Carmel's side, helping her settle the estate, solicitous but retaining a proper distance, steadfastly refusing to discuss his own future and always deflecting conversation toward her options and the new practicalities of her life.

One day last March he had phoned from the airport to announce he was on his way to Zurich. A business trip. He couldn't talk, his plane was on the tarmac, but he'd return as soon as possible. Carmel had thought in terms of days and then weeks. That had been five months ago.

Was Wolf planning to come back at all? His aunts in Munich had no idea and she had never been able to catch him here at his home in Berlin, though she had called often enough. Why had she thought phoning him from only a few blocks away would improve her chances?

Determined not to let brooding spoil her homecoming, Carmel unpacked a few things, then grew restless. Throwing on her tweed coat, she left the mansion.

Otto, the Adlon doorman, greeted her with a friendly wave. "Frau Berg! We've missed you. Heil Hitler!"

"I've missed you too," smiled Carmel. "Grüss Gott!" By Otto's answering grin, she knew next time he would greet her with "God Bless," indicating they shared certain political sympathies. It was a game Germans played, the way children mocked adults with a secret language.

Grandly he hailed one of the black carriages that now plied Unter den Linden, drawn by a moth-eaten nag with a sway back. "Our horses have also gone to war," apologized Otto.

To the little driver with oversized top hat that rested on his shoulders, Carmel instructed: "The Red Fox, please."

The leisurely *clop-clop-clop* up Unter den Linden Boulevard was comfortable and fun. Though bomb damage seemed more extensive in this older, more official part of Berlin, the chic canopied cafés buzzed with women in silk dresses and slouch hats, diplomats from the eastern embassies, secretaries from the ministries on Wilhelm Strasse. Lulled into somnolence by the gentle sway of the carriage, Carmel awakened with a cruel jolt. The door of The Red Fox was barred and padlocked. A picture of Frau Fuchs had been slashed with the insulting words HOUSE OF JOY. Even more ominous was the official seal, six white stamps with a spread eagle gripping a swastika in its claws and bearing the legend CLOSED BY THE GEHEIME STAATSPOLIZEI.

"Oh my God, the Gestapo! When did this happen?"

Melodramatically rolling his eyes under the brim of his hat, the driver replied: "Two nights ago."

"What happened? Do you know?"

"She told one too many jokes that the party didn't like. The Gestapo took her straight to Dachau." Shooting eyes right then left, he added a hasty "Grüss Gott" as if crossing himself, then sent his nag galloping out of the alleyway.

Shocked, Carmel huddled in the open carriage as it trotted back over the Spree river then down Unter den

Linden. As they stopped for a red light, she numbly watched a corpulent man with a white napkin tucked under his chin waddle out the door of Café Schön, waving his arms. "Stop!" Assuming he wanted to commandeer her taxi, Carmel prepared for resistance. Instead he jumped on the running board and clasped her hand.

"Frau Berg!" he panted. "That incomparable profile – I thought I was dreaming."

Inspecting the round face with bright-red mustache and cropped head, Carmel recognized Willi Bliss, critic for the *Berliner Tageblatt*.

"Will you join me for dinner? Forgive the early hour but we Berliners who like to eat do it early. Before Churchill drops his loaded peanuts."

Willi Bliss's warm hand and chocolate-truffle eyes moved Carmel in the manner of a pleading dog. "I might like some company tonight."

Dismissing her driver, he ushered her to a table in the window of Café Schön. "Best seat in town for the best show. Everyone worthwhile passes here eventually, as you've just proven." Filling their goblets with Bernkasteler Doktor, he gave the Bavarian royal toast: "Hoch! Hoch!" then smacked his lips and inquired: "And now, dear lady, what lures you to Berlin? A film comeback, I hope."

Still numbed by concern for Frau Fuchs, Carmel nodded. "Perhaps. I'm seeing Dr. Goebbels tomorrow."

"Not alone, I hope. Since the Führer put an end to his disastrous affair with that Czech star Lida Baarova, he seems bent on raping every actress taller than himself – which means every actress. The only woman who doesn't know about the salon attached to his ministry office is his wife, Magda. He even keeps foreign diplomats waiting." Chuckling, Willi asked: "Why did the Führer move the Angel of Victory column? Answer: So Goebbels couldn't get at her."

"What concerns me more is the quality of the scripts he has to offer," murmured Carmel, in no mood for jokes.

"Ahh, then it will be a testy few hours. Have you seen the 'No' list? No film that presents marriage as anything but idyllic. No film showing German soldiers dying. No film mentioning any religion other than Führer worship. No political films since today's friend may be tomorrow's foe – witness Russia. No spy films and no films displaying luxury since either one might give Germans ideas. No films with Jews unless they're stridently anti-Semitic. . . . When the propaganda ministry screened *Gone with the Wind* last year, the lineup of petty officials who just happened to be passing was longer than the one for visas outside the American embassy."

Carmel stuck her fingers in her ears. "Don't. This is my first day. You're depressing me."

"I'm depressing myself." Snapping for a waiter, Willi complained: "Service is slower here than in the Adlon bomb shelter. I was caught there last week, a wall away from the French burgundies without being able to get at them." Reversing Göring's vow that if bombs fell on Berlin he'd change his name to Meyer, Willi quipped: "I informed the Oberkellner that I wouldn't return till Herr Meyer changed his name to Göring."

At last they caught the waiter, placed their order and received a plate of Bismarck herring. Picking at it without appetite, Carmel asked: "Can you tell me anything about the closing of The Red Fox?"

Wiping his mouth on his bib Willi nodded. "A little. It wasn't just Frau Fuchs' jokes. It was her cheeky delivery and the fanaticism of the crowd. Here's the one they hauled her in for. Staring deadpan at the audience, she announced: 'I saw the strangest sight the other day. Imagine! A great big 12-cylinder Mercedes was driving through Berlin *without a single Nazi in it*.' Now you'd have to know something about the hate and fear in this town to understand why the audience went hysterical then gave her a standing ovation. Five minutes after curtain, presto! The Gestapo was at the stage door with flowers."

"What will happen to her?"

Indulging in the shrug that was part of every German's defensive arsenal, Willi lamented: "I'm a journalist, not a soothsayer. Perhaps six months' detention. Perhaps a year. I'm not as well informed as I used to be. Did you hear? I'm no longer the critic for the *Berliner Tageblatt*. Goebbels sacked me."

Still distracted, Carmel murmured: "I'm sorry, Willi."

"Well, it was getting harder to squeeze in that little bit of truth disguised as metaphor. Since Dr. G became the patron of all the arts, anything the regime produces is art by definition – mistake that at your peril. My nemesis was Karl Ritter's *Stukas*. Have you seen it?"

"I've seen almost nothing in a couple of years."

"Lucky you! It's about a shell-shocked flier who is cured through the inspiration of hearing *Siegfried* – not even the whole opera, just Wagner's "Grand March." Foolishly I expressed some skepticism about the completeness of such a cure."

"What will you do now? The *Berliner Tageblatt* and the *Frankfurter Zeitung* are the only papers still respected."

Willi grimaced. "I'm working for the propaganda ministry, where Goebbels can keep his eye on me. Try not to despise me."

"How could I? If I make a film I'll be working for him too."

"I was given a choice. Either write news releases with a patriotic slant or be dispatched to the hottest front with a water pistol. That's how this regime disposes of its critics – you artists should have been so lucky."

Arriving with their main course, the waiter set a Norwegian trout before Carmel, then presented Willi with his Weisswurst. Stabbing a link with his fork, he addressed it somberly: "What is a Bavarian?" He answered himself: "Someone who eats a Weisswurst even if he knows it's poisoned." That ritual done, he delicately peeled it with his knife. "My new job does have its compensations. Observing the German war machine is like watching a collaboration between D. W. Griffith, Max Reinhardt and

Cecil B. De Mille. I've actually been as close to the front
as Maxim's. . . . Paris on the day of capitulation – what a
sight! All those magnificent monuments like picture post-
cards without a Frenchman in sight. Shutters down,
streets deserted, nothing open except the bordellos. That's
how it was for a couple of days while the French sulked,
then *all* Paris became a bordello. A few hundred marks
and you were a king – forget the uniform. Imagine – it
took six hundred thousand dead Germans to try to take
Verdun in the last war, and this time we got it in one day!"

Popping the Weisswurst into his mouth, Willi chatted
around the bulge in both cheeks. "The French are shame-
less. The Resistance was spearheaded by the Communists
and when Stalin and the Führer climbed in bed together,
that finished it. Why the British refuse our generous offers
of peace is beyond my comprehension. Can't they see we
love them better than the French ever did? That's why the
Führer let them go at Dunkirk. He and Göring didn't
think they had the guts to sacrifice their cities over their
air force. That's something the French would never do –
Paris is now the safest capital in Europe. They're even
hauling away their sandbags."

As Willi jabbed the air with knife and fork, spewing
words in staccato bursts, Carmel gratefully let his verbal
blitzkrieg steamroll over her, marveling at his adaptabil-
ity. What Axel used to call "adjusting to the Realities," as
if they were troublesome but well-meaning neighbors.
How tempting to do the same. What good did her inner
resistance do since she never acted it out beyond the game
of Grüss Gott?

Aloud, she challenged: "Admit it, Willi, you secretly
admire the French because they do what you'd like to."

Instead of answering, he offered up another of his Bavarian jokes. "The other day I was sitting in a beer garden
when a waiter picked up a drunk by his lederhosen and
tossed him out.

" 'Why did you do that?' I asked.

" 'Every time that rascal passes by he pisses in the

sauerkraut. Of course, he does no harm, but after thirty years I ask myself, what good does he do?' "

Later they went for a *shuffle-shuffle-grope-bump* along the Kurfürstendamm. After a year of blackout, Germans negotiated their glass and concrete jungle like confident night animals, small flashlights in their pockets with phosphorescent party buttons burning like eyes on both lapels. Tiny red lanterns were mandatory for car bumpers, while bars advertised themselves with blinkered blue lights that cast a sinister Mephistophelian glow.

"I'd take you out on the town, but what would you see? At the Golden Horseshoe, a ring where women can trot a horse for seventy-five pfennigs while the men ogle their thighs. A foggy basement called the Bluenote where the band thinks it's bold when it smuggles American jazz into German folk songs – like spiking the sauerkraut with cola. Even the Scala and Winter Garten feature the kind of 'talent' that used to play the streets – party-approved magicians who juggle the rings through their noses, barrel-chested, arm-pumping sopranos who are funnier than the clowns. What Goebbels calls cultural diffusion – meaning leveling down." Snarling under cover of darkness, Willi groused: "We Germans don't play Shaw or Schiller or Shakespeare anymore. We wrestle and lift weights. Bahh! That Poison Dwarf is his own worst propaganda failure. No one gets better press, because he writes it himself, yet no one is more hated."

Relieved to hear someone indulge in a Berliner's inalienable right to grumble, Carmel slipped her arm through Willi's. "I'm glad to hear victory hasn't ruined everyone."

At the Romanische, once the home of left-wing radicals and artists, they selected a marble–topped iron table from which the graffiti of the famous and infamous had been carefully sanded. While Carmel ordered a Berliner Weisse,

Willi – like a fat brown bear preparing for winter – chose a second dessert and a beer.

"Five years ago, this place would have been jammed with friends," mourned Carmel. "Now I don't see anyone I know."

"That table by the door holds what's left of the American press," pointed out Willi. "They used to be the spoiled darlings of the Reich, with double rations, no censorship and both Goebbels and Ribbentrop competing to entertain them. Since Roosevelt started lending Churchill ships, Hitler hates him even more than he hates Churchill. In a single editorial in the *Völkischer Beobachter*, Roosevelt was called a gangster, a butcher, a cannibal in white collar, a Negroid maniac and a depraved Jewish scoundrel. Last month a friend of mine was ordered out of a café for speaking 'American,' and when she cheekily explained she was British, the owner apologized and invited her to stay."

Willi stopped talking. A cold hush had crept over the café, beginning at the door. Swiveling to look where he and everyone else was staring, Carmel saw an erect and haughty SS officer, like a whiplash of polished leather, tapping his white gloves against his palm while he gazed from drinker to drinker as if card-cataloging each one.

"Ahhh, the Blond Beast," muttered Willi, lips unmoving in the style Berliners had perfected. "Reinhard Heydrich, the biggest and blackest of the Big Black Ones. He owns a brothel near here, where he entertains. In my opinion, you're looking at the next Führer of the Third Reich."

As Carmel stared in fascination, Heydrich inclined his skull so its waxy skin and sharp planes caught the light, while his eyes remained shadowed. Then, with a braying laugh, he spoke to someone behind him – another man, dark-haired, aristocratic and slender. The intruders abruptly turned to leave. Heaving a collective sigh, everyone chattered at once as if filling a hole ripped in the air. Carmel sprang to her feet. Pushing to the door, she was just in time to see the men climb into a black Mercedes.

"Wolfgang!" she shouted, but she was too late. If, indeed, it had been he.

TWO

I T TOOK eight hours to metamorphose Carmel Kohl out of cosmetics, clothes and sealing wax. The skin had to be cleansed, buffed and moisturized, the hair trimmed and tamed, the eyebrows plucked, the cheeks hollowed, the mouth reddened and extended, the eyes blackened. Though the extra five pounds Carmel had put on in five years of country living had improved her figure, this excess did nothing for the clothes so precisely molded to her Rhinegold Maiden frame. At last she settled on a slippery black dress, high-necked, long-sleeved, with a black velvet hat and veil: the widow, a warning to Dr. Goebbels to keep his hands off. Fortunately, Wolf had taught her physical self-reliance. The daily phoenix flight of Carmel Kohl from the ashes of Kara Nobody had never been a task entrusted to menials who might fall ill, have marital troubles, go mad, move away or withhold their services for an increase in pay. Emotional self-reliance, that had been different. Always before she had had Axel, Frau Fuchs, Professor Stein, Wolf . . .

Picking up her bedroom phone for the eighth time, Carmel dialed his number, let it ring ten times for a total of eighty, forcing her to conclude Wolf was not at home and never had been. Probably she had manufactured him out of Reinhard Heydrich's shadow and her own desires, the way she recreated Carmel Kohl at whim and will.

Used to working precisely to curtain time, Carmel was

finished at five minutes to three, which meant she was fifteen minutes early since she planned to be fifteen minutes late. As the seconds ticked by, she experienced the worse case of stage fright in her career. During five years of retreat in Munich, the tough and nervy extroverted part of herself had fallen away so she felt like a clam without a shell. She was terrified to be confronted once again by the needs, drives and responsibilities of the glamorous Carmel Kohl – the result of a conjuring trick she performed with bright lights and mirrors. Or perhaps it was just that she was used to a script, whereas this afternoon she'd be working out of instinct, with someone else's fate in her hands.

Anxiously Carmel rifled Axel's desk, searching for the Balkan cigarettes he used to keep for Wolf. She found a pack somehow missed by Rudolf, who she now knew had been robbing her blind. It wasn't so much that she wanted to smoke the cigarette as to sniff it – a smell she associated with successful opening nights. Closing her eyes, she puffed without inhaling, improvising lines on behalf of Frau Fuchs, whose case she intended to plead, remembering how she had written her own dialogue for *Our Motherland*.

At 3:10 Carmel stubbed her cigarette and rang for Rudolf to bring around the white Mercedes – provided he hadn't already stole it, tire by tire. Though it was only a couple of blocks to the Ministry of Propaganda and Enlightenment, Carmel Kohl had to arrive as a star.

Stepping out her front door, she blinked in the sun, a zillion times harsher than klieg lights. Carmel wasn't used to matinees. Seeing the audience in their raincoats and tweeds made her feel overdressed, which she was.

Fortunately Rudolf had two virtues. With his polished silver hair and wax features he looked like a chauffeur from Central Casting. Secondly, he seldom spoke. This last especially pleased Carmel as he eased the limousine around the corner, past the Adlon onto Wilhelm Strasse, traveling at a snail's pace the way an ambitious walk-on performer plumps his part.

Ribbentrop's palatial foreign ministry was painted a sickly yellow, including the decorative snakes strangling a sphere that looked like the world. The bronze doors from Hitler's starkly imposing new chancellery, designed by Albert Speer, had been melted down for guns.

Rudolf drove up the ramp of Dr. Goebbel's stately propaganda ministry – a converted Hohenzollern palace designed by Schinkel. Alighting under the portico festooned with Nazi banners, Carmel strolled by the guards, enjoying the snap of their heads. One even allowed his mouth to gape. It was amazing. All she had to do was slip into her alter ego as if it were a one-piece stage costume and a marquee light flashed overhead: STAR!

Soon heads were popping from gilt and red plush halls bearing the names Throne Room, Blue Gallery, Red Hall. She heard the familiar silky rustle as office boys and flunkies in braided uniforms whispered her name – a talisman passed from mouth to mouth.

A former Hohenzollern prince who perhaps came with the palace ushered Carmel ever inward, through two doors and by several secretaries to where Dr. Goebbels held court. It was a large office, surprisingly austere, with the minister at an outsized desk flanked by a giant globe and a telephone possessing some fifty colored buttons that lit up like a pinball machine. Behind him was a bookcase bearing a photo of his glamorous wife, Magda, and a bouquet of yellow mums, while overhead hung the de rigueur oil of Frederick the Great in a romantic pose contrasting painfully with the little doctor's own awkward and twisted pinstriped ambience. With his gaunt, sallow face and coarse dark hair, his noted resemblance to a rodent was fair rather than malicious.

As Carmel entered his office, he rose to greet her – not more than five feet tall and a hundred pounds as he dragged his orthopedic right shoe while managing, through self-propaganda, to make Carmel feel she was the wrong size. As he clasped her hand, an infectious wrap-around grin transformed those same ratlike features into Mickey Mouse.

A silly young fly challenged a wise old one to a race from one side of Goebbels' ridiculously wide mouth to the other. Thinking to pull a fast one, the young fly zipped along the top lip, leaving the lower "outside" track to the old one. When he arrived, panting, at the other side, the wise old fly was already there, dozing. "How did you do it?" demanded the youngster. "Simple," revealed the old-ster. "I jumped across the back."

Stifling a nervous giggle, Carmel reminded herself that Dr. Goebbels, the No. 3 man in the Nazi hierarchy, was an amoral manipulator of radio, film and press; the man who turned Nazism into a religion with banners, rallies, mar-tyrs and marching columns; the mastermind behind Kris-tall Nacht.

Before he could guide her by the elbow to his black leather couch, she slid into an armchair, now deeply into the persona of Carmel Kohl, anticipating how Wolf would direct her for the drama she intended to play from the upstage position, as aware as if she were in the spotlight of her hands, legs and facial expression.

To her relief, Dr. G accepted the sycophantic role sug-gested by her aloof manner. "I was distraught to hear about the death of Herr Berg," he sympathized in his rich and flexible baritone. "A double tragedy – for you and the party. Still, you were unkind to make his illness your excuse to deprive the Reich of your talent. That's unfor-givable! The sooner we get you back on the screen, the more gratifying my job as patron of the arts."

With a fluting laugh, Carmel protested. "Not, I hope, using any of the scripts you've already sent me. Please, Herr Doktor, no more peasant women yearning to breed soldiers for the Fatherland."

He bristled. "We Germans have a lot to learn about the art of cinema, Frau Berg, but a little nationalism is good for us and the world. UFA was founded to counter the lies the Americans spread about us in their movies after the First War. Have you seen the technicolor film *Swanee River*? I must say I found it fascinating. The Americans are masters at taking their cultural heritage, pitiful as it is, and modernizing it to conquer the world. We Germans have a far greater fund of artistic treasures but we're too loaded down with piety and tradition to capitalize on it. That has to change if we're to dominate the world market and make large profits for the party, as we must."

Still testing her power, Carmel retorted: "But, Dr. Goebbels, what about *The Blue Angel*, *The Cabinet of Dr. Caligari*, *Faust* and *M*? Many people think Germany has had her golden age of film."

"Nonsense. Nationalism will take us over the threshold of greatness. At present we're so soft, so generous, so innocent that we lack political opportunism entirely. Send a director to Paris or Vienna or Prague, and instantly he becomes imbued with that country's nationalism over his own. I've had to veto every script our Paris office has sent to us." Using his voice like an organ while gesturing with eloquent, slender hands, Goebbels mounted to an indignant climax. "If we dared to manipulate our audiences the way the Americans do, they'd throw us out. The German people wouldn't put up with anything so immoral. The Americans are so groggy with Roosevelt's lies, they can't tell the difference between truth and fiction."

Carmel knew she was observing a skilled but technical performance. Once she had witnessed Goebbels drive an audience of five thousand at the Sports Palast into a frenzy, then stroll offstage without a drop of sweat, whereas the Führer lost several pounds during such an ordeal. Grudgingly, she allowed: "I hope it will be possible for us to come to some agreement."

"Possible? With the finest script, the best director, your choice of leading man, we'll make it impossible for you to refuse!"

"That may be difficult, Herr Doktor. Leo Warner, Ernest Lubitsch and Peter Lorre are in Hollywood. Piscator is in New York. Conrad Veidt has gone to –"

"Surely you aren't suggesting there are no talented people here a thousand times better than those betrayers! What about Karl Ritter for director? Werner Kraus or Christian Jürgens for the lead?"

"I'd love to work with Christian again. Since I don't have Axel, such continuity is important. But one other person is *essential*."

"Tell me his name so I can hire him."

Sweat trickling under her slippery black dress, Carmel warned: "there may be complications."

"If he's within the Reich, I'll get him for you!"

"Frau Hildebrand Fuchs, my mentor. The person who nurtured my career from –"

"Ahhhcht!" spat Goebbels. "That Bolshevik pervert."

Haughtily Carmel reminded him: "Cabaret has a long and honored tradition in Berlin. It's no threat to a healthy regime."

"I'll be the judge of that, Frau Berg." Fingers in a steeple, voice cruel, he lectured her as if from a great height. "In the Third Reich we don't shy away from corrective treatment. All governments must control the people they rule, but we're more honest and sensible about it. The story of UFA is the story of how hard a few patriots had to fight against Jewish-Bolshevik efforts for control. The sole aim of this regime is to weed out such people. I will *not* put those dregs to work on any production, and that's final!"

Anguished, Carmel started to cry.

Though continuing to sermonize, Goebbels modulated his tone. "What you don't seem to understand, Frau Berg, is that the Third Reich, like any other government, is a bureaucracy with something called spheres of interest, presided over by various ministers. While Herr Heinrich Himmler and Herr Reinhard Heydrich may sometimes grumble about having to round up a few thousand Jews and Bolsheviks and perverts, they can become even testier when asked to pick back through the garbage they've collected."

"All I know is that as an artist I must be surrounded by people I can trust."

"Homosexuals?"

"Peers! Transvestism also has a long and honored tradition in Berlin."

Staring at her coldly, Goebbels demanded: "What are we really talking about, Frau Berg? Is it the genuine need for a pervert's professional services or an exchange of favors? If you're suggesting you'll do a film for UFA if we release your 'mentor,' then say so. Your name is of use to us, since you're the German star most admired in America, where your filthy colleagues are spreading Jewish-Bolshevik lies about us."

He gave Carmel a clue to the real reason he was humoring her. "The Führer often asks for *Lorelei*. He's seen it more times than any other film. All our ministers understand favors, so let's be frank."

"I'll do a film for UFA if you'll release Frau Fuchs."

He nodded dismissively. "I'll see what can be done."

THREE

Mullhorig, Bavaria

December 1940

S ET IN RURAL Bavaria amidst gently rolling hills where the villages are counted by church towers, Mullhorig had its Gasthaus, its post office, a variety store and a cemetery with the family plots reaching back a dozen generations. Estranged both by location and philosophy was a three-story stucco building with red-tiled gables and shuttered windows, extended by barracks. Once a Catholic welfare home run by the Sisters of Mercy, it now flew the red-and-white Lebensborn banner and the black-and-white SS rune.

In the head nurse's office on the second floor, Ilse Schmidt could gaze out her frosty window both at the village snuggled to its red roofs in snow and over unbroken fields to the sharp blue line of the Alps. Often this view reminded Ilse of home, but today her nostalgia was disturbed by the sight of four Dachau prisoners in blue-and-white striped uniforms. Dragging a snowplow intended for horses, they were clearing ground for tonight's bonfire celebrating winter solstice. Even with her windows sealed, she could hear the crack of whips as they split the icy air, the grunts of the men as they labored under a breathy cloud of steam. A cruel and inefficient method of work, no matter how "therapeutic," Ilse couldn't help thinking. She watched their clogs slip in the snow. One had no socks, another no gloves. Did they have underwear beneath their cotton uniforms? From the scrawniness of their chests, she doubted it. Ilse decided she must talk to Dr. Zuckmayer about this. She was sure he would tell her such things were not her business, but how could she ignore them when they took place outside her window? What was the point of playing lullabies and erecting a Julfest tree to cheer expectant mothers, while forcing them to witness scenes of medieval horror?

In Ilse's view, this was the sort of thing that soured the village folk against the Lebensborn. Last week she had advised her girls not to go into Mullhorig unless necessary, and then in threes or fours – enough for protection but not so many as to overwhelm. Her memo had resulted from her own attempt to buy solstice candles at Flesch's variety store. As Frau Flesch was checking her stock, an old crone had flown into Ilse's face like a black crow. "Slut! Strumpet!" she had hissed, crossing herself. "Whore of Satan!"

Instead of apologizing for the old woman, Frau Flesch had caught her craziness, as if it were a virus. Scornfully, she insisted she had no more candles to sell, though Ilse could see a box of them.

Mullhorig was a Catholic village. Old ideas died hard. The gossips cursed Ilse's girls as prostitutes when they should have honored them as progenitors of the Thousand-Year Reich.

Ilse gazed at her Lebensborn poster. A romanticized version of herself in a corn field breast-feeding Bruno, it was painted from a photo taken by her brother Erich. Though she felt vain hanging it here, it bucked up her spirits by reminding her of Lebensborn ideals. Not only did the Mullhorig home produce five hundred babies each year for the Führer, but the movement had spread like a tender vine over all of Germany and occupied Europe.

Ilse checked her appointment book.

"4:00 p.m. Helga Hewel, applicant for student nurse." That was the term the Lebensborn used for girls selected to bear children in "biological marriage" with SS volunteers. Examining the photos and information form, Ilse saw Helga was 5′10″ with broad hips and sturdy thighs. Wide-set blue eyes, blond hair in a single plait. A solemn mouth – or was that sulky? Age twenty-three. Eldest of seven. Born in Dresden. No birthmarks or blemishes. No serious childhood illnesses. Perfect teeth and vision. Highest Aryan rating: completely in accord with SS selection principles.

Since last month Ilse had requested to see all applicants with No. 1 ratings. At thirty-three, with only one child and a history of miscarriages, she had to face the fact that she was a reproductive failure. She also knew she must compensate by arranging a biological marriage for Kurt.

Ilse remembered the exact moment she had come to her decision. On leave at their Berlin apartment, she and Kurt had taken advantage of Bruno's afternoon nap to make love. Afterward Kurt lit a Muratti cigarette and sat naked on the side of the bed, his flaxen hair ruffled into tufts.

"I've been turned down for the front," he brooded. "When this war is over, I'll still be converting vacuum cleaners to anti-aircraft guns. Maybe someone'll hire me to turn them back again."

Though retooling factories for the armament industry kept Kurt working eighteen to twenty hours a day, it also kept him safe. Ilse's heart flooded with joy, but then she felt a backwash of guilt. Why should she be so pleased when thousands of women had already sacrificed their husbands to the Fatherland?

"Kurt," she blurted. "You need a biological wife." As soon as the words were out, Ilse knew they had weighted her mind for a long time.

Kurt protested he wanted no child other than hers. Ilse persisted, arguing that it was a matter of honor and privilege for both of them, feeling the lift of a burden she hadn't realized she was carrying.

Helga was the fourth applicant Ilse had interviewed with Kurt in mind. The girl had stated she intended to give up her baby for adoption, but was she likely to change her mind? Would she demand further contact with the father to attempt to extort money? Since Ilse's dream was to adopt Kurt's biological child as a brother for Bruno, she had to be careful.

At exactly 4:00 p.m. Ilse pressed the buzzer on her desk. Before she had a chance to tuck in her brown blouse, a blond Amazon filled her doorway. "Sit down, please," she invited, keeping the desk between them to show authority, though she would have preferred to share a hot chocolate on the couch.

After Helga had seated herself, hands folded in the lap of her navy skirt, thick ankles crossed, Ilse got down to particulars.

"With how many men have you had intercourse, Helga?"

"My fiancé, Rolf, who was killed in France, and another friend, Arnulf. He decided to marry my sister."

"Why do you want to join our program?"

"To help the Fatherland. I know I'm never going to marry. I'd like to have a baby. The one Rolf and I would've had."

"Your application says you plan to give up any child for adoption. Is that likely to change?"

Helga's voice was firm. "No. I work long hours in a munitions plant. If a good German couple can give my child a home, I'd let them."

Beaming her approval, Ilse explained: "If your application is accepted, you'll be hired for six months as a student nurse. For three days each month, at your highest fertility, you'll be assigned to one of our impregnation centers where you'll meet with your SS volunteer. After you become pregnant, you can stay with us, beginning at your third month, learning child care by helping other mothers, or you may return only for the birth." With more emphasis than she intended, Ilse coached: "Coming from a large family you may think you know about children, but I'm sure, Helga, some of our new scientific concepts will surprise you. Reichsführer Himmler has devised a diet and exercise program that practically guarantees the production of a boy."

Helga's face glowed with enthusiasm. "I'd love to stay at the home!"

Studying the girls' eyes, Ilse warned: "Please understand the strictest confidentiality must be maintained. If the father wishes to reveal more than his first name, that's his business, though something we discourage. The same with you. Marriages from our biological unions are very much the exception. Under no circumstances can you urge further contact. As the Reichsführer says: 'A forced marriage is an unhappy marriage.' Besides, *your volunteer partner will very likely have a wife and other children.* Does this meet with your expectations?"

A vigorous nod. "Ja!"

"Good. One more matter. Often our German wives are more broad-minded that those in other countries. Sometimes the biological father and his legal wife will want to adopt his Lebensborn child. That's the solution we consider the best."

"That would be my choice."

Ilse felt almost giddy. "We've talked of the difficulties, now I'll tell you the benefits – comfortable quarters, delicious food, the best medical treatment, companionship and a heightened sense of purpose only a soldier risking his life for the Fatherland can understand. The Lebensborn is the nurturing cradle of Aryan civilization. You are the fountain of life! And I'll tell you a little secret: Our greatest asset is the love Reichsführer Himmler bears us. Despite his crushing responsibilities, the detail of his correspondence would astonish you. Toilet training, milk production, the shape of a nose – all these interest him personally. When a child happens to be born on his birthday, October 7, his kindness knows no bounds. Gifts of candlesticks, a bank book with small sums deposited. . . . Oh, we care about our girls, Helga. We give them dignity and fulfillment in advance of our times."

Afterward Ilse felt pleased with the interview – even

exhilarated. It felt good to speak idealistically to a girl and see the kindling fire in her eyes. Camaraderie among women with the same reproductive dreams – that was something a man could only imagine. She had felt that bond with Helga. The girl was perfect.

Ilse checked the time: five o'clock. Though she usually toured the Lebensborn, seeing her new babies, keeping her nurses on their toes and cheering up her mothers, tonight was Julfest – December 21, the longest night of the year when the Lebensborn celebrated the rising of the sun from the ashes of the winter solstice. A date from the old Teutonic calendar, the Führer was encouraging all Germans to honor it instead of Christmas.

As Ilse climbed the stairs to the common room, she heard the lively sound of music and laughter mixed with the squalls of babies. Clustered around an upright piano, mothers with children on their laps were singing "O Tannenbaum," while a competing group was rehearsing a new anthem for winter solstice. The Julfest tree cast a magic glow. The room smelled of the fir bows looped over the rafters.

Keeping an eye out for her son, Bruno, Ilse greeted mothers by name – no small task since one hundred might be living here at peak periods.

"Signe, I'm delighted you're up so soon. It would have been a shame to miss Julfest."

"Oh, he's beautiful, Maria. Have you thought of a name? Dr. Zuckmayer will be so pleased when he gets back from Norway."

To Elisabeth, the wife of an SS captain, Ilse enthused: "That's three for you. Next time it's a bronze cross." That was the award presented in the name of Klara Hitler, the Führer's mother, to women who had produced four children. A silver cross was for six, and a gold for eight. Though irreverently dubbed the Order of the Rabbit, this honor entitled a woman to special allowances, a Polish housemaid and the prestige of receiving the Hitler salute.

Ilse spotted Bruno's fuzzy red head a split second

before he saw her. Throwing down his rubber ball, he fought his way from the arms of Rosa, his student nurse, and slithered toward her on his belly in a rapid, crab-like motion. He seized Ilse's leg, then let loose a stream of gibberish.

"Liebling." Swinging him up in her arms, Ilse buried her face in his familiar smells and textures. "Have you been nice to Rosa?"

How much like Kurt he looked, with intense blue eyes set close to the bridge of his sharp nose, yet how much like her brother Bruno, as if a photograph of one had been superimposed on the other. She brushed her lips through the red curls that were distinctly his own, though Kurt said his mother had red hair.

"You must help Mutti finish her rounds."

Ilse put her son down, causing a piercing howl. As heads turned, Ilse scooped him up again. At one year and eleven months, Bruno had been slow to walk and spoke only a mishmash of words that required a mother's intuition to decipher. All this Ilse blamed on his premature birth. Besides, why should he learn when it was more convenient to imitate the babies around him?

At the Julfest tree, Bruno at last allowed her to release him so he could admire the candles reflected in silver balls. "See the lady on the gold star at the top? That's Klara Hitler, the patron saint of mothers." Prizes to be distributed in her name were strung on the branches – pink and blue teething rings, SS pendants for mothers with the highest milk production, booties for twins.

Under the tree, in cotton batting stolen from medical supplies, Ilse had created a miniature village into which she had smuggled the crèche she purchased on her honeymoon. As she plugged in a string of bulbs, illuminating the cellophane windows of the houses, she enthused: "Mother was born in a wood house like this. In the mountains." Oh, how she longed to scoop up Bruno and run home with him! To see the chalets sparkling with icicles, the skiers in their bright mittens and caps, the snorting horses with their red harnesses jangling with bells, the church hung with evergreens and tinsel stars, while all around them the mountains glowed like the golden crown of the Magi.

Marthe Schultz had never even seen her first grandson. Instead of taking pride in Ilse's achievements, she had ostracized her daughter as the official black sheep. Not only had she refused to participate in a Catholic christening unless Ilse renounced Bruno's naming ceremony as a sin, but she had also accused Ilse of "Satanic acts" in encouraging pregnancy outside of marriage, just like the crazy women of Mullhorig.

Ilse had only to close her eyes to see her mother's flushed face as she vigorously punched down bread dough while chiding her: "You've always beaten your wings too hard for a woman. That's something God punishes in His own way."

"Frau Schmidt." Rosa was holding up Bruno's red snowsuit. "The sun's already setting. If we don't hurry we'll miss it."

Glancing out the window, Ilse saw an orange disk resting on the horizon as if it were a silver plate. "Five minutes till the solstice bonfire," she announced to the rest. "Bundle up warmly."

Ilse threw her ski togs over her party uniform, then hurried out into the brittle twilight. Pine trees, cut by prisoners, had been stacked into a cone two stories high. Around it stood several doctors in party uniforms, drinking schnapps, with two SS officers assigned to work the water pump should the bonfire get out of hand.

As Ilse exchanged salutes, she saw Dr. Zuckmayer. "I wasn't expecting you until tomorrow."

With a gold-toothed grin, he raised his schnapps. "I don't like to miss a good party. Will you see me afterward in my office?" He gestured toward a line of pregnant women as fat as winter bears in their fur coats. "I could be pretty busy on the wards tomorrow. I understand there's quite a competition to produce the Julfest baby."

By now the sun had slid halfway below the horizon. While others drank milk and warm beer, the mother with the most children climbed a stepladder beside the pile of firs, carrying a lighted torch. Two pregnant fiddlers waited, bows poised. Just as the last glowing fragment of sun extinguished itself, the Julfest mother hurled her torch into the pines. The trees ignited, the fiddlers fiddled and the Lebensborn mothers sang the solstice song:

> "From the loin of the dying sun
> We pluck the seed of Life.
> We nourish it during the long night.
> We keep it pure, guard it from taint.
> Burn fire against the darkness.
> We pray for the rise of the new day."

All that night those who could manage it without medical mishap intended to take turns playing accordions, flutes, lutes and guitars till dawn when the group would reassemble to sing:

> "We give birth to the light
> From the womb of the night.
> Sun rise! Sun rise!
> Maidens of the Holy Grail,
> Vessels of the pure blood,
> Daughters of the Fatherland,
> Brides of our sweet Führer
> Companions of the Black Order,
> Untainted by darkness,
> Free of imperfections,
> We greet the dawn
> Of the new Teutonic Age.
> Sun rise! Sun rise!
> Light our Thousand-Year Reich.
> Sieg Heil! Sieg Heil!"

Dr. Zuckmayer touched Ilse's arm. "Whenever convenient, Frau Schmidt."

"I'll get my reports."

"No, nothing so serious. I just want to chat. My feet are cold. I figured yours might be."

As Ilse handed Bruno to Rosa, he grabbed her scarf and refused to let go. When she tried to peel away his fingers, he screamed.

"Just bring him along," suggested Dr. Zuckmayer.

"He's overexcited – his first real Julfest, the tree, the lights."

"Ja, Ja, of course. Just bring him."

In Dr. Zuckmayer's unpretentious office they settled on a red plaid chesterfield crowded by filing cabinets, with Bruno between them. Drawing a bottle of kirschwasser from a desk drawer, the doctor offered some to Ilse in a paper cup.

"I'm anxious to hear about your trip. Was it a success?"

"A qualified one. Our homes in Norway and Denmark are working well. With our common blood bond, Nordics have no trouble understanding Lebensborn aspirations. In countries like France and Belgium, I'm afraid our Reichsführer proceeds with more hope than pragmatism. There's so little good blood worth saving that I'm afraid our presence only encourages our troops to look on the native women too favorably. I intend to make a point of this in my report. Any problems in my absence?"

"Nothing internal. Our big headache is the locals. One or two of the women in Mullhorig have stirred up the rest against us. They treat us like whores and witches."

"All in good time," soothed Dr. Zuckmayer. "When the veil of secrecy is lifted, Reichsführer Himmler and the rest of us will be hailed as visionaries. Until then, the Lebensborn is a private dream shared by an intimate few, but all the more precious because of it."

"The prisoners from Dachau," blurted Ilse. "I think that's part of the problem. You see them on the bitterest days without even socks . . ."

"Those are hardened criminals – homosexuals and agitators," cut in Dr. Zuckmayer coldly. "No use feeling sorry for them. They'd just as soon slit your throat. You'll have to toughen up." More gently, he inquired: "How's your own personal project coming? Have you found a suitable recruit?"

"Just this afternoon. A lovely girl, quite responsible, I think. Helga. Mature enough to know her own mind."

"The more I see, the wiser I think you are to make the choice. It's amazing what even our most reliable officers come up with when left on their own. It's the Jewish press and their trashy image of womanhood that are to blame – emaciated Jewesses flashy with jewels, glossy American housewives too lazy to do anything but shop, modish French tarts." He sighed. "All in good time . . ."

Bruno began to fuss. From the warm, wet feel of her skirt, Ilse knew what the problem was. Since the stain was obvious, she had no choice but to apologize. "I'm afraid I'll have to change Bruno. It doesn't happen often, just when he gets excited. He's like a little puppy."

"Perhaps I should see the boy in my office, check his development. Maybe there's some problem."

"No!" Unable to control the panic in her voice, Ilse protested, "It happens so seldom. I've given him all the tests. He picks up my tensions when I'm overtired. He spends so much time with younger children that it's easier for him to crawl and jabber so he can play with them. He's a little con artist." Smiling brightly, she added: "I wouldn't dream of taking your time from real problems."

Scooping up Bruno, Ilse rushed him to her own washroom. A sweat had broken out over her body and she could feel her heart ache with a pain Dr. Zuckmayer had diagnosed as angina. Stuffing Bruno's dirty diaper into the overflowing hamper, she washed him, changed him, comforted him, then tucked him into his own bed.

"Stille Nacht, Heilige Nacht . . ."

Ilse took a midnight tour of the nursery. In darkness except for a night light, it contained eleven babies, mostly newborns, all visible through a glass partition.

After putting on white smock and mask, Ilse asked one of the night nurses: "Any problems, Agnes?"

"Baby Manfred has colic, but he seems to have settled down."

"Good."

"And Baby C . . ."

"I'll look after things for a while if you and Eva want to join the others in the common room for apple cider."

Ilse went from bassinet to bassinet, checking weight charts, food schedules, doctor's comments. Baby Marguerite was awake but hadn't yet decided she was hungry. Baby Johan needed to be untangled from his comforter. A quiet night.

Baby C's crib was pushed away from the others – a natural response but one Ilse fought. All babies were to be treated equally, according to their needs. No exceptions, and right to the end. Though his feeding schedule had been maintained, his weight had not been marked, and no comments from the doctor had been recorded. Not here on the public record, though the correspondence had been voluminous.

Lifting him out of the crib, Ilse cuddled him, suspecting she was the first person to do so all day. The mother: Louisa Thomsen, age seventeen, a student nurse with No. 1 rating, accepted last December. Biological husband: an SS lieutenant with three children. Impregnation after two mountings. A boy, eight pounds two ounces, born November 3 – with an inoperable cleft palate. Nothing in either genetic chart to suggest such a tragedy, a heart-breaking act of fate.

All had been done that could be done. Decisions had been taken – not hers, thank God! Tomorrow at dawn Ilse would transfer Baby C to a portable bassinet, pinning his covers so he couldn't throw them off during his long journey. To keep his head warm, she would put on a yellow helmet she had knit for Bruno. Then she would install him in the back of a heated L-van for the trip to the psychiatric hospital at Brandenburger-Gorden near Potsdam. Last of all, she would administer morphine to dope him, then pin a brown envelope to his pillow.

The brown envelope contained Baby C's death certificate, post-dated two weeks to allow for examination and autopsy, and citing pneumonia as the cause. When confirmation had been received from Gorden, she would send a memo to Dr. Zuckmayer. Though Reichsführer Himmler flew into a rage if he was not immediately informed of the death of a normal Lebensborn baby, he did not want to know about the defectives. No one in the SS did, including the father.

Ilse had already interviewed the mother. Most were so anxious to get rid of their tainted babies that no cover-up story was necessary, and when offered an urn of ashes, most refused. Louisa Thomsen had proved no exception. What concerned her more was the report of the Reich Committee for the Scientific Investigation of Grave Hereditary Disease and Defects, and how that would affect her future. Such an attitude, Ilse supposed, was healthier and more modern than her own. After all, it was a blow to a girl, told she was perfect, to produce a child out of pain and patriotism only to discover she had borne a reject.

Baby C began to whimper. Feeling him nuzzle her breast, Ilse opened her blouse and let him suckle. Her milk had never ceased to flow, and she saw no harm, though she knew Dr. Zuckmayer would berate her for her foolishness. The fate of defective children was one thing on which she vigorously opposed him. Baby C felt no different from other babies. He smelt the same. To her he looked the same. In her village a Mongoloid child named Gunther had been a pet, and when he died at age eleven, after never hurting another soul, everyone had mourned. The strongest skier had been deaf. Against such sentiments, Dr. Zuckmayer quoted the Reichsführer: "Every garden needs weeding. In a chicken coop the stronger peck the weaklings to death. It's the law of nature. Perfection isn't possible without pruning."

Ilse had had her first attack of angina the day she committed the first defective child to an L-van for "collection."

From the nursery Ilse could see the moon shining on the onion dome of the Catholic church in Mullhorig. How she yearned to disguise herself in a shawl, and make her confession. She remembered with chagrin how irreverently she and her sisters had abused that privilege when they were young, mumbling so low old Father Todt couldn't hear their real crimes, then shouting trivialities for half the valley to hear when he urged them to speak up: "*I refused to eat my porridge without sugar on it.*"

Thinking up ways of incriminating each other:

"I confess to thinking mean thoughts about my sister *after Hilde snitched thirty pfennigs from our mother's sewing basket.*"

When Father Todt took on a shy young assistant, how the sisters tortured him with sexual crimes, real and imagined. "Father, I confess to touching my breast. Was that a sin? What about the nipple? Where exactly would touching be a sin? Father, is it a sin to break wind in church?"

Now Ilse imagined herself, a figure draped in black, slipping into the confessional in Mullhorig:

You have something to confess, my child?

Yes, Father.

And what is your sin, my child?

In the past year and a half, my Father, I have sent thirty-three children to their deaths, one for every year of my life. . . .

Tucking Baby C into his bassinet, Ilse drew a vial of water from under her smock, unstoppered it and traced a cross on his forehead.

I have something else to confess. This time to Dr. Zuckmayer.

Yes, my child.

I named every one of those thirty-three babies. I baptized each with holy water left behind in the chapel by the

Sisters of Mercy when we kicked them out of here. O Holy Mother of God!

Agnes and Eva returned from the solstice celebration in high spirits. Ilse looked in on Bruno, then tried to sleep, but kept imagining a black crow with her mother's face trying to scratch out her eyes. "Whore of Satan! Slut! Strumpet!"

At dawn, as she went down for Baby C, she heard the solstice celebrants singing:

> "Companions of the Black Order,
>   Untainted by darkness,
>   Free of imperfections,
>   We greet the dawn
>   Of the new Teutonic Age."

FOUR

Nibelheim Castle, Swabia

April 1941

RAIN PELTED the trees of the Swabian forest. It gushed down hillsides, washed out roads, tore at the roots of grapevines, spattered apple blossoms like pink confetti and bulged the banks of the Neckar, yet it could not erode the self-satisfaction of SS Captain Kurt Schmidt, riding in a black Mercedes. For the past two weeks he and ninety-nine other SS officers had been on spiritual retreat with Reichsführer SS Heinrich Himmler and SS Lieutenant-General Reinhard Heydrich at fabulous Wewelsburg Castle, the legendary home of the Black Order. Located in Westphalia, it had been rebuilt by the Reichsführer on the ruins of a medieval castle at a cost of thirteen million marks. A massive black-and-white structure, with round towers soaring over the forest from a triangular base, it was the physical embodiment of the Order of the Teutonic Knights, founded in 1198, and filled every German boy's head with romantic thoughts, while haunting his manhood with impossible standards.

They came from many lands, having proved their knightly spirit in battle under many sovereigns and flags, but when they entered the austere precincts they abandoned their personal shields and their single emblem became the Cross. They sought no other identity but as selfless Members of the Order, and no other honor but to die in battle so they might gain eternal life.

The walls of Wewelsburg were hung with massive tapestries celebrating German heroism. Heavy brocades shaded the high blue granite-framed windows. Carved doors were embellished with precious metals and stones. The grand staircase had a forged iron banister etched with runes. Only the finest craftsmen had constructed the solid oak furniture, fashioned the iron candlesticks, sculpted the marble statues and decorated the rooms dedicated to German rulers – Henry Fowler, the first of the great Saxon kings (whose reincarnation Himmler believed himself to be), Frederick Barbarossa (always reserved for Adolf Hitler), Otto the Great, Henry the Lion, Philip of Swabia. No item in any room was duplicated in any other. Each contained swords, shields, garments and jewels of its period, sometimes those of the luminary himself. With Wagner's "Grand March" from *Siegfried* swelling through the corridors, so each precious item glowed with its own inner music, Kurt felt like a human chalice undergoing an electrical charge.

After such titillation, Kurt's new assignment proved a bitter blow, fulfilling the Reichsführer's warning: "In the SS we give our worst jobs to our best men."

For over a year the Reich had buzzed like a wasp's nest with indignant rumors spawned by a spate of sudden deaths in hospitals for the insane, the handicapped, the senile and the incurable. With rare courage a few pastors of both Catholic and Protestant churches had accused the party of conducting a euthanasia program which they branded murder.

Kurt now knew such a program did exist, and on a scale as yet unappreciated. During one session at Wewelsburg, Dr. Alfred Zuckmayer of the Lebensborn Movement had shown slides of patients selected for disinfection – the crippled, the crazed, the retarded. "Our Lebensborn breed the superrace of tomorrow. Our disinfection program purifies the one we now have," boasted Dr. Zuckmayer. "In the New Reich, these wretches would never make it past the first year."

Lieutenant-General Reinhard Heydrich took the

podium in front of the gold eagle with thirty-foot wing-span. Leaving zeal to Dr. Zuckmayer and the Reichs-führer, he coldly endorsed the euthanasia program on pragmatic grounds: "We can't afford to let vegetables take up valuable room in our hospitals. Before our Führer can open another bold offensive, we need space for the wounded. Now that the munitions industry is in high gear, we must put the technological skills of men like yourselves in the service of human resources." In summation: "Never waste time thinking if the thing you must do is right or wrong, if it's pleasant or unpleasant. Just ask yourself: 'Am I up to the mark? Am I tough enough?'"

From the moment Heydrich arrived at Wewelsburg, Kurt had watched him like a dazzled adolescent. Whether dueling or hurling the discus, he seemed like Siegfried incarnate – as authentic a part of the castle as the swords and armor. While Himmler was a chinless fuddy-duddy with the handshake of a wet trout, Heydrich seemed carved out of a single piece of crystalline, without vulnera-bility and hence without blemish.

The first night at the bar Kurt attracted Heydrich's attention by protesting his eagerness for active service with the Waffen SS in their invasion of Yugoslavia. Touch-ing his silver tankard to Kurt's, Heydrich confided: "I know exactly how you feel. I detail myself for action with the Luftwaffe as often as possible. It's a tonic. In the Norwegian campaign I flew an ME-109, and afterward I indulged in ME-110 reconnaissance flights over Britain." He grinned. "Can you imagine how Himmler and the Führer feel about the head of their Security Service duel-ing with Spitfires? Hitler grounded me as soon as he spot-ted my bronze bar for combat missions. Of course I still sneak off. I figure it's a man's right."

The next day, when Heydrich asked for volunteers from the elite corps of one hundred to participate in a test of courage, Kurt had been first to come forward.

Standing alone in the courtyard of Wewelsburg, he was challenged to remove the pin from a live grenade and to balance it on his helmet until it exploded – presumably upward in the path of least resistance.

Jaws clamped, sweat pouring down his face, Kurt had spent the longest few seconds of his life before the world shattered, knocking him unconscious with the impact.

Afterward Heydrich commented: "I never forget a name or face. Don't be surprised if I contact your commanding officer within a year. I have plans that are unprecedented. Who knows? You may become a part of them."

As the Mercedes whistled along the slick asphalt, with the sun at last breaking through, Kurt determined to use his skills to get an odious task done as quickly as possible.

He was irritated when the car had to slow for a barbed-wire barricade guarded by SS men with machine guns. A sign warned: KEEP AWAY. DANGER OF PESTILENCE. This, Kurt knew, was the welcome mat for his new assignment. Surely the party would do better to acknowledge its euthanasia program rather than to feed rumor through secrecy. If the bleeding hearts could see Dr. Zuckmayer's slide show, they might form a more sensible definition of humanitarianism.

Rolling down a window, Kurt smelt the moist air, tangy with pine. Nibelheim Castle loomed through the mist. Its Gothic towers, crowned with shafts of sunlight, cast an eerie spell over the forests and glens. At the drawbridge across a muddy red creek, Kurt showed his pass and received permission to drive up to the black marble archway. An SS corporal, thin as a stork, with an Adam's apple that looked as if he'd swallowed an egg, opened the car door. Though an example of the sad decline in SS standards caused by war, he threw Kurt a snappy salute. "Corporal Albert Eike. Shall I take you to your quarters, sir?"

Kurt checked his watch. "We were delayed by weather.

Perhaps you'd better take me directly to Captain Hammel."

"He's seeing to a new shipment, sir," informed Eike, his Adam's apple bobbing with each syllable. "Over that grassy knoll behind the castle."

Guided by Eike, Kurt slogged through a muddy parking lot containing some two dozen gray vans. Pausing on the other side, he wiped red ooze from his shiny boots onto the coarse grass, then crested the hill. Before him lay a natural amphitheater, as moody as a Druid's circle, surrounded by black forest swirled with wispy fog like spun glass.

Despite Dr. Zuckmayer's provocative slide show, Kurt was not prepared for the pageant in progress below. In a freshly dug clay pit, dozens of naked bodies, slippery with blood, were packed like fish in a barrel. They exuded the high-tension hum he had mistaken for the rush of wind through the pines.

On a platform extending over the pit, six naked people stood with their backs to a six-man firing squad, while an SS captain sat on the pit's edge eating his lunch. As he signaled with his sandwich, six rifles split the air. Six people jerked, jackknifed, then exploded into the pit. Another six were herded into place by two guards wielding whips. In all, the process from one volley to the next took three minutes.

Kurt stood at attention, not a muscle twitching, conscious of Corporal Eike's eyes upon him, feeling blood drain from his face. Some of the bodies still convulsed in the last throes of death. Others emitted piercing wails as they struggled to claw their way out of the bloody mass, arms waving like the feelers of some evolutionary being struggling from a red primordial sea.

While the platform was wheeled to a less congested spot, Captain Hammel spotted Kurt and beckoned.

Kurt strode forward, offering a twist of a smile that was a reflex from the tightening of his sphincter muscles. Declining a seat on the slimy pit, he delivered a heel-clicking Heil Hitler, which Hammel returned with the casual backflip of his hand.

Gazing at Hammel, Kurt felt a revulsion equal to the horror he was repressing. The man was unshaven, his hairy belly protruded through his spattered SS tunic. He stank of sweat and whiskey, and the furry hand clutching his sandwich looked like an ape's. How could such a filthy beast inhabit an SS uniform even in wartime?

Stuffing his sandwich into his mouth, Hammel delivered an assessment of his own. "So you're the pretty one with the engineering degree from Wewelsburg. Well, you're welcome to it. I've earned my leave. I prefer the naked girls of the Moulin Rouge, d'ya mind? Some don't think this is so bad. Better to shoot subhumans than be shot by them in the cast, d'ya see?" He offered an Ariston cigarette, which Kurt declined. "Hoped to have this mess finished but the weather, d'ya know?"

Six more naked men and women were hustled from a low barracks onto the platform, discharged by a wave of Hammel's cigarette, then replaced. Few protested. Many were old and pathetically handicapped, as in Dr. Zuckmayer's picture show. Some seemed disturbingly normal. Quite a few were quietly weeping. Some comforted each other. An old lady rocked an imaginary baby in her arms. Another twisted a rosary.

One young girl, about twenty, with lovely auburn hair, insisted on facing down her executioners. Kurt heard the report, saw her body jerk over the pit in an antic dance, her head explode in a red star. Conscious of Hammel sizing him up, he kept his gaze steady, holding himself as still as an animal in a trap who senses the only escape is to gnaw off a leg. Though his heart was thudding, he knew it couldn't be seen or heard. His bowels – that was another matter. Despising himself, he remembered Reinhard Heydrich's motto: *Don't ask if a thing's right or wrong, pleasant or unpleasant. Just ask: "Am I up to the mark? Am I tough enough?"*

Hammel passed a tin flask to Kurt. Though he intended to decline, his hand snatched for it.

"That's one good thing about this job – all the booze you can drink," sympathized Hammel. Gargling a mouthful, he added slyly: "And you'll find you drink one shit of a lot. A large bunch of carrots and a long stick – that's the secret of keeping men working here, d'ya know? More money, better grub, plenty of smokes and a chance to pilfer the cast-off clothes. On the other hand, get uppity enough to refuse an order and it's the loss of a badge or two, and a one-way ticket to the front, d'ya see?"

Flicking his lighted butt into the twitching pit, Hammel eased himself up with a sharp breaking of wind. "That's most of it for today. Not much left except for bashing the crazies in the straitjackets." To a sergeant in the firing squad, he ordered: "Carry on." Then he slapped his pants with his gloves, as if that could possibly rid them of their red mud.

Side by side the captains trudged up the hill, with Eike behind. "So you're an engineer," repeated Hammel. "Nice to be replaced with a little class. You never know what's going to be useful these days. Can you believe it? I used to be a pig farmer."

As they crested the hill, Hammel grew technical. "This operation could use some streamlining. Like anything else, you fall into habits. It was me invented the platform into the pit – they don't teach you them things at Wewelsburg. There's tricks to every trade, like holding back the better ones to dig and cover the pits. After a few days the bodies swell. It's the gas, d'ya see? It pushes up the mounds six to ten feet. My men don't like that at all. They don't like to see graves that move, and they don't like to hear the gas hissing out of them. That's what spooks them most, d'ya see? It's a funny thing. Sky'll be clear as a cow's eye everywhere else, but over the pits you'll see this clammy cloud just hanging. I'm sure that makes sense due to the lie of the land, but sometimes it has a peculiar look." He grunted. "No, I'm not going to miss this place at all."

Hammel's voice grew more impersonal. "The big thing is finding a new way to do the weeding. Bullets are too slow and pricey. They use too many men, and they're demoralizing. Some of the Hitler Youth graduates are tough little shits. Hard to tell where the gun leaves off and they begin, but my older guys are retired from the army. They're not used to shooting at things that don't shoot back. You've got to respect a man for that. As for hanging – cheap but messy and too slow." Hammel grinned. "If I had my old pig-farm team, I'd go for the under-the-chin smile. A few seconds and it's done, *zip-zip*. That's my style."

"Have you tried injections?" inquired Kurt, trying to match Hammel's matter-of-fact tone.

Hammel nodded. "Too hard on medical supplies. The muckamucks bitched like hell."

"What about burning the bodies?"

"Too much diesel fuel. We have a crematorium to man-ufacture ashes for 'grieving' families, but that's a small operation, thank the devil!" Holding his bulbous nose, he confided: "The stench of that is an advertisement that hangs over this place for a week."

By now they were at the black marble archway into Nibelheim Castle. "I've cleared the office. You'll find the death certificates for this lot on your desk. Thought I'd get them signed, but the rain lost us a couple of days. I'm off to Paris first thing tomorrow. Eike will tell you more than you want to know. Can't risk missing my chance, d'ya see? I smell something big coming in the east."

By mid-afternoon Kurt was installed in his drafty office with its gloomy gray stone walls, vaulted ceilings and thin Gothic windows, facing a sea of gray trucks. On his stout oak desk, in three neat piles of approximately one hundred, were the death notices.

> Dear
>   We regret to inform you that your   , who was
> recently transferred to our institution by ministerial order,
> unexpectedly died on   of   . All medical
> efforts were without avail. In view of the nature of your loved
> one's incurable ailment, this death, saving the patient from a
> lifelong institutional sojourn, is to be regarded as a release.
>   Because of the danger of contagion existing here, we are
> forced by order of the police to have the deceased cremated
> at once. If you wish to receive the ashes, please notify us by
> return mail. Otherwise we will dispose of them, with full
> respect to religious affiliation. Heil Hitler.

All the blanks had been filled in by Albert Eike's round childish hand, with cause of death listed as smallpox, influenza or diphtheria. The first one hundred had been signed with Captain Hammel's bold, erratic slash, the shaky downstrokes indicating ample liquid refreshment.

Using a fountain pen with black ink, Kurt signed in a scrawl somewhere between Eike's inhibition and Hammell's lack of it. After the first fifty, he stopped to relax his hand, picked up one, then another, of the personal files. The majority were listed as incurables from mental hospitals, but a few were political detainees, as Kurt suspected. The picture of a beautiful girl with auburn hair fell from a folder – the girl who had faced down her executioners. Opening her file, Kurt discovered she was Frieda Rees, age twenty-four, from Freiburg near the French border. Known to the Gestapo as a troublemaker who refused to display the Führer's birthday picture in her pastry shop, last month she smuggled a downed British pilot across the Swiss border to Basel. As cause of death, Eike had listed advanced syphilis. Offended, Kurt blacked this out, wrote in "brain hemorrhage," signed the document, then reached for a dozen more.

At the two-hundred mark, Kurt again faltered. Filling

his office sink with hot water, he soaked his right hand while gazing out the window. Though sun now sparkled from slick green foliage, a gauzy gray shroud hung over the knoll, as Hammel had predicted. Der Todesengel, the Angel of Death. He could hear tractors begin to scoop up red clay to dump over the corpses. Pulling his blackout curtains, Kurt wondered how long he would have to stay in this shithole. To buoy his spirits, he conjured up scenes from Wewelsburg:

They wind down marble steps to an underground room with arches, where the stones give off the chill of old bones. A black stone altar is blazed with the white rune of the SS. As each candidate receives a resin torch lit by the Reichsführer, he wends his way even deeper into the crypt. Kneeling in a black marble alcove flickering with firelight, he receives the Blood Grail, from which he drinks.

Now the Reichsführer rests his dagger on Kurt's head: "Arise, Captain Schmidt . . ."

Kurt signed in rapid succession. Then, to reward himself, he reread parts of the letter he had received from Ilse that morning.

> . . . Dr. Zuckmayer confirms chances are excellent that Helga will give birth to our new child on October 7, the Reichsführer's birthday. That it will be a boy seems likely, since Helga religiously drinks the herb tea the Reichsführer has recommended, and Dr. Zuckmayer confirms the position of the fetus is typical for a boy. Rather than returning to her munitions job, Helga has received permission to stay on at the Lebensborn to help look after Bruno and the new baby. I think the delicious food and the occasional chance to sleep in have played their part in her decision! I have to urge her to exercise so as not to put on too much weight, thus complicating our delivery . . .

Ilse had included two snapshots taken with a camera Kurt had given her for her birthday. One was of his son Bruno, nearly two and a half, holding a cardboard shield in one hand and a wooden dagger in the other. On the back Ilse had printed: "B is so excited by the dagger you sent that he won't play with anything else. I'm afraid he's making quite a pest of himself!"

Studying the picture, Kurt saw an awkward little boy with knock-knees and an oversized head. Or did all kids look that way? Kurt tried to feel love for his son, but all he could manage was a vague affection. Ilse did her best, with chatty letters, but he had seen too little of Bruno to form an easy, natural attachment, and he had nothing in his own background to teach him what fathering was. He thought of Ernst Schmidt, estranged from his family for four years by war, and felt empathy.

The second snapshot showed Ilse with her arms around a blond girl in dirndl skirt with ballooning belly. Knowing that he owed his promotion to that human enterprise, he felt a surge of gratitude toward Ilse. How lucky to have a wife who would put aside petty jealousy for a principle! So few women were capable of seeing a political issue over a domestic one. As for the girl Helga, Kurt stared at her belly, trying to imagine his son in there. He remembered the large body, almost as tall as his own, with fleshy thighs and small breasts, but if he saw that unremarkable face on the street, he wouldn't recognize it. The girl had become pregnant on the first mounting, and while she had been responsive enough, he had felt self-conscious and formal. His only sex experience had been with street girls and with Ilse. His psyche couldn't assimilate this other event.

A vision of the lovely girl with auburn hair flashed vividly and erotically into Kurt's consciousness. Though he had seen her for only a few seconds, he was amazed how every contour of her face and body had become imprinted on his memory – the long legs and small waist, the full breasts, the heart-shaped face with eyes like liquid fire as she poured contempt over her murderers.

On impulse Kurt took her photo out of its folder. From a left-hand drawer of his desk, he drew another file – a few poems by his father, a wedding picture of his mother, a letter of praise from a schoolteacher. He found what he was after – a program from The Glass Slipper, dated 1925, featuring Carmel Kohl in *The Rhinegold Maiden*. He set the two pictures side by side. Though the girl Frieda was wearing a baker's smock and Carmel a gold fishtail jacket with tights, he noted a definite resemblance beyond the red hair. By chance he also noticed some similarity to his mother in her wedding gown.

Kurt fingered the *Rhinegold* program, personally autographed. He still saw *Lorelei* whenever he had a chance. It flattered him into thinking he led a secret life, apart from the others in the theater, apart from Ilse. He had read that Carmel Kohl was making a comeback film for Goebbels and knew he would be one of the first in line to see it.

Impatiently Kurt swept his mementos back into their drawer and returned the auburn girl to her folder. Ringing a handbell for Eike, he demanded: "Bring me blueprints of all the buildings at Nibelheim."

From the instant he had looked into that bloody pit on the other side of the grassy knoll, Kurt had vowed to find a more efficient and humane way of carrying out the Reich's disinfection program. All the time he had been signing death certificates, ideas had been percolating in his unconscious, and now they were surfacing.

Half an hour after Eike had delivered the blueprints, Kurt zeroed in on his target. A building twenty yards by seven, once a stable, now an equipment shed. Made of stone, it should be easy to insulate. Carbon monoxide could be introduced by hose from trucks in the parking lot. . . . Neat and clean. Faster and cheaper than bullets.

FIVE

Berlin

June 1941

W ORKING dawn to dusk, wrapped in fantasy at UFA
film studios, Carmel Kohl could pretend the war did
not exist.

The film was tripe – little better than the scripts Goebbels had bombarded her with in Munich. Entitled *Passion
and Purity*, it told the hanky-dabbing story of a Rhenish
wench who immigrates to Berlin in 1918 to earn money to
save her parents' farm, stripped by the French under the
Treaty of Versailles. In the city of sin, showpiece of the
Weimar Republic, she is seduced into wanton degradation
by "gross foreign elements." Rescued through the pure
passion of a hero from Adolf Hitler's 1923 putsch, she
returns with him to the family farm, which they restore to
prosperity. Blissfully happy, the heroine bears her Aryan
prince a son, whom they dedicate to the Führer.

In the original script, the heroine was allowed to enjoy
her life amidst the cornfields. In the final version, revised
in green pencil by Dr. Goebbels, she must die in childbirth
as penance for allowing her Aryan blood to be sullied by
"gross foreign elements." This script change had required
an extra two days of shooting, with Carmel writhing to
the strains of Handel's "Hallelujah Chorus," while pictures of dying soldiers were superimposed over her thinly
clad flesh, conveying to the thickest blockheads that giving birth for the Führer was as heroic as engaging in
battle.

Increasing Carmel's impatience through this farcical denouement was the fact that Frau Fuchs had been released from Dachau two days ago, at the end of the original shooting schedule, as agreed by Goebbels. Now as she rushed off the set, her one desire was to escape to The Red Fox.

Carmel's dressing room had been converted by a bank of wreaths, each signed with Dr. G's thick green pencil, into what looked like a crying chamber for a Mafia funeral. Sprawled amidst the flowers was Christian Jürgens, her co-star for *P & P*, dead drunk.

"Heil!" he greeted her, raising an empty bottle of Courvoisier in mock salute. "But I'm not drinking to you. I'm drinking to Tristan Drexler, my favorite soprano." He was referring to the actor who played the "gross foreign elements" in *P & P*. When Christian had objected to Drexler's falsetto Jewish caricature, Drexler had converted his character into a lecherous gypsy – a more personal insult since Jürgens' wife, Renate, was a gypsy.

Waving a copy of Goebbel's newspaper, *Der Angriff*, Christian remonstrated: "Look!" A publicity photo of himself and a malevolent Drexler in gypsy costume bore this lengthy caption: "So impressed was Christian Jürgens with co-star Tristan Drexler's portrayal of the devious and filthy gypsy seducer in their film *Passion and Purity* that he announced he will divorce Renate, his gypsy wife of ten years. Twin sister of the Bolshevik painter Raymon Arno, she wrote obscene novels during the lurid days of unrepentant republicanism, proving once again that bad blood flows in families. The Arnos are mulattos as well as gypsies, this paper has discovered. Saddened by his experience of mongrelization, Jürgens told friend Drexler: 'Those people have different morals than we do. I even doubt that the children who bear my name are my own.'"

Showing Carmel a photo of his wife and two children Christian raged: "This is the angel that sadist wants me to divorce! Last week it was Eleanor Roosevelt Goebbels discovered to be a mulatto. Now it's my Renate. It would be funny if it weren't such a tragedy."

Kicking over Goebbels' floral tributes, sending daffodils and daisies, wicker and water and wire and glass in all directions, Christian cursed: "I confess it. Once I longed for fame in the cheapest way. I saw myself as a matinee idol, with women fighting for a lock of my hair. Now it's happened and it's a nightmare. Reporters dog me, demanding to know when the divorce will be."

"But, Christian, can't you bargain with Goebbels to leave your personal life alone?"

"Bargain with the devil?" exploded Christian. "I'd sooner eat shit!" Collapsing, hands over face, he confessed: "I tried to bargain. Do you know what he wants me to play? The lead in Hans Westmar's 'masterpiece' on the life of Horst Wessel – that ponce! that pimp! Wessel's the real stuff Nazi heroes are made of!"

Tugging at his white-blond hair, yanking it out by the roots, he roared: "Even this is false! Though that Beelzebub is as black and twisted as a snake, he couldn't stand a matinee idol who doesn't look like Siegfried. When they ask me to play Adolf Hitler, what color will Goebbels want me to dye it? When do you become what you don't resist? Renate is my integrity, my guiding star, but some things I'd be ashamed to do for my darlings."

It was nine before Carmel had delivered Christian to a worried Renate and was speeding along Unter den Linden toward The Red Fox in her new Opel. The Opel was a gift to herself so she could avoid driving to Babelsberg studio chauffeured by Rudolf. Carmel now paid the two snoops in her attic just to keep out of her way. She would have loved to fire them, but who knew what information they'd collected on her and her friends? She should never have allowed Christian to let off steam in her dressing room. No doubt Dr. G's daffodils were disguised ear trumpets, while the tiger lilies were all tongues when it came to blabbing in high places. Usually she and Christian were more careful, with code words and hand signals. Artistic license only went so far, as the case of Frau Fuchs had proved.

A mounted policeman signalled Carmel to pull over just as she reached Friedrich Strasse. After the usual anxious reflex, she realized he only wished her to allow a summer solstice parade to pass. A golden disk was being held aloft by the sun god, its yellow streamers carried by children dressed as sunbeams. Flocks of butterflies, water nymphs and skylarks ushered in beauteous summer, dressed in green with her skirt spangled in daisies. Though annoyed by the delay, Carmel had to admit it was a damned sight better than the Hitler Youth shaking everyone down for Winter Relief, which went directly into party coffers.

The delay at least caused Carmel to appreciate that it was summer. The chestnut trees bordering Unter den Linden were in bloom, their clusters of white flowers like luminous bunches of grapes. A balmy breeze stirred the scent of lindens and acacias.

Twelve virgins, chosen for their flaxen hair and lovely faces, carried a golden grail and sang in high, innocent voices:

> "We are maidens of the Grail.
> Vessels of the pure blood.
> Guard our Aryan heritage.
> Preserve us from the unclean Jew . . ."

As Carmel watched and waited, she admitted she'd been thrilled to be back before the cameras after six years, despite her fear of toadying to National Socialism. The scenes of "wanton degradation" set in the Weimar Republic had evoked in her only happy nostalgia for the three-pronged devil's assault she, Axel and Wolf had made on all of life's possibilities, and she hoped this would be the vitality to which the audience secretly responded. Drexler's vicious portrayal had taken her by surprise but, she reasoned, she had used the film to rescue a friend. Surely that counted for something. In a society in which most restaurants bore the sign NO DOGS OR JEWS, did a movie like *Passion and Purity* matter?

Now Carmel was being pressured to do a tearjerker called *Love Shield*, in which a long-suffering wife's faithfulness protects her warrior husband from death. In fact, her letter in his chest pocket deflects the fatal bullet from its course. All this seemed suitably innocuous. Perhaps she could use her leverage to get Christian as her leading man, thus saving him from the ignominy of Horst Wessel. What else could either of them do but play for time? Since Axel's death, she had discovered that nationalization, graft and inheritance taxes had prevented her from becoming the wealthy widow her husband had intended. She needed to work to survive, to blot out loneliness and grief, to save herself from missing Axel and brooding over the past. She needed an outlet for her energy so it didn't explode in her face. She also needed to throw an occasional bone to Goebbels to prevent the party from finding a more mischievous use for her than yet another banal movie.

Or did she? Had she other options? Now that Goebbels had transformed Eleanor Roosevelt into a mulatto, as a fitting consort for her allegedly Jewish husband, a travel permit to America was not likely. Peace was the greater possibility. Though Göring's Luftwaffe had bungled the Battle of Britain, the Führer seemed to be winning everywhere else. How long would the British bother to fight now that their own shores were secure? Why would the United States enter a war so far away? When Europe again had peace, then people such as Christian and Renate and Frau Fuchs and she herself could openly fight back. But how could you attack your leadership in wartime? That was the "stab in the back" that had caused Germany to lose the last war.

So fervently did Carmel wish for the convenience of peace as she navigated the familiar alleys of her childhood

that she managed to convince herself it – like summer –
was just around the corner. Turning into the lane containing The Red Fox, she was startled to find her way blocked
by a boisterous crowd, some blowing horns and slapping
tambourines. At first she thought it was another summer
solstice celebration. Then she saw a white sheet strung
between fire escapes:

FRAU FUCHS TONIGHT!
ONE PERFORMANCE ONLY!

Abandoning her car, Carmel fought her way up the
teeming alleyway. Where had all these people come from?
There must be several hundred of them, summoned by
"mundfunk," that astonishing word-of-mouth Berliners
had developed to counter Goebbels' official news.

Falling into the arms of The General, acting as doorman, Carmel gasped: "Where's Frau Fuchs? She can't go
on tonight! It's too soon. They'll arrest her again."

Rolling his rheumy eyes, The General passed Carmel on
to Fritz, who helped her elbow her way to the front of the
cabaret.

"Take me backstage," shouted Carmel over the din.

Pointing to his watch, Fritz gestured: *Can't. It's curtain
time.*

As if in corroboration, the houselights dim. Fans cheer
and clang, whistle and toot.

All eyes focus on the faded red curtain illuminated by a
spotlight. A hush sweeps the room. One, two, three . . .
ten . . . twenty . . . thirty seconds. Tension builds. Just as it
becomes unbearable, a hand fingers the curtain. Frau
Fuchs steps through – but not the Frau Fuchs of old. The
outrageous blond wig is the same, and the gaudy mask of
makeup, but instead of a busty red satin gown, she sports
an SS tunic, breeches and black boots. Forty pounds
lighter from her sojourn at Dachau, she seems to consist
of her own head grafted onto a Blackshirt's body. Yet the
expression too is wrong – sober, even fearful.

The silence is ruffled by nervous whispered questions:

What's wrong? Gnawing on her thumbnail, Carmel hears the terrifying word – *brainwashed*.

When it seems that something must happen or the place will explode, Frau Fuchs fixes a monocle in her right eye. Obsequiously wringing her hands, she apologizes in a timid voice: "My friends, what I told you last time I stood here was wrong. Then I announced that I had seen a great big twelve-cylinder Mercedes without any National Socialists in it. Well, I took another look. There were two of the buggers in there after all!"

Now The Red Fox does explode. Mugs are banged, cowbells are rung, bells chimed. Fans scream in relief. Carmel sobs.

Deadpan, Frau Fuchs waits till all are hushed by the thunder of her silence, then she announces: "Folks, I can tell you from experience that Dachau does have a high-voltage fence, a moat, a wall and dozens of machine-gun towers. I don't understand why it's guarded so carefully. If I wanted to, I could get inside in a minute . . ."

And: "My Viennese friends tell me, before the annexation of Austria, things were good. Since the annexation, they're better. We hope they'll soon become good again."

Question: "A plane crashes carrying Himmler, Göring and Goebbels. Who is saved?" Answer: "The German people."

"Did you hear that Göring is ordering a larger phone? He wants to be able to dial it with his mace."

"All clubfooted men are degenerate. In all of history there's only one exception – a clubfooted man of compelling oratory, a revolutionary, a man of courage and unselfish devotion to his ideals. I'm speaking of Lord Byron."

Some of the jokes are corny. Some are so familiar the audience mouths the words like children listening to a favorite fairy tale. None of that matters. Someone is standing up on the stage, giving them hell. Even listening is a revolutionary act.

When a group of Blackshirts enters the cabaret, creating a dark and silent pool, that only adds to the titillation. One heckles Frau Fuchs. "You dirty Yid!"

She snaps back: "You're wrong, sir. I only look intelligent." Shading her eyes so she can see the SS officer, she taunts:

"Adolf Hitler and Heinrich Himmler are out driving when they run over a dog. Orders the Führer: 'Go and find the owner of the dog and apologize, but come back quickly.' Hours later Goebbels returns, very drunk. 'I found the house and reported: Heil Hitler, the dog is dead.' 'Thank God,' cheered the man. 'Let's celebrate.'"

Throwing kisses to the audience, Frau Fuchs shouts: "How deep are we into the shit?" She raises her hand in the Nazi salute. "This is how deep we're in the shit!" Slipping through the curtain, she is gone.

The patrons of The Red Fox clap, stamp, plead for the return of their heroine. The SS officers stand against the wall, temporarily at bay. They're too few to take on this crowd when animal power is on the other side. While they block the exits, awaiting reinforcements, Carmel plunges backstage.

Frau Fuchs is at her mirror, a towel over her SS tunic, removing her makeup. Fiercely embracing Carmel, she apologizes. "I'm sorry, Liebling, but I couldn't help myself. Not after all that rehearsal time. Ten months' solitary for one show – that's a luxury!"

"You were wonderful," cries Carmel. "But what's going to happen now? They'll arrest you again."

"They'll have to catch me first." She hands Carmel a note with her name scrawled across the envelope in purple ink. "That tells you what to do if you need me. Mind, not for torte and a tankard. For an emergency."

As she's explaining, Frau Fuchs attaches the badge and epaulettes of an SS lieutenant to her tunic, along with an eight-year service pin and an oak-leaf cluster. Then she tosses off her blond wig.

For the first time Carmel sees her friend of thirty years

without makeup: a bald-headed male of fifty, with lashless eyes and a face as bland and featureless as an egg.

"SS Lieutenant Helmut Fuchs," comes the introduction, with a how-deep-in-the-shit salute. "Bye-bye. I'm going down the coal chute."

Carmel returns to the theater knowing what will occur since she saw it here once before. Though still awaiting reinforcements, the Blackshirts blocking the exits are waving their Lugers. Unintimidated, the high-voltage crowd mills and snarls on the verge of rushing them.

Something else happens: A newsboy tosses a stack of *Völkischer Beobachter* papers into the lobby. An SS officer takes one, then shows it to another. Word spreads. Papers are being snapped up by anyone with ten pfennigs. They pass from friend to friend, and then from stranger to stranger.

Soon papers are scattered over the theater as if swirling in a high wind. Carmel reads: RED INFAMY SHOCKS FÜHRER. Knowing from bitter experience exactly how to interpret such a headline, she gasps to Fritz: "My God! Hitler has attacked Russia."

The story by DNB, the official news agency, confirms: After a period of "decency," the Bolsheviks have shown "their true and treacherous colors." Once again, the Soviet Union is The Red Terror, from which Hitler vows he'll save the German people.

"Having learned through superior intelligence of the ruthless and unconscionable intentions of the lying Kremlin, our Führer has ordered German troops to cross the eastern border for protection of our Fatherland."

Even now, shells are exploding over Russian military installations. The first Russian barracks have been taken. In a matter of weeks, if not days, a triumphant German army will be goose-stepping down the Russian steppes on its way to Moscow. The Russian people await liberation from a corrupt tyranny.

Other headlines proclaim THE GREAT HOUR HAS STRUCK and TO BE GERMAN IS TO BE INVINCIBLE.

This stupendous news has drawn the SS away from the exits and undermined their desire to bash other Germans. They realize as well as everyone else that Germany is faced with the harsh reality that caused her defeat in 1918: a two-front war!

Carmel remembers the Victory Arch, so confidently erected last year in Pariser Platz, now with the gilt running from the wings of the eagle and the superstructure buckling. Peace, she fears, is a long way off.

"Did he lead me away from myself? Yet whatever I may say or write, the complicated feeling of being bound to him persists to the present day. In view of that, might it be more accurate to say that he actually led me to myself? . . . He communicated to me a strength that raised me far above the limits of my potentialities . . . through him I first found a heightened identity."

  – Albert Speer, Minister of Armaments and Munitions

"It was granted to me for many years of my life to live and work under the greatest son whom my nation has produced in the thousand years of its history. . . . I regret nothing. If I were standing once more at the beginning I should act once again as I did then, even if I knew that at the end I should be burnt at the stake. No matter what men do, I shall one day stand before the judgment seat of the Almighty. I shall answer to Him, and I know that He will acquit me."

    – Rudolf Hess, Secretary to Hitler, at Nuremberg

"We shall go down in history as the greatest statesmen of all time or the greatest criminals."

                              – Josef Goebbels

"In fifty or sixty years there will be statues of Hermann Göring all over Germany. Little statues, maybe, but one in every home."

               – Reichsmarschall Hermann Göring

ONE

Berlin

January 1942

Parking her Opel under an icy spiderweb supporting the elevated railway, Carmel stepped into air so cold she felt her nose had been clamped by a metal clothespin. She was in a genteel section of the West End with gray stone houses like fat dowagers squatting on lots too small for them. Arched windows primly veiled in lace. Domes like tea cozies. Handkerchief lawns edged in wrought iron.

Not only had Carmel sold her Pariser Platz townhouse to an ambitious SS colonel and his wife, but she had managed to acquire a comfortable flat. As usual in Berlin in the winter of '42, such good luck was based on someone else's grim reality. The flat had been hastily abandoned by an American correspondent six days before the Japanese attacked Pearl Harbour, on December 7, and ten days before Germany declared war on the United States.

Carmel checked the address Willi Bliss had written out. Her new home was next to the S-bahn, a nostalgic reminder of the elevated railway that rattled dishes in the East End flat where she was born.

She pressed the brass buzzer in the centre of an outsized mahogany door. Seconds later it was opened by a wiry porter in his seventies – courteous, correct, unsmiling. Hissing through ill-fitting false teeth, he introduced himself as Herr Schnell. Yes, he had been expecting her. Yes, her flat was ready and her bags had arrived safely that afternoon. Yes, she was very lucky. Flats were as hard to

come by as duck's eggs, but of course the American gentleman had to leave.

Herr Schnell ushered Carmel into a white marble vestibule decorated in art nouveau scrollwork, then up a steep
staircase, leaning forward like a tree struggling against a
prevailing wind. Stopping at a stained-glass door, he exhi-
bited a ring of three keys, as if about to perform a magic
trick. "No. 1 is for the front door. No. 2 is for this corridor
door. No. 3 is for your flat. Insert each key notch side up.
You will have precisely sixty seconds before the stair light
switches off and the corridor light comes on." To Prussian
exactitude he added Prussian conviction. "All locks in
Berlin turn to the right."

Carmel entered an ochre corridor still smelling of the
gas once used to illuminate it. As predicted, the stair light
switched off while a line of tulip corridor lights flashed on.
Two women in black flung themselves against the wall in
dismay.

"Guten Tag," smiled Carmel.

Averting their faces, they scurried past. Carmel
glimpsed a gold star on the elder one's chest. Since September 19 Jews in Germany and Bohemia were obliged to
identify themselves with a six-pointed Star of David. As
Goebbels had editorialized in the *Völkischer Beobachter*:
"Racial comrades, when you see this emblem, you see
your death enemy. In the eastern campaign the German
soldier has met the Jew in his most disgusting, most gruesome form, accounting for cruel atrocities. This experience forces the German people to deprive the Jew of every
means of camouflage at home."

Herr Schnell whispered: "Nice people, the Vogels."
Then raising his arm as stiff as a broomstick, he broadcast
for public consumption: "Heil Hitler!"

Carmel's flat stretched down the south side of the building, with the rooms elongated like railway coaches. The
parlor was illuminated by stained-glass lamps and cathe-

dral windows hung with lace. The rolled-arm sofa was flanked by matching chairs. Over a mirrored sideboard hung a portrait of Bismarck, while Frederick the Great held court over a roll-top desk.

The tiny kitchen had a gas burner and refrigerator. The dining room was furnished in mahogany, with cranberry accents. The bedroom had a bolstered bed overhung by a lamp with beaded fringe. In the green-tiled bathroom a seashell tub evoked Botticelli's "The Birth of Venus." Switching on a gold tap, Carmel received a pleasant shock – hot water.

She sprawled on her beige sofa, still wearing her red fox coat, the only one she had retained from her collection. By drastically reducing her overhead, she hoped she would never have to humiliate herself by making another propaganda film for Dr. G. She was even planning to resuscitate her nightclub career. Though Axel wasn't here to pick her up if she faltered, his stability had allowed her to establish a bedrock of confidence. Frau Fuchs was no longer a phone call away, but she had bequeathed Carmel an example of courage. Professor Stein, still missing and presumed dead, had taught her to appreciate that vital causal link between past, present and future.

The ghost of Wolf gave Carmel more trouble. It was two years since he had abandoned Germany for Switzerland. Occasionally she heard a rumor he had been sighted in Berlin, but if so, he had shunned his old haunts and good friends. Though his silence worried her, she realized he was being true to his most essential quality: elusiveness.

Carmel hunted for her phone and was not surprised to find it inside a vacuum-cleaner bag stuffed with cotton batting. Since it was whispered that the Gestapo could bug telephones even when not in use, many people considered this a normal precaution. Dialing Christian and Renate Jürgens, she was disappointed when they didn't answer. Carmel had wanted to celebrate with friends, but she had made no new ones since returning to Berlin sixteen months ago. Those who didn't support the regime kept to themselves while the rest were lethal.

Deciding to explore the neighbourhood, Carmel sauntered out her three doors into the street piled with snow no one had time or energy to remove. Despite the Reich's continued military success, the bubble of plenitude had long since burst. As Carmel wandered the streets, she was shocked to see how sad and shabby the city had become, like a papier-mâché movie set left out in the rain. Much of Berlin's once-lavish metalwork had been gathered for scrap, and even buildings undamaged by bombs had deteriorated for lack of men and materials. Bars, shops and cafés were cracked and peeling, their windows blacked out like missing teeth. Because of acute shortages resulting from the British-Russian blockade, most were forced to close until they accumulated enough product to open for a week or even a day, with their signs euphemistically declaring: CLOSED FOR LUNCH. CLOSED FOR REPAIRS. CLOSED FOR REDECORATION. Everything but the truth: CLOSED BECAUSE WE HAVE NOTHING TO SELL.

Willi Bliss argued that the barometer of both civil and military morale was the digestive tract. As Carmel examined Berliners in the harsh light of their third winter of war, she realized they were so undernourished and exhausted after ten or twelve hours of work that they shuffled like sleepwalkers and slept while standing. Bundled in frayed overcoats, multiple sweaters, earmuffs and galoshes lined with cardboard or bound in cord, they waited in a queue with net bags for whatever was available. One line three blocks long was for cigarettes, two to a customer, rumored to be made of camel dung, thanks to Rommel's success in Africa. Others were for runty potatoes, rotten turnips, moldy cabbages – a separate line for each, with housewives forbidden to save places. Grocery windows that seemed full of cakes and liqueurs contained only pretty boxes or bottles of colored water discreetly labeled: FOR DECORATION ONLY. Ordinary items such as string, toilet paper, elastic bands and paper clips were permanently out of stock. The only products that did seem in good supply were patent medicines, aphrodisiacs and sunbathing magazines posing as art, since pornography had been banned in 1933.

For clothes each German received 100 ration points a year, to cover everything from yarn (7 points) to a suit (45 points) or a dress (30 points), but the greatest problem was finding these things. Shoes could be purchased only by special permission, so it was not unusual to see fashionable women clumping in wooden clogs with canvas tops. What was sometimes worse: Since ersatz soap, toothpaste, deodorant and shaving materials were scarce, Germans on crowded subways stank like soiled lederhosen. Even soldiers on leave looked derelict in bleached-out SS uniforms redyed gray-green for the military, or wearing restyled enemy uniforms.

Carmel imagined a whole battalion outfitted in the red fox coats she had donated to Winter Relief, then concluded they had probably all been diverted to the backs of party wives and mistresses. She had bet Christian she would spot one before winter's end, and had collected at last week's screening of *Love Shield*, when a starlet turned up at the Promi in Carmel's Norwegian jacket and hat.

Apart from such perversions, most Germans now experienced the war as a bitter reality affecting every hour of every day. Russian regiments had not, as confidently predicted, thrown down their rifles to embrace their German comrades. So many letters to soldiers in the east had returned stamped FALLEN that Goebbels forbade the publication of death notices. To further smother truth, he issued red cards to be hung on radios: "Loyal Germans. It is your duty to refuse to listen to foreign stations. Those who do will be mercilessly punished." The Victory Arch in Pariser Platz had long since been treated to euthanasia before it collapsed of old age. Troop trains east were dubbed the Frozen Meatball Express, while soldiers who marched through Berlin singing. "We're going to England, to England!" were not expressing patriotism but relief. The Russians had reverted to being the Red Peril, so monstrous in defeat they burned fields of wheat to deprive starving Germans of bread. They even booby-trapped toilet seats.

It was four o'clock. Carmel watched black figures creep out of doors as if from caves – emaciated, threadbare, their gold stars pinned on their chests as they slid like a dark frieze around Berlin. Of the 160,000 Jews in the capital when Hitler seized power eight years ago, only 40,000 remained, their ranks thinned by emigration, suicide, murder and the eastern transports begun last October. Allowed to shop only from 4:00 to 5:00 p.m. and required to wait till Aryans were served; banned from great avenues like the Kurfürstendamm, from streets with government buildings, public washrooms, parks, places of entertainment and bomb shelters; forbidden public transport, radios and telephones; forced to work up to fifteen hours a day, regardless of age or sex, at the dirtiest jobs for minuscule wages from which "contributions" were subtracted; governed by a nine-o'clock curfew and confined to their own districts; restricted to their food rations, refused clothing allowances and forced by Goebbels to donate their warm coats for German troops in Russia, the Jews were such figures of pathos that all but the most pig-headed party members pitied them. Instead of exposing them, their gold stars caused Berliners like Carmel to avert their eyes in shame, ironically rendering them more visible.

Depressed, Carmel again attempted to phone the Jurgenses from a booth beside a news kiosk. When they failed to answer, she escaped into the Dürer Haus restaurant.

Though she and Axel had come here often, she no longer recognized the Oberkellner presiding over this sedate silver-and-crystal world. Ancient and correct, he had been drafted out of retirement and a different epoch.

For each year of the war, Berlin's waiters aged ten years. In high starched collar and frock coat, he greeted her with a dignified bow. "Guten Tag, Fräulein." Seating her at a linen-covered table massed with silver, he inquired: "May I offer you a drink?"

Though Carmel craved a martini, she knew the cocktails celebrated under such glowing euphemisms as Pink Passion, Ecstasy and Himbeergeist were fake vodka or wood alcohol flavored with phony fruits and packing enough wallop to knock her out for the evening. Deciding on dinner only, she accepted a thick menu embossed in gold. Where once it listed three dozen entrees, now it offered two: roast chicken and fish.

"I'd like the chicken, Herr Ober."

Soulfully casting his eyes to the art deco ceiling, fingertips touching, the old gentleman disclosed: "The chicken is finished for the day."

Since the just-opened restaurant contained only three customers, Carmel guessed the chicken had never been available but was the face-saving device of a once-proud establishment.

"Then the fish, please." No point in asking what kind it was. Like most food in Germany, it had just been invented.

The waiter inclined his head. "Your ration book, Fräulein, please."

After removing tickets for fish, potatoes and bread, he sympathized: "I'm sorry but I'll have to collect a few grams of your butter ration. For frying your fish in grease."

When the waiter returned, he was wheeling an enormous silver salver. Snapping off the lid with white-gloved grace, he displayed an indiscriminate hunk which he treated with a delicacy inverse to its charm. Swamping it with watery red sauce smelling of chemicals, he added potatoes. "Enjoy your meal, Fräulein," he murmured with downcast eyes and the hint of an apology.

The red sauce tasted like iodine, while no matter how

determinedly Carmel tackled the fish, her nose assured her it was inedible. Pushing it under the corner of her napkin, she did what she could with the potatoes thinned by additives then bulked with sawdust. Still hungry, she picked at the fish then held her napkin discreetly to her mouth to keep down what she had unwisely eaten. Observing that now-familiar gesture, the waiter tactfully swished away her entree, replacing it with a roll that was stale, so she would chew harder and feel fuller. Another customer – a red-faced burgher who had managed to retain all three of his chins – snapped for attention. "Herr Ober!" He berated the aristocratic old waiter. "My fish portion weighs less than required by law. I demand you bring the weigh scale. Don't you realize I have Beziehungen?" That self-important boast, meaning influence with a party big-wig, filled Carmel with contempt. Paying her bill, she fled the restaurant.

It had begun to snow, thick wet flakes that flung themselves suicidally against her face. As she trudged toward the S-bahn, she saw crying women clustered around a news kiosk, ghoulishly illuminated in blue lamplight. She wondered what new disaster in the east had overtaken Germany, then decided she didn't want to know.

As Carmel scurried by, she glimpsed a photo of Christian Jürgens. Assuming it to be a publicity shot for *Love Shield*, she took half a dozen more steps before remembering her unanswered phone calls. Carmel fumbled for ten pfennigs, then snatched up a newspaper:

TREASONOUS COUPLE SIGNS DEATH PACT

"An hour before their arrest for treason, the matinee idol Christian Jürgens and his gypsy-mulatto wife, Renate, obliged the German people by putting bullets through their own heads. Best known for portraying the high-minded Aryan in films such as *Passion and Purity* and the newly released *Love Shield*, Jürgens proved anything but savory in his personal life, beginning with his obstinacy in embracing a woman of tainted blood and then by allowing this filthy union to corrupt his morals. Though the whereabouts of the two mongrel children – Lise, age nine, and Hanna, age four – is not known, be assured they will be dealt with using the ruthless mercy which such circumstances demand."

Carmel dropped her paper in the snow. Though she wanted to scream, all she managed was to throw up whatever dinner she had gagged down. Collapsing in the doorway of a bombed-out building, she tried to be sick again but produced only dry heaves, remembering how Christian had joked that they had sobbed over each other's corpses so often in make-believe that they wouldn't know how to produce tears for the real thing.

The crowd thinned. The news vendor closed his kiosk.

"Are you all right, Fräulein?"

"Yes, thanks."

"I know how it is. You see someone like that on the screen and it's like losing a friend. Never sold so many papers so fast. These senseless times!"

A clock struck six. Looking up at the tower, Carmel saw the big hand pointed north and the small one south. Still stunned, she decided to travel south, up one street and down another, through blind and crooked alleys, like a mouse running a maze in a lab experiment everyone has forgotten, feeling cursed with heightened awareness, so it was as if the skin peeled away from Berlin, revealing a rotted, black-ribbed corpse with its putrid breath leaking up from sewers, hearing rats gnaw the wood legs of World War I tramps, the thud of skulls in Gestapo cellars and the shuffle of Jews and gypsies to their caves, while overhead the six-pointed stars shone brightly.

At dawn Carmel found herself back where she started, with the boarded-up news kiosk, the clock with its hands again at six and the empty booth in which she had attempted to phone Christian.

Warmings pfennigs in her palms, she inserted them one

by one, then dialed the digits as they popped into her head. She let the phone ring three times, as Frau Fuchs' note instructed, with her breath vaporizing on the cold mouthpiece. Then she hung up, reinserted the coins and dialed once more.

On the second ring a masculine voice barked: "Ja!"

She stammered: "My name is Carmel Kohl. I understand you have two silver candlesticks to sell."

A long pause, then: "Ja."

"Could you see me this morning as soon as possible?"

"Ja. At seven. They're at St. Nicholas Church. Do you know where that is?"

"Near Savigny Platz."

"Ask for Father Klausner."

A stately Gothic edifice veiled in snow, St. Nicholas Church was in acute disrepair, with letters missing from its sign and the stained-glass windows boarded. Though religion had never been banned in the Third Reich, boisterous Hitler Youth songs reflected the official attitude:

> "No evil priest can prevent us from feeling
> That we are the children of Hitler.
> We follow not Christ but Horst Wessel.
> Away with incense and holy water!
> The Church can go hang, for all we care."

Entering the shadowy sanctum, Carmel saw a tiny priest, his body crippled into a question mark. "I'm Carmel Kohl. I've come about the candlesticks. Are you Father Klausner?"

"I'm Father Bauer," wheezed the priest in a light dry voice, nothing like the one over the phone. "Father Klausner will see you in the confessional in five minutes."

Only three candles burned in the church. Stuffing a 100-mark note into the collection box, Carmel lit one for Christian and another for Renate. Then she entered the confessional to the left of the altar. Of battered wood, it smelled of cough drops and mildew. She waited. Silence. "Father Klausner?"

"Ja!" The raw Saxon accent from the phone.

"My name is –"

"Ja, ja!" he interrupted, each word as abrasive as a cat's tongue. "I know. But why are you here?"

"Christian."

"Yes . . . a terrible tragedy." He murmured in compassion: "The children are safe."

"Are they with Raymon?"

A pause, then a sharp: "You ask too many questions! Why did Christian's death bring you here?"

"I want to help."

"Who?"

"Myself."

"Good. Does the word treason scare you?"

"Yes."

"It should. Everyone is useful sooner or later. To deliver messages, to transfer money. But you must remember: no matter how little we ask, the price will be the ultimate if you're caught. Not just for you, but for anyone you involve."

"I understand."

"Then write your address and phone number on a piece of paper."

A black-gloved hand reached through a half-moon in the confessional screen. "We'll contact you about the purchase of a string of pearls and arrange a place of meeting. That last will be a cover. Come here at the agreed time."

TWO

Zelbec, Poland

February 1942

K URT SCHMIDT stared from the train at a sterile sheet
of snow sweeping in an unbroken line to the horizon,
oppressed by a skyful of glowering clouds. At Nibelheim,
upthrusts and outcroppings had shared the weight of the
sky, allowing him to breathe. Here he felt like that thin
horizon line, stretched at unbearable tension between
heaven and earth, until you had to ask: When will it
break?

The train had taken three days, composed of blackouts,
bombings, breakdowns and strafings by British Spitfires,
to travel from Stuttgart to Warsaw. Now it seemed to be
taking another two to push the last two hundred miles
through glutinous snow clouds, southward on the Lublin-
Lvov line. The slam of the wheels, the jerky stops, the
swaying of its belly made Kurt feel like a sluggish fetus
long past its time.

Poland. The wastes of Russia would have been prefera-
ble. Indeed, he had pleaded for them. Though the Axis
were winning in most war theatres except Suez, the cost
had been high. Of 160,000 Waffen SS who had attacked
Russia with the regular army, nearly 1,000 officers had
been killed along with 25,000 other men. In repeated letters to his superiors, Kurt had requested to be transferred
to the front, even daring to hint at the disgrace of recruit-
ing Belgians and Frenchmen into the Waffen SS when
Aryan officers were eager to serve.

He knew he had performed well at Nibelheim. In a year and a half, the disinfection program had eliminated 70,273 worthless lives. Most importantly, SD chief Reinhard Heydrich had requested a blueprint and description of the Nibelheim operation. Observing the stable Kurt had converted into a gas house comfortably accommodating thirty, and disguised for humanitarian purposes as a communal bath, he had commended Kurt for his innovations.

Kurt felt gratified, both as a technician and as a decent German. Thanks to him, about ninety percent of candidates for disinfection walked peacefully to their deaths. As for potential troublemakers, they were drugged with morphine, scopolamine shots or soporifics when supplies were available, run off together or shot as before. With that, he had nothing more to do beyond signing the death certificates. In fact, he had never again ventured from behind his blackout curtain during a "weeding." His job was strictly administration, reorganization, cost accounting.

After ten months Kurt had had enough. He was tired of using his talents to shoot broken-winged birds as they struggled in a net. He wanted to fight men with guns, as his father had done.

At last the train shunted into Zelbec – a detention camp consisting of a handful of new buildings tossed on the snow like unpainted blocks. Spotting the sign SS ZELBEC OFFICE, he carried his suitcase in that direction, resentful no one had met him. The snow crunched with a dry, hollow *plock-plock*, like boots on skulls, while the wind was an invisible wall against which he struggled as it snatched up powder and recirculated it. What Kurt hadn't expected was the greasy texture of the air, with its sweetish, pestilent odor, staining the dark clouds yellow so they hung like a severed chicken's foot over Zelbec. The coal soot of his boyhood home of Dortmund seemed wholesome in comparison. Kurt set down his suitcase at the door and, resisting the urge to pull his scarf over his nose, made the hand-washing motions so habitual that his staff at Nibelheim had dubbed him The Washerwoman.

Everything inside the office was of plywood, linoleum and steel. Kurt identified himself to the desk corporal, who informed him: "The Commandant will see you now."

Kurt was ushered through a double door, the first one of plywood. The second, of wormy maple, opened onto a scene of Oriental splendor – Iranian rugs, an Indian brass gong, a Japanese lacquered screen, an ivory table with Japanese tea service.

Plump and succulent like an oyster, Commandant Graf sat at a wormy maple desk in front of a bullet-proof oval window. His hand, as he saluted, was soft and dimpled like a woman's; his pearly eyes were so pale you couldn't distinguish the whites from the irises; his nose was snubbed; his mouth a wet pink hole between fleshy cheeks. In his left hand he held a peacock feather with which he teased a white Persian cat. He oozed the scent of jasmine cologne.

Waving the feather at Kurt, he enthused: "At last. The man I've awaited for two days. No, don't apologize. Don't you think I understand the train service? How else could I import my treasures to this wasteland?" He scratched his cat under the chin. "The trains are our life's blood, aren't they, Sofie?" Flirtatiously he used his feather as a fan. "I understand, Schmidt, that you're a wizard of efficiency. We can certainly use that here. As you see, I like to keep a clean desk. I also like to keep a clean compound – one day's work in one day's space. With the increase in our quotas, we'll have to increase our output. That's where you come in. I'm looking for big things."

Groggy from the trip, Kurt felt more resentful than flattered. How could he take praise seriously when the transfer had not involved a promotion to major?

Commandant Graf pushed the belly button of an ivory Buddha and spoke into its mouth: "My sealskin, Weber." Checking his diamond watch, he informed: "Our next shipment left its checkpoint seventeen minutes ago. It will be here in another six. I'll personally show you around so we'll understand each other sooner and better."

Outside it was waiting for Kurt as he had left it, like a book with a turned page corner: the wailing wind, the recirculating snow. In sealskin coat and hat, Commandant Graf trekked to a two-track station near a row of barracks. A puff of soot marked the approach of a train from Lemberg. The puff turned into a smudge and then into a trailing black cloud, underlining the greasy yellow one.

As the train slithers and snorts like Fafnur the dragon on its silver rails, the doors of the barracks burst open. Hundreds of broad-faced Ukrainians, well-bundled but ragged, sweep over the rise, yelping and wielding whips. Before the train comes to a full stop, they swarm around Graf and Kurt, exuding steamy clouds of animal energy.

Now they pry open the train doors. They yank out men, women and children, some carrying suitcases, as dazed as rabbits circled by baying hounds.

"Attention, all detainees!" bawls the loudspeaker, repeating itself in three languages. "Enter the hut marked CLOAKROOM. Deposit suitcases, coats and parcels at the wicket marked VALUABLES, then claim your receipt. I repeat . . ."

Wielding hair whips like Medusa tossing her tresses, the Ukrainians herd the new arrivals into the cloakroom. Good at such calculations, an astonished Kurt estimates the fifteen-car train to contain some twenty-five hundred people. As the first are emptied, the Ukrainians leap inside. They heave bodies onto the platform, creating a stench that causes Kurt's nostrils to twitch as if a hairy fly had flown up one. Refusing to react or assess, he concentrates on stilling his nose, while behind his back his hands engage in a persistent and desperate washing motion.

"I enjoy my work in the winter," pipes Graf, his girlish voice like splintered crystal in the dry cold air. "In the summer there are too many flies. Shall we follow the process further?"

Inside the cloakroom, hysterical with noise, Kurt watches confused detainees reluctantly hand over parcels and coats for what he sees are blank scraps of paper. When one brings this oversight to a guard's attention, he receives a fist in the face, bloodying his nose and shattering his glasses. "That's our answer to troublemakers."

Pressing the bewildered Kurt's arm, Graf directs him to a room marked HAIRDRESSER, containing one hundred chairs where women are having their heads shaved. A child of about twelve is clamped into a chair. Ignoring her screams, Graf runs her waist-length black hair sensuously through his fingers. "This will make fine felt slippers for our U-boat crews. We use everything in this camp but the squeal."

In the final room, loudspeakers again bray multilingual instructions: "Strip! Everyone strip for delousing. Put each piece of clothing in a separate pile, shirts, underwear, dresses. Men to the right and women to the left. Important! All shoes must be tied together. If you don't have laces, ask for a piece of string. Then line up for the showers."

As soon as Kurt hears the word "showers," his suspicions crystallize. Ahead he can see a hundred-yard corridor strung with barbed wire and open to the wind. Arrows point: TO BATHS AND INHALATION ROOMS. Graf guides Kurt parallel to the passageway, now filling with naked and shivering detainees, guarded at five-yard intervals by Ukrainians with whips. A diesel truck is parked by the bathhouse, labeled: COURTESY OF ZINK RECREATION FOUNDATION. Exhaust hoses feed from it into the bathhouse.

A numbed part of Kurt's mind flexes into indignant life. Has Graf gone mad? He knows of the resettlement of Slavs and Jews in Poland, but this is something different. Who has authorized it?

Keeping his voice neutral he inquires: "Why are these people standing naked in the cold?"

Eyes glistening like the underbelly of a fish, Graf deliberately misunderstands. "Yes, it is unfortunate, but if we let them take 'showers' with their clothes on, the financial loss would be too great. Do you think the poorest German, in the coldest winter, will consent to wear clothes that have had Jewish shit on them?" Waving his hand like the Dauphin his hanky, Graf signals for two burly Ukrainians to unbar the bathhouse. The death march begins.

A stout woman with a baby at her breast wails: "What's going to happen to us?"

In an unctuous voice, Graf soothes: "You're going to be disinfected, that's all. Remember to breathe deeply to strengthen your lungs." He demonstrates like a conscientious gym instructor. "In, out. That's it, you've got it. Inhaling prevents infectious disease, especially in the little ones."

"But what's going to happen to us afterward?" persists an elderly man, dignified even without clothes.

"You strong young men will build roads," snickers Graf. "The women will do housework – if they feel like it."

Though some take hope from these teasing words, most know the truth as well as Kurt. This is no lineup of wretches so ill or deformed that death is a release. The gassing house has not been disguised as a shower to soothe, but to mock.

A woman with eyes that could stare down the sun curses Kurt and Graf as murderers, while a blind man worries about Jewish ritual, repeating piteously: "Who will give us water to wash the dead?"

As detainees enter the bathhouse, a Polish boy of about seven in cut-down fur coat distributes soap, proud of his responsibilities, while beside him a pyramid of grinning false teeth bears the sign: PLACE YOUR SMILES HERE. Kurt involuntarily runs his fingers through the boy's hair as his father used to do, now understanding the meaning of that gesture – helpless resignation. Grinning, the boy offers him a sliver of soap and Kurt simulates the washing of hands. Catching Graf's curious eye, he stuffs the soap into his pocket.

Kurt calculates the bathhouse must be filled, but Graf orders: "Pack 'em in, at least 700 or 800 for every 270 square feet or we'll be here forever."

Kurt struggles to protest but is incapable of challenging authority. The best he manages is relief he's not carrying out the orders and a sense that "someone" must be informed.

The line shuffles through pinwheels of swirling snow, like a long white slug with two rows of chillblained feet. Kurt's stomach churns and his bowels liquefy. The shooting of the handicapped into the pits of Nibelheim was more gruesome, but that was accomplished in the name of humanity, no matter how crudely. By now he admits Zelbec can't be Graf's doing alone. The operation is too large and well organized. This must be authorized, but by whom? He closes his eyes, instinctively aware that as soon as the door is hermetically sealed and the carbon monoxide pumped in, the moral conceit behind which he has functioned will be stripped away, leaving his conscience as naked and helpless as the victims.

The impossible quota is reached. The doors are closed. A shivering girl, left outside, complains: "We'll catch our death of cold!"

"You'll not die of pneumonia," teases Graf. "Trust us."

An SS sergeant, with an ox's square body and flattened head, attempts to start the diesel. Graf stands over him, tapping his toe, *pitty-pitty-pat*, and staring at his diamond watch. "Damn you, Zink!" he explodes, thus explaining the joke on the bathhouse: COURTESY OF ZINK RECREATION FOUNDATION. Fifteen minutes tick by while Zink and his Ukrainian assistant struggle with cold hands to start the motor. Inside the bathhouse the sobs and moans and shrieks rise till Kurt half expects to see it spin off as if lifted by a cyclone. Many, he knows, must already be dead.

"That's the sound they make in their synagogues," Graf

cheerfully discloses. Grabbing a whip from a guard, he slashes Zink's Ukrainian assistant. "I'll put *you* into the bathhouse. I'll trade you for a Jewish physics professor!"

After an hour and thirty-nine minutes, the diesel growls. Kurt hears a *bzzz-bzzz-bzzz* like a hive of bees as the carbon monoxide feeds through vents. It swells to a crescendo then slackens off as the tomb grows quieter. After another thirty-two minutes, Graf pronounces: "Kaput."

Prisoners, awarded their lives and a percentage of the take for their grisly work, open the doors.

"Watch closely and you'll see something interesting," promises Graf.

Since the corpses have no room to fall, they stand erect like pillars of salt, with families holding hands even in death, making it difficult for workers to separate them. One by one they're tossed out – blue, slippery with sweat and urine, soiled with feces and menstrual blood. Volunteer dentists tear open mouths with iron hooks, then hammer out gold teeth to a tune from "The Moonlight Sonata," plucked out by a little man on a large harp. Another team inspects anuses and genitals for money, gold and jewels.

"You wouldn't believe the wealth from assholes alone," gloats Graf, shaking a shoe box of rings and uncut gems. "This is the result when you pit Aryan know-how against Jewish deceit. We figure a prisoner-laborer earns us 1,431 marks after nine months, which is the usual life expectancy. A dead prisoner earns us 1,631 marks for the same period, including interest. Of course we expect you to improve on those figures."

Impatiently ordering the harpist to play something more lively, Graf confides: "That one holds the Iron Cross. He used to play in the Berlin Philharmonic. He's instructing me on the harp, but when I know what he knows, then he's finished. Like the rest of this gang, he's seen too much."

Outside once more, Graf volunteered: "Now let me tell

you the true genius of this operation. The prisoners do it to themselves! How else could we Germans undertake such a massive program? Here's another little secret: The luckiest are the ones who move direct from the trains into the gas houses. At least they preserve their innocence. No one can survive, even for a day, in one of our installations except at the expense of someone else. Every morsel of food a prisoner puts in his mouth deprives someone he can see with his own eyes, who needs it more and will die without it. Here we tear the veil man has woven between himself and his animal nature. We expose the chain of life, the process by which one insect hatches his larva on the eggs of another. In doing so, we blur the line between persecutor and persecuted. Everyone participates so everyone must share in the guilt of living. Only death is noble."

"Why don't they fight back?" demanded Kurt.

"Because they don't dare to see. The prisoner who buys time by collecting the clothes blinds himself to the fate of the one's who's naked. The one who stands in line blinds himself to the one who has just stepped in the gas-house door. But it's the same as in life, don't you understand? We all know we're going to die, but we refuse right till the bitter end to see the person who's a step ahead of us on the same conveyor belt. In here we merely press the speed-up button."

Graf pointed to several buildings Kurt recognized as crematoria – the cause of the yellow stench raining down like chicken grease. "Unfortunately, those are a necessity," he apologized, daintily putting his sleeve to his nose. "If I had my way, we'd bury the corpses under bronze obelisks the size of Stonehenge, saying who we are and admitting our courage in carrying out such a gigantic task. Unfortunately, the opinion of those who fear future generations may 'misinterpret' our efforts have carried the day. Frankly, if a generation comes along so soft they don't understand something as obvious as this, then, Herr Kapitän, the whole National Socialist movement has been in vain." Checking his watch, he sang: "Time for tea! Sofie will be waiting for her snackies. Let's leave the crematoria till after lunch.

Back in his office, Graf directed Kurt to a silk settee. Tossing up his tunic like a ballet skirt, he sat beside him, pressing so close their thighs rubbed. The odor of his jasmine cologne, now set with burning flesh, forced itself up Kurt's nostrils and into his pores. Edging away, he tried not to soil his lungs by breathing.

With Sofie on his lap like an apron, Graf poured tea from his delicate Japanese pot. "What a relief when the Führer signed the tripartite agreement with Japan! Then I could bring my Oriental collection from storage. Some sacrifices are almost too much to make for one's conscience."

Rolling his buttocks on the silk settee, he simultaneously shifted subjects. "As of tomorrow, Schmidt, your job at Zelbec will be the practical running of this camp, with Sergeant Zink as your right-hand man. I'll do the administration that occupied too much of your time at Nibelheim."

Kurt pictured himself like Captain Hammel, black hair covering his body and blood on his boots. Nauseated, he refused the shortbreads Graf was urging on him. "Why has my application for active service been denied?"

"Ahhh, yes, the front," mocked Graf. "Medals to wear on parade." Dipping his little finger into a pot of molasses, he teased Sofie by smearing it on her nose. "Those of us who won our spurs in the T-4 extermination units are the true elite of this war, Herr Kapitän. Our skills, so carefully honed, can't be spared."

In despair, Kurt at last challenged the authority by which he lived. "We have a two-front war. Why waste energy waging a third front against cripples and Jews?"

"Surely after ten years in the SS your indoctrination

can't be so lacking, Herr Kapitän! Have you no respect for the Führer's pan-Germanic vision?"

"I can't connect this slaughter with anything visionary."

Ratting his teacup in its saucer like the tail of a rattle-snake, Graf remonstated: "How can you despise the work you spawned? Where do you suppose we got the blueprint for Zelbec except from your innovative work at Nibelheim? Gas instead of guns. Shower stalls and bathhouses. I thought today you might have felt some pride, even amusement, at seeing your ideas implemented on a grand scale."

"I did what I could to finish a dirty deed quickly. I never tormented healthy people!"

"Healthy? Can tainted blood exist without corrupting everything it touches? I'm beginning to think, Schmidt, your views may be painfully at odds with party ideology. The Jews have declared war on us by their existence. The fact some look almost human only makes it worse. Like cancer, you can't always see the diseased cells just under the surface. Have you heard of the Final Solution?"

Kurt nodded. "The export of Jews and gypsies and other unreliable elements to a reservation in the east. After the war they'll be shipped to Madagascar."

Licking molasses from his fingers, slipping each one into his wet pink mouth, Graf chuckled: "I'm afraid that's the one before the final one. Our Russian campaign made that solution anachronistic. At the Wannsee conference held last month a more realistic plan was endorsed, calling for the extermination of all Jews and gypsies in Europe. That's at least eleven million people, a task requiring all our will, our courage, our humanity. Zelbec is a test case. In a few months we're hoping to operate at full capacity – 15,000 liquidations a day. And there'll be other camps. With the Jews gone, we'll tackle the Poles and the Slavs and the Ukes. When perfection is the goal, the standard must keep rising."

"How can you justify such things to the German people?"

"I've told you. It's the Jews and the Slavs and the other subhumans who'll do it to themselves. Their organizations will select victims to fill our quotas. Then we'll conscript the strong to liquidate the weak. How else could a nation of eighty million rid itself of eleven million? Eventually, all Germans will find out, despite our oath of secrecy. You can't hide a slaughterhouse for subhumans any more than one for animals. Noses will discover what eyes dare not see. Word will spread, but by then everyone will feel too culpable to protest. Besides, if you didn't complain when your neighbour was selected for slaughter, why bother after he's gone up in smoke? Those who have troublesome consciences will be the blindest. Only the cynical, the amoral or the strong who understand our ideals will dare to see. The masses will shrug and sigh and turn their eyes. How often have you heard a German say: 'I didn't hear that' when someone has been too frank? Afterward, when the tough work is done, they'll open their eyes like Rip van Winkle, see the paradise we've created and want all the credit."

"Does the Führer know?"

"We're the shock troops of his will!"

"And Lieutenant-General Heydrich?"

"He's the one entrusted with organizing the Final Solution from deportation to liquidation. He chaired the Wannsee conference, involving state as well as party officals, and I must say I've never seen him in such high spirits. It took us only one and a half hours to decide the fate of eleven million. The principle was never at issue. Most of our time was spent debating whether one-half and one-quarter Jews should be exterminated or merely sterilized."

Patting Kurt as if he were Sofie, Graf cautioned: "Who are you to judge or even question? One ant in an anthill! If we'd had another year of emigration, we might have resolved the problem, even with British resistance. We'd already cleared out two-thirds of them from the Reich – some 460,000. But we were overtaken by our own success in conquest. Suddenly we had three million more Jews from Poland alone. The mania for resettlement was causing chaos in our transportation system and food supplies. Even then, if the war had ended last year, we could have kept the Madagascar plan. You see? All these things have been thoroughly gone into on a higher level. Since the Führer's every utterance is law, he lifts the burden of decision from you. You need not consider the matter further. Not only are your instructions a military order, but they're also the law of the land. When you challenge them, you challenge German history."

Graf folded his hands neatly, like a punctuation mark. "Any questions?"

"Why me? Why must I run Zelbec?"

"As I've told you, those in T-4 are invaluable, the heart of the program, but because of your training as an engineer and your experience in industry, you have special qualifications. Are you familiar with Zyklon B?"

"A prussic acid gas." Kurt had experimented with it at Nibelheim for the bathhouses, then discarded it as too efficient, too horrifying.

"I've ordered a ton from Degesch Pest Control in Hamburg."

Enough to liquidate one million people! "I used prussic acid as a disinfectant and delouser at Nibelheim but found it too unstable," lied Kurt, washing his hands.

"We need it to meet our 15,000-a-day quota."

"The slightest impurities in the containers, and corrosion begins," insisted Kurt. "I had to bury a hundred kilos because of decomposition."

Graf stared at the convulsive hands. "Our camp at Treblinka boasts excellent results. With your technical experience I'm sure you'll have no trouble inventing solutions. You should be flattered. I wasn't the only commandant who vied for your services."

"Why me?" agonized Kurt once more. "If I'm so valuable, why wasn't my rank raised to major when I was transferred?" He expressed a fear far greater than any snub to his ambition. "What blot do I have on my record? Why am I being punished?"

Graf chuckled, a soft eruption like the bubbling of poison gas deep in his throat. "You're right. There is a problem. A most distressing one. In your own family." Pausing to scratch Sofie's ear, Graf revealed: "When you and your wife were married, the Reichsführer had high hopes such a union would prove fruitful. Unfortunately . . ."

"But that's been looked after!" interrupted Kurt. "I've taken a biological mate. We have a daughter, and the girl may be pregnant again. She's only twenty-four. I'm thirty-five. Think how many children such a fertile union can produce."

Eyes as unblinking as ping-pong balls, Graf allowed: "Oh, I know all that, Herr Kapitän. The phones work even in this wilderness. The problem is not your daughter. The problem is your son."

"Bruno?"

"Himmler's godson. Which makes him a double embarrassment. How old is he now? Three? The situation grows more critical with the passing of each month. The fourth birthday seems to be a natural cutting-off point of such matters, don't you think? Before that, a baby. After that, a young boy progressing toward Hitler Youth. How humiliating if a godson of Himmler doesn't make it! That can't be allowed to happen." Graf advised: "It would be best for this to remain a family matter – something for you and your wife to attend. A lengthy correspondence has already transpired betwen the Reichsführer and Dr. Zuckmayer. Not only is your son causing ideological tensions at the Lebensborn home, but it's the good doctor's professional view that it's your wife's sick attachment to this sick child that renders her incapable of conception. The retardation has no genetic base. The child's brain did not receive sufficient oxygen at birth. What sort of life can a halfwit lead in the Führer's New Eden? I urge you, Herr

Kapitän, to remember your ideals. Remember the blood oath you've sworn. Remember your work at Nibelheim and how satisfying it was to end so much suffering."

Kurt closed his eyes as if drawing a blackout curtain to hide the view.

"Don't think I fail to sympathize," wheedled Graf, laying a dimpled hand on Kurt's knee. "In weak moments I too can feel overcome with pity for these poor wretches whose worst crime was to be born. The weeping and wailing of women, the snatching away of babies – at such times the strongest among us must struggle to maintain our idealism. I've even seen Reichsführer Himmler almost faint when a 'model' firing squad failed to execute two women with the first volley. If you enjoyed your work in T-4, you'd be no better than the subhumans who wield their whips to save their own worthless hides for a few miserable months. I can honestly say I'm glad you're squeamish."

Fluttering his peacock feather, Graf enticed Sofie into dancing across the tea table. "I'm a pretty good student of human nature, Herr Kapitän. I study men the way you study machines. I can predict exactly what will happen to you over the next few months because I've watched other men struggle with the same problem.

"For the first few weeks, you'll feel sorry for the subhumans that fate has placed in your hands. You may attempt to save lives. With Sergeant Zink, it's his infernal diesel engine that keeps breaking down. He doesn't know why. I do. With Lieutenant Weber, my adjutant, it was a trainload of Jews rerouted to safety in the ghetto of Lodz. Weber deliberately betrayed his position. So will you. You'll come to me a week from today, your face all puckered and breathing heavily, to announce the Zyklon B arrived in such a shocking state of decomposition you've had to bury it."

Graf sighed with indulgence. "Such a stage, like adolescence, passes. Faced with the futility of your efforts, you'll ask yourself the point of risking everything to save a few lives for a few months. With the shock of extermination worn thin by repetition, the highly trained SS man inside you will reassert himself. Estranged from the organization that nurtured you, even from your own identity, your conscience will begin to bother you more for *not* carrying out your duty. Once again you'll yearn for the approval of your superior so you can get on with your life and career."

Fanning himself with his peacock feather, Graf embarked on a personal odyssey that increased in intensity. "It is at this crucial turning point that the more sensitive among us come up against the true horror. If what we're doing at Zelbec is wrong, then the Führer is wrong, National Socialism is wrong and our lives are an abomination! All the blood we've shed is on our own hands. We're thugs and mass murderers! Perhaps we may even consider killing ourselves in despair.

"Out of that dark pit the first seedlings of hope sprout. Wrestling with our bourgeois conscience, we stare at the deportees shuffling by, hour after hour, naked, heads shaved, without teeth, eyes blank, faces mournful, reeking of self-pity, some sniveling, some still whining about the loss of their luggage, knock-kneed, puckered with age, *shuffle-shuffle-shuffle* without protest to their deaths while the more aggressive compete for a chance to perform their indignities on the corpses of their kin, rifling mouths and stomachs and assholes, outdoing each other in cruelty to ingratiate themselves with the German guards. Pity shrivels into contempt. We try to imagine Germans behaving that way and we can't. Then it dawns on us in a single stroke of lightning: *They're subhuman, as the Führer has said!*

"With the return to sanity, we cease to say: 'How horrible!' Now we say: 'How horrible I must carry this heavy burden.' Instead of saying: 'Is this right?' we say: 'Am I tough enough?' Taking up our hard task with zeal, we once again dedicate ourselves to the Reich and its future instead of to the subhumans who perverted us. We become excited by the vastness of our task and wish to

raise our daily quotas. Though we find our work no plea-
santer than before, we see where Zelbec fits into the
Führer's glorious vision."

Watery eyes glittering like albumen, Graf enthused:
"You see, Schmidt, the reason we Germans can take lives
is because we live in harmony with Der Todesengel, the
Angel of Death. We know nothing is worse than life with-
out honor and nothing more heroic than death for our
Fatherland."

Gripping Kurt's hand, he revealed: "I'll tell you a little
secret that the Führer confided to me. If we Germans lose
this war, he's considering mass-gassing as many of us as
he can as a mercy death."

By now the sickly sweet smell of Graf's jasmine perfume had grown so powerful Kurt gagged, unable to catch
his breath.

"You're finding this hard to swallow," interpreted Graf,
"but when you achieve redemption you'll have the
strength and the will to rid your wife and yourself of your
burden."

Fondling Sofie, he waited till Kurt had stopped choking
before promising: "When you can say to me, 'Yes, I love
the Reich more than a few million subhumans, and the
Führer more than my halfwit son,' then we can speak of
rewards. If you still want heroes' baubles, I guarantee you
can go to the front if you choose. But what a waste!
Consider the alternative."

Graf paused dramatically, hoping to fan a flicker of
interest even in the shell-shocked captain's eyes. Easing
Sofie from his lap, he ambled over to his wormy maple
desk and drew out a letter which he brandished.

"This, Schmidt, is a request from Lieutenant-General
Reinhard Heydrich for your record and my recommenda-
tion. Now that he's Reich Protector of Czechoslovakia, he
needs tough, pragmatic men for rapid advancement.
You've stayed in his mind – that all-important first impression. Well, I won't stand in your way, Schmidt. If you
reorganize Zelbec's facilities for Zyklon B without too

much fuss, then clean up your domestic mess, I'll release you to follow your rising star. Otherwise . . . your career is stuck. Right here, at Zelbec. Forever. No transfers, no promotions, no leaves. *Forever*."

He laid his manicured hands on the tea table. "See these pretty little fingers, so soft and dainty? The hardest work they do is to crochet doilies. I can afford such lovely hands because my heart is hard. Like Sofie, my claws are retractable."

Stroking the cat from head to tip of tail, he purred: "Sofie is my darling. Nothing pleases me more than to midwife her annual brood, yet if her little kitties turn out to have dark hairs or badly shaped skulls, I wring their necks without a qualm. Is such hardness necessary? Yes, and yes again. For it's the fruit of the poisoned womb that will later destroy us."

THREE

Harz Mountains

March 1942

As the cog car chugged up the Harz mountains, Carmel Kohl stared into black pine forest, a darkling vertical world where Faust and Mephistopheles once consorted with witches on the Brocken. She had anticipated this trip into the Kingdom of the Brothers Grimm since Herr Klausner had proposed it from that other mystery – his confessional. After three months, she was going to meet the man who barked orders in a disembodied voice as if from God Himself.

Who was Father Klausner? Without knowing more than his name, undoubtedly assumed, Carmel had launched a nightclub act enabling her to deliver false passports, coded notes and money to Hamburg, Innsbruck, Frankfurt and, most recently, Prague.

The procedure was simple. If she had a message for someone, she would pass from table to table in the nightclub, distributing white roses and singing:

> "Alone am I in the night,
>   My soul awake and listening.
>   The wind has told me of a song
>   And happiness beyond all dreams.
>   He knows what my heart is missing,
>   And to whom it belongs,
>   And for whom it beats . . . come . . . come . . ."

Backstage she would await a note from a writer whose

initials were always W.R., for White Rose, and embedded in a friendly greeting she would find an invitation: "Perhaps you will remember me? We were introduced by Josef, the owner of The Kubchick Toy Shop on the corner of Mostecka and Saska." Or: "It was wonderful to hear you again! Can we possibly meet for drinks after the show at The Sailors' Wharf on Zirkusweg in St. Pauli? It's so long since we've seen each other, perhaps I should warn you I'll be the fat one with the brown hat and the tweed overcoat."

Though Carmel had begun her underground work with a healthy sense of fear, she discovered the obverse to be exhilaration. For the first time since her days as an urchin, she was living by her wits, improvising, making dangerous decisions. She had reconnected to an earlier self, and though she often heard Axel's voice offering wise parental advice, their years of seclusion in Munich now seemed blurred and distant, like a movie role remembered with tenderness.

At the same time, Carmel's professional self had undergone dramatic change. Standing in a single spotlight, simply dressed in black or white, hair tousled and with little makeup, she would belt her songs from some inner place full of the smoky sadness that seemed a permanent part of wartime Germany.

Ironically, the more "real" Carmel became on stage, the more the glamorous star who was a trick of mirrors took on the functions of Carmel's private life – flattering Goebbels into granting her travel passes; concocting lies to explain to theater managers why she had to leave immediately after a concert; flirting with customs officials to avoid scrutiny.

Sometimes Carmel felt her real self was the puppet and this alter ego the twister of strings. Sometimes the cynicism with which this brittle self manipulated others aroused her contempt, but always the songs restored her emotional balance. In the world of the Third Reich, where else could you hide true feelings except in the guise of make-believe?

Carmel cleared the frosty window with her breath. The sun had slid behind a rosy stand of larch sprinkled with powder snow. Hers was the next stop. She could see a dilapidated station illuminated by one blue light. Uncramping her legs, she made her way down the crowded aisle with her overnight case.

The train lurched to a stop in a massive exhalation of steam. Turning up her fox collar, Carmel stepped onto the platform and into air like iced champagne. The station was closed. Wading around it through knee-high drifts, she stumbled upon a double row of snug shops with snow piled up to their peaked roofs, their chimneys puffing smoke into a twilight sky.

In front of the first waited a red sleigh with a gray horse and roly-poly driver in reindeer skins, a wreath of steam over his head. He turned – a broad-faced Ukrainian with a steel-toothed grin. Before she could introduce herself, he hefted her luggage onto the sleigh. Tucking a reindeer robe around her, he cracked his whip by the flank of the gray horse.

With a jingle of bells, they slithered across hard-packed snow, through the silent village and over a gurgling stream. Ears flat, the horse strained up a mountain, snorting and heaving, the mist whitening over its head. The runners bit with a whine while the driver murmured encouragements like an auxiliary motor. Everything glowed in the moonlight as if each twig had been dipped in a bucket of phosphorescent paint. Fence posts looked like beer steins with their crowns of foam. The wind played through the pines while the horse's hooves added a gentle *oompah-pah-pah*.

Smoke curled in a potato peel over the next rise. Carmel glimpsed an impressive log hunting lodge, with gables and balconies. Quickening its pace, the horse whinnied in anticipation of its oats.

A path led through four-foot drifts to a red door. Tucking Carmel's case under his arm, the driver lumbered ahead. As he shouldered his way inside, light slid in a golden welcome mat across the snow.

Stamping flakes from her galoshes, Carmel entered a pine vestibule two stories high, lit with a chandelier of candles. An astonishing tapestry depicted a stag being attacked by baying dogs.

Smiling, with the same broad features as the driver, a stout woman greeted Carmel, her face shiny with firelight. She led her up a spiral staircase, using a paraffin lamp.

Carmel's room, under the eaves, had a fourposter bed, wolfskin rugs and a Delft porcelain stove. On the down comforter she found a card: COCKTAILS IN THE LIBRARY.

The library lay to the right of the vestibule. A cut-glass decanter of sherry with two glasses rested between a deer-skin couch and a birch-log fire.

Carmel examined leatherbound books lining the room: on wildflowers, birds and taxidermy. German literature from the fourth-century Bible translated by Wulfila to Schiller and Goethe, Kafka and Brecht. German history, particularly Charlemagne, Frederick the Great and Bis-marck. Tales of German's pagan past – of the Valkyrie, who carried dead heroes from the battlefield to Valhalla; of Wotan, the father of all; of the Norns, weavers of des-tiny. An early edition of Wolfram von Eschenbach's *Parsi-fal*, on which Wagner based his opera. Books of witch-craft, magic, alchemy and prophecy. Books of German philosophy, including a few Carmel had struggled through under Professor Stein's tutelage: Nietzsche, whose hatred of the meekness of Christianity and democ-racy combined with his glorification of a race of supermen inspired Hitler's political rationale. Hegel, whose concept of the omnipotent expression of Divine Will strengthened Hitler's religious rationale. Luther, whose rabid anti-Sem-itism legitimized Hitler's racial rationale. Karl Haushofer, whose space-power theory of geo-politics provided Hitler with a blueprint for global conquest.

Rifling through volumes, Carmel found their pages spliced with rice paper on which the reader had disputed the text in a meticulous hand.

A door led from the library to a gallery lit by gaslight. Glass cases contained lead soldiers depicting famous German victories, while the walls were covered with artwork – Matisse, van Gogh, Cézanne, Braque. Masterworks banned in the Third Reich. Among contemporary German artists, Carmel discovered the portrait of herself by Raymon Arno.

A voice behind her commented: "Raymon's best, don't you think? That exquisite line of the throat alone makes it worth possessing."

Carmel froze, then wheeled. A familiar figure posed in the doorway, one hand in black velvet pocket.

"Wolf!"

As he stepped toward her, Carmel threw her arms around his neck and burst into tears. After holding her firmly till she recovered, Wolf moved back. "I guess I should have worn my beige wool dress," he teased, referring to that time in Munich when they had dressed identically after three years' separation.

Carmel dabbed at her eyes. "Why didn't you tell me? Why did you pretend to be Father Klausner?"

"I guess I didn't want to influence you. You had to make your own decisions about how far you would go."

"You influenced me just as much as Father Klausner. No man has influenced me more than you – not even Axel."

He offered a lopsided smile. "More's the pity."

Ushering Carmel to the deerskin couch, Wolf poured the sherry. "Our old toast? To reunion."

She drained the glass. "Damn! All the things I wanted to know, and now I'm speechless."

"Let's begin with names. I know your list. The two Jürgens children are in London."

"With Raymon?"

"No. They were. He smuggled them into Switzerland. Now they're with Sara Stein." Again he raised his glass. "To reunions, everywhere."

"You should be proud of your old gang."

"Yes. We turned out to be capable of more than arguing in cafés. You did your part on this one too. Remember Heinrich Heine's *Die Lorelei*? You delivered it to a bookstore in Stuttgart."

"It contained a false passport between chapters two and five."

He nodded. "For Raymon. Even my mother contributed. By forcing me to spend my boyhood copying other people's masterpieces, she turned a mediocre painter into a master forger. I've come upon few documents in the Third Reich I can't reproduce, and even fewer photos I can't retouch into a good likeness. I decided to make Raymon an importer so he could transport two large packing cases. One contained part of Göring's Dürer collection, filched from Poland and sent to Basel for safe-keeping. The other contained the Jürgens girls. The risk was appalling. Children cry. Children get the hiccups. Children, unlike Dürer sketches, leak. They were only an hour in transit, but it was the longest hour of my life. At last Raymon called from Basel: 'The shipment arrived safely. No breakage, no leakage.'"

Carmel nodded solemnly. "Couldn't Christian and Renate have escaped too? I've cried myself sick thinking I might have helped them."

"No, you couldn't change the facts. If Christian had defected, he would have known the Gestapo would retaliate against his mother and father. If Renate stayed in Berlin, she would have been arrested. So many of Christian's friends had committed suicide, I guess he considered it a reasonable option. He also knew his death would give Goebbels a black eye. Another one."

"Where's Raymon now?"

"He's safe . . . for the time."

"In Switzerland?"

"No." Using Father Klausner's Saxon accent, Wolf rasped: "You ask too many questions."

Wolf's housekeeper entered the library, carrying a tray bearing white and cobalt-blue Meissen plates and silver cutlery. Carmel examined the Friedrich crest engraved on a spoon: a wolf and a fox supporting a cross with the motto COURAGE AND CUNNING. She laughed. "That much I know. Now tell me, where have you been living up to the family motto?"

"In Switzerland. In London. Even in Germany. Reinhard Heydrich wanted me to join a seminary to infiltrate the Catholic church. I think I was to be the next pope – I'm not sure I'm joking. Fortunately, Hitler felt I lacked certain sublime qualities, so I was dispatched more informally to sound out as many priests as I could. At the same time, the British Secret Service thought I was working for them."

"A double agent?"

"On paper. In my own mind I was just collecting information until my direction clarified. I discovered most priests couldn't be corrupted by Nazi bribes or the promise of power, but neither could they be swayed by compassion for human suffering. Common sense meant nothing to them either. The words Jew and Communist were such an anathema they couldn't see that what was happening to those two groups would eventually happen to them. My one convert after ten months' work was wonderful little Father Bauer. I'm sure he has more courage in his arthritic bones than all those corpses in the Vatican archives awaiting sainthood."

The housekeeper re-entered, this time bearing steamy salvers of pheasant stuffed with wild rice, boiled potatoes, turnips with real butter.

Wolf uncorked a bottle of wine. "Kitzinger Main Leite 1938. Good enough for Göring's funeral!" He complimented the housekeeper. "You've surpassed yourself, Frau Kublek."

"I'd forgotten such food existed!" reveled Carmel.

"Country wisdom. If you want something, grow it. If you can't grow it, barter. My housekeeper knows the system well. To her the great inflation was a piece of foolishness that happened somewhere else." Reversing Göring's pre-war slogan of "Guns before butter," Wolf quipped: "Turnips before grenades."

Putting aside her cutlery, Carmel tore her pheasant with her fingers.

"More country wisdom!" approved Wolf, deftly continuing to carve.

By the time they had reduced the entree to a heap of bones, the pressure of unspoken words was building between them. Accepting a cup of Brazilian coffee and cognac, Carmel asked: "Well . . . am I to be told something about the organization?"

A rueful laugh. "Organization is too large a word. A few students and professors, stretching from Munich to Hamburg, who believe we're being led by a gang of criminals. Some of the Old Guard who remember the true meaning of honor, or who understand enough about men and supplies and two-front wars to understand Germany must eventually collapse. A few clerics of assorted faiths in touch with their consciences or who fear a loss of Church power. Sometimes their actions are spontaneous and symbolic, such as the distribution of anonymous leaflets across Germany denouncing the yellow star. Sometimes they're individual and humanitarian, such as the hiding of illegals one step ahead of the Gestapo. When we're 'organized,' it's usually because we're acting with the undergrounds of occupied countries or directed by British and American agents. So far there's been no resistance in the sense of blowing up munitions plants. We have no common ideology beyond disgust Adolf Hitler is ruler of Germany."

Carmel asked another question that had been nagging her: "Where did you get the portrait of me by Raymon?"

"I rescued that from the Exhibition of Degenerate Art

held in Munich in '37. One hundred and twelve works by
the world's finest artists displayed unframed in a mad
jumble as if by fools – which was the literal truth. The
caption under yours read: 'Aryan beauty as lusted after by
a sick Yiddish mind.' That show was the most popular
ever staged in the Third Reich. Two million visitors – five
times as many as turned up for the party-approved show
in the House of German Art. I managed to save half the
works one way or another. The rest, if you can imagine the
stupidity, were mutilated and burned."

"Raymon stayed here, didn't he?"

"How do you mean?"

"This was where he came to 'dry out' and to unblock
his painting. Don't deny it. Christian and Renate used to
visit him somewhere in the mountains. Now I know it was
here."

Wolf studied her through the amber eye of his cognac.
"Do you want to see where he lived? He unblocked, all
right. You'll find it interesting. Take that fur rug or you'll
be chilly."

Picking up a kerosene lamp, Wolf led her back into the
gallery where she had seen her portrait. With the toe of his
boot, he kicked up a faded rug, revealing a door in the
floor. Hefting it by its metal ring, he volunteered: "This
was the root cellar of the original kitchen. Whenever I lost
something as a child, Frau Ulrich, our housekeeper, told
me it had disappeared down here where I would go some
day. Shoe or beloved pet, it didn't matter. Naturally, I was
terrified. It still turns up in nightmares."

As Carmel followed Wolf down steep stairs, he shifted
his lamp to reveal a nook with a cot, a washstand, a
bureau and a stove.

"Raymon had the run of the lodge, but he seemed to
relish it down here. Come, I'll show you his Sistine
Chapel."

Wolf unlatched a wooden door. "This used to be a coal
cellar."

Carmel stepped inside, then recoiled. Walls, floor and

ceiling were painted with a collage of bitter quotes and violent images. Across one panel rampaged four apocalyptic horsemen, recognizable as the tribunal Hitler had appointed to purge the Reich of non-Aryan art. The words of one of them were splashed in yellow across the floor: "The sublimest image, recently created in Germany, has not come out of an artist's studio. It is the steel helmet." This was satirized by a half-dozen viciously caricatured beer-bellied Germans using swastika helmets as chamber pots.

Another panel showed Goebbels' steel fist smashing onto the heads of artists murdered by the regime, while across his elegant cuff was inscribed: "We wish to relieve creative people of the feeling of forlorn emptiness by giving them the consciousness that the state is holding its protective hand over them."

Emblazoned in red was a statement by Hitler: "Art should be uplifting rather than disturbing. The public should be allowed to see only the beautiful and the picturesque." This was illustrated by Aryan supermen goose-stepping through bloody poppies, carrying rifles which proved to be severed human limbs.

Another panel featured an eagle, with Hitler's face, raping a blond milkmaid representing Germany. Entitled "Leda and the Swan," it referred to Hitler's well-known obsession with Caravaggio's painting by the same name.

A ceiling mural, imitating Leonardo's "Last Supper," depicted Hitler and eleven henchmen ranged about a table devouring grapes, sausages and spaghetti which, on closer inspection, were eyeballs, penises and entrails torn from corpses hidden under the table.

Even more dynamic were the panels in which the artist had broken free of satire to recreate, with realism and rage, scenes of Gestapo torture and mass murder.

"God, the power!" gagged Carmel. "I can't breathe. It's crushing me."

Leading her from the room, Wolf slammed and bolted the door. "Arno blasted through five years of artistic paralysis with his fury. The work is powerful, all right. Years ago I would have argued it wasn't art. I can hear my voice, 'Mere political cartooning.? The classical part of me still insists words are for books and anger for the prizefight ring. It still mourns a tragic corruption of a major talent."

Back in the library, Wolf put another birch log on the fire. As he poked and prodded, scowling into the ashes, Carmel asked: "What does White Rose mean?"

"It's a historic German name." Reluctantly, he added: "It derives from an ancient occult society opposed to black magic."

"Do you believe in the occult?'

"Certainly not!"

"I've heard Christian claim that Hitler and Himmler were Satanists. He said they belong to a black arts society called Thule."

Wolf snorted. "Christian was a romantic. A racist society by that name did exist. Hitler and some of the early Nazis did belong. What fantasies they held about themselves I can't say. I wish there were a Satan to account for evil. That would let off us humans rather lightly, don't you think?"

Remembering books she had noticed earlier, Carmel pulled down one entitled *The Devil: A German Meditation*.

Wolf laughed. "Sorry to disappoint you but my study of devilry is a scholarly one. Demons are vital to the German imagination and to the dark side of the Nazi dream. Our pagan ones were smuggled into our version of the Christian religion as the court of the anti-Christ, and our church fathers tortured witches in greater quantity and further into modern times than anywhere else in Europe. That doesn't make these things real, though often the persecutors performed with such conviction that the poor wretches came to believe in their own black powers."

Fanning the fire with a set of bellows, he warmed to his tale. "Even as a child, I had my own convert – old Frau Ulrich, our housekeeper, whom I've mentioned. I was obsessed with her pilgrimages down into Raymon's coal cellar, about which she'd already fired my imagination. Convinced I was ridding the world of evil, I tried to set fire to her. Fortunately, I overestimated the power of a single match. Or did I? My childish persecution persuaded her she did have evil powers. She even convinced the more gullible villagers that all the normal tragedies of their lives were traceable to her. That was far more exciting than inciting one small boy."

Wolf dispensed with his bellows. "That's the kind of Satanist Hitler is. He's Dr. Caligari, while the rest of us are dull-witted Cesare hypnotized into carrying out his will. To me that's what evil is – a puny and undernourished awareness of the power of good. Which is not to deny a dark romanticism runs like black lightning through German history. When that becomes wedded to Prussian authoritarianism, the result is violent and excessive."

Since Wolf had bothered to rekindle the fire, Carmel thought they would at least talk for a while. Instead, he placed a chaste kiss on her forehead as if laying a flower on a tombstone. "I know it's been a long day for you. We're both tired. Frau Kublek will see you to your room."

Carmel awoke to the sound of church bells. Icicles framed blue sky laced with a birch branch on which two birds were singing. Her nose twitched appreciatively – fresh coffee.

"Guten Morgen."

Frau Kublek was setting a tray before the porcelain stove: Breakfast for one, Carmel noted. Slipping into a white velvet robe, she devoured plump homemade rolls crusty on the outside, with real butter, a boiled egg and Westphalian ham.

As she licked crumbs from her sticky fingers, Wolf

strode in wearing a military greatcoat and an envelope of
frosty air. Clicking his heels on the pine floor, he ordered:
"Dress warmly. We have work to do."

Under a fall of snow, the world was as clean and snappy as
freshly washed sheets. Seeing her cuffed red ski pants,
Wolf nodded. "Good. Come with me."

Bemused by the unexpected emergence of his family's
military tradition, Carmel struggled to match his long
stride through heavy snow.

At the stable behind the lodge, Wolf halted, withdrew a
Mauser pistol from his greatcoat and laid it on her palm
so she felt the icy steel bite through her gloves. With their
breath mingling in a shiny cloud of ice needles, he
explained the action of the precisely balanced death
instrument, then pointed to a straw target. "You must hit
that with this."

Though Wolf's tone suggested he was confident she'd
never handled a gun, Carmel had whiled away sunny
afternoons at the Berg estate in Munich learning to shoot
everyone in Axel's collection. Taking aim, she squeezed.
Not a bull's-eye, but close. Surprised, Wolf offered a curt
nod – the same stingy praise through which he'd controlled her acting career. Irritated, Carmel directed her
aggression toward the formal target, hitting bull's-eyes
even when instructed to draw from her pocket. After an
hour, Wolf pronounced her "competent."

"Keep this gun but don't carry it unless you think you'll
need it." Wheeling toward the lodge, he barked: "Come!"
still playing the general with one private.

Exasperated, Carmel belted, "Turn around, Rat!" – the
beginning of a speech from their favourite musical *Broadway*. Aiming the Mauser at Wolf's head, she warned:
"The last thing you're gonna see before you go straight to
hell is Axel Berg's woman who swore she'd get you."

Jerking up her hand, Carmel fired, snapping a cedar

branch burdened with snow so the tree dumped its cold white load on Wolf's startled head.

With the sulphurous sound of violence re-echoing, she tossed away the pistol and, lowering her own head, rammed like a fist into his midriff, sending him sprawling. Her anger converted into laughter, she flung herself upon him, passionately kissing his face while thrusting her hands like burrowing animals into his greatcoat. Unfastening his breeches, she took him into her mouth, felt him mount a brief protest, then quicken and surrender like the snow tree falling to its fate.

"You raped me." Both burst out laughing. "You've unleashed a monster." Carrying her to the stable, he dropped her on a bed of straw. Then he peeled open her red snowsuit and made love to her without control, the sweet scent of the hay blending with the randier odors of the sweating horses.

They gazed at each other in laughter and tenderness. "Your eyes are green," mused Carmel. "I thought they were black. You always kept them so tightly closed behind your camera."

Wolf slapped her lightly on the bottom. "You don't think I'm going to lie here and listen to such terrible dialogue, do you? How would you like to go for a gallop? No doubt you've mastered the hunt as well as the shoot?"

"I've ridden, yes," she admitted. "Quite a lot."

Wolf knocked hay from both of them with his gloves, using stinging slaps that pushed Carmel away. "Let's go," he ordered, reverting to the Prussian mode she now recognized as his last line of defense against intimacy. Linking arms, Carmel fit her stride to his. Wolf understood she was attempting to relieve him of his habit of distance as if she were a butler collecting hat and cane, and he squeezed her hand.

Herr Kublek, Wolf's Ukrainian groundsman, produced a chestnut filly for Carmel, along with Wolf's black mare.

The horses' hoves stirred swirls of powder, their snouts spun clouds of steam as they trotted by ponds of blowing grasses, shaded from beige to wine-red. Carmel marveled at the intricate tracings of hoof and paw prints, the night's legacy. Wolf pointed out deer, fox, rabbit, even mouse, explained the difference between white pine and red, identified deciduous trees by their skeletons, not instructing her but sharing his enthusiasm. She imagined him, a solitary child curled in the deerskin couch in the library, learning the labels of wild things as a way of controlling them, domesticating them, so he would not fear them.

Affectionately patting a pine branch, Wolf mused: "Last time I was in England I stood on the cliffs of Dover looking out to sea, with the world reduced to a gray horizon line. How different it must have been for our ancestors growing up in the mist and mystery of the forest, with leaves deadening sound and feet falling silently on moss. With the eye forced upward to sun and moon and stars, instead of sweeping unimpeded across a broad plain. How much does that affect the German character? How much my own? In a forest you're never sure you're alone. Behind every bush the imagination hides an enemy warrior, a bear, a demon, an elf, a shadow. The British could see the Spanish Armada almost from the time it left home port!"

Reaching for his hand, Carmel inquired: "Were you happy as a child?"

"What a question! Was I supposed to be? Only someone born into the lower classes would ask. It's your luxury to hope an improvement in fortune will bring happiness. Mine was a life of privilege in which such considerations never arose. Displaying that privilege to best advantage was a full-time job, like a peacock supporting his tail. So many things to learn!"

"What things?"

He squinted down a line of larches. "How to enter a room, what to say in what tone and order. So many things for a boy to do with his hands and feet, whether sitting with a sword on a dais or dancing at a Hohenzollern ball.

All those customs passed from one generation to the next, along with the monogrammed china. Now such things are smashed."

"Are you sorry or secretly relieved?"

Watching a magpie flit from branch to branch, he shrugged. "When you apply the knowledge of structure, order and detail to a royal ball, then it's tedium. When those things help you appreciate the nuances of art or music, such knowledge becomes a scaffold to climb higher, to see farther and deeper. I would have preferred the old order to continue because I had learned to manipulate it, but I wouldn't wish it to return. I'm repelled by retired generals, their chests covered with outdated orders, and ladies-in-waiting in tarnished tiaras who yearn for 'this nastiness' to pass so they can recall the Hohenzollerns to their former stupidities."

"What would you have become, Wolf, if the old world hadn't ended?"

"A priest," he replied promptly. "For all the wrong reasons. As an adolescent, I went through a state of religious ecstasy – seeing visions, fainting at the altar – the natural result of my father's relentless attempt to turn me into a soldier. As Hegel says, for every thesis expect an antithesis. My father, with his love of uniforms, was offended by that Roman skirt, so I was attracted. Heydrich was shrewd enough to pick up on that."

"What was your father like?"

Remembering a disciplinarian, forever in the grip of rage, Wolf allowed: "Stern."

"And your mother?"

Remembering a blue-veined beauty with stiff black hair, he repeated: "Stern. My father was not a person but an order. My mother was needed to duplicate that order, and I was to be the vehicle of future perpetuation. Haven't you noticed how all the Kaiser's officers looked alike? Large and handsome with waxy mustaches, blank eyes and fewer changes of expression than uniforms. Such men do not age in the usual way. One day they topple over and you discover nothing was inside but sawdust. My father lasted only six months after the Kaiser's abdication. My mother, six months after that. Still, can you imagine what preoccupied my father in making his will? Instructions for his most reliable officer to force me, age fourteen, to drink glass after glass of schnapps, then do military drills till I learned never to show the effects of drinking – something the officer caste has always done in great pride and quantity. Form was everything, an acid that ate up content." His laughter was rough-edged, like a rusty can. "Even my father's ghost didn't wish to be disgraced by a tipsy son, and in that I can boast I've never disappointed him. After a few lessons, I was leaving the 'reliable officer' under the table."

"But how can such proud, rule-loving men support Hitler and his gangsters?"

"Because he caught them like fish in their own net of formalism. From infancy they were taught all life, all honor, all duty belonged to the Kaiser. Then his abdication threw a thousand years of history into the garbage. Out of that chaos Hitler brought order, constitutionally and with a good deal of foreign admiration. He bound his generals to him with oaths, and then he had them trapped. All the loyalty that had belonged to the Kaiser now belonged to him."

"But that makes no sense. Brutality is brutality even if it's legal."

"I guess you'd have to belong to a military family to understand the tradition of the oath, its mysticism combining law with an inner code that's more powerful than religion. The oath stands above the men it binds. By requiring it of his generals, Hitler has them doubting even their right to doubt. Besides, the longer the war continues, the more gravely the professional officer is implicated in the regime's misdeeds and the less his scope for individual choice. Only a few dare break from the herd."

"Like those who belong to White Rose."

Wolf frowned. "Can't we forget such things? To talk in

this magic world is like crackling cellophane bags during a Mozart concert." Pulling down a pine bough so it dumped its hand of snow on Carmel, he galloped his mare around a frozen pond stiff with bullrushes like soldiers. Carmel's filly followed as she clung lightly to the mane, exalting in borrowed power and the keening rush of the wind.

That evening they made love in front of the fireplace in Wolf's room, then fell asleep in the master bed bearing the Friedrich crest. When Carmel awoke in the morning, Wolf was already bending over her, his tongue making hot curls on her cheek so that the night felt seamless, as if they had been joined even in sleep.

After having breakfast, they drank coffee, watching a gentle fall of snow. Inevitably the conversation drifted toward the darker side of the winter of '42.

"How have you avoided joining both the SS and the army, Wolf? Does Heydrich still think you're working for him?"

Wolf blew a smoke ring. "He knows I am. I provide a very valuable service."

"As a double agent?"

"Something more suited to my talents. I serve Heydrich's ego, just as it pleased Goebbels to hire Prince Christien of Schaumburg-Lippe to carry his briefcase. The Nazis love employing their betters at déclassé jobs."

"But what's the job?"

"I run a brothel for Heydrich."

Carmel started to laugh, then remembered the night she glimpsed Wolf with Heydrich at the Romanische Café, with Willi Bliss whispering: "Heydrich has a brothel near here for party big shots."

"The last thing the party wants is yet another general's son pressing for advancement, but a good brothel-keeper – that's different. Salon Kitty – a nine-room mansion off the Kurfürstendamm, offering high-class facilities to ranking members, diplomats and the like. As Gestapo chief, Heydrich planted microphones in all the rooms, though he's been less involved since also becoming Reichs Protector of Czechoslovakia. My method of gathering information is more informal. Since the girls often despise their 'patrons,' they line up for the privilege of squealing. I feed this incriminating stuff to Heydrich, Göring or Goebbels, wherever I figure it'll do most damage, securing their patronage while fanning party factionalism. The important stuff goes to the British Secret Service, but that's a sideline I'd prefer not to brag about. Now how about you? Has Goebbels asked you to make another movie?"

"He bombards me with scripts, all so silly I find it easy to refuse. After three winters of war, Brownshirt epics are box-office poison, so UFA has gone in for the most asinine comedies."

"Does Goebbels give you any personal trouble?"

Carmel giggled. "I'm too old for him. Besides, I have another protector. The Führer. I'm told he calls me The Woman in the most flattering way. Like the loyal secretary, Goebbels projects the feelings of his boss."

"Good. But accept another movie soon, something innocuous. It's protection and keeps you circulating in the highest party circles. White Rose has begun a new phase. If Germany wins this war, the party must not. If Germany loses, some of us must prove this country worthy of an honorable peace. Either way, a few Nazi linchpins must go. There'll be assassinations. And bitter reprisals."

"Who?"

"One is obvious, but he leads a charmed life – bombs that don't explode, bombs that do two minutes after he's gone. We've settled on an interim target. That much you should know to prepare yourself."

"Are you directly involved?"

"In the planning. Beyond that, no, but yes. We all are, including you."

"What's going to happen?"

Wolf stared out the window. "A quiet street. An open car. Two assassins, one parchuted in from Britain, the other a local man." Sardonically, he inquired: "Any more questions?"

"Yes. The one Father Klausner always refused to answer. Where's Frau Fuchs?"

He shrugged, then smiled. "Neither Father Klausner nor I know. That's the truth. Though I could contact her in an emergency."

"How long since you've seen her?"

"Oh, she pops up from time to time. When you're least expecting her. She was one of the men who hefted the case containing the Jürgens children onto the train to Basel. Sometimes I recognize her and sometimes I don't. Remember the toy shop you visited in Prague?"

"Of course."

"Frau Fuchs sold you the bugle with a list of names from the Czech Resistance."

"Not the toymaker with the square glasses and the mound of white hair?"

Wolf laughed. "I don't know. I didn't see her, but I know she was there. I cease to think of her as real anymore. To me, she's a guardian angel."

He looked at his watch and frowned. "Eleven. Today the witching hour comes at noon. I think you'd better get packed."

Though Wolf lounged on Carmel's bed observing her every gesture with a lover's indulgence, he did not interrupt her or suggest she stay longer, as Carmel had hoped. Fastening the clasp of her suitcase, she asked that sad, hopeful question: "When will I see you again?"

Wolf avoided her eyes. "I can't say."

"A week? Three years?"

He smiled. "Somewhere in between."

"As Father Klausner?"

"No. We mustn't endanger Father Bauer anymore. He has his own work to do. I'll see you as myself – whatever that is. But we can never meet in private again."

"Why?"

"Because it's too dangerous. We'll be followed. Our

conversations will be taped. I'll say too much, as I already have."

"Why did you invite me here, Wolf?"

He butted his cigarette and reached for her bag. "To warn you. To retire Father Klausner." He took her hand. "Because I'm not immune to temptation."

"Can't we enjoy each other and accept the risk?"

In a kindly but firm voice, Wolf advised: "You must put aside all your bourgeois yearnings, as I have done. As I had done until this weekend. The war is no time for a personal life. To do one's job, one can't afford to want to live too much."

FOUR

Mullhorig, Bavaria

April 1942

THE SCENT of lilacs drifting in Ilse's window made it difficult to finish her memo to Dr. Zuckmayer. At the end of each paragraph, her eyes slid out to the swaying purple clusters, then followed the breeze downward to the Polish prisoners turning the wet loam into tulips and daffodils. A few Lebensborn mothers were playing lawn croquet, including Helga, now five months pregnant with Kurt's second biological child. Given Helga's girth, knocking the ball through the hoop was proving difficult, especially with Bruno and Ursula clamoring for attention. A clever, energetic child, nine-month-old Ursula was already able to stand up and say a couple of words, including Mutti for Ilse, her adoptive mother, and Gugga for Helga. Bruno, age three, was sharing her playpen, a thing Ilse had forbidden. She headed indignantly for the window, then told herself to let it go for now.

Though Helga had proved to be a lazy girl with an overfondness for Mullhorig's luxuries, she was fulfilling her promise as a biological mate for Kurt, and she was helpful with Bruno. Ilse was willing to overlook a few bad habits. She also confessed she hadn't been heartbroken when Helga produced a sister for Bruno instead of a brother. Given Bruno's slow start in life, he didn't need competition.

With a burst of energy Ilse finished her memo, outlining problems likely to need Dr. Zuckmayer's attention:

the three babies from Nursery B, now in quarantine with a mysterious rash that might be infectious; the student nurse she suspected of stealing food for the prisoners working the grounds. If her accusations proved true, the girl would be dismissed, the guards demoted and the prisoners executed. Dr. Zuckmayer was meticulous about moral matters, believing one rotten apple ruined the barrel.

Ilse looked at the Polish prisoners tilling the soil, their faces so spare they were like skulls with gouged eye sockets, then at the plump-cheeked mothers with their babies, and then at Mullhorig's onion-domed church ringed with apple blossoms. Impulsively she ripped up the part of her memo dealing with the prisoners. She had no proof. She would just warn that foolish girl to watch out!

Again Ilse let her eyes drift with the dandelion fluff to the distant Alps fringing green wheatfields. In an hour Kurt was coming to take Bruno and her on a vacation – the first time she'd seen him in five months. Since his transfer to Poland, his letters had been sporadic, dark and disjointed, full of his impatience for active service. After his depressing work at Nibelheim, Ilse thought he would rejoice at being part of the Reich's eastern resettlement program. Perhaps a time came for every German soldier when only the front would do. Since the beginning of the Russian campaign almost a year ago, a number of women at Mullhorig had become widows before they had become mothers. Ilse reached for her pink pills, prescribed by Dr. Zuckmayer for her angina. So far she'd been lucky.

An SS officer was hurrying across the drawbridge into the compound, his body stiffly held as if he were pushing against an invisible barrier. Ilse glimpsed the saw-toothed profile. "Kurt!" Leaning out the window she waved like a schoolgirl. He squinted into the sun, recognized her and saluted.

Using her Lebensborn poster as if it were a mirror, Ilse tucked in tendrils of hair, then raced down the steps. Kurt seemed leaner, but sinewy and tanned from the Polish plains. Inhibited by the security guard and her husband's reluctance to show feelings in public, Ilse held herself back from embracing him, clasping his hand instead. She poured out words: "Bruno is so excited. So am I. You're early. That's wonderful!"

"There was no traffic. I guess no one has gasoline." Though he barely smiled, he squeezed Ilse's hand while seeming to search her face.

"Did you see Helga as you came in? She has Bruno and Ursula."

Linking arms with Kurt, feeling elation and desire, Ilse escorted him to the lawn where Helga had been playing croquet, conscious of envious glances. To her relief, Bruno was no longer in Ursula's playpen but on a sandbox digging with his wooden SS dagger.

Helga nodded wordlessly, not sure how to behave toward this stranger whose second child she carried.

"Bruno, see who's here," enticed Ilse.

The boy's face lit up. "Papa."

Since that was what he called all men in SS uniforms, Ilse underlined: "Your father came to take us to the mountains. He gave you your dagger last Julfest."

Crawling sideways like a crab, Bruno grabbed Kurt's boot. Waving his dagger, he stammered: "Dag-dag." Then he reached up to be held.

Conscious of so many eyes upon him, Kurt shook Bruno's hand. When his son persisted, he stepped back paralyzed and began wringing his hands.

Ursula pulled herself up the side of her playpen, clamoring for attention. Kurt scooped her up in gratitude, burying his confusion.

A jealous Bruno slashed his father's legs with his SS sword.

"Big boys over three shake hands with their fathers," soothed Ilse, but Bruno would not be comforted until Helga produced a candy from her pocket.

Wearing a red dirndl and white blouse with flowered scarf knotted around her braids, Ilse sat by her husband in their rented BMW with Bruno wriggling between them. As they sped southward on the autobahn, she watched the mountains rush toward them, already imagining the smell of the pines, the wet granite, the icy alpine flowers. Though Kurt was still remote, Ilse reminded herself that it always took him time to warm up after separation. She could pick up their relations in mid-sentence, but he had to find his way back to her like a stray dog that never takes its welcome for granted.

"Did you have much trouble getting a berth to Munich?"

Before Kurt could do more than nod, Bruno had interrupted by banging his SS dagger against the dash and blowing saliva bubbles.

"You must stop that, Bruno," chided Ilse. "Show your father how grown-up you can be. Look – see those goats? Your mother used to milk one every morning. We called her Clothespin because she liked to eat them. Isn't that a silly thing for a goat to do? Like you trying to eat your wooden dagger."

As Ilse wove a little story around the adventures of Clothespin the goat and how he used to chase butterflies thinking he could fly, she tried to draw Kurt into the net of innocent intimacy, but he remained aloof, like a boulder that had tumbled down the mountainside and lodged behind the wheel.

This road preoccupied Kurt. Every tree, every pothole seemed intensely familiar, though he had driven it only once eight years ago . . . the grim convoy of Mercedeses with the Führer in the lead. Their surprise destination – Hanslbauer Spa Hotel. The gaping jaws of the hotel clerk as the Führer led his escort, with guns drawn, through the lobby and up the stairs. The puffing red face of SA Chief

Ernst Röhm, twisted in soiled bedsheets as he pleaded his case . . . and afterward.

The troublesome aspects of the SA purge had filtered from Kurt's memory so his most enduring legacy was a prideful sense of having been chosen for a difficult task. He inflated himself with that emotion, conscious of his SS dagger against his thigh, signifying he could be counted upon: *My Honor Is Loyalty*.

Bruno's bleats were an irritant. The scenery invited Kurt's admiration, but he had every reason to avoid the present by dwelling on the past and spinning pipedreams of the future.

Switching gears, he started the BMW on its upward climb.

Nothing could dampen Ilse's spirits as vista upon vista opened up and she felt the mountains wrap round her.

Bruno had fallen asleep.

Ilse stole a sideways glance at her husband, saw him shove back from the wheel to stretch, beginning to relax.

He smiled at her for the first time. "Commandant Graf says Reinhard Heydrich has asked for my record. He's interested in me for something important in Czechoslovakia. That would be much better than the front. After the war, all those top administration jobs will still be open."

"When did this happen? You didn't mention a word!"

Kurt started to reply then clammed up.

"Your letters worried me," prodded Ilse. "You never said what you were doing. Just a few lines scrawled on memo paper."

Kurt looked at Ilse, then at the sleeping Bruno. He worked his mouth like a fish before protesting: "Believe me, when you're dealing with deportations the size of those at Zelbec, every day is a load! Thousands of emigrants, all claiming to be special cases needing special treatment, and only a few of us." He gave Ilse the first real clue to his mood: "After a while natural pity dries up.

Working with subhumans makes me appreciate submachine guns."

They stopped at a Gasthaus with balconies and flowerboxes, cuckoo clocks and crucifixes. The scent of pine and goat cheese, sauerkraut and beeswax, evoked happy memories in Ilse. "I can almost see my grandfather sitting in that corner by the fire smoking his pipe, and my brothers waxing their skis."

When the Schmidts sat down to their evening meal of pig's feet and red cabbage, Bruno kept up his chattery demands, using words only Ilse and Helga could understand. Kurt again turned inward, eyes blank like disks. What was he thinking? Ilse assured herself they would talk when Bruno was asleep.

Kurt could hear Ilse settling Bruno in his cot as he bathed in a round wood tub with water piped from natural hot springs. Using a brush of pig's bristles and a bar of homemade soap, he scrubbed and scoured every taint of the slaughterhouse from his flesh till it was raw. Then he went to work on his hands and nails. He could hear Ilse telling a bedtime story, frequently interrupted by Bruno's shrill gibberish.

Turning up the water, Kurt drowned out the noise, feeling a dangerous buildup of frustration as if steam were passing through his pores to expand inside his chest. When he left Zelbec, he had thought he was ready for this tour of duty. Under Graf's tutelage, he had come to accept the liquidation camp as an unpleasant necessity. Now returned to ordinary life, Zelbec seemed entirely mad, unreal. He felt his will disintegrate.

Instead of telling Bruno another sunny episode in the life of Clothespin the goat as she intended, Ilse stared at puffs of steam curling around Kurt's black SS tunic as it hung on the bathroom doorknob and began a darker tale:

"Once upon a time there was a little goat with fuzzy red hair and a wooden dagger, who would not obey. Whenever anything angered him, he kicked his heels and screamed, despite the pain he knew this caused those who loved him. One day he kicked so hard the crust of the earth cracked open as if it were an egg. Out sprang Black Goat with two strokes of lightning between his silver horns. Stamping his silver hoof, he pointed to a boulder balanced on a mountain peak. 'Every time you're naughty or tell a lie, the stone will spin, and the earth will tremble, and one day it will roll down the slope and crush you.'

"The little goat ran to his mother who was in the churchyard munching the nettles growing between tombstones. 'Save me, Mother!' he pleaded. 'If I'm naughty or tell a lie, the stone will spin, and the earth will tremble, and the rock will roll down and crush me.'

"The mother felt sad to hear this news, but when she tried to comfort her son, the only word that filtered through the nettles was 'Obey!'

"Brandishing the dagger his father had given him, the little goat boasted: 'If you won't help me, I'll fight Black Goat myself. I'm not afraid.' That was the first lie. Black Goat stamped his silver hoof, and the stone began to spin and the earth to tremble. The little goat bleated: 'Oh Mother, save me, save me!'

Stuffing his head under his pillow, Bruno protested: "Stop! I hate that story."

Tucking in his blanket, Ilse apologized: "Mutti's sorry, but it's time to sleep anyway."

Ilse dabbed on perfume she had been saving, then stretched out on the double bed, waiting for Kurt, wearing the nightgown she had sewn for her honeymoon, the sexual hunger which had been building all day now undercut by self-rebuke. Why had she frightened Bruno with that disturbing tale? When she was a child, her paternal grandmother used to hunch over the fire, jabbering about kobolds and witches and monsters and demons as if they were hiding under the bed, causing Ilse's eyes to bulge from their sockets, transforming her dreams into nightmares.

In one story, a father had cut off his daughter's hands because the devil ordered him to. In another, a willful girl was buried alive for disobedience, and when she clawed through the earth, begging for comfort, her mother beat her hands with a rod. Later Ilse found these dreadful tales in a book of German fairy stories, with beautiful but terrifying illustrations. The theme of each, however gruesome, was the same: Obey!

In a cloud of steam, Kurt emerged from the bathroom, his hair wet and spiky, his skin flushed. Without a word, he climbed in bed, lifted Ilse's nightgown, then burrowed hard and hungry, desperate to lose himself between her breasts and thighs, grinding his bony pelvis against her fleshy one and scraping her mouth with his teeth.

Ilse stiffened against the shock of his invasion, made fists of her outrage, struggling against an urge to push him away.

A few agonized thrusts, then Kurt collapsed inside his wife. As he lay panting with his defenses down, he knew now was the time to confide in Ilse, to expose Commandant Graf's morbid logic to the harsh light of another person's reality, to share the burden of Zelbec. Yet even while the temptation was strongest, so was the inhibition. If Kurt questioned Zelbec and refused to obey his orders no matter how repulsive, he was doomed to return till the slaughter of millions was completed and the ovens grew cold. If he acted on faith, he was free. Burying his face in his wife's breasts, Kurt burst into humiliated sobs.

Bewildered, Ilse comforted her husband with her nipple, the same way she still soothed Bruno, running her hands through his hot hair, feeling herself drawn to climax by the greedy pull of his lips.

Kurt's labored breathing gave way to erratic snores. Holding back tears, Ilse drifted into a waking sleep. Some deeply troubled part of herself compulsively continued the story of the little goat, unable either to anesthetize herself with sleep or to stop the flood of words and images.

Tears spring to the eyes of the mother goat when she hears the first lie, and she sees the stone spin, and she feels the earth tremble. Since she's not strong enough to fight Black Goat, she decides to seek protection from the most powerful goat she knows.

Wrapping herself in a cloak the color of earth, she rides on a plow laboriously dragged by four blue-and-white-striped goats with blisters on their hooves. They halt before Big Brown Goat, cross-legged under a black-and-white banner and drinking kirschwasser from a paper cup.

"Help me, Big Brown Goat," clamors the mother. "My child has been threatened by Black Goat, and you are the most powerful goat I know."

"That may very well be," agrees Big Brown Goat. "Unfortunately, I can't help you. You're a reproductive failure. The Reich Committee for the Scientific Investigation of Grave Hereditary Disease and Defects has been looking into your case. They insist Black Goat is only doing your duty. Do you dare question the decision of such men?" He hands the mother a bottle of pink pills. "Take two of these whenever your heart aches, and wash them down with vinegar. You're going to have to toughen up."

When the mother returns, her son is playing with his dagger in the sand. "Mother, I'm hungry," he bleats. "Please give me your teat."

The mother chastises: "You're too old for that. Goats over three shake hooves. You're going to have to toughen up."

The little goat waves his dagger at his mother. "I don't want your milk, you stupid cow. It's sour anyway." That was the second lie, and this time Black Goat didn't have to stamp his silver hoof for the stone to spin and the earth to tremble."

The little goat shrieks: "O Mother, Mother, save me!"

Though tears spill down the mother's cheeks, she isn't wise enough to fight Black Goat so she decides to consult the wisest goat she knows.

Wrapping herself in a cloak like a raven's wing, she allows a raven to carry her by piercing her heart with his claw.

The Black Queen perches on a black peak in apron and headdress of precious jewels, surrounded by crucifixes, and dozens of cuckoo clocks ticking at once.

"Help me, Black Queen," pleads the mother goat. "Your grandchild has been threatened by Black Goat, and you're the wisest goat I know."

"That may very well be," agrees Black Queen, puffing her meerschaum pipe. "Unfortunately, I can't help you. You've always beaten your wings too hard for a woman, and that's something God punishes in His own way."

Opening a pine trunk, she withdraws an urn inscribed BRUNO. "Give this to your son. There's room for more ashes if he's baptized first. As for yourself, you've never learned the difference between pleasing God and pleasing man. Don't come near me till you've absolved yourself with the Sisters of Mercy."

When her daughter reaches out in supplication, the Black Queen beats her hand with a rod. "I'll cut them off if you come closer!"

The mother goat returns to her son.

"Mother, Mother," he bleats. "I've been so lonely. Come and play with me."

"Take this urn of ashes, put a cross on your forehead and contemplate your sins," orders the mother.

Grabbing the urn, the little goat smashes it. Now the stone begins to spin and the earth and sky to tremble. The little goat stretches out his arms. "O Mother, Mother, save me!"

Though sobs catch in the mother's throat, she believes

she isn't pure enough to fight Black Goat so she seeks comfort from the purest goat she knows. Wrapping herself in a cloak of blood, she travels through moldy crypts in search of the Sisters of Mercy. When she calls to them, all she hears is the *drip-drip-drip* of salty water, like tears, and her own voice echoing: "Confess!"

Kneeling at an altar, the mother goat intones: "When I was a child I refused to eat porridge without sugar on it."

Crossing herself, she looks inside herself for an even darker sin: "I had mean thoughts about my sister Hilde *after Hilde snitched thirty pfennigs from our mother's sewing basket!*"

Offering up her blackest sin, the mother goat declares: "I have sent forty-seven children to their certain doom."

The subterranean winds set up such a howl they knock over the altar, revealing a crystal chalice filled with tears.

"Now I have holy water to baptize my son."

When the mother goat returns, the little goat is still playing in the sand.

"Look what mother has! Holy water to baptize you."

The little goat brandishes his wooden dagger, first at his mother and then at Black Goat, leaning against the boulder, playing his flute. "I don't want to die. I hate you both," he shrieks, and that is the third and most terrible lie. Ravens' wings blot out the sun. The stone spins. The earth trembles. Streams moan, while pines wrap themselves in their limbs.

The little goat pleads: "O Mother, Mother, save me!"

A bolt of green lightning strikes the spinning stone like a hammer cracking a skull. As the mother gazes up in horror, half the mountain falls away and the stone rolls, end over over, toward the little goat. . . .

Before dawn, the Schmidts hiked up Sulphur Peak, named for hot springs that burst forth in abundance, creating meadows of unnatural beauty. Their destination was a cave on the western slope, where they would spend the night. Ilse and Kurt zigzagged upward, with Bruno strapped to his father's back, the gravel crunching under their boots as the tangy pines knotted darkly around them.

Gazing up their scaly trunks to a patch of night sky, Kurt recited one of his father's poems:

> "The pine tree stared into the eye of God,
>   Its green hair tangled in a net of stars,
>   A prisoner of its destiny. . . ."

Kurt, too, considered himself a prisoner of destiny. He had made up his mind to take the path fate had shown him.

From the cool mystery of the forest, they emerged onto sun-baked rock. Now as they ascended, the snowcapped peaks encircled them, while below stretched the valley with shining pools like silver coins.

Before crossing the glacier, Kurt released his boisterous son but insisted they rope up. Patiently he demonstrated the correct knots, but they were far beyond Bruno's understanding, and he was too excited to watch. As they tramped over the glacier, they entered a garden of awesome wind sculptures – mostly blue or green, some a sulphurous yellow. At the first crevasse, Bruno pulled on his rope. "See down. See!"

Kurt clasped his hand, allowing him to peer far down into its perilous blue-green throat, rimmed with dripping icicles like shark's teeth . . . knowing he had only to release his grip.

With a grunt Kurt set his son's feet back on the ice. Turning frisky, Bruno leapt over a crack, shouting: "Goat! Goat!" Kurt severely yanked his rope, as if pulling himself from a brink. "Even a glacier with a beaten track must be respected."

This sudden scolding caused Bruno to cry. Kurt laid his hand upon his son's red head, as if in benediction, yet his voice was stern. "The most important thing a German must learn is to *obey*."

Ilse resisted interfering between father and son, though she sensed a chilling counterpoint to the flawless beauty of the day. As she admired an ice lake with the frenzied waves frozen at the height of a storm, she translated her own inner turbulence into morbid reality by recalling her father's death twenty years ago on a neighboring mountain.

Later, while Bruno napped, Ilse told Kurt the story in vivid detail:

"Two Oxford students insisted on climbing, though everyone warned them of avalanches. My father spotted their flares and organized a rescue party. Though he allowed me to go along, he wouldn't let me climb the last slope. I watched from the base camp as he and another man from the village chopped footholds in the glacier, then mounted the white wall into the sun. They made contact and signaled. No injuries, just two adventurers scared as treed cats. I watched them descend, with the students roped between them. It grew dark. An electrical storm was crackling and sizzling around them. A bolt of green lightning struck just above. I can still hear that sound, like a hammer cracking open a skull. Half the mountain fell away."

Continuing over a boulder-strewn moraine, the Schmidts veered upward with Bruno again riding his father's shoulders. On a neighboring peak, they spotted hikers roped in a vivid caterpillar.

"Before the war, this mountain would've been crawling with them," observed Ilse.

"Everyone's in Russia. No one's left to climb," growled Kurt.

From his tone, Ilse knew he wished he were with them, and her own moodiness deepened.

After half an hour's labor, they reached a ridge that ran a mile along the top of the world before soaring up in a jagged dinosaur spine, with a dizzying drop of a thousand feet. Though the sun was hot, the wind carried an edgy chill. Donning windbreakers, Ilse and Kurt roped up again.

Mist swirled from rock pockets, blotting out the dazzling panorama. Ilse fastened her hood, waiting for the sky to clear. Instead the fog grew more opaque till large wet flakes obliterated Kurt two yards ahead. Anxiously Ilse checked to see how Bruno was taking this change in his adventure. She was relieved to glimpse him waving through a gap in the cloud.

Wet snowflakes clung to Ilse's face like a blindfold, reducing her world to puddles of rock and the sound of tramping feet. Bruno began to whimper then to cry with hysteria. Catching his panic, Ilse wondered if he had soiled himself. Though more than three, he would never tell her. Why should he learn with Helga and her as his servants? Though not wishing to draw Bruno's disgrace to his father's attention, she was on the verge of calling out when Kurt began to play his flute, the Pied Piper luring her on with poignant notes like silver beads strung on a silken cord, more real to her than the one encircling her waist and turning the hike into something magical. As the sounds trembled then ceased, Kurt flung down a sad yodel that ululated through the valley, peopling it with his own voice, sending a shiver through her.

Again the weather shifted. The fog brightened as a yellow pinwheel burnt through, melting the ice from Ilse's eyelashes. Erased by a giant hand, the mist disappeared. Kurt, with Bruno on his back, stood under a stained-glass sky in blinding light. He beckoned. Before them was a meadow of unnatural beauty, thick with purple and gold flowers, its air clamorous with the rush of water.

"It's paradise," murmured Kurt.

Releasing Bruno, he untied their rope and began to strip. Bruno imitated him. Ilse did the same.

Leaving footprints in the lush and dewy grass, they wandered around a promontory to a grotto where water gushed from a glacier into rock bowls. The first two were silty blue with cold. The third was fed by a sulphur spring. Moving from hot to cold, they bathed till their bodies were neutralized against change of temperature.

Feeling as if he were wearing an invisible raiment of light, Kurt proclaimed: "My parents searched all their lives for this. We Germans aren't afraid of our natures. We aren't afraid to open ourselves to elemental forces. Our ancestors celebrated summer solstice by capturing the sun with their naked bodies. This is part of the heritage our Führer has restored to us. He has promised us this perfection, this Eden."

Still naked, Kurt checked the cave, found it habitable, and laid out their sleeping bags. Ilse unpacked the lunch, unexpectedly finding Kurt's SS dagger tucked in a pocket.

Unsheathing it, she instructed Bruno: "When you've outgrown your wooden one, this is what you'll have. See the writing on the blade? *My Honor Is Loyalty*. That means even grown-ups have to do what they're told."

Ravenous, they devoured goat cheese, bread, dried fruit and blood sausage. Kurt again turned to his flute, piping a melody more melancholy than before.

Noticing something glinting in the grass, Ilse picked it up. A miniature of the Virgin Mary. She showed it to Kurt, then to Bruno. "In fall, when shepherds bring down their herds from the upper meadows, they decorate the horns of the bulls with ornaments and pictures of saints." She recalled her thrill as a child when the herd passed her in a thundering golden rush, with the lead bull wearing a decorated fir between his horns, as tall as himself.

"Remember the Julfest tree with all the silver balls and the candles?" she coaxed Bruno. "Remember the solstice bonfire and how excited you were?"

No light of recognition kindled in his eyes as he played with his father's SS dagger, trying to yank it from its scabbard. Frustrated, Ilse took it from him, then laid it on the rock where it couldn't be forgotten. She repacked the food into its knapsack.

Ilse turned to see what her son was up to. She asked

Kurt, still playing his flute: "Where's Bruno?" Both turned. Both spotted him at the same time, crawling from the cave. Ilse gasped. He was smeared, head to toe, with excrement!

Proudly waving his father's dagger, he stammered: "Dag-dag."

"Bruno!" Ilse ran toward him, caught his leg as he squiggled into the cave. He had soiled both Kurt's sleeping bag and her own, laid side by side, before smearing himself. As she pulled Bruno outside, the day's dark undercurrent seemed to have erupted through the shiny surface. Walloping her son, Ilse screamed: "How could you do such a thing? Why didn't you tell me? You swine! Even animals don't foul their nests."

As Ilse broke into hysteria, Kurt padded up behind her, caught Bruno by the hand, then gripped her arm so tightly she let go. "I'll look after the boy," he promised.

His voice was so compassionate even Bruno allowed his sticky fingers to be peeled from his father's SS dagger and then to be meekly led to the grotto.

Composing herself, Ilse rolled the sleeping bags to be washed and aired, and scrubbed her hands in hot water. Then she dressed, combed and replaited her hair, grateful to Kurt for sparing her the worst of the crisis. As she coiled her braids about her ears, she admitted: Something would have to be done about Bruno. Dr. Zuckmayer had strongly hinted the boy needed more attention than Ilse could give. Perhaps Erich's wife, or one of her sisters, might take him for a summer in the mountains, where he could develop at his own pace until he caught up.

As Ilse returned her comb to her pocket, her hand closed on something cold and smooth. Absently, she withdrew it: a vial of holy water. Staring at it, she asked herself: Why did I bring that? At the same moment she remembered: Kurt had not put Bruno's sleeping bag inside the cave. It lay by the mouth as tightly rolled as a new leaf.

The grotto was overhung by a thick sulphurous mist.

Stunned, Ilse walked toward it, her hand pressed against her chest.

She rounded the promontory.

Kurt stood to his waist in steamy water, swirled with rust-red. He was scrubbing blood from his hands and his SS dagger. Stretched on a rock lay her son Bruno.

Screaming, Ilse ran toward him. Kurt caught her by the wrists. Staring fiercely into her eyes, he rebuked: "You knew it had to be done." He offered the comfort she spoke to mothers whose babies were condemned by the disinfection program: "The Reich has acted mercifully to relieve you of this burden."

FIVE

Prague

May 1942

W ITH ITS seven graceful spans across the Vltava river, its cupolas and spires, Prague was one of Wolfgang von Friedrich's favourite cities. Dressed in overalls and workman's cap and carrying lunch in a wrinkled brown bag, Wolf strolled through the Gothic watchtower onto the St. Charles bridge. A shimmering haze blurred flowering trees and weathered stones, enhancing the timeless beauty of the Czech capital so it looked like an old and delicate painting.

Office workers spilled onto the pedestrian bridge for their noon break, along with a mix of laborers from the waterfront. Wolf noted the burly slouch that seemed to go with the cap and overalls, and imitated it with adaptive skill as he meandered past iron lamps and baroque statues to the central arch where Christ hung from a stone cross. Leaning against the bridge rail, he surveyed Little Town, dominated by Hradcany castle, more than one thousand years old, once the seat of Bohemian kings and now the office of Reich Protector Reinhard Heydrich.

As the hands on the watchtower slid to five then ten past noon, Wolf's gaze narrowed as he searched each approaching figure for the familiar silhouette and gait of Raymon Arno. To avoid suspicion, he opened his brown bag and chewed on a stale roll, though food was the last thing he wanted.

At 12:35 two women in print dresses gave way to a

slight, olive-skinned figure in mended jacket with cap pulled over shaved head. Turning his back to allow Raymon to approach him as if by surprise, Wolf again focused on Hradcany castle with its black-and-white SS flag.

"Friend!" Raymon slapped Wolf on the back, then joined him at the rail. "I thought I recognized you."

With his head shaved as well as his mustache, and tauter lines shaping mouth and eyes, Raymon closely resembled the doctored photo on the forged paper buried in one of Wolf's bread rolls.

They clasped hands, two good friends meeting by chance.

Eyes as hard as peach pits, Raymon announced: "I'm ready."

Speaking through slit lips to avoid being detected by spies trained as lip-readers, Wolf advised: "The papers and ten thousand korunas are in a bread roll. You're Otto Weiss, a German-born bargeman. You'll travel downstream till the heat cools."

"Good."

Holding onto his lunch bag, Wolf insisted: "I still prefer the other plan. I've made up a separate set of papers for it."

"Shit on you! Then you've wasted your time," exploded Raymon. "Do you dare bring that up again?"

Exaggerating the stiffened lips to urge Raymon to caution, Wolf argued: "Not again. I've never wavered."

"Nor have I. It's impossible. You don't understand what's needed for this job. I'm a true revolutionary, by class and motive. I *hate*!"

"You also paint. You have genius, Raymon, and I don't use that word lightly."

Raymon gave a strangled laugh. "I'm a genius who no longer wants to paint. Can't you get that through your skull? I could cover this bridge with pretty bourgeois images in a weekend, but I no longer have anything to say with my brushes. Throwing a bomb – that's what I want to do with my hands. If I could spare the time, I'd burn all my paintings and save the Nazis the bother. They are trash."

"I know the plan as well as you. I know the contacts even better," persisted Wolf. "I have more choices if things go wrong. I can throw a bomb as well as you."

Raymon snorted. "No doubt, but look at you. Your overalls are dirty because you've rubbed mud into them, but they don't stink. You wear your cap as if you were slumming at a costume ball. No!" He snarled the worst insult he could think of: "You wear revolution like Leo Warner. Some Communist, off in Hollywood with starlets on his lap. He hung slogans across a stage and claimed to have radicalized me. Having my sister hounded to death and my family hunted because we're gypsies did that job."

"You aren't the only one who suffered the loss, Raymon. What happened to Renate and Christian wasn't a crime against one race or class. It was a crime against humanity. I loved them too."

Raymon rubbed his hand over his bullet head. "Give me my papers. Do you think I've come to argue morality in the middle of the Vltava river while the madman I'm after signs death notices? If you won't give me my papers, I swear I'll punch you out, then accuse you of stealing them."

The intensity of the argument, no matter how silent, was in danger of attracting attention. Stepping back, Wolf gestured grandly toward shore. "A lovely day, isn't it?" he asked sarcastically, yet with an appropriate look of bland enjoyment on his face. "You must be hungry, my friend. Would you like a lunch roll?"

Offering Raymon the brown bag, he mocked: "Try the one with the Russian caviar. Stalin gave me the recipe. I'm sorry I forgot the vodka. Don't choke on the ten thousand korunas."

With the papers in his hands, Raymon relaxed against the stone wall, chewing as if he were actually hungry. He confided: "It isn't as an artist I'm ruined, Wolf. It's as a human being. I *do* hate. I'm consumed with it. I haven't the skill to see the overall picture the way you do. You're more valuable than I, even in war."

"Another general in the family, sending his troops off to battle," retorted Wolf bitterly.

"I don't mind dying," assured Raymon as he stared at the SS flag on Hradcany castle. "I'm still enraged at Christian. Not because he killed himself, but because he didn't take some bastard with him."

Stuffing the roll into a battered satchel, Raymon clasped Wolf's hand. "Friend!"

The two men embraced. "You're a revolutionary in your guts," Raymon relented, "but you'd make a lousy bargeman."

"Good luck."

Three hours after his meeting with Raymon, Wolf sped along the west bank of the Vltava in his Alfa Romeo, dressed in tweeds like a gentleman out for a Sunday drive circa 1920. As he turned left up a steep hill, three linked red trolleys rattled down one side of a double silver track, their electrical arms sparking through a grid of cables. Wolf imagined Raymon pacing them on his bicycle, completely exposed, entirely vulnerable as a fleet of SS men on motorcycles pursued him full throttle. It wasn't good luck he should have wished Raymon in the shadow of the crucified Christ, but a miracle.

The three-way hairpin turn was exactly as Raymon had drawn it – one of the advantages of wasting a master draftsman on an assassination. Set back from the street was the house with the overgrown garden that created a two-way blind, contained by an iron fence with ten stone pillars. As Wolf completed his turn, he saw No. 14 stop where the residents of the suburb of Holesovice waited for trams that took them into the heart of Prague. Two middle-aged women chatted, while a man lounged, foot against a fence post, smoking. Across the street was the phone booth from which Raymon had three times called

Wolf, and the tobacco kiosk where he had once sought change. Under a red sign, OUT OF STOCK, the proprietor read his newspaper.

Tomorrow morning at 9:30, when the green Mercedes belonging to SS Lieutenant-General Reinhard Heydrich raced down this hill to Prague, his chauffeur would have to brake almost to a halt to negotiate the blind turn. For five seconds, Heydrich would be an open target for Raymon Arno and Lubos Valkova, an exiled Czech trained as an assassin in Britain. Lubos planned to step into the path of the Mercedes, drop the raincoat concealing his Sten gun, and blast the Reich Protector. Around the corner, Raymon, serving as backup, would lob into the car a British-made Mills bomb set to detonate on impact. Then he would run for the bicycle he had hidden farther downhill, and pump the mile to the river, while Lubos escaped by bicycle on a different route. Both had a list of places where they could shelter, including Kubchick's Toy Shop where Carmel had unknowingly encountered Frau Fuchs. If all went well, each would be on the river by midnight of the following day. Otherwise, they would hide in the crypt of the Czech Orthodox church on Ressel Street.

Wolf accelerated up the hill through the sleepy suburb of Holesovice, soon to become notorious. On this long slope, two other accomplices would be stationed at three-hundred-yard intervals to warn the assassins of the approach of the green Mercedes by flashing hand mirrors into the sun. In practice, this had provided Lubos with thirty seconds' warning so he could remain screened till the last second.

Hand mirrors! What if it rained? The whole scheme fell apart in Wolf's head, each absurd piece more fragile and unlikely than the next. He hadn't wanted to approve it, but Raymon and Lubos had insisted.

As Wolf left Holesovice on the trip to Panenske Brezany where Heydrich had his villa, every scene was so familiar from photographs and drawings that he felt as if he were the daily commuter. That white sign across the street said PRAGUE TWO KILOMETERS on its reverse side; the red brick cottage with a flock of geese belonged to a resistance family surnamed Sojchik.

Turning onto an avenue of chestnuts fluffy with white blossoms that swayed in a gentle breeze, Wolf recalled one of the grimmer blueprints submitted by the assassins: to decapitate the Reich Protector in his open car by stringing invisible wire between two trunks. That plan had been discarded because it couldn't be tested. Another called for booby-trapping Heydrich's Mercedes, but that required access the conspirators didn't have. A third had them blow up Heydrich's saloon car attached to the Prague-Berlin Express, but that involved too much advance information about his schedule. Better to turn a man's ingrained habits against him than count on special circumstances.

Wolf made a sharp right through Libeznice, with its cobbled streets and stately church. Though the plot had been in the active planning stage since December when Lubos parachuted in from a British plane, final arrangements had been made in four days. That was after Heydrich had phoned Wolf to urge him to visit Panenske Brezany on May 26 to discuss "a personal matter of some delicacy. Since you've turned down my friendly invitations, now I'm summoning you. This is your last chance to see me in splendor. I'm flying to Berlin the next morning for a conference with the Führer." He could not resist boasting to the friend of his adolescence: "It's confidential, but the Führer is posting me to France to oversee the Vichy government and to crush the Resistance. I'm leaving immediately after the conference. I'll send for Lina and the children when I'm settled."

So there it was: May 27, the last possible date for Operation Anthropoid.

At the village of Predbon, Wolf left the tarmac for a dusty narrow road through rolling country. As he admired mustard fields against the starkness of pines, duck ponds, glowing orchards of apple and pear blossoms, women in bright kerchiefs hoeing, he brooded that these would be the images Reinhard would take to his grave. Though Wolf had smothered such sentiments with details of the plot and concern for Raymon, he acknowledged . . . a man's life after all.

Wolf sorted through the reasons why this assassination must be.

As a brilliant technocrat, Heydrich was Hitler's most dangerous inheritor in a court of fools and deviates. At thirty-eight, he controlled the Reich's security system. In seven months he had turned Czechoslovakia from a hostile territory into a model Reich state, securing an armament industry second only to the Ruhr. This he had accomplished through selective terror in which all deemed enemies were ruthlessly punished, and by seduction of the Czech worker through incentives. So startling was his success, the Czech government-in-exile, headed by Eduard Benes, had endorsed the assassination partly in expectation that harsh reprisals would end the "sweetheart" arrangement between occupied Czechoslovakia and the Reich.

Aware of how horrendous those reprisals might be, the local Czech Resistance had pleaded through Wolf, code name Silver, to repeal the assassination order, but on May 13 a decision had been returned: Operation Anthropoid, as scheduled.

The drive from Prague to Panenske Brezany took half an hour, as Raymon predicted. Heydrich's impressive white chateau set in dense forest was wrapped in a ten-foot wall roofed by red tiles. A detachment of security police, billeted in the village, mounted permanent guard – the reason Raymon and Lubos had never considered ambushing Heydrich here.

Slowing his Alfa for the gate, Wolf saluted the sergeant. "I have a four-o'clock appointment with the Reich Protector."

Checking Wolf's identification against his visitor's book, the sergeant waved him through.

As Wolf parked beside Heydrich's dark-green Mercedes, then strolled across well-groomed lawns, he speculated on what Heydrich's "personal matter of some delicacy" might be. Something to do with Salon Kitty? Surely a phone call would cover that. By now they had enough code words to discuss the operation of Heydrich's brothel at the Führer's birthday party without anyone being the wiser.

So engrossed was Wolf that he didn't hear Heydrich call. The Czech maid who answered the door pointed out the Reich Protector under a magnolia tree, his tunic off, his tie undone.

Heydrich's hand was raised, but not in salute. "Over here," he waved, grinning. He clasped Wolf's hand as warmly as Raymon had. "I thought I'd better enjoy myself since this is my last day."

Wolf felt his face drain. Then he realized Heydrich was referring only to his transfer to France. Forcing a smile, he complimented the Reich Protector on his new home. "At last you have a residence reflecting your rank. Now Göring and Goebbels will have to add extra turrets."

Heydrich chortled. "This was requisitioned from a Jewish sugar baron with pretensions. At first Lina complained bitterly about being tucked away out here, but now she loves it. You'd be amazed the change decadence has made in my habits. Now I bring work home like other domesticated husbands."

He escorted Wolf around the grounds, past bushes sculpted into swastikas, even naming a few flowering shrubs. "Nature bored me till I discovered you could put a ten-foot frame around it and add a dozen gardeners. These flower beds might even pass muster with Himmler." With a braying laugh, he related: "Knowing our fussy Reichsführer's passion for gardening, Lina spent several days on her hands and knees weeding our yard at Fehmarn for his first visit. At last she announced it weed-free, and even invited our neighbors in to inspect. Of course, Himmler hadn't stepped from his car before he was pointing to a shoot three inches high: 'That will have to come out!' "

After showing Wolf the lily ponds with a Japanese bridge and the white gazebo spattered with plum blossoms, Heydrich fastened his collar and tightened his tie. "Perhaps we'd better go inside to talk. I don't like being spied on by the groundsmen."

He ushered Wolf into an elegant office paneled in rosewood.

"Your sugar baron had a good eye for antiques."

"That cabinet you're looking at is mine, purchased at auction. I've taken a passionate interest in local history, even to the point of devouring novels on St. Wenceslas. It's the relationship of Bohemia to the German empire that especially interests me – a modern problem." Opening a refrigerator concealed behind rosewood, he brandished a bottle of wine. "Though I know what a snob you are, I'll risk this champagne from Bratislava. It's quite potable. I've been experimenting with a view to export."

Serving the champagne in two fine Bohemian goblets, Heydrich confirmed: "I've really felt at home here. Would it ruin your image of me to know I've even allowed myself to be consulted in the hanging of pictures and drapes?"

Wolf flicked a piece of cork from his champagne. "When you learn to serve champagne without 'flies' in it, I'll believe in radical change. I can be as fussy about things like that as Himmler with his dandelions." He mimicked: "This will have to come out."

Laughing, Heydrich raised his glass. "Prosit!"

To which Wolf contributed the Czech equivalent: "Na zdravil."

Once behind his desk, Heydrich came directly to the point. "As I hinted, I want you to do me a personal favor, Wolfgang. The kind only you have the background and sensitivity to understand. It's my pedigree again. This time it's Himmler in league with Martin Bormann, who's spreading rumors. Since Bormann became Hitler's secretary, no cruder boor or worse hypocrite exists. He claims to have a secret file proving conclusively I have Jewish blood. We both know it has to be a forgery, but I want you to get your hands on it and destroy it. *How* is up to you, though I suggest Salon Kitty might be useful. Despite his puritan airs in front of Hitler, Bormann's randier than a bull in heat. And brutal."

"I know his reputation. Some of our girls have come across him. I'll do my best."

"Really?" Heydrich slammed down his glass so vigorously it overflowed on his desk blotter. "Your best? That would be a change." He berated Wolf with a bitterness that suggested he'd been storing up a long time. "You've given so little service for my patronage, I've had to ask if you're a dilettante incapable of commitment, or if it's your loyalty I must question."

Deadpan, Wolf allowed: "I warned you I had no taste for causes, but you said you didn't care."

"I don't. If the person makes up for lack of faith with ambition, or brilliance, or cunning, or hard work, or brutality. You haven't shown much of anything." Leaning back, Heydrich studied Wolf through slit eyes. "If you manage to please me on this personal errand, we may still find a use for each other. Czechoslovakia has been a test case for me. I see its reclamation in two stages. The first – political integration – I've already accomplished. Now I wish to oversee its cultural integration by blending the best the Czechs have to offer with Germanization. That's where you may come in. As cultural director. Think of it! Your own little fiefdom to play with, like your family of old. On weekends, you can even reinstitute The Hunt."

It was clear from Heydrich's jubilant tone that he was sure he'd fixed on a temptation Wolf could not resist. While Wolf was framing his answer, a tap on the door and a woman's voice interrupted them. "It's Silke's bedtime."

In the past Heydrich would have responded with impatience. Now he welcomed his wife, Lina, a well-bred blond about six months pregnant, carrying a chubby little girl.

"You see? I *have* been overtaken by domestic bliss," enthused Heydrich as he affectionately gave his daughter her good-night kiss.

Frau Heydrich's pretty features, once marred by a permanent scowl, also seemed softer, more feminine. As the door closed behind them, Wolf admitted: "Perhaps you've changed a few of your spots, Reinhard. What's made the difference?"

"The chance to do something positive," rejoiced Heydrich. "With the Gestapo I'm always cleaning up someone else's mess. Here I've formulated my own policies and built a model satellite in which all but the soreheads are happy. The last seven months have been the most satisfying of my life, except perhaps when I was a naive young man in the navy and saw myself as next year's admiral. I can't tell you what a tonic they've been. I've even managed to convince the Führer the Czechs may be worth saving. I don't want my work here ruined, and while I'm no longer sure how far I can trust you personally, Wolf, suspicion keeps me on my toes. I know I can trust your good taste." He poured more champagne. "Tonight Lina and I are going to a chamber music concert at Valdstein Palace. Why don't you join us to get the feel of this place?"

This was a possibility for which Wolf had rehearsed.

"I'm sorry, Reinhard. Your suggestion fascinates me and I appreciate the invitation, but I'm on a tight schedule."

"You can fly back to Berlin with me tomorrow. I'm taking my own plane. We'll have a chance to talk. Klein, my chauffeur, can return your car."

"But it's Munich where I'm headed."

"Why not cancel? There's my phone."

"Not that easy . . ."

Heydrich sniffed his champagne. "Have you poisoned me? Is that why you're so anxious to leave?"

Wryly, Wolf reminded him: "The cork flies and the bad

vintage are yours. If anything's in danger of being murdered, it's my taste buds."

"Good." Heydrich's blue eyes were steely. "Because if ever you get any ideas about using our friendship to liquidate me, I urge you not to bother. There's already a lineup. Not my Czechs, of course. Aliens. The last one was a Russian agent picked up in March. He was passported as a German musician, but his too-new trumpet case contained a gun with silencer and telescopic sights. Perhaps the cello player at the concert tonight has my number. Is that why you don't want to go?"

"Your fame is spreading, Reinhard," parried Wolf.

"Unfortunately. I no longer have Himmler to hide behind. But as a son of Germania, I believe in fate, not luck. When time runs out, well, it runs out. It wasn't jumping her horse that my mother broke her leg. It was in her larder reaching for a wheel of cheese."

Heydrich checked his watch. "Are you absolutely sure you can't stay over? We can have an early-morning joust at Vladislav Hall before the flight."

"Impossible, another time . . ."

Sighing, Heydrich corked the champagne. "I admit I'd bypass the evening too if I could, but the Bonnhardt Quartet from Halle is playing a work by my father. A piano quintet. Since my mother stopped speaking to me when I arrested the Bishop of Meissen, I don't want to offend my father's ghost as well."

Wolf allowed silence to gather between them, an invitation to dismissal. Reinhard stood up. Wolf did the same. As he edged toward the door, Reinhard suggested: "Since you won't join me for the concert, perhaps you'll play a duet with me? I have my own music room attached to my office."

Reluctantly Wolf followed Heydrich into a soundproof cubicle of mirrors containing two easy chairs, a grand piano, a violin and a podium.

"You'll find a Mozart sonata on the rack." Tucking the violin under his chin, Heydrich began to play. Seating himself, Wolf joined in. Though technically rusty, Wolf's skillful touch and instinctive feeling for the music remained. They played for over an hour, more Mozart, some Haydn and a little Brahms, the way they used to practise at Heydrich's father's conservatory in Halle.

"Let's try the Toselli 'Serenade,'" suggested Reinhard.

Though surprised by such a sentimental choice, Wolf played his part. Afterward Reinhard confessed: "When I was in the navy, a Polish captain used to call me out of bed night after night to serenade him with this. After he puked on the floor, he'd say: 'Well, heavenly Jew, you've given me peace.' Then he'd fall asleep. I've never been able to listen to that music again. Now you've given *me* peace."

Returning his violin to its case, Heydrich murmured almost as an afterthought: "You know, Wolf, sometimes I get very depressed bumping people off." Then he reached under the piano and withdrew a Luger. Taking deliberate aim at his own reflection, he shot himself through the heart. The little room shattered. Silver shards rained down around both men so it seemed a miracle neither was cut.

Twirling the gun on his finger, Heydrich defiantly quoted four lines from his father's opera, *Amen*:

> "Yes, the world is a barrel organ
> Played by God Himself.
> We must all dance to the tune
> That just happens to be on the roll."

He saw Wolf to the door. "The file," he snapped. "Get that file from Bormann."

A mile away from Heydrich's estate, Wolf stopped and lit a cigarette to calm his nerves, knowing how it felt to deliver a Judas kiss. Then he pointed his car toward the German border and shot it like a gun.

SIX

*M*AY *27, 1942. 9:30 a.m.* Major Kurt Schmidt sits in an arbor on the estate of Reich Protector Reinhard Heydrich, his briefcase at hand. Twenty yards away he can see the Reich Protector in a white wicker chair, his daughter Silke on his lap. Heydrich's sons, Klaus and Heider, have their school work spread on a picnic table under the magnolia tree, while his wife, Lina, serves coffee.

A Czech maid shyly brings a cup to Kurt. Dropping a curtsy, she intones: "The Reich Protector wishes you to know his trip to Berlin will be delayed for family reasons."

Although they are half an hour late, Kurt is entranced at this rare opportunity to observe the Reich Protector with his family, and instinctively knows he'll get the benefit with increased cordiality. Though he can't hear the conversation, the charming tableau speaks for itself. Impressed by her powerful daddy's uniform, Silke has managed to pull off a silver swastika button. Heider is sent for thread, which Frau Heydrich uses to sew it on again.

Kurt imagines himself in such a setting, the white chateau, the blossoming trees, little Ursula and other babies as yet unborn. A sour taste seeps into his mouth. Though Ilse has been under sedation much of the time since the death of their son four weeks ago, Dr. Zuckmayer insists she's a hardy SS woman who'll come to understand that Kurt acted in everyone's best interests, and especially the boy's.

Sucking in the perfumed air of the Heydrich estate, Kurt knows it's been worth it. He would do it again, and far worse, to rid himself of Zelbec.

10:00 a.m. Reich Protector Heydrich dons his black SS tunic, newly sewn, and his peaked cap with the death's-head emblem. Picking up his briefcase, he kisses his daughter and his wife, shakes hands with his two sons. Then he lopes across the lawn toward Kurt, his gait becoming more military. "Glad you could make this trip, Major Schmidt. I think you'll find it interesting."

As the two officers stride toward the parking lot, Heydrich commiserates: "I know you've had to perform hard tasks, but in France you'll enjoy the positive work that's possible only under authoritarian government."

Heydrich's chauffeur, a six-foot-seven bruiser with meaty hands and pugilistic face, stands with one foot on the running board of the forest-green Mercedes. Grinding out his cigarette, he salutes, his chest of medals flashing in the sunlight.

Touching his own array, to which a silver bar and the Iron Cross first class has been added, Heydrich acknowledges: "Corporal Klein and I are all decked out today. A guard of honor is greeting us at the airport."

Klein climbs into the driver's seat of the lovingly polished Mercedes, which Kurt identifies as a twelve-cylinder, three-and-a-half-liter model, costing fifty thousand marks. Ushering Kurt into the back, Heydrich throws his briefcase in front and sits beside him.

"Hope you don't mind a little wind, Major Schmidt. Klein and I never put up the hood even when it rains. That's how we keep our heads cool, eh, Klein?" Winding up the side windows, he urges the others to do the same. "At least until we get outside the grounds. It impresses my security guards, though what they think a window will do against a bomb, I haven't any idea." He gestures contemptuously toward the fortified gate. "Himmler and the other party grandpas think this sets a good example, but my Czechs would never harm me."

10:05 a.m. Klein turns onto a narrow, unpaved road through rolling country, traveling at a cautious speed to keep the dust down. Watching the sturdy peasant women working the fields, Heydrich opines: "The Czechs are sensible people once you get to know them. My first decision was to crush opposition more ruthlessly than my predecessors but to avoid those useless, provocative acts that arouse the ire of captive peoples. I'm talking here about Germanizing the names of Czech towns and forcing everyone to drive on the right side of the road. Why rub the fur of the cat the wrong way if you want it to purr? I decided instead to appeal to my Czechs through their stomachs. By declaring war on the black marketeers, I made sure every worker felt each pig held back by a farmer meant one less slice of ham on his own plate. Then I hung the German racketeers as well as the Czech ones. The first German butcher whose feet left the ground proved my case. At the same time I made goodwill visits to factories, improved pensions, wrote sympathy letters to war widows, stopped the flood of black market geese to Berlin and provided incentive holidays at luxury spas. After a weekend at one of my hotels, comrades came home and turned each other in! The cat now purrs and rubs against me so affectionately. I intend to deliver a Czech unit for the eastern front. It's more than a symbolic gesture. When the Führer understands this country can be reclaimed as a decent province, you of all people will understand what that saves in terms of liquidations. I set my sights on political enemies more than racial ones. The best blood must be the first to go if it's opposed to us. That's how we'll work in France. Trust me. You'll find the work unprecedented."

10:15 a.m. At the village of Predbon, Klein accelerates onto the tarmac. Reaching over the front seat, Heydrich rifles through his briefcase. "I want to recheck some figures in my report. Enjoy the scenery. You can study this while I'm flying us to Berlin."

Klein makes a sharp right turn at a cobbled town called Libeznice then sails onto an avenue of chestnuts so straight it looks as if it were laid out by an architect – a further invitation to speed. Minutes later they wheel onto a two-lane highway.

To the right Kurt glimpses Prague in a misty valley cut through by the Vltava river. A suburb identifies itself as Holesovice. Klein slows for a milk cart, then swerves around a dog sunning itself on the road.

10:28 a.m. They dip down the hill, in rapid descent to the Vltava river. Kurt idly watches a double tram on silver tracks disappear around a corner. A sudden flash from the roadside attracts his attention. Turning, he notices a workman wheel away his bike, and assumes the light came from his reflector.

Ahead is a tram stop where a lone woman waits with a shopping bag. As Klein begins to brake for the blind turn, Kurt braces himself so as not to fall indecorously against Heydrich, still absorbed in his report.

A man steps around the corner into the path of the Mercedes. He drops his raincoat and raises something hard and metallic to his shoulder. As Kurt instinctively reaches for his Luger, the man fires. Nothing happens. The Sten gun has jammed. Mouth agape, the assassin jumps back on the curb as the heavy Mercedes swerves around the corner.

Both Kurt and Heydrich have their revolvers drawn as Klein, cursing, slams on the brakes. It's a foolish mistake. A second man is running uphill toward the Mercedes, a heavy object in his right hand. In the long second before he lobs it, Klein stares into his hate-filled eyes and knows this one isn't going to miss.

The bomb lands in the front seat as a second tram bustles uphill on the left. It explodes in a belch of orange. Klein smothers it with his enormous body. Kurt is forced back as if by an invisible hand against the upholstery while simultaneously the windows of the tram shower glass. Klein's tunic, ripped from his ruined body, dangles like a black flag over the tram wires. The car bucks once, twice, then pitches to a stop.

Kurt and Heydrich bolt through the gaping side of the green Mercedes as screaming spectators mill. The woman who had been waiting for the trolley falls to the pavement, her skirt over her head, as if not seeing might protect her, while passengers pour from doors and windows.

Impelled by blind rage, Kurt pursues the bomb thrower downhill as Heydrich takes off after assassin No. 1. A second tram draws up behind the first. Darting between the two, the bomber shouts: "Out of my way! Have guts. This is a revolution."

"My Czechs" have difficulty sorting out what's happening and whose side they're on. One man shakes his walking stick at both pursued and pursuer. While the bomber pulls a bicycle from the bushes, Kurt squeezes off two bullets, but his leg is gushing blood and he can't catch up.

A woman with a scrub bucket throws her sudsy water at the biker, scolding: "Fool! You'll get us all killed." That slows him down enough for Kurt to take another good shot. He thinks he wounds him through the shoulder, but can't see for blood gushing into his eyes. Too late the woman throws her bucket.

The biker is now out of range, pumping toward the Vltava. Stumbling back up the hill where he can hear pistol fire, Kurt finds Heydrich behind a stone post, exchanging shots with assassin No. 1 behind a tram car, while spectators gape from poles and shrubs and windows. Though Heydrich's hand continues to jerk convulsively, no bullets shoot from the barrel. Waving with his empty pistol, he hails Kurt: "After him, man!" Then he collapses across the iron fence.

Kurt manages one clear shot at the assassin before he produces a bicycle from behind the tobacco kiosk. In spasms, Kurt stops running. His leg buckles under him like a tire that flattens when the wheel stops spinning.

A Czech policeman is on the scene. While a blond woman cradles Heydrich's head, howling: "It's the Reich Protector!" the policeman waves down cars.

"Assassination!" shrieks the blond, frightening away one driver. A second bellows out the window: "Let him walk!"

A baker's van stops. Policeman and driver attempt to lift Heydrich into the van but he gains consciousness long enough to insist on climbing in himself. He collapses on the floor as Kurt limps in.

Klein, of course, is dead.

With the policeman on the running board, the van races to Bulovka hospital. The nun who bathes Kurt's ankle is trembling so much she spills most of the antiseptic. Though doubled in pain, Heydrich perches on the examining table, his empty revolver still in his hand, refusing to let anyone touch him till a surgeon arrives.

"I'm Dr. Snajdr," the surgeon announces in Czech. Silently Heydrich raises his arm.

With the nun's assistance, the clothes are cut from his body. Another doctor attempts to administer an anesthetic, but Heydrich snarls: "What's this? You want to put me under to finish the job?"

With tweezers and disinfectant, the surgeon removes particles of glass, metal, leather and horsehair from the Reich Protector's body. Despite the pain, he doesn't flinch. He insists on pushing his own wheelchair to the x-ray room.

Kurt is assisted onto the examining table. As he passes in and out of consciousness, he hears the doctor remark:

"You're the lucky one. Not much besides the leg injury and head gash. How did you miss the shrapnel?"

Kurt envisions the grossly oversized Klein smothering the bomb with his body, absorbing the blast but perhaps also directing some of it backward to Heydrich.

Beginning at 4:30 p.m. Prague Radio continuously announces: "This morning, at 10:30, a brutal and inhuman attack was perpetrated against the life of Reich Protector Reinhard Heydrich. Thanks to the intervention of a merciful destiny, the Reich Protector escaped death with only superficial injuries. Be assured, enemies of the Reich – you worthless worms! you ghouls! you monsters who have done this vile and immoral deed! – you will be hunted down and slaughtered. Be assured, loyal citizens, you will be avenged. A reward of ten million korunas will be given for any clue leading to the arrest of the assassins. Whoever hides them or gives them help of any kind, or has knowledge of their identity, or a description of their appearance, and does not inform the authorities, will be shot with his whole family."

Martial law is declared in Prague. All public transport grinds to a halt. All rail and road arteries into the city are blocked. All cinemas, theaters, restaurants and bars are closed.

From 9:00 p.m. on May 27 till 6:00 a.m. the following day citizens are ordered to remain indoors or risk being shot after the first challenge.

At 10:00 p.m. the largest police search in European history is launched. The Gestapo, security police, Waffen SS, local force, Czech police, the SA and even Hitler Youth conduct a house-to-house hunt, bullying and intimidating, breaking into cupboards and stripping boards from attics.

Though important clues such as the Sten gun and raincoat are recovered from the scene of the crime, no direct information leads to the identity or whereabouts of the assassins. The population of Prague has clammed up.

By dawn of May 28, reprisals instigated by Himmler and Hitler begin. Ten thousand Czech suspects are arrested, with one hundred to be shot each night until the assassins are captured.

Heydrich is diagnosed as having smashed ribs, a punctured diaphragm and pierced spleen. A team of surgeons from Prague and Berlin tend him round the clock in a hospital converted into an armed camp.

SS Lieutenant-General Reinhard Tristan Eugen Heydrich died of blood poisoning at 4:30 a.m. on June 4, after an arduous nine-day struggle. On the night of June 5, The Black Order kept a torchlight vigil and next day the body was paraded by gun-carriage through silent streets lined with thousands of SS men. Beneath a monumental Iron Cross and flanked by pylons with flaming bowls, Heydrich lay in state in the courtyard of Hradcany castle on a promontory overlooking Prague, the city of bridges and spires. Thousands of mourners trekked past, many of them "my Czechs" in native dress, bearing bouquets.

On the afternoon of June 7, the body was hauled by special train to Berlin, where it again lay in state at the Central Security Department of the Reich. June 9 it was transferred to the Mosaic Hall of the Reich chancellery and mounted on a dais banked with flowers and backed by Nazi insignia, including a floor-to-ceiling SS banner.

While the Berlin Philharmonic played the funeral march from Wagner's *Götterdämmerung*, the state's chief mourners assembled: Adolf Hitler, in drab gray decorated with Iron Cross first class and bronze wound badge – a stranger to Berlin since the eastern campaign. Reichsmarschall Hermann Göring, corseted in white suede, his chest brilliant with medals. Minister of Propaganda and Enlightenment Josef Goebbels, wearing party khaki.

SS Reichsführer Heinrich Himmler held Heydrich's two sons, Heider and Klaus, by the hand.

Positioning himself at the podium, Heinrich Himmler eulogized the deceased as "one of the best educators in National Socialist Germany . . . a gentleman by birth and behavior . . . a shining example . . . a model of modesty . . . a character of rare purity and an intellect of penetrating clarity . . . feared by subhumans, calumniated by Jews and criminals . . . irreplaceable . . . an ideal to be emulated but perhaps never again to be achieved."

In summation: "You, Reinhard Heydrich, were a truly good SS man. For myself, I am privileged to thank you for your unswerving loyalty and wonderful friendship, which was a bond between us in this life, and which death can never put asunder."

Though Himmler later admitted to Dr. Zuckmayer that he felt squeamish to think he might have had two little Jew boys by the hand, publicly he testified: "As you have continued the line of your ancestors, doing them nothing but honor, so you will live on with all your qualities, decent and clean, in your sons, the inheritors of your blood and name."

Placing a wreath of orchids on the coffin and so moved he could scarcely choke out the words, the Führer confined himself to a single sentence: "He was one of the best National Socialists, one of the strongest defenders of the Reich concept, and one of the greatest adversaries of the enemies of the Reich."

Pinning a Wounded-in-Active-Service gold badge to the ceremonial cushion, he murmured, "Heydrich, he was a man of iron." Then the Führer touched the heads of his two sons as if offering a benediction.

The funeral procession formed in Wilhelm Strasse, its destination the Veterans' Cemetery designed by Frederick the Great. To the strains of Beethoven's "Funeral March," three Waffen SS companies led the parade, followed by the wreath and insignia bearers, and then the gun-carriage drawn by six black horses and bearing the swastika-draped coffin of the Martyr of Prague, topped by steel helmet and sword.

Reichsführer Himmler conducted the privileged mourners to the graveside. These included Major Kurt Schmidt, awarded a bronze combat bar for his role in defense of the late Reich Protector, and using a cane to support his bandaged left leg. Disconcerted, he found himself mated with the only man in the procession not in uniform – Count Wolfgang von Friedrich, correct in formal mourning attire, but managing to look, in Kurt's jaundiced eyes, like the master of ceremonies in an all-night bistro.

Under Kurt's scrutiny, the count's face did not change during the lengthy ceremony. Kurt's dashed hopes, his grief, his fury found its focus as he hissed: "Schieber, Schieber, Schieber!"

As the two men marched up, side by side, to pay their respects, the count plucked a white rose from one of the bouquets and placed it on the coffin. The theatricality of that gesture further infuriated Kurt as he vowed to track down and destroy every person who aided in this cowardly murder.

As chief witness, Major Kurt Schmidt was appointed by Reichsführer Himmler to head the investigation into the assassination of Reinhard Heydrich.

Under the most thorough of tortures, conducted in the basement of Petschek Palace, Major Schmidt pried from reluctant informers information that the assassins were hiding in the Czech Orthodox church on Ressel Street.

The morning of June 18, a force of nineteen officers and 740 NCOs, led by Schmidt, stormed the church. After a gun battle of two hours, they razed the superstructure, discovering a crypt which could be entered by moving a slab commemorating a Bohemian knight.

When neither machine guns nor tear gas could drive out the fugitives, Major Schmidt ordered gasoline poured into the crypt, then set fire to the assassins along with the priest who had sheltered them and members of the Czech Resistance.

Afterwards the bodies were laid on slabs in what remained of the nave of the church. With satisfaction, Schmidt identified the subhuman face he had confronted as the fatal bomb had been hurled. Investigation conclusively identified this person to be the gypsy Bolshevik Raymon Arno, twin brother of pornographic novelist Renate Arno, and brother-in-law of the tainted matinee idol Christian Jürgens.

Meanwhile, from May 28 to September 1, 3,188 Czechs were arrested for offenses such as illegal possession of arms and "approval of assassination." Of these, 1,357 were sentenced to death by summary courts. Others already in prison were executed.

The deporting of Jews was accelerated. In Berlin alone, Goebbels ordered five hundred arrested as his personal tribute. Aktion Reinhard, a campaign for robbing Jews of their wealth, including their gold teeth, was launched. Since Heydrich's life might have been saved had penicillin been available in the Reich, a program of "humane experiments" with sulfonamides was begun at Ravensbrück concentration camp.

Still unappeased, Hitler ordered the destruction of Lidice, a village of five hundred, twenty miles northwest of Prague, where rumor indicated assassin Lubos Valkova had contacts.

With Major Kurt Schmidt again directing the action, Lidice was surrounded on the night of June 8 and all inhabitants driven from their homes. At dawn, the men were shot against the wall of the village café, with their families forced to watch. When this proved too inefficient, the rest were herded into a barn and burned, bringing the total to 199.

Babies were drowned in cattle troughs, four pregnant women were aborted and 191 were dispatched to concentration camps or prisons.

Of ninety-eight children ages one to sixteen, ninety were sent to concentration camps, many to be gassed, while eight were deemed worthy of Germanization and adoption.

The village of Lidice was burned with flame-throwers and the ruins blown up. All this was filmed. The movie-makers were presented with a medal of Heydrich's profile stamped with the word REVENGE.

Thus did the Third Reich mourn the passing of its most perfect SS man, its Crystal Knight.

For his efficient resolution of the Heydrich assassination, Kurt Schmidt was promoted to lieutenant-colonel and made a special deputy of Heinrich Himmler, new chief of the Gestapo.

PART VI

"If the human features are going to be missing from the portrait of Hitler, if his persuasiveness, his engaging characteristics and even the Austrian charm he could trot out are left out of the reckoning, no faithful picture of him will be achieved. Certainly the generals in particular were not overwhelmed by a despotic force for a whole decade; they obeyed a commanding personality who frequently argued on the basis of cogent reasoning. . . . He was sustained by the idealism and devotion of people like myself. Criminals and their accomplices are always around; they explain nothing."

– Albert Speer, Minister of Armaments

"In the world of absolute fatality in which he moves, nothing makes sense; neither good, evil, time, space, what men call success, can be used as a criterion. Hitler will bring us to catastrophe. I doubt that he has a single friend who knows him, outside of myself. Is he really human? I would not want to swear on it. There are times when he gives me the chills."

– Josef Goebbels,
Minister of Propaganda and Enlightenment

ONE

Berlin

April 1944

E VERY NIGHT Carmel Kohl was torn from sleep by a vampirish shriek that inflated her skull till she thought it would burst. Stubbornly she would cling to her mattress like a life raft tossed on waves of sound, while the sirens rattled her windows, swirled around stairwells, turning her building into a piercing howl of outrage. To escape the sirens, she would throw on her now-tatty fox coat and plunge down dimly lit corridors filled with swinging doors like flapping bat's wings. Then she would huddle for two or three hours in the basement, smelling of coal dust and mildew, with twenty-three others sharing the thirteen cots Superintendent Schnell had scrounged for them. Dividing thirteen cots among twenty-three people was not easy, but it was the kind of tactful mathematics Berliners in cellars all over the city were learning: *Sleep faster, comrade, your brother needs your bed.*

That's the way things were in the capital of the Third Reich during the fifth winter of war: not if the bombers would come but when. How many hundreds would be injured or killed that night? How many thousands would be left homeless?

The major exodus from Berlin had begun last August when British pamphlets, dropped during a ninety-five-degree heat wave, urged women and children to leave, thus creating a panic in which thousands clogged railway stations like leaves in a sewer. Berliners were refused tickets unless they had been bombed out and then were bribed with increased rations into staying.

The population had taken to the earth. Public shelters were excavated under Pariser Platz and Wilhelm Platz, while the one under Zoo station was enlarged to accommodate ten thousand.

Beginning in early March American planes had joined the British in bombardment of Hamburg, Hannover, Cologne, Dortmund, Düseldorf, Essen. The Yanks in their Liberators and Flying Fortresses with P-51 escorts preferred daylight attacks in clear weather, lasting two to three hours during which they leisurely picked their targets, while the Brits in their Lancasters and Halifaxes with Spitfire escorts preferred dark nights and bad weather when they would carpet-bomb for forty-five minutes. Any time of day or night Berliners could look up at a sky of silver invaders churning like smelts in a spring run – four hundred or a thousand. Even the birds had become restive and confused in the screaming black smoke that turned day into night and the fire that turned night into day. The best thing one Berliner could wish another was: "Bombenlöse Nacht!" Have a bombless night.

First casualty of the night raids was sleep. Berliners had learned to snooze standing up like horses as they waited in line, leaning against the shoulders of other passengers jammed into the wood-burning, gas-driven buses.

The second casualty was privacy. Carmel had not wanted to know what pot-bellied Herr Tafel from apartment No. 6 looked like in his too-short red flannel nightshirt, or Frau Giesseler from No. 2 without her teeth. She had never yearned to hear the Boldt children urinate into chamber pots on demand because their grandfather, a veteran of World War I, was convinced urine fumes neutralized poison gas. By now she was so used to seeing Fräulein Karnau in her curlers, Carmel doubted she would recognize her without them.

More depressing was the war talk divided between the pessimists and the optimists, few in number and mostly male. In two years the enemy had gained superiority on land, on sea and in the air. North Africa had been lost to American invasion and British sea power. Germany's 6th Army had capitulated at Stalingrad with appalling losses. Italy had fallen then declared war on Germany. An allied landing was expected on coastal France, and many Germans prayed it would happen soon enough to save them from the Russians sweeping through Poland.

Against all this, the optimists promoted the New Eastern Offensive, which they claimed would be launched any day, and the Führer's secret Wunderwaffe. A superpatriot who claimed "internal injuries" kept him from the front, Herr Tafel expounded: "A friend of a cousin of mine saw those wonder weapons tested over the Russian border near Pinsk. *Pooft*, and a town ceased to exist! Soon the whole world will be licking our boots again." It was Herr Tafel who had tried to urge everyone to sing Trutzlieder, Songs of Defiance, on sheets issued by the propaganda ministry. Then group wisdom had countered: "Shut up, Big Mouth! That's worse than listening to Churchill's exploding turds."

Despite Herr Tafel in his red flannel nightshirt, Carmel became fond of her cellar group the way she supposed people grew to tolerate the idiosyncrasies of their own families. Sometimes she fantasized that Hitler's wonder weapons had wiped out everyone but this gang of twenty-three, forced to listen to each other's complaints through eternity. At other times she imagined she was sharing a grave with the people whose bones would molder with hers till some enterprising archeologist dug them up in a few million years, figuring he had found the Missing Link. Perhaps a primitive tribe of Homo sapiens at prayer. Enough odd artifacts existed to justify any theory: the Boldt family's photo album, Fräulein Karnau's love letters, Herr Schnell's fishbowl, Frau Giesseler's astrology charts, the sweater Frau Stengel knit to sooth her nerves, then ripped out and reknit because she couldn't get wool for another.

Along with personal peculiarities came group rituals. In Willi Bliss's cellar, where he was a prisoner with sixty-two others, everyone faced north to counter bomb blasts – something to do with the magnetic poles. In another, the habitués covered their eyes to prevent flash blindness. In a third, tubs of water were needlessly filled and carted.

Carmel's cellar group had bonded around a guilty secret: the presence of the Vogel women in apartment No. 4 across from Carmel's.

On February 27, fourteen months ago, Goebbels had launched Fabrik Aktion – a roundup of all Jews in an attempt to render Berlin Judenfrei. Thousands were swept up for deportation east. Others committed suicide. A handful, estimated by Goebbels at four thousand, went into hiding.

Frau Vogel and her lame daughter had been passed over. Was it an oversight or consideration for the fact she was the widow of a World War I hero? No one knew. As word leaked through the cellar community, a feeling developed that the Vogels were good luck. Since they were too terrified to show themselves on the street or to answer the door for anyone besides Herr Schnell, Carmel and some of the rest donated food through the superintendent. Though Herr Tafel's mouth was hardest to seal, even he became convinced by Frau Giesseler's astrology charts that "two dark angels will protect your house" must mean the Vogels. When houses on either side fell in the same raid, he rejoiced: "We're safe forever. It's written in the gold stars."

Tonight Carmel had to squat on a mattress against the wall like the inhabitant of a pre-war dosshaus, while thirteen others snoozed on the cots. Restlessly she lay her ear against the air vent. A sensitive antenna tuned to survival, it was capable of interpreting the drama she could not see. First, the drone of approaching planes – a slurred and jerky buzz like a swarm of lazy bees, with the throb of individual engines becoming distinguishable. Then the bombs would fall – distant thuds like the footfalls of an approaching giant. Now the answering clack of artillery fire. A crisp, clean explosion with a lighter echo meant the guns were close and facing her. A muffled explosion followed by rumblings meant the guns were pointed away. When the *akk-akk* was followed in two or three seconds by metallic bursts, that was shrapnel.

At last Carmel heard the sound she hankered for: all-clear. Stumbling out of her cellar, she found the pre-dawn sky crisscrossed, tangled and looped by vapor trails like lethal chalk marks on a blackboard. Pointless to try to sleep. Mounting the bicycle that had long since replaced her Opel, she pumped east along the Kurfürstendamm.

Other Berliners were tumbling from their caves, shaking off the night like a dog ridding itself of dirty water. Morale had never recovered from Stalingrad over a year ago. Though slow to admit the enormity of the defeat, Goebbels was quick to pick scapegoats. Certainly no one could blame the party or the leadership, eager to take credit for lightning victories during the plummy days of blitzkrieg. For the architects of defeat, one looked to a failure of nerve in the army and the unwillingness of the German people to sacrifice their all.

After calling for three days of mourning, Goebbels closed all places contributing to frivolity – hairdressers, sweet shops, the better restaurants. Since few Germans still believed they were fighting a righteous war and the myth of invincibility had been exploded, Goebbels turned from carrot to stick, vengefully beating the populace like a broken-down horse with too heavy a load. Remember what happened to you last time you lost a war. Remember the shameful Treaty of Versailles. Remember the occupation of the Rhineland where we Germans had to enter public buildings by the back while the French and British swaggered in the front. Remember the signs on restaurants, swimming pools and railway compartments, "No Germans Allowed." Remember the seven o'clock curfew,

with those who disobeyed being shot. Remember how our
telephones were disconnected, our postal service ended,
our radios confiscated, our newspapers censored. Remember
reparation. Remember how the victors starved our
children with a blockade so they died like flies. Remember!
Remember! Remember! Since Goebbels was telling
Germans a historical truth, it was hard for them to disbelieve
when he raged: *If all that happened to you last time,
imagine what they'll do to you if you dare lose again.*

The only other high-ranking party member still interested
in civilian affairs was Reichsführer Heinrich
Himmler, who engaged with Goebbels in a campaign Berliners
dubbed "Strength through Terror" after the
"Strength through Joy" vacations the party had once
sponsored. To convert Germans into spies who would
report "treasonable utterances," Himmler wove his Gestapo
network like a black spiderweb through every neighborhood.
Derelict buildings were turned into headquarters.
Block wardens were instructed to exploit petty
jealousies and family conflicts to create informers in every
home.

In Willi Bliss's cellar Himmler and Goebbels forged a
heroine out of a woman who denounced six friends who
told her they'd heard over the BBC that her son, reported
dead, was a POW.

Yet as Carmel pedaled along Leipziger Strasse on this
lovely spring morning, she could see that Berliner
Schnauze – the caustic wit for which the city was famous –
had not died. At the corner of Hermann Göring Strasse
one of Goebbels' Red Menace posters was defaced with
the scrawl: "Don't worry, Dr. G, the Reds will never make
it across the Rhine." A row of bombed-out buildings bore
the banner: ALL THIS WE OWE TO THE FÜHRER – a slogan
coined by Goebbels when Berliners still had Danish butter
for their bread. Yesterday Herr Schnell – wheezing so
hard he almost lost his dentures – handed Carmel a cartoon
worn thin by many hands. Goebbels under Soviet
fire was holding up a sign: RUSSIANS, YOU HAVE CEASED TO

EXIST. Over his shoulder he complained to Göring: "These stupid Russians don't understand a word of German." Twice this morning Carmel spotted work parties under SS guard scrubbing off the anti-Nazi slogans, which had blossomed overnight with the crocuses, and replacing them with Goebbels' patriotic banalities:

WHAT CAN'T KILL ME STRENGTHENS ME
HALF MEASURES ARE NO MEASURES
THE FÜHRER'S WHOLE LIFE IS STRUGGLE, WE MUST STRIVE TO
TAKE THIS LOAD OFF HIS SHOULDERS

Carmel parked her bike at Alexanderplatz. In her purse she carried a Leica IIA given to her by Wolf at a brief meeting last week in the Tiergarten. Her job: to photograph some of the thousands of guns and searchlights concealed in parks, on buildings, in rubble, including the four anti-aircraft cannon mounted on a 100-foot tower in the Tiergarten; heavy industry and rail intersections; conspicuous landmarks now camouflaged. The East-West axis running through Brandenburger Tor, where pilots oriented themselves, had been disguised with a green tarpaulin to blend with the Tiergarten. A radio station at one end was also covered in green with a gray center strip simulating asphalt. Lamp posts had been transformed into trees and the gold Angel of Victory had been tarnished so it wouldn't reflect moonlight.

Though Carmel had agonized over taking pictures of the city she loved so British and American bombers could pulverize it, Wolf had convinced her that by pinpointing military targets, they might save historic and residential ones.

Last night's raid did not inspire hope. While the warehouses around Alexanderplatz were in flames, blocks of apartments had also been reduced to hulks from which hundreds of homeless picked their belongings like hot potatoes from a bonfire. Carmel saw a woman weeping over a teapot, its pieces spread on the sidewalk, incapable of comprehending the larger tragedy, while wardens using an opposite set of defenses passed around dead dogs and even babies as if they were cordwood. For blocks around Alexander station, thousands of burned and bandaged refugees covered with dust waited for trains that would never come, while the trek of those pulling belongings in anything with wheels started earlier each day, grew faster and continued longer.

Unter den Linden was a tornado of flame. Most of the chic restaurants, the embassies, the National Library and several of the grandiose Hohenzollern folies de grandeur had been reduced to rubble. Thousands of soldiers strung barbed wire and arrested looters, while firemen salvaged furniture and dug out bodies. Craters were filling with water from hoses strewn like black spaghetti. Iron lamp posts had snapped like matchsticks. In Pariser Platz the French embassy was leveled along with the townhouse where Carmel had lived for ten years with Axel Berg. Crowds of Germans squatted before the former American embassy the way desperate Jews used to wait for visas. Now it was a soup kitchen.

Wilhelm Strasse had become obliterated by smoke. With the exception of the Promi, most ministries had been evacuated with the first burst of gunfire, their occupants fleeing like garden party guests before a thunderstorm. Nobody missed them. It was as if the bureaucracy were the top layer of a wedding cake ornately wrought of paste and cardboard, for show only.

Positioning herself on a viaduct overlooking a crisscross of silvery railway tracks, Carmel noted a long line of boxcars newly arrived from the east, containing hundreds of wounded soldiers. As she focused her camera, she heard the tramp of boots.

"Achtung!"

Spinning, she confronted an enraged Wehrmacht captain with a growling Alsatian.

"What are you doing here, Fräulein?" he demanded.

She noticed his "Frozen Meatball" badge from the

eastern campaign, accompanied by a Silver Wound badge, meaning he had sustained at least three injuries.

"I felt moved to take pictures of our wounded. I refuse not to see or feel just because of orders from Goebbels."

That name "Goebbels" struck him like shrapnel.

"Ja. From the Dutch we got chocolate. From the French, fine wines. From the Russians – *corpses*." Bewildered by the honesty his anguish had wrenched from him, he shot up his arm: "Heil Hitler!" Snapping his dog to his side, he fled across the viaduct.

Carmel charged in the opposite direction, not stopping until she felt warm bodies press around her. Collapsing against a pylon she felt her own body convulse, the result of raw nerves, too little sleep and too much sadness. Though she had had many more dangerous encounters, what shocked her was her own carelessness. That's when they caught you – not smuggling forged papers across the border but shooting pictures of wounded soldiers with your guard down.

The Adlon Hotel, where Carmel was lunching with Willi Bliss, showed minor ravages of war.

The linen cloths were gray from too few washings; stuffing bulged from chairs; the orchestra had been reduced to a single violinist who played Liszt's "Liebestraum" as if he wanted to rush home before bombs fell. Yet the dining room was crowded and lively with the air of partygoers on a luxury liner in a stormy sea.

Willi was waiting with a bottle of burgundy, a napkin tucked under his chin. War had not come between him and his appetite. He and Göring must be the only two fat men left in Berlin. Kissing Carmel's hand, he flattered: "Still so beautiful. Fräulein. I look around me and despair. Have you ever seen so many fashionable women with gray hair? The weekly trip to the beauty parlor is sorely missed."

After requesting a stack of empty plates, he drew a

hamper from under the table – ham, potato salad, smoked oysters, croissants and butter. As other diners gawked, he heaped Carmel's plate then his own. "I just returned from Paris, and I intend to spend my last days eating as well as those we are supposed to have conquered. The Third Reich is like Carthage, unwilling to make peace and incapable of waging war."

Ordering another bottle of burgundy, he updated Carmel on his love-hate relationship with the French. "Nothing has changed. Do you realize even coffee is still available on the black market? The prices are sky high, not because of scarcity but because the damned French are saving it for the Yanks. Those people – they're so selfish and deceitful you have to admire them. Maxim's carries on as always. The girls still dance at the Lido. Suits and dresses, even gowns and jewelry, fill shop windows. You see those French girls on the Champs-Elysées in their clogs and the turbans they wear now that felt is in short supply, then you spot one of our Bund deutscher Mädchen in her dreadful uniform with no makeup and braids, and you feel pity."

Though embarrassed by envious stares, Carmel couldn't resist the splendid buffet. Tasting the potato salad, she raved: "No sawdust. No ground bones."

Snapping his fingers, Willi complained: "Where's our burgundy, Herr Ober?"

Sniffing the oysters, the old man barked: "Don't you know there's a war on?"

With hauteur, Willi retorted: "May I inform you, my good sir, the distance from my table to the wine cellar is not one inch longer in war than in peace." Stuffing a croissant in his mouth, he returned to Carmel. "Have you started another film?"

"Not yet, but soon. With trains so unreliable, I can't keep my nightclub act going. I'm reading a script on Lola Montez and King Ludwig I."

"Good. We Germans have no trouble identifying with mad men – Dr. Caligari, Nosferatu, The Student of

Prague, Dr. Mabuse. I could update that list with real-life figures but I would have to be mad to dare."

"The script's okay, but Goebbels wants Werner Kraus as my leading man. His Jewish caricatures in *Jud Süss* were nauseating."

"But didn't you see King Richard III? His murderous cripple was unmistakably Goebbels. Werner is apolitical, as artists should be."

"That's what I used to think. The only reason I agreed to do Lola is I'm sure we won't finish it. Goebbels wants me to sign the contract next month with Hitler at Berchtesgaden so as to bolster his own prestige. I yearn to do something decent. I saw a rehearsal of Gustav Gründgens in Schiller's *The Robbers*. He's magnificent! His villain is a ringer for Hitler, even to the plastered hair."

"Good luck to the fool. The man I envy is Leo Warner. I saw a pirated edition of his *Maidens of the Rhine* when I was in Paris. He stole everything from you and Friedrich, down to the last sequin. America loved it, though to me it was like warm champagne. What a pity you and Wolfgang never went to Hollywood. You could have had the stars off the American banner."

Willi received his burgundy from the waiter and pronounced it potable. Carmel inquired: "How are things for you at the Promi?"

He chuckled. "It's the cheeriest place in the Third Reich since even the cockroaches insist we're winning the war. This morning I worked out rules governing servants. Can you beat it? Show me a gardener left in Berlin, yet I'm writing a memo detailing how many hours he gets to sleep each night."

"Sleep? Who sleeps?"

"My alleged gardeners, butlers and chauffeurs. I feel like a street cleaner during the last days of Pompeii."

"The Promi must be the only ministry undamaged."

"Like Satan, it can't be consumed by flames. It just gets Browner. Closest call came when the warden demonstrated a stirrup pump by starting a fire in a wastebasket.

He took out two offices." Belching, Willi cursed: "What the hell does it matter who wins or loses? This war will have to be re-shot in a few years. Churchill, Stalin and Roosevelt? They'll be at each other's throats, with Germany holding the balance of power. Germany belongs to Europe and Europe to Germany. We're the heart of the civilized world. Even the British will have to join us, despite the fine airs their channel gives them."

Carmel returned home an hour before blackout. A group of ragged women carrying string bags pressed against the door of her building. As she squeezed through, several elbowed her. "Wait your turn."

She showed her key. "I live here."

Puzzled, Carmel unlocked the door to the south wing. As a row of tulip lights switched on, she readied her third key.

No. 4, the Vogel women's apartment, was sealed with white tape. Stamps bore a swastika with a spread eagle and the words: GEHEIME STAATSPOLIZEI. Carmel spun around as the corridor door burst open behind her. "Herr Schnell. What's happened to the Vogels?"

In a loud voice, a byproduct of his deafness, he replied with his usual precision: "This morning at 6:45 two men identifying themselves as Gestapo arrested the Vogels. In a few minutes an auction of their belongings will be held." With disgust, he whispered: "A woman of sixty and her lame daughter sent east to lay railway tracks!"

"Where were they taken?"

A sharp rap on the corridor door interrupted them. "Geheime Staatspolizei."

A bullish Gestapo officer in trenchcoat and fedora pushed by, followed by a small man in blue serge suit. Self-importantly he broke the seal on the Vogel's door, then directed Herr Schnell with his thumb. "Let the herd in."

Propelled by the stampede, Carmel found herself inside

the Vogels' flat. Closet doors and bureau drawers had been yanked open, offering a pitiful display of threadbare linen, mended clothes, worn shoes, dinted pots and pans. In the shuttered room was the smell of fear, of despair, of people huddled against an inevitable doom.

As the auctioneer in blue serge offered each item, the bidding grew quarrelsome then mean-spirited. Squabbles over two yards of faded calico. Complaints that a pot had a broken handle. When a woman accused the only man in the crowd of being a Gestapo plant to force up the bidding, she was arrested, proving her point.

Stunned, Carmel fought her way to her own flat. She poured herself a drink of the calvados Willi had brought from Paris, and then another, while the voices shrilled then silenced.

Herr Schnell tapped at her door. "Frau Berg." He was hoarse with excitement. "I told you a white lie. I got wind of the Gestapo an hour before. I play cards with the policeman for our block – a decent man called in from retirement. He doesn't like the new ways. The Vogels are in the basement, but there's bound to be a house search. Do you have any contacts?"

Wolf was in Hamburg till next week. Carmel thought: Father Bauer. She said: "I'll try."

St. Nicholas Church was shabbier and draftier than Carmel had remembered. Only one candle burned. As she lit another, placing five hundred marks in the poor box, tiny Father Bauer shuffled from behind the confessional.

"How good to see you, Fräulein. I've missed you. I don't talk to many young people these days."

"I'm afraid I have a favor to ask. Two Jewish friends – a widow of sixty and her daughter . . ."

He clasped her hand. "Don't say another word. There are crypts in this church only the Holy Ghost knows about."

"Thank you, Father Bauer." Carmel embraced him in relief.

He dabbed at his eyes with his sleeve. "No, Fräulein, I thank you. I used to turn away Jews that weren't baptized. One young couple had a baby, couldn't have been more than a month. I've often felt like the innkeeper in Bethlehem who turned away Mary, big with God's child." He held out his hands. They were trembling. "I'm not afraid of the Gestapo. What can they do to my body that life hasn't already done? I fear meeting the Holy Father in Heaven, but how can our pope be infallible when he tells God's servant to turn away little babies?"

TWO

Mullhorig, Bavaria

May 1944

I LSE SCHMIDT sat at her desk surrounded by piles of
papers. A second desk confined her in an L formation.
Cabinets lined the walls with reports on top waiting to be
filed. In an outer office two secretaries worked shifts – two
of them, one of her. It had been months since she had seen
the oak grain of her desk. Even the Polish cleaning
woman had given up attempting to dust it.

Ilse's eyes shifted to the silver-framed desk photo of a
child waving a wooden dagger. Bruno Kurt Heinrich
Schmidt (1939–1942). Not once in two years had she awakened without an aching sense of bereavement so that she
had to struggle to catch her breath and then to agree to go
on breathing. For six months after her son's death Ilse
had lain in a coma, passing in and out of sedation, unwilling to live and yet unable to die. Dr. Zuckmayer, sitting
by her bed and gripping her hand, had pulled her through.
Kurt, he insisted, had acted compassionately under
Reichsführer Himmler's orders to relieve them of a
burden which would have grown worse with time and
which she had not been prepared to handle.

Though Ilse understood that Kurt could not be with
her, she felt angry and hurt that he would never talk to her
about Bruno. Ironically, at the point she overcame her
anguish enough to forgive him for being the instrument of
it, he had become resentful of her. Now Kurt behaved as if
Bruno had never existed. He had even wanted to burn his

photos. That would have shocked Ilse if she hadn't seen how often mothers of babies sent off in the L-vans adopted the same defense. To Ilse, everything had purpose. Perhaps that was the result of her Catholic upbringing. With Dr. Zuckmayer's help, she had come to feel that Bruno had been given to her and then snatched away to make her tough enough to carry out her Lebensborn tasks.

Sometimes she faltered. Twice this month after blackout she had wrapped herself in her old nursing cape and stolen into the cemetery of the Catholic church in Mullhorig to put flowers on the graves of the little ones buried there. She knew Dr. Zuckmayer would be angry, but what could be the harm? Lifting the miniature of the Virgin Mary, which she had found in the alpine meadow, from between her breasts where it hung on a gold chain, she gazed at the shining face and illuminated heart. Hail, Mary, Mother of God. Only another mother could understand her anguish. A Mother who had lost a Son.

Ilse jolted out of what had become a trance. She looked at her watch: eight o'clock. Guiltily she realized she had missed Ursula's bedtime for the second time that week and vowed to make it up to her with a special treat tomorrow. Ruefully she admitted that her adopted daughters Ursula and Marlene meant no more to her than the other children at the Lebensborn. She loved all babies, but she had had only one child, and he was dead.

Retreating from such cold thoughts, Ilse took Kurt's last letter from the wire basket marked "Hold."

A month ago, without warning, Kurt had used their savings to purchase a villa and its contents for a fraction of its value. Located in Wannsee, a palatial southwest suburb of Berlin, it had belonged to a baron arrested for treason then executed by the Gestapo. Ilse gazed in disbelief at the photo of the gingerbread castle floating on a magic green carpet to Havel Lake. She tried to picture herself living there, ordering servants about, but retreated from that image in confusion.

For two weeks Kurt had been living in this ridiculous place he referred to as "my villa," commuting to Gestapo headquarters. She reread a part of his letter, dictated to his secretary: "The oils on the wall cover the price I paid, and more are wrapped in canvas in the attic. I've already discovered a small landscape by Caspar David Friedrich and a nude drawing by Cranach."

Friedrich? Cranach? Who were these people? Kurt had also included an itemized list of the dining-room contents, prepared by a curator:

Augsburg silver, 8 8-piece settings
Art Deco glassware, 4 goblets in service for 12
KPM porcelain, 18th-century, 6 teacups and saucers. 2
chipped Dresden Swan Dinner Service, single piece made for
Czar Nicholas. . . .

Ilse's head reeled. The Third Reich crashing around their ears, and her husband was counting teacups. She read: "I realize you might consider the real-estate market too volatile, but the risk is worth it. Sometimes when I sit with a drink in the window of my villa watching the bombers head for Berlin, I feel I'm watching a newsreel. Everything around me is so untouched."

Ilse pushed the letter from her. Not a word about how he was or how she and Helga and the children might be. Not a word to say he missed her. She remembered the letters he wrote in their first year of separation, full of the unself-conscious detail of his life. She still had some of those by heart: "Today when the captain commended me for my handling of field maneuvers, I thought: 'Ilse would be proud of me.' I showed your picture to the others in the officers' barracks and they congratulated me. Imagine how jealous they'd be if they could see you the way I do. I put a large X through each day, waiting till next weekend."

Today's letter had been signed by Kurt's secretary. Though the forgery was a good one, he had accidentally processed it with a batch of others so it ended: Colonel Kurt Schmidt.

After years of laboring at thankless tasks, Kurt was now being spoiled by attention and Ilse feared it had gone to his head. She remembered his haughty words when she phoned in a panic to protest about the villa: "My rank requires it. Everybody who counts lives this way. If you don't, you're not respected."

Ilse had thought the tragedy of Bruno, bravely faced, would have drawn them closer. Instead, Kurt seemed to want to use it as a barrier to block off the past. The little time they spent together had become an ordeal – the strain of not letting herself weep, of feeling his growing contempt for her weakness while she had to endure the sight of him preening himself over his good fortune. Kurt was still more interested in the death of Reinhard Heydrich, whom he had turned into a tin god. His obsession repelled her – the files he kept on anyone who had seen the man since his appointment to Czechoslovakia, the photos of the assassination glued to his office wall, the death mask of Heydrich he had begged from Reichsführer Himmler, the film the Führer had made of the ghastly slaughter of the village of Lidice, which Kurt had directed, the medal he wore around his neck stamped with Heydrich's profile and the word REVENGE.

Ilse reread the last line of Kurt's letter: "My investigations are taking me into the highest circles. The Reichsführer and I are to be the dinner guests of the Führer at Berchtesgaden. He wishes me to inspect the bunker system of the Berg. Also present will be Carmel Kohl, who is signing a contract with Dr. Goebbels for her new movie. . . ."

All those names, dropped so casually. No suggestion that she might accompany him, or regret that she hadn't been asked. Kurt's life as second-in-command of the Gestapo had opened a new world both socially and professionally. The villa was just a symptom.

Ilse felt overwhelmed by futility. What did any of it

matter? She forced her attention back to her desk. Though
an excellent organizer of people, space and supplies, she
had always been a wool-gatherer when it came to paper-
work and since Bruno's death her concentration had suffered. She shifted a bunch of photos to the center of the
desk, telling herself she must keep her wits about her for
Dr. Zuckmayer's sake. The Lebensborn was facing
serious problems stemming from Reichsführer Himmler's
Polish Recovery Program. Though she and Dr. Zuckmayer had fought it from its inception, they no longer had
the luxury of opposition. Many of the practical tasks were
theirs.

Established in June 1941 out of Himmler's impatience
with the slowness of Aryanization through selective breeding, this program aimed at the recovery of Nordic blood
from populations now under German control. Simply
stated, its proponents argued that through the flukes of
mixed breeding, parents of inferior blood might produce
offspring of an almost pure Aryan type. As proof they
cited the number of blond-haired, blue-eyed children in
Poland.

The first step was acquiring these children from
orphanages or parents sent to labor camps; through selections during which children were herded into a public
place and sorted into "recoverable" and "non-recovera-
ble"; through kidnapping by Brown nurses trained to
apprehend suitable children on their way to school or to
snatch them from their buggies.

Two million Polish children had been acquired in these
ways for the Third Reich.

The second step was processing these youngsters for
adoption by German parents. At Polish transit centers,
babies were given Germanized names and false identity
papers. Older children up to age ten or twelve were told
their natural parents had abandoned them, were forbidden to speak their native tongue and taught the German
heritage. Recalcitrants were punished with beatings, star-

vation and isolation. The more stubborn cases were discarded.

As head nurse and manager of the Lebensborn at Mullhorig, Ilse was expected to oversee the adoption of many of the quasi-Nordic children. Even in the best of times, the recovery program was an ambitious and labor-intensive one. With the Third Reich fighting for its life, it was becoming impossible to administer. Not only were rail communications in a constant state of disruption, but something seemed to have gone tragically wrong with the selection process.

Of the thirty-one babies newly arrived from Poland with their German papers ready for adoption, seven had failed to meet Ilse's exacting standards. Some were so pathetically unqualified that even if they had been of pure German blood she would have considered them for the disinfection program. One eight-month-old boy had eyes so slanted he looked Asiatic. A girl of about a year had the left leg shorter than the right. One baby had a deformed ear, another a disfiguring birthmark. Three had dark hair, and five brown eyes. How could such obvious mistakes be made by trained personnel?

The more Ilse checked the photos and measurements of the naked children against the Aryan ideal, the more agitated she became. Rejected photos meant rejected children.

Ilse buzzed her secretary, then ordered through the intercom: "Get Helga Hewel and the other two scouts responsible for the last shipment from Poland."

As she waited, Ilse brooded. Lazy and deceitful, Helga was turning into a problem for which Ilse had full responsibility. Even the girl's story, of wanting a biological child because of her fiancé killed in France, Ilse now suspected had been concocted to help her ditch her munitions job. In recommending Helga for training as a Brown Scout, Ilse had tried to give her the chance to prove her worth.

Within twenty minutes Helga and the two other nurses were in front of Ilse's desk, their blouses hastily stuffed into their brown skirts, surprised to have been recalled to duty.

Looking at the Lebensborn poster of herself breast-feeding Bruno, and squeezing the medallion of the Virgin Mary in her hands, Ilse prayed: Help me to be strong. Ease this pain, O Virgin Mother. Make me selfless and pure. Help me to do my duty . . .

She turned to the nurses. Helga looked sulky, while the other two were frightened rabbits. Distributing photos on which she had stamped REJECT, Ilse instructed: "I want you to take a good look at these." In a well-modulated voice she continued: "I suppose all of you know the difference between black hair and blond? Can you count the number of toes on a child? Do you know how many an Aryan child is expected to have?"

Her voice rising, Ilse demanded: "Eva, did you think you were doing this cripple a favor by bringing her here?

"Gudrun, did you go along with the others because it was easier than having an opinion of your own?"

Staring into Helga's resentful face, she shouted: "And what about you? Were you drunk? Were you out the night before with some Pole you met in a beer garden? Do you know what happens to these children you bring to me that I must reject? Do you expect others to cover up for your blind eyes and poor judgment? Do you realize how rapidly a small taint in a small baby grows into a big deformity in a big child? How would you like to deal with heartbroken German parents who adopt an Aryan child, only to have it turn into a subhuman with brown eyes?" The words spewed like vomit from Ilse's throat. "Do you realize how much better off these bastards would be if you left them with their natural parents and let fate take its course?"

Flinging her arms toward the door she shrieked: "Go study your physiognomy manuals. Get your eyes tested. Just don't bring any more of this trash to me!"

As the nurses fled, Ilse collapsed on her couch, overwhelmed by hate, eaten by it, humiliated and helpless in its grip, hatred of the nurses, hatred of the babies who forced her to reject them, hatred of Helga and her two healthy daughters, hatred of Kurt and Dr. Zuckmayer and Himmler and even hatred of the Führer, hatred for all who were not Bruno and who had deprived her of her son, feeling her body ache for the softness of his flesh, as if he were an amputated part of herself. She thought of the Polish mothers who lay on the train tracks to prevent their children from being taken from them, and those who stormed the stations with bricks and brooms, and those who waited at darkened windows for children who never came home from school. Gasping for breath, Ilse massaged her chest, feeling pain like a corkscrew boring through her heart. Surely it couldn't go on this way. Surely it would be better tomorrow or in six months. Hail, Mary, Mother of God. . . .

Berchtesgaden, Bavaria

May 1944

O NCE THE Bavarian village of Berchtesgaden was noted only for its soaring peaks, breathtaking gorges and foaming torrents that crashed into blue-green König See. Since Adolf Hitler transformed a modest alpine cottage on the ridge called Obersalzberg into an imposing retreat, the area had become famous as Führer Mountain.

From the balcony of the Grand Hotel, Carmel Kohl used high-powered binoculars to scrutinize the road as it toiled upward. At 12:50 she spotted Adolf Hitler's convoy completing its three-hour drive from Munich, traveling at sixty miles per hour, with other cars forbidden to pass. In the lead Mercedes, open to the beautiful weather, was the Führer with Goebbels and Himmler, followed by another Mercedes with Hitler's two secretaries and his mistress Eva Braun, flung back on the trunk sunning herself. A third Mercedes carried luggage.

At three o'clock the Führer's valet collected Carmel and her overnight bag for the serpentine trip upward through forests, skirting a precipice that offered startling views of the valley. Posing as groundsmen, SS men tended camouflaged machine-gun nests. Twice they had to stop at high-voltage gates to show passes.

"A necessity even for Reich ministers," apologized the valet. "Martin Bormann's orders."

Of natural materials and as extensive as a hotel, Hitler's Berghof with its gables and carved balconies blended tastefully with its mountain backdrop. The valet escorted Carmel to a flagstone terrace wrapped by a low stone wall, providing a commanding view of misty Unterberg where the ghost of Charlemagne was said to sleep.

A dozen casually dressed women with men in assorted uniforms were drinking cocktails amidst the red-gingham, white-wicker furniture. As Carmel made her entrance, heads snapped even here. Smiling like a cat about to claim a plump mouse, Dr. Goebbels limped toward her. "The Führer sends his greetings. He'll join us shortly. Do you know you're the first outsider to be invited to the Berg in almost a year?" Taking her arm, he steered her toward her hostess Eva Braun, a pretty, toffee-haired woman in skimpy blue halter, carrying a black terrier.

"I adore your movies, especially *Love Shield*," she gushed. "We used to see two pictures a night until the Russians. Now the Führer thinks that's too frivolous. He only watches newsreels. They're so upsetting and boring, don't you think? Who wants a movie of something you can see looking out your own window?"

Though charmed to hear Eva express the unguarded thoughts of many Berliners, Carmel was disconcerted when her hostess continued: "Wasn't Christian Jürgens wonderful? How lucky you were to know him. We all felt terrible when he killed himself, but he must have been unstable to marry a gypsy. What could have made him do such a thing?"

"Love and decency," snapped Carmel. Then, turning to the mountains, she enthused: "Such a gorgeous view. Do you every go sailing on König See?"

Trained to hear only what she wanted, Eva responded easily to the change of topic. "We used to picnic there then go into town so the Führer could meet the children. Dozens would bring him bouquets. It was very sweet, but Martin Bormann put a stop to that. Sometimes I go myself, but I have to take SS guards. Besides," she wrinkled her nose, "the Führer likes me to stay out of sight. He things it's best for the German people to see him as a bachelor. Marriage is out of the question, because he feels offspring of geniuses usually have too hard a time. The world never forgives them for being average."

Having staked her territory, Eva returned to the gossip that fascinated her. "Is Zara Leander as sexy as everyone says? What's Emil Jannings really like? Once at a reception he talked to each piece of food as he ate it: 'Hello, oyster. Emil is going to eat you.'"

As Carmel attempted to answer, Eva took a cigarette from her shoulder bag, all but dumping a pearl-handled revolver. Stuffing it back, she confided: "That's a gift from the Führer. He makes me and his secretaries practise shooting because of the nightmare he keeps having. It's about a naked German woman, chained to a bed, being attacked by a Jewish lecher."

While Carmel stared at the bulge of the gun, imagining what a courageous person might do with it, an SS man in waiter's white tunic whispered to Eva: "The Führer is on his way."

Stubbing her cigarette, Eva scattered the smoke. "He hates me smoking but I can't quit. We'll have to pretend it was you."

All guests stopped talking to face east. Adolf Hitler strolled onto the patio, with Reichsführer Heinrich Himmler glued to his right side and his secretary Martin Bormann to the left. The Führer's body had slumped and fattened in the two years since Carmel and the rest of Berlin last observed him at Reinhard Heydrich's funeral. His misshapen nose was but a lump of putty over the bushy mustache, while the broad cheekbones had submerged in pallid flesh.

After greeting Eva, aglow with hero worship, he took Carmel's hand and caressed it like a sacred object, while staring into her face, seeming to search her inner self as if it were a periwinkle to be turned from its shell. Though she wanted to blink, she was hypnotized by the iceberg-blue eyes striated with gray, slightly protruding, lashless, their expression piercing, startling, unforgettable.

At last breaking the connection, Hitler kissed Carmel's hand. "You are Germany's other wonder weapon."

Goebbels, who had been hovering in the background like the father of the bride, moved in. Seeing him, the Führer nodded. "Ahh yes, business first." He ushered Carmel to a table decorated with swastikas. As she signed a UFA contract committing her to star in the movie *Lola* based on Lola Montez and King Ludwig I, an SS man took publicity photos, as did Eva Braun.

The Führer donned his broad-brimmed fedora and exchanged his field-gray tunic for a hiking jacket. The group on the terrace put down their glasses. As he took Eva's arm, he called his Alsatian, Blondi. Himmler and Bormann fell in behind, his black and brown shadows. Goebbels took his place beside Carmel. The twenty-minute trek to the teahouse had begun.

Constructed like a stone silo, the teahouse had six windows offering a panorama of the Ach river valley and the distant towers of Salzburg. Rejecting one place after another at the round table, Hitler selected a chair with its back to the view.

"The Führer hates to look at snow since the eastern campaign," whispered Eva. "He's developed a phobia." As Bormann seated Eva to Hitler's left, Goebbels placed Carmel to his right. They were joined by Himmler and Hitler's two youngest secretaries, Frau Gerda Christian and Frau Gertrud Junge, while other guests filled other tables.

SS men served peppermint tea and platters of chocolate éclairs, black forest cake, tortes and fudge. The Führer piled three desserts onto Carmel's plate, then onto the plates of the other women. To their squeals of dismay, he retorted: "Nonsense. You women are too thin. Eva was pleasingly plump when I met her. Now she's like a bird. It's not for men that women undergo such sacrifice. It's to make their girlfriends jealous."

Eva protested: "The Führer used to eat chocolates by the box and take seven teaspoons of sugar in his tea. Now that he's disciplined himself he makes us eat for him."

As the raillery continued with Hitler playing the eccentric and lovable old uncle, Eva spotted a stag on a nearby crag. "Look. I'm going to take a picture."

"The Führer's property is a game preserve with herds of chamois, roe and deer," informed Goebbels. "He has hundreds of feeding stations stocked with grain."

As Eva snuck up on the stag, it raised its antlers, nostrils flared.

"What a magnificent beast!" admired the Führer. "Who but a sadist could harm such an animal?"

"Hermann Göring," chuckled Goebbels. "When you made him chief forester, you put the fox with the chickens. Even today he's seen more with a bow and arrow than a gun."

In bad odor because of personal excuses and professional omissions, the Reichsmarschall was an easy target.

"If it's meat our Göring enjoys, perhaps I should send him blood pudding from the leeches my doctor uses for bleeding," sniffed the Führer. "After the war I intend to make Germany vegetarian. It will take only one trip to a slaughterhouse – I know just the one in the Ukraine. I saw girls wading in blood to the tops of their boots."

Pushing aside his éclair as if eating were no longer possible, Himmler spoke with a preacher's fervor: "I would ban blood sports altogether. To attack a poor creature, innocent and defenseless and unsuspecting, is murder. Nature is so marvelous. Every animal has a right to live. I was extraordinarily interested to hear Buddhist monks carry bells through the woods to scare off insects and animals so no harm comes to them."

"When choosing between corpse-eaters, I take the poacher," informed Hitler. "At least he kills at some danger to himself. That's why I released poachers from prison and placed them in provisionary battalions."

"I wouldn't even allow vivisection," asserted Himmler.

"Except for military purposes," interposed Bormann, with a sycophantic glance at Hitler.

"Yes, that's right," approved Hitler. "Otherwise I see no reason to snuff out the life of a dog, with its ability to feel and think, just to help a civilian bent on selfish pursuits."

"We Germans are the only people who have a decent attitude toward animals, including man," praised Himmler. "That's why we're the only people who understand subhumans."

Tapping on the window, Hitler urged Eva, still taking pictures. "Come in, my little patscherl, my honeybun. Your tea's getting cold."

She returned in high spirits, her camera over her shoulder. Again the Führer coaxed her to eat more pastries. When she refused, he tempted her with his fork, like a mother bird with a nestling. "You must have this morsel, it's good for you."

Eva relented piece by piece till the last one. Then, wiping her mouth, she refreshed her lipstick.

"If only you women knew how that stuff was made, you wouldn't touch it," mocked the Führer. "It's grease from waste water."

"This is from Paris," insisted Eva.

"Paris waste water is the worst. French girls turn our sensible German heads. They send our women high heels to break their ankles."

Snatching Hitler's broad-brimmed fedora, Eva modeled it. "I suppose, my Führer, you think your clothes are beautiful."

"Only on you. On me they're sensible."

Though a narcissistic woman with little grasp of issues outside her circumscribed world, Eva appeared confident and content. To her the war was the occupation that competed for her lover's time – a newsreel to be turned off when it became boring. As she clowned in the Führer's hat, Goebbels urged: "Why don't you do your Al Jolson imitation?"

"Not with a real movie star watching!"

"Then lend me the hat." Arranging it on a chair like a crown on a dais, Goebbels performed one of his favorite party pieces – a dissertation as to why Germany should return to monarchic government. In the nasal tones of the former crown prince, he seemed rational and impassioned as he launched each argument, oiled with tricks of oratory – poignant expression, subtle gestures, even a voice that cracked as he built to a feverish climax, thus proving his pathological insincerity to all who doubted it.

Laughing behind his hand to hide his crooked, yellow teeth, Hitler snatched back the hat. "Now I must have my turn." He delivered a monologue from *Richard III*, cruelly basing the crippled prince on Goebbels, as actor Werner Kraus had done.

Humiliated and furious, Goebbels pretended to laugh.

"Our Führer has a wonderful sense of humor," gloated Bormann.

More innocently, Eva underscored: "Just the other day we were in stitches over a painting sent by a fan of him standing nude on a diamond, flashing a sword." To Carmel she confided: "The Führer could have been a genius of the theatre. Sometimes he designs stage sets and he's especially good at lighting, though music is his passion. He's got the whole of *Die Meistersinger* off by heart."

Carmel felt swept by unreality. Their world was threatened by a tidal wave, yet here they sat with the chief windmaker in the still eye of the storm, talking about vegetarianism, leeches and the preservation of insects by Buddhists carrying bells.

The Führer readjusted his felt hat – the signal for returning to the Berg. Cars awaited. Striding to the lead one, Hitler called Blondi to heel. When the Alsatian bounded after a squirrel, he repeated his command in a higher pitch of irritation. Again the dog ignored him. Smashing his walking stick against a boulder, he screeched: "Imbecile! Obey me. Obey this instant!" As the dog pursued its canine destiny, the Führer thrashed the rock, screaming, cursing, bellowing in impotent rage like King Lear on his heath.

Violence poured from every pore. The air crackled, making plausible Willi Bliss's stories about the old carpet-eater on his knees tearing the chancellery rug with his teeth.

For five minutes the leader of the Third Reich raved at his dog, his face livid with powerlessness, the veins pumping in a jagged claw across his forehead, while everyone stared in frozen silence.

Losing track of his squirrel, Blondi loped back to its master, then plunked on his haunches to scratch a flea. Cutting his tirade as if with scissors, Hitler nodded in satisfaction. Face flushed, limbs trembling, he proceeded to the lead Mercedes with Blondi trotting after him. Everyone began chatting and laughing, opening and closing doors, sorting out seats as if nothing unusual had happened.

The sun was setting as Colonel Kurt Schmidt left the village of Berchtesgaden and began to climb Führer Mountain in his souped-up BMW. Though he had been to the Berghof twice before for meetings with the Führer, this was the first time he had been invited to stay the night – a distinction not lost on him. His assignment was a simple one. Tomorrow he would inspect the bunker system under the Berg and make suggestions for its expansion – his first engineering job since Zelbec. He had already studied the blueprints. Ninety percent of the task lay in its confidentiality, which was why he had been asked.

Kurt's spirits soared as he climbed higher. The assassination of Heydrich had closed some doors and opened others. Gestapo work appealed to him. He liked pitting his mind against the enemies of the state, flushing them out of their nice warm holes and disposing of them. Especially the highborn, like the baron whose villa he had inherited.

Though he was not on intimate terms with anyone in the Führer's inner circle, he had files on them all and they knew it, a legacy from Reinhard Heydrich. Like Heydrich, he was not well liked but he was respected.

After years of struggle, the current under Kurt was running fast and smooth. For the first time he felt a sense of privilege – what the wealthy and titled took for granted. Nor did the possible collapse of the Third Reich entirely deflate him. He knew now how such things worked. A few heads would roll. The government would change and the nation would be required to suffer. After a few concessions, the wealthy would continue as before, with the chaotic period of readjustment providing unlimited new opportunities for expansion.

It was Kurt's intention to be part of that elite. Already men of the highest rank in the party were sounding each other out, testing loyalties and friendship to see how much weight they would bear, calling in old favors, consolidating, altering records, burning diaries, preparing to jump one way or the other or both at once. Kurt was keeping his options open. Himmler, Göring, Goebbels. . . . Whoever was asked by the victors to take charge of the New Germany, he would be ready with invaluable experience and a willingness for hard tasks.

Kurt stopped at the first checkpoint, then waited with impatience as a phone call was made to the Berg and permission received. "Proceed."

Driving faster than he should to make up for these few minutes of lost time, Kurt turned the next corner too sharply, saw the pavement give way into empty space, and wrestled the car back from a dizzy trip down to König See. Pausing, he lit an Ariston cigarette, then continued his upward journey more soberly.

Reluctantly Kurt admitted to one conspicuous problem – a part of his life that no longer worked. Why couldn't Ilse let the past be? Her constant tears, her need to go over the same ground, rationalizing and justifying, were getting him down. He had done his suffering before the death of

their son. That had been his crucifixion. Even Reichsführer Himmler had written to him commending his courage and toughness in accordance with SS ideals. "You
were given a unique opportunity to serve, and you did not
falter." Did Ilse think because he failed to weep and whine
with her that he was without heart? Kurt tightened his
grip on the wheel. He couldn't stand the past. He wondered now how he had gagged his way through it. He had
spared Ilse the details, made his own decisions, borne his
own burdens. Was he to be penalized for that?

Once Ilse had identified with his ambitions as if they
were her own. Once he had respected her feminine wisdom and better education. All that had changed. She had
been slow to conceive and then had injured the fetus. It
was her job at the Lebensborn that had demanded from
them a greater purity as parents. The Helga solution had
been a face-saving one, but what did Kurt get from that?
Goebbels had a beautiful show wife and a thousand starlets to cater to his desires. Göring had a wife who pleased
him, a love match. Himmler had taken his secretary as his
second wife, and had children by her. Why should he be
the only man in the SS whose biological wife was chosen
by his legal one?

Kurt felt he deserved more. After a good beginning, Ilse
had not lived up to expectations. Though he had forgiven
her her biological failure, she had not proved tough
enough to forgive herself. For that, she was punishing
him, dragging him into an unhealthy morass. The rewards
for selfless dedication were now his and he intended to
reap them.

Kurt slowed for the second checkpoint, surprised at the
anger his thoughts had aroused. As the SS guard returned
his pass after confirmation from the first checkpoint, Kurt
noticed a coffee stain on it and snarled: "This isn't a lunch
paper. Be assured I shall report you."

Resuming his climb, Kurt tried to regain his buoyant
mood. Switching his thoughts from his wife to his new
villa, he pictured the rolling lawns, the shrubs bursting

into yellow and pink bloom, then found his mind circling back to the one woman he could imagine as chatelaine in such a splendid setting: Carmel Kohl.

As soon as Kurt allowed her image to fill his mind, he realized that seeing her was the reason he was so impatient to get to the top of the mountain. Her visit to the Berg, coinciding with his, was fate. Kurt had inherited a modest file on her from Heydrich. As he had watched it thicken through his own dogged efforts, he had wondered how he might confront her. To visit her would be demeaning, but to call someone of her fame into Gestapo headquarters required him to present evidence to Gestapo chief Heinrich Müller. This he was unwilling to do. As yet the incriminating details were circumstantial. Besides, secret information meant power. Kurt's power over her. It would please him to present his case to her in private, then to discover how anxious she was to protect herself. Around this fantasy his mind had embroidered many scenes.

What could be better than an intimate party at Berchtesgaden, where she could see firsthand how far he had risen and how much he was respected?

As the forest opened into a broad clearing dominated by the Berghof, Kurt determined to seize this opportunity to talk with her even if that meant risk. Should the Third Reich collapse, it would not hurt to have a wife or mistress who had been disloyal to the regime. Besides, he relished the adventure.

Showplace of the Berg, the grand salon was dominated by a picture window and a timbered Gothic ceiling. The massive fireplace, red marble stairs, giant chandelier and outsized furniture took their scale from the mountain. The carpets were as thick as moss, the walls were hung with medieval tapestries interspersed with German and Italian masterworks.

In a white Grecian gown, Carmel was introduced by Goebbels to those added to the afternoon group, now formally buffed and polished: Hermann Göring, in a Master-of-the-Forests uniform so tightly corseted he looked like a green apple core, and his wife Emmy, along with the wives of the adjutants.

Arriving after the more formal introductions, Reichsführer Himmler was accompanied by a Gestapo officer with a profile like a saw, intense blue eyes and thinning white-blond hair. He brought the man to Carmel. "Colonel Kurt Schmidt has been chosen as your dinner partner. He's a fan of yours, as we all are."

Smiling in acknowledgment, Carmel found the colonel's handsome if chilly presence ruined for her by his too-sweet cologne. Used to gamier but more honest human smells after five years of shortages, she suspected he was a man who knew something about his animal nature he wished to hide.

The Reichsführer's introduction proved even more unsettling when he added: "Colonel Schmidt solved the Heydrich assassination. Even after two years the smallest clue sends him halfway across the Reich. When he's through, even those who sold the assassins their last set of underwear will have been destroyed."

When all the guests were assembled, the Führer made his appearance. Shaking hands with everyone, including those he had seen that afternoon, he inquired about families and pet projects. Though his intention was to relax the room, the guests grew tense in the competition to make a good impression. Striding to the dining room through a colonnaded corridor, he was followed by Martin Bormann escorting Eva, with other couples falling in behind.

As Schmidt linked arms with Carmel, she found something about him challenged her memory. Did it have to do with the Heydrich assassination? Had pictures of him appeared in the papers or was the connection a more dangerous one?

Eva was seated to the Führer's left in the paneled dining room, Carmel to his right. An SS waiter served the Führer Fachinger mineral water from a fresh bottle, another poured Moët et Chandon champagne for his guests. Selecting two white roses from a silver vase, the Führer laid one on Eva's plate and the other on Carmel's. "Now I'm a thorn between two roses," he joked.

Jarred by the underground significance of this gesture, Carmel stammered her thanks, then found Colonel Schmidt gazing at her with inappropriate intensity. Tongue-tied, she forced a smile while asking herself: What does Schmidt know about White Rose? Have I betrayed myself? Is this a trap? Shrewdly she studied the faces around the table. All but Schmidt's seemed unaffectedly friendly.

As an SS man served the guests leek soup with a nutty aroma, the Führer's waiter brought him Nudelsuppe prepared to his own eccentric tastes but also kept separate as a safety precaution even here. Asparagus and carrots, grown by Bormann in the Führer's own greenhouses, were accompanied by steak for the guests, a Russian egg and yogurt for the Führer.

Though at the teahouse dialogue had been allowed, now only the Führer declaimed. In the course of an hour he asserted that more Shakespearean productions had been staged in Germany than in Britain over the past three hundred years. Only the classical Greeks knew how to build a perfect roof. Red is the best color for political posters. The same speech has a different impact in the afternoon than in the evening. The father of Jesus was not Joseph but a Roman legionnaire who was an Aryan. All great American inventors were immigrants from Swabia. The Jews are perverting the culture of Lapland. Birth control killed the Roman empire. A diet of vegetables prolongs the life of elephants.

Though relieved not to have to make conversation with Colonel Schmidt, whose eyes seemed always to be on her, Carmel became obsessed by the nagging sense of having met him before. As dessert was served, she confronted him. "I have a memory I can't get hold of. Do I know you from somewhere?"

He smiled slightly, while redevoting himself to his baked apple.

Rising, the Führer kissed Eva's hands and Carmel's, signifying the end of the meal. Then, after the women had filed back to the grand salon for coffee and liqueurs, he led in the men.

Again the Führer concentrated his attention on Carmel as guest of honor. "I'll show you the three most important things in this room." He guided her to a portrait of Frederick the Great, his acknowledged military idol, by Anton Graf. "I take this everywhere. On planes it occupies the seat beside me, even if one of my generals must stay behind. My finest hours are spent in its contemplation." He displayed his thumbs. "See these? They're exactly like Frederick the Great's. The enlargement means strength of will. Like Frederick, I know something about overcoming reverses."

Now he led Carmel to a bookcase containing the leatherbound works of Karl May, a German author who wrote about the American West without ever seeing it. "I'll never have to go to America because I've learned all I need to about its soul from Karl May. You're familiar with his books?"

Carmel laughed. "*Pshaw and damnation, sir*. My mother was a fan. Those were the only books in our flat. Old Shatterhand, who could shoot through a hangman's noose and who defeated the Injun hordes through will-power and treachery."

Solemnly the Führer nodded. "Such nobility is inspiring. I've ordered my generals to carry these books into battle because Russians are like Indians. They hide behind bridges and trees then come out for the kill."

Passing up a sea nymph by Böcklin and a Botticelli nude, the Führer showed Carmel a portrait by Franz von Stuck. Entitled *Sensuality*, it was of a naked dark-haired beauty with a large black python undulating between her thighs. "This is my favorite. See how the eyes burn like Medusa's. My mother had eyes like that. Stuck's influence on me is second only to Wagner's." Fixing Carmel with the same smoldering gaze, he extended his arm in the Hitler salute. "I can keep it up for hours without wilting. I've trained myself."

After this extraordinary tour, the Führer sat by the fireplace, again drawing Eva and Carmel around him, while the others ranged themselves in a circle, with Colonel Schmidt off by the window.

"Play the overture to Rienzi," he ordered his SS sound engineer. Eva and the secretaries called the record's number, indicating how often they had heard the Berg's repertoire. With the overture swelling into the room's cathedral spaces, the Führer discoursed on the importance of music to the German psyche. "We Germans go to a concert the way others go to church. With the sacrament of song we celebrate our heroes, our youth march to battle, our spirit explores infinity. Any person who doesn't know Wagner doesn't know National Socialism. He's our supreme prophet. He awakens us to the grandeur of our ancestry and the superiority of our blood. When I listen to *Rienzi* or *Lohengrin*, I hear the secrets of the cosmos, shock waves from a bygone world but also of our future – a power like electricity that science will someday measure.

"It was on a summer's night in Vienna after being transported by *Rienzi* that I received my mandate to lead the German people from servitude to the height of freedom. As I, a penniless youth, poured out my heart to my dearest friend, it was as if another spoke from my mouth, and I could only listen with astonishment to the elemental forces bursting the dykes like floodwaters."

The Führer stared at the full moon and glowing peaks, allowing the silence to lengthen. Then, in an anguished voice, he shrilled: "I hate the moon, that pale ghostly fellow. It's dead and terrible and inhuman. Adolf comes from Athalwolf, meaning noble wolf. I'm the eternal wolf baying down the moon."

For the next several hours, while eyes glazed and heads drooped, the Führer sermonized unchallenged, shifting in time and from the personal to the mythic, selecting topics like seashells cast by a storm onto his inner shore, turning them over then discarding them. "My mother had eyes like Medusa. I have eyes like my mother. Once my father caned me while I counted the blows and my frightened mother stood outside the door. Two hundred and thirty strokes! When I wouldn't cry, my father didn't dare beat me again."

Simultaneously the Führer agitated the fire, sending out smoke, sparks, tongues of flame, alternately striking and wooing it with poker and bellows. Fixing his eyes on one person or another, he engaged in eye duels, daring him or her to blink. Twice he caught Göring snoozing, with his chins cascading down his green uniform like a flesh stream. "Am I keeping you from your nap, Herr Reichsmarschall?"

Nudged by his wife, Göring jolted to attention. "Just meditating on your point, my Führer." To prove attention, he told an anecdote from the days when he was a World War I ace – a tale which would have fit as snugly as a jigsaw piece into the conversation fifteen minutes back.

Tunelessly whistling "Who's Afraid of the Big Bad Wolf?" the Führer let Göring finish before snarling: "All my Luftwaffe brass are lazy. All are crooks. All drag their feet when they should be marching forward. The battle against those nincompoops is worse than the one with Russia. All should be hanged. I myself will put up the gallows. Fortunately it's easier to fire a Reichsmarschall than a janitor because they're easier to replace."

Goebbels seemed to have mastered the art of sleeping with eyes open and a smile propping the corner of his mouth. Bormann, the ambitious secretary, took notes, while Himmler, with the flame blotting out his steel-rimmed eyes, remained inscrutable as a Buddha.

Posed by the window, his frosty profile like that of the mountains, Kurt Schmidt remained outside the circle of fire, as if afraid it might melt his glacial substance. Whenever Carmel looked up, his eyes were on her, gleaming from the dark like those of a night animal. Shifting uncomfortably, she tried to remember where she had met him, but every time she caught some tag-end of memory, it wriggled from her like a worm through the beak of a bird.

As if aware of a counterforce in the room, the Führer broke off, gazed from Carmel to Schmidt, then demanded: "Herr Colonel, after two years of working on the assassination of Heydrich, what have you to say about this kind of crime?"

Without hesitation, the colonel testified: "That it's the dirtiest offence against the state, and one for which the punishment should be prolonged and unforgiving."

"And what's the best advice you can give against such jackals?"

With the same assurance, Schmidt answered: "Never fall into the luxury of set habits."

"Ja, ja, ja. The Reichsführer and I are in total agreement that Heydrich's postures were almost provocative," approved the Führer. "By confusing bravery and foolishness, he made himself a sitting duck for every sorehead and lunatic. I feel safest in my car because I never let anyone know where I'll be or when, not even the police, but in a crowd I'm also protected by enthusiasm. If anyone took out a gun, my people would tear the assassin apart."

After staring into the glowing coals to recharge himself, the Führer shifted his gaze onto Carmel. As if speaking for her alone, he warned: "In my extreme youth four of my brothers died, while I alone survived. Destiny had taken me up in her loving arms. Fighting in France, I passed unscathed through the fires of hell. When my comrades on both sides were shot, my commanding officer concluded with awe: "There's no bullet with your name on it.' So it is today. No bullet or bomb bears the name Adolf Hitler. I am the living embodiment of the legend from Charlemagne through Frederick the Great."

At last shifting his eyes, he exalted: "In Berlin, which I

shall rename Germania, there will arise a city of unequaled magnificence. Through the heart will run Pracht Strasse, the Street of Splendor, with triumphal arches and a superdome seven times that of St. Peter's. On the Urals I will recreate our medieval cities with their charming crooked streets and Gothic towers. Rothenburg, Augsburg and Heidelberg will be our models. Already I've made careful calculations as to how long it will take to drive a Volkswagen at sixty miles per hour from Berlin to the Ukraine. The year after the war we'll have a million Volkswagens in production.

"Since we are a people who value tradition, we won't forget our glorious dead. We'll build gigantic tombs three hundred feet high on our main avenue." Pausing to pile more logs on the fire, he drew his chair so close to the flames they seemed to rifle his hair and melt his face as he stared into their molten core. "The western democracies are decadent and feeble. If it hadn't been for us, they would have fallen prey to the more virile races of the East. The Anglo-American plutocracy, the Marxist-Bolsheviks, the Jewish financial conspiracy, the Freemasons and the Jesuits will regret this struggle they have forced upon us. We have lost one opportunity to raze London, but we'll have another. Our miracle weapons will fly like lethal silver birds into its heart. New incendiaries will breed fires everywhere in London till all unite in one conflagration.

"Why wasn't Paris set aflame? Ahh, what a funeral pyre that will make. But all is just practice for the show to come. The destruction of New York in a sea of flame, skyscrapers turned into torches and collapsing one upon another, their skins melting, leaving twisted black super-structures like agonized beasts screaming for water . . . not a city burning but imploding, while around us we hear the glorious music of Wagner. . . ."

Words spewed like lava as he raved, binding those in the room with his mad fantasies. At a point of unbearable tension his speech climaxed, then he collapsed, draining himself and everyone else.

Eva Braun left the room.

"Get me tonight's air-raid reports," the Führer demanded of Bormann. Rising shakily, shoulders stooped, he shuffled after Eva like an old man.

The others stared at the space where the Führer had been, held by aftershock. Several smiled at Carmel, as if grateful to her for offering a fresh pair of ears. She realized something more powerful than devotion or even opportunism held these people in thrall. By rescuing each from obscurity, then proclaiming himself a god, the Führer had become the sun to which they were attached with a force akin to gravity. While creating their own dependent satellite systems, they had to return to the source of their energy, no matter how humiliating or boring that might prove. The alternative was psychological death.

As Carmel uncramped her limbs and murmured the appropriate exit lines, she noticed with relief that Colonel Schmidt had already slipped from the salon. A thoroughly nasty presence, she concluded.

Carmel's room was on the second floor. As she strolled down halls with Roman arches lit by moonlight, she was alarmed by the sudden, too-sweet scent of jasmine. The shadow stirred. Colonel Kurt Schmidt stepped across her path. "I have a message for you. Meet me in twenty minutes in the cave below the Berg."

"Why? Who's the message from?"

A slight hesitation. "Me."

Carmel stalled. "What about the security guards?"

"I've checked all that out. Two sets will challenge you. Say you can't sleep and need the fresh air." He wrung his hands as if washing them. "I've told them I expect a lady to join me. Take the left path from the terrace, then follow the left fork down thirty yards."

Controlling her distaste, she demanded: "Why should I compromise myself for a stranger?"

He leaned forward as if offering news of the highest confidentiality. "Twenty years ago I used to drop in

Saturday nights at The Red Fox. Herr Berg took us to the
Adlon." His smile for once held charm. "We stole
spoons."

Suddenly Carmel did remember, every detail etched
clear. The hungry young man in pink cardboard shirtfront
and Frau Fuchs' tuxedo, stuffing bread into his pockets.

Kurt waited in the cave thirty yards down the mountain –
a natural indentation extended deep into the rock by tunnels, part of the bunker system where the leadership of the
Third Reich could hold out as long as their supplies. To
destroy it, the mountain top would have to be sheared off.
No weapon existed that could do that, not even the
Führer's rockets.

He smoked a cigarette, feeling sweat trickle inside his
uniform. She was already five minutes late. He must be
careful. He desired her, but not enough to jeopardize his
life or his future. One woman in a world of billions. *He*
was in the position of power.

A light footfall, the stirring of gravel. Stubbing his cigarette, Kurt retreated into the cave. She stood in the moonlight, ghostly pale despite the red hair. Sensibly she had
changed to hiking clothes and soft-soled shoes.

As Carmel entered the cave, she smelled the colonel's
cologne and knew he was waiting. She played it boldly
like a stage entrance. "Hello, Colonel Schmidt. What a
unique opportunity to become reacquainted. This regime
has done very well by you."

Stepping into the moonlight, Kurt relit his cigarette.
"I've paid my way."

"You said you had a message for me."

"A warning. I know all about your shady activities, as
did Reinhard Heydrich. Don't bother to protest. Our files
go back to the day you arrived in Berlin – careless acts and
treasonous utterances reported by two loyal party members who served as your chauffeur and housekeeper. That
would be enough to send an ordinary person to a concen-

tration camp. Fortunately for you, you've never been ordinary." His tone was unsympathetic, full of repressed violence.

"Why are you telling me these things?"

"So far the most serious evidence against you is circumstantial – your bad companions, especially Wolfgang von Friedrich. Lieutenant-General Heydrich suspected his loyalty even while using him for certain distasteful tasks. Though your playmate is doomed, Fräulein, I'm offering you a chance for life. The investigation was mine. Your complicity is known only to me, and files have been known to disappear."

"I haven't any idea what you're talking about."

"Don't play games. We haven't time."

"You still haven't told me why you brought me here."

"You're a sophisticated woman. I don't think I need spell things out. With me as your protector, you may live to see the end of the war and share in the fruits of victory."

Every instinct warned Carmel to humor him, perhaps pretend to agree till she could come up with a scheme of her own, but anger and fear pushed her beyond common sense. "Victory?" she jeered. "You must know in your heart Germany can't win. Any day the allies will land in France. Help shorten the fighting. Save what's left of Germany. Save lives. Save yourself or at least your soul."

"Soul? I know only this life, which I like very well. I've made you an offer – one many women would jump at without any need to save their skins. Leave your worthless count. Have nothing to do with him till his arrest. That man is scum. A traitor who spits on honor and duty and loyalty. I should let you sink with him, but out of a soft heart I'm giving you a chance to account for your shame."

"Leave Wolfgang for you? He's not a lover, he's a friend. But either way my answer is the same – you aren't fit to lick his boots."

Grabbing Carmel by the shoulders, Schmidt shook her with violence. "Don't say another word. Instead of wasting your sympathy on subhumans, think of the German soldier. Think of how he's suffered. I've killed many enemies of the state with these two hands and sometimes that's been difficult. I'm only human, but I rejoiced to do my duty."

Compulsively he began washing his hands. "Do you know my hardest professional task? At Stalingrad. Shooting wounded German soldiers in the snow. Thousands of them perishing because the German army doesn't retreat."

Kurt had intended to stop there, but his tongue ran ahead of his ability to control it, turning what was intended as a testament to duty into a confession of misery. "Afterward, as the other officers and I took off in the Reichsführer's private plane, soldiers mad with hunger hung by their hands from the wings. We were ordered to shoot them like dogs. And why was there no room for these healthy men in the plane? Because of a special cargo I was returning to Reichsführer Himmler. Tin cans containing heads of Jewish-Bolshevik commissars for the Institute for Anthropological Research at Strasbourg University. I personally oversaw the measuring of the skulls on the living victims before shrinkage from death ruined the biological data. *I* was the officer who instructed the firing squad to aim low so as not to damage the goods. *I* was the one who watched the physicians claim their trophies with scalpel and hacksaw."

Sweat and the smell of despair oozed through Colonel Schmidt's cologne – not a human scent but the odor of a trapped animal. Groaning, he reached out to Carmel as if for comfort. Repelled, she struck his face with her fist. "Get away from me, you foul thing!"

Humiliated by guilt and rejection, Kurt flung her against the cave wall. To regain control, he pulled his revolver from its holster and waved it melodramatically. "I'm going to count to ten, then I'll shoot. Compose yourself for death. Nothing can save you now. Even the Führer will pin a medal on me when he knows you've been involved in assassination. . . . One . . . two . . . three . . ."

He fixed a silencer to his revolver, unable to retreat.

"Four . . . five . . . six . . ."

She had often imagined her death, but this was too absurd, this crazy man in this crazy place.

"Seven . . . eight . . . nine . . ."

He cocked the gun.

"Ten . . ."

He fired.

Carmel slumped to the ground. For several seconds she lay inert. She felt nothing, no explosion or pain. Just shock and disbelief. Blood gushed from her forehead, though her skull was intact.

Kurt Schmidt sagged against a pine tree outside the mouth of the cave, his gun in his hand. At first Carmel thought he had shot himself, then she saw him straighten, a vacant look on his face. She realized he must have deliberately shot over her head into the cave, spattering rock that gashed her forehead.

Darting past him, she scrambled up the path, putting space between herself and this man who had mutated into his uniform, conscious of the damp and loamy scent of the air, losing her footing on the slippery pine needles and sliding five yards before struggling up again, afraid to turn to see if she were being pursued.

FOUR

Berlin

May 1944

WOLFGANG von Friedrich sat on a bench in the Tiergarten, tossing bits of bread into Neuer See and watching the greedy splatter of ducks.

Bombed several nights in succession, the Tiergarten looked like a scene from *Götterdämmerung*. Oaks and beeches had been ripped out by their roots and flung like clubs discarded by a race of giants. Even more surreal were the ones left standing, their charred and denuded limbs hung with tinkling strips of tinfoil dropped by British Mosquitoes to confuse the city's radar defenses.

Wolf draped half a dozen streamers over his shoulder like a guest at a child's birthday party. As a boy he had never been alloyed to have such a party. His mother hadn't believed in them. Too messy. Decades too late he grieved for her. How unhappy she must have been, a figure frozen in a crystal paperweight with the artificial snow recirculating. Wolf wondered why his parents had bothered to have a child, then decided he was a statement of their good intentions.

As the ducks departed and the waters stilled, Wolf looked at his reflection in the opaque green pond. In the two years since Heydrich's assassination, he had suffered much torment, not from remorse but from the knowledge of evil which made such a barbaric act necessary. At forty-two he had as much gray hair as black while his eyes looked like broken eggs from lack of sleep. That he didn't regret. Suffering had stripped him of his superiority and his masks so he was no longer a spectator of life but a man joined to his own species, and hence all others, through compassion. Colors seemed more vibrant, sounds richer, tastes sharper, textures more complex. As he sat on his bench he imagined he could hear grass grow, feel fingers of sunlight massage his back, see the finely veined maple leaves reach out like children's hands.

He had begun to hear snare drums in his sleep and to see columns of cavalry stream through Brandenburger Tor. Whose funeral was he reviewing this time? He had a feeling it was his own. At least it would not be a military funeral. Of all the able-bodied men in the Third Reich, Wolf was one of the few who had never donned a uniform or insignia of any kind – infantile rebellion against his father, but more. He had never had to wear the lies and compromises implied by every uniform in Nazi Germany, had never found himself trapped by corrupt codes that scratched and pinched like too-tight armor.

Some of Wolf's contemporaries had argued that they had joined Nazi organizations to change them from the inside. It was better for them to take such jobs, they rationalized, to prevent "real" Nazis from getting them. Yet when next he saw them they were often acting more like Nazis than the real ones, to preserve their cover. Some had even begun to protest their virtue on the grounds that they had murdered fewer resisters or Jews or Bolsheviks than they could have.

Wolf felt satisfied that the lies he had worn had been of his own choosing, and the raiment he had woven from them was of his own design.

When the Nazis came to power, Wolf had wasted time wondering what his father would have done if he had lived. Then he realized how fatuous that question was. His father had committed suicide by heart attack as surely as if he had fallen on his sword. That was the old general's answer, and his mother had joined her husband in an act of unconscious will as surely as if she had committed suttee. That was his flinty legacy along with the family silver. Perhaps it was this example that had prevented him from falling to the temptations of Reinhard Heydrich.

As Wolf lit a cigarette, the bushes to his left quivered and parted. He was mildly surprised when an ostrich trotted past, looking like his Aunt Gertrude out for a morning's jog wearing his tennis shoes. Since the British had scored several direct hits on the zoo, thousands of exotic animals had been released, spawning fantastic rumors. Crocodiles, it was said, now lurked in Landwehr Kanal. Boa constrictors coiled around the limbs of linden trees. Apes were turning up in clothing lineups. Two months ago Wolf had been in Café Kern when a wandering tiger gobbled a tray of pastries, then took a convulsion and died. When a customer complained the tiger had been killed by Kern's inferior cakes, the pastry chef had sued for libel. An autopsy proved the animal had died of glass splinters and the chef won his suit. All this with bombs raining down like hailstones.

Wolf saw Carmel coming through the same bushes as the ostrich but far prettier in a yellow dress and sun hat. She had phoned him on her return from Berchtesgaden deeply upset. Removing his tinfoil strips he rose to greet her. "Still among the living, I see."

Taking her hand he drew her down beside the bench, using courtliness to conceal a powerful and treacherous tenderness. "You must let me hold your hand. Love. That's our cover. That's how everyone all over Berlin is dealing with anguish. I almost tripped on two couples in the grass while I was trying to avoid the amorous advances of a moose. Another couple was making love in a phone booth with two giraffes lined up outside. Whether the giraffes wanted to use the phone or were seeking carnal knowledge I can't say, though one was a little forward when I passed. The male. It's like old times on the Kurfürstendamm except everyone is older, sadder and hungrier. All this we owe to our Führer."

Too anxious to laugh, Carmel clutched his hand. "Wolf, you're in danger."

He laughed. "Oh, yes. I've noticed. Several hundred bombers of assorted nationalities, bellies painted white to resemble clouds, are even now crossing the Rhine. In an hour you'll be able to say the same about everyone in Berlin."

"No, please listen. It's more serious. Colonel Schmidt of the Gestapo. He's still working on Heydrich's death. He knows about you."

Briefly Carmel recounted the curious tale of Kurt Schmidt. "Don't bother telling me I was a fool. I know that."

"Your instincts are usually right. That's why you're a fine actress. You might have behaved in exactly the right way to checkmate the bastard . . . It's odd. I thought I remembered every detail of the night I heard you sing at The Red Fox, but I don't recall our socially mobile Colonel Schmidt. I was aware someone by that name was working on the assassination of Heydrich. The worst kind of Nazi – idealistic *and* opportunistic. A switch-hitter."

"He said the Gestapo was going to arrest you."

"Could be bluff."

"You must go into hiding."

"My dear Carmel, you seem not to grasp the world we live in. Thousands of Germans are working in munitions plants and waiting in lineups who'll be dead tomorrow. Did you hear the one about the two corporals in a trench on the eastern front? One warned the other: 'You're in danger. You must go into hiding.' Or what about the Luftwaffe pilot who taxied back in his ME-109? 'Whew, that was lucky. I just read the statistics on those things. I could have been killed.'"

"Wolf, this is deadly serious. You have to hide."

"I know it's serious. That's why I can't hide. Raymon was right. I'm not tough enough to be a revolutionary. The first threat of reprisals and I'd give up anyway. I can't stand the sight of other people's blood on my hands."

He recited:

> "Yes the world is just a barrel organ
> Played by God Himself.
> We must all dance to the tune
> That just happens to be on the roll."

Carmel demanded: "What's that supposed to mean?"

"It's the last thing Reinhard said to me. A stanza from his father's opera entitled *Amen*. When he recalled that, then shot his reflection in the mirror, I knew our assassins couldn't miss because they had another accomplice – Reinhard himself. Why, I don't know. That's trickier. I always envied him as a man without conscience. Perhaps the Aryan side of him executed the Jew. Or perhaps the Jew sought vengeance on the Aryan. I don't even know if he was Jewish or not. What an exquisite irony! I doubt he knew himself, but the split in his personality was widening. You could see it in his face. One half of him relaxed and happy as violinist, father and husband, the other champing like Genghis Khan to cut a swath across France. With so much mediocrity in the world, the perfectionist in me hated to kill a man who was go good at his job."

"What does all this have to do with you and Schmidt?"

"Can't you see? The rules are the same for both sides. The rules of fate. I feel my own death fattening inside me the same way Reinhard did."

Carmel threw her arms around his neck just as the sirens wailed. "That's garbage. You're convincing yourself. You have to fight back."

Wolf untwined her like a gardener uprooting vines. "I have to go."

"Where?"

"Home. Didn't you tell me to protect myself? There's an air raid. I'm following orders – yours and the Führer's."

"Take me with you."

"That's impossible."

"Why?"

"I'm proscribed. You said so. You'd be safer here. Even with the bombs. Your colonel gave you good advice – stay away."

"That's for me to decide. You always insist I make up my own mind. I just have."

She recited:

> "We must all dance to the tune
> That just happens to be on the roll."

"Unfair."

"The Gestapo won't raid with bombs falling. Let me come with you till the raid's over. At least we can have that."

Untouched by bombs, the Friedrich mansion conjured up an era of carriages and ladies in hoop skirts. As they walked arm in arm up the cobbled drive, Carmel remembered the first time she had been here – for her wedding.

The rush of blue-liveried servants for hats and gloves, the swirl of glamorous guests – princes and pretenders with almost as much gold braid as the doorman; generals with complexions as waxy as their mustaches; glittering names from stage and screen with glittering gowns to match; diplomats as stiff as their starched shirts; industrialists as fat as their cigars; financiers trying to get the hang of their new monocles. And scattered about like ominous Black and Brown shadows, members of the National Socialist party to which Axel Berg had generously donated.

As Wolf unlocked the door, Carmel mourned: "My list of wedding guests reads like a proscription one."

Together they went over the names: Professor Max and Sara Stein, the first imprisoned with fate unknown, the other in exile. Christian and Renate Jürgens, by their own hand. Raymon Arno, executed. General von Blomberg, last of the Old Guard, fired and disgraced. SA Chief Ernst

Röhm, executed and unmourned. Security Chief and Reich Protector Reinhard Heydrich, dispatched by bomb.

"I'd say the survival rate was about like that for Henry VIII's wives," agreed Wolf.

The hall felt as clammy as a mausoleum, with faded burgundy rectangles marking where Wolf's ancestors had hung. Dust covers lay on the floor like broken chrysalises from which priceless antiques had been sold. In several places pans of white plaster had been shaken from the ceiling.

Wolf guided Carmel up the staircase smelling of mold into the oval ballroom with its dome painted in plump cupids and Italian Renaissance maidens. As they crossed the inlay floor, the hollow echo of their heels created an unbearable tension, like soldiers marching in lockstep across a bridge.

Taking Carmel in his arms, Wolf waltzed her to the other side of the room, conjuring up Max and Sara Stein as they had spun around the silken blue walls before the barbed wire tightened. He ushered Carmel through the leatherbound library where she and Axel had spoken their vows, then out a second door into the servants' wing. Flinging open a third door, this time unpainted, he announced: "My studio. You're the first guest I've had."

Carmel stepped into a solarium choked with tropical growth and cluttered with canvases and paint tubes. Sunlight struck an easel bearing a portrait. Carmel stared at it, feeling a powerful explosion in her chest like a firecracker going off in a tin can. Wolf's face had been grafted onto Reinhard Heydrich's, suggesting the masks of triumph and tragedy, but with the expressions so mixed it was impossible to tell which was which.

"You did this."

"Some part of me. The day after Heydrich's assassination my arm started to move without conscious control or awareness. I finished it the morning he died, though that's something I didn't know till afterward."

"It's a masterpiece."

"Unlikely. But it is very good. I call it 'A Study in Black and Dorian Gray.'"

Carmel scrutinized it then stepped back, marveling at the power, the agony. "Why has Heydrich's death disturbed you so much among all the others when you know what a monster he was?"

"Don't you see? That only makes it worse. I saw him as a projection of my coldest most logical self, the part of me that envied his apparent lack of conscience. It was Reinhard's Saxon accent I used for Father Klausner as my way of dealing with that. Reinhard showed me what evil I'm capable of."

"You'll live forever in your portrait, Wolf. It's the gift of self-expression you've always wanted."

Acknowledging that nothing that has existed can ever be destroyed, he agreed: "Yes, but I'd sooner live in you."

They made love in a jungle of palms, like the paint of two portraits running together, while the golden light faded to indigo.

"How would I survive without you?" asked Carmel.

"The way you would have if we'd never met. We're all messages in bottles tossed on a stormy sea." More practically, Wolf instructed: "If you need help, go to Frau Fuchs."

"But where is she?"

"Where she should be." He put his hand over her mouth. "Not another word."

The darkness was shattered by more sirens and the coming of a false dawn. Searchlights pierced the night like electric swords as metallic birds laid their lethal eggs, hatching fire. Now Wolf and Carmel made love fiercely in the still center of the exploding universe, their nostrils expanded with the stench of sulphur and loam torn from the bowels of the earth, poignant with the knowledge that the world was spinning out of control.

Amidst the chorus of thumps, thwacks, crunches and thuds, they heard a new sound, prolonged and muffled as if giant hands were ripping the rotting black velvet of the sky. An explosion eliminated the house next door, sending shock waves through the Friedrich mansion. Debris shot skyward, creating a cloud that hovered like a vulture before raining down plaster, wood, metal and glass.

The new glow in the east was the rising sun. Leaving the solarium, Wolf and Carmel found the Friedrichs' terraced garden whitened with plaster like the tiers of a wedding cake. Flakes of confetti fell from trees. Carmel snapped a branch, releasing a cascade of warm snow on Wolf's head. Laughing, he presented her with a white rose powdered with ash. "I return good for evil."

"This is how the roses looked in our garden after I sprinkled Axel's ashes . . . black roses. Is that what's going to happen to White Rose? Are we going to die after coming through so much together?"

Smoke hung over the city, glowing like a red-hot stove. Some streets were impenetrable with acrid fumes. Others were strewn with high-tension cables. The Kurfürstendamm was blocked by shredded camouflage nets and paved with glass. Mannequins with severed heads advertised the real corpses buried in basements while burglar alarms rang in shops whose doors and windows had been blown off. In one house half a room had been demolished, leaving a table set for dinner. Of another, all that remained was a fireplace chimney, with a portrait of the Führer – a lure to photographers from the propaganda ministry.

"The unpredictable laws of chance," murmured Wolf.

In most areas cleanup had begun. Polish prisoners, wearing purple Ps, boarded windows, swept plaster and posted signs forbidding looting on penalty of death. Despite such severity, the rules of ownership were changing. What used to be stealing had become acquiring.

"When will people start fighting over the spoils?" wondered Carmel.

"Survival of the fittest has always been the message of National Socialism. Wouldn't it be unfortunate for Goebbels and Hitler if everyone suddenly got the message."

Yet in the midst of chaos women were delivering papers to the doors of houses still standing. Berliners picked their way through rubble to work. An old man walked his wolfhound. Courting couples held hands. A woman carried a portable radio that blasted "Request Concert," a program linking soldiers with their families by musical requests. Lineups formed outside Gloria Palast, despite a hole in the roof, for a revival of Carmel's *Love Shield* touting the miraculous properties of love, while on Hardenberg Strasse at the UFA Palast *Victory in the West*, circa 1941, was shunned.

"On my street some people are living in houses without roofs or walls," marveled Carmel. "You see them carrying on as if nothing had happened."

"Maybe some are relieved. Suddenly the past, with its debts and responsibilities, is canceled. Ritualized bad habits are swept away. You've no choice but to live for today."

At the auction house of Hans W. Lange, collectors could still buy quality paintings. An elderly man in mismatched clothes confided to Carmel: "Last month a woodland landscape by Dutch painter Koekkoek was valued at 25,000 marks but went for 64,000. Do you know what its normal value would be? Four thousand marks. It's the great inflation all over again."

At the Natural History Museum the bones of dinosaurs protruded from the wreckage as students unearthed them for another time.

"A warning to Homo sapiens," commented Wolf. "Species destruction."

The curator, waving his arms like a corner preacher, lectured all who would listen. "Priceless treasures. Irreplaceable. You can't lump this with the ruins of a few stores and churches. It's the history of civilization."

A policeman maneuvered a wheelbarrow covered with burlap, from which gnarled feet extended. Somberly Wolf and Carmel watched his slow progress, with his frail but difficult load through indifferent crowds. Wolf recited from Tolstoy's "The Death of Ivan Ilych": " 'The awful

terrible act of his dying was reduced by those about him
to the level of a casual, unpleasant and almost indecorous
incident, as if someone entered a drawing room diffusing
an unpleasant odor.'"

They walked arm in arm to the Tiergarten. "I'll leave
you here," announced Wolf.

"I'm going with you."

"I believe in fate, not stupidity."

"Don't patronize me, Wolf. If the Gestapo want me,
they'll take me. If they don't, they won't. That's the way
it'll be whether I'm at your house or mine. And I intend to
survive."

"I believe you will. You have elemental force. You exude
it. I remember something Max Stein said when he began
to understand Jewish culture might not be a match for
Nazi primitivism: 'People like me need to touch earth
with our bare feet again. It's easier for monkeys to learn to
speak than for a man to swing from trees with the tail he
no longer has.'"

They found a cab with two doors off and the roof
patched by tarpaper, perhaps the last in the city, and
returned to Wolf's. They made love with tenderness, as if
bruised by the day's events, remembering the gnarled yellow feet, decapitated mannequins, dinosaur bones and
black roses.

As they savored Rauenthal wine, Wolf pushed a second
easel into the light then removed its canvas shell.

"Oh God, Wolf. It's wonderful."

Again Wolf had superimposed two images – Carmel's
public persona and the private self she thought no one
could see. Adding about ten years, he had emphasized
vulnerability, compassion, a knowledge of suffering.

"Not me. How I would like to look."

"You. My gift of prophecy. The repayment of a debt. I
found my best self in your eyes, though I couldn't stand
looking for long. You never needed Axel and me. We
needed you. Look again and remember what you see." He
grinned. "The name is very original. I call it 'Kara.' I

never should have changed your name. It's the sort of thoughtless thing men do."

"If I hadn't come back, you wouldn't have shown it to me."

"I didn't know if I could stand seeing it and you together. I didn't know if I dared let us both see what any fool would know: how much I love you."

At 2:22 a.m. a brick was thrown through Count Wolfgang von Friedrich's solarium window. Seconds later it was as if the whole dark night had poured through the hole as a dozen Gestapo swarmed around the room.

FIVE

ONCE THE hulking gray building at 8 Prinz Albert Strasse had been an art school with a pleasant garden. Now it was Gestapo headquarters patrolled by steel-helmeted guards toting machine guns.

Inside it looked like any other office – glass partitions, desks and typewriters – where people gossiped and ate their lunches while filing reports such as "Prisoner Weiss expired at 6:17 a.m., 5/27/44, of heart failure after prolonged interrogation."

In the basement was The Labyrinth with detention cells and interrogation rooms, containing the instruments of persuasion that gave the building its distinctive reputation. In Kurt Schmidt's view, the workers in this antiseptic maze were merely a necessary extension of the bureaucracy on the five upper floors, established by Reinhard Heydrich, "the good SS man."

In his windowless office – walnut-paneled, steel-plated and bullet-proof – Colonel Kurt Schmidt was enjoying a moment of personal satisfaction. After years of liquidating thousands whose names he had never known and for whom he had too frequently felt an ill-advised pity, he was about to preside over the slow and agonized death of a man he despised – a parasite who, along with the Kaiser and his family, had for generations sucked the blood of the German people; a degenerate who had fought on neither the battle front nor the home front; a brothel-keeper who had maintained himself in privilege by licking the boots of one party satrap after another; a Jew-lover responsible for the murder of Reinhard Heydrich.

Scrubbing his hands in the washroom attached to his office, Kurt Schmidt stared at the death mask of his mentor hung over the basin instead of a mirror – the high-minded forehead, the sculptured cheekbones, the nose broken twice in pursuit of athletic excellence. His interrogation must be hard, thorough, impersonal and very unpleasant, in accordance with the highest SS standards. Under no circumstances could he allow a repeat of the self-indulgence that had marred his performance in the cave at Berchtesgaden.

Drying his hands, Kurt cracked each knuckle then donned fresh white gloves from dozens in cellophane bags in his desk drawer. Flanked by an armed escort, he marched to a basement door guarded by more SS men with machine guns. Schmidt gave the password, "Raven." Then they filed down into the white glare of The Labyrinth. Lit by bulbs at five-foot intervals, it was the business part of 8 Prinz Albert.

Count Wolfgang von Friedrich stood barefoot and blindfolded in a brick cell, surrounded by one SS officer and four SS men with truncheons, his stance as casual as if he were waiting for his tailor to measure him for a new silk dressing gown. Twisting his arm, Schmidt forced him to his knees while the SS officer stripped him of the robe he was wearing. At a second signal, also silent so as not to give warning, the four SS men fell upon him with truncheons, methodically striking face, kidneys and genitals. Blood gushed from the count's nose and one ear. Gasping for breath, he choked up more blood and several teeth.

At another signal, the assailants forced their victim into a dentist's chair, to which they manacled his wrists and ankles. Yanking off his blindfold, the colonel stared into his eyes. "My name's Kurt Schmidt. We've met before. You are in the hands of the Gestapo. The equipment in here is the sort only a specialist would understand." He gestured toward the pallid young officer propped by one foot against the wall. "Captain Frick is such a specialist. He's going to question you with the skill of long experience. I'll be frank, there's no question of your leaving alive. It's a matter of how quickly you'll be allowed to die. The more you tell us about other resisters, foreign agents and assassins, the quicker and more merciful we'll be. But have no illusions. We'll get the information from you. It's just a matter of efficiency with us. Notice the sign carved over the door. AT THE END STANDS VICTORY. The victory of us over you. The victory of the Führer over the world. Both are inevitable."

Allowing himself one piece of theater, Schmidt removed the medal bearing Reinhard Heydrich's profile and marked with the word REVENGE from his own neck and placed it around the count's. "A gift from Lieutenant-General Heydrich."

Dragging a chair into position, Frick straddled it with his grasshopper legs. He thrust his nose into the count's face, then accused him of everything from the election of Roosevelt to the fall of Stalingrad. After this barrage had its numbing effect, he zeroed in on specifics. "Who is your British contact? Since he's already squealed, you might as well tell us. Why did you visit Reinhard Heydrich the night before the assassination? Who else did you contact in Prague?"

When Count Wolfgang von Friedrich made no response during three hours of interrogation, including pauses for truncheon beatings across belly, kidneys, soles of feet and genitals, Schmidt grew impatient. Snatching Frick's whip, he smashed it across the count's left cheek, extending his dueling scar in a way that did real damage. "Perhaps you fail to understand what's in store for you, Count No-Account. Not the simple roughing up you've had, but with the lash, rusty nails, lead pipes applied with precision so the flesh falls in raw slabs from the bone."

Dipping a sponge in vinegar, he laid it on the count's slashed cheek, creating an involuntary convulsion. "So you *do* have nerves. Good. You'll feel every one after we place electric shocks with terminals on your hands, feet, ears, penis and rectum. Then you'll think you're frying in a pan of oil with a pain so hideous you'll plead for death."

Stripping off his soiled gloves, Schmidt flung them to an aide, then received another pair sealed in cellophane. "After the electric shock we'll progress to baths of ice water into which you'll be plunged naked, held under till you're nearly asphyxiated, then yanked out so you gasp for breath, only to be forced under again."

Schmidt scrutinized the count, still as haughty as if he were checking the Adlon's wine list. "Have you nothing to say to spare us this trouble? You've saved so many sub-humans, can't you save yourself? What good do your titles and money do now? Where are your powerful friends when you need them? It's useless, you know. All this well-bred stubbornness. We still have the ultimate weapon God has provided . . ."

Schmidt reached into the pocket of Wolf's blue silk dressing gown and withdrew a gold lighter with a discreet swastika, the one he had coveted in The Red Fox so many years ago, or its twin. Snapping it in its owner's face so he could feel the lick of the flame, Schmidt exalted: "Fire. We of the home-front war know its persuasive powers."

He lit a Balkan cigarette, also from the count's dressing gown, then slid the lighter into his own pocket.

Filling his lungs, Schmidt exhaled the sweetish smoke into the count's face. "What flesh can resist the agony of flame as it renders it into butterfat?" When the count didn't flinch, Schmidt ground his cigarette into the man's other cheek and felt gratified to see his hands tighten into fists.

"Yes, I know, you want to strike back. Reinhard Heydrich too was a fighter and in his prime. He too wanted to live."

Schmidt poured a glass of vinegar, then held it to the count's cracked lips. "Smell that bouquet, the finest wine from the Gestapo's own cellar. Drink to all that makes life worth living. Drink to Reinhard Heydrich."

As two SS men held the count's head, he poured the vinegar down his throat.

Kurt Schmidt sat at his desk, surrounded by photos of him shaking hands with Lieutenant-General Reinhard Heydrich, Reichsführer Heinrich Himmler and Adolf Hitler, each representing a step upward. He tried to feel triumph, even satisfaction, but all he could find within himself was emptiness. Depletion. Acute depression.

What had he expected – that the count would beg for mercy? Blurt out names of friends? Lick his boots like a dog? All Kurt had so far received for nine days' labor was silence. Silence and those two black eyes following him around the interrogation cell, gaining in luminosity. He had forgotten the power of things to mutate into their opposites. The eyes of his enemy into the eyes of his deepest self. The golden castle of Wewelsberg into the rat-shadow of Nibelheim.

Kurt tried to revive the humiliation, anger, bitterness and sorrow that had given his life its forward thrust – poverty, the early loss of a mother and a sister, the murder of a father, but for every pair of eyes demanding vengeance, ten thousand stared back in accusation, all melded into the eyes of the dying count.

After the first surge of power, Kurt had felt only a grudging envy for the man who could still find something worth suffering so much for. As the days had ground by, he had had to rev himself up for the routine of reducing a man's body to a pulp while still allowing him enough consciousness to feel. Even the steely Frick had begun to show strain. It was the silence that had hexed them. Since the moment of his arrest, the count hadn't spoken a word or uttered a syllable. What occupied the man's thoughts during the long dreadful hours? Kurt longed to know, but the count's face remained inscrutable, as if his spirit had flown to some impregnable citadel, leaving only the eyes. Kurt tried to conjure up an image of Count Wolfgang von Friedrich peering in condescension through his monocle, a Balkan cigarette dangling from his lips, but he could no longer connect the battered hunk of flesh on the floor of the cell with that storied dandy.

It was the morning of June 4, the second anniversary of the death of Reinhard Heydrich. Returning to the interrogation room, Schmidt ordered his henchmen: "Wrap our guest's hands with kerosene-soaked rags." He informed Count von Friedrich: "The next time I snap your gold lighter, your 'mittens' will burst into flame. Eventually you'll pass out from the excruciating pain. If you awaken, you'll be without hands. Do you have anything to say that will save you from this pointless torture? Why not use your hands to write out the names of all your accomplices in Czechoslovakia and Germany? Purge yourself of guilt for your crimes against the Fatherland."

Propped in the dentist's chair, the count stared at him through two black holes.

"No? Then you have chosen."

He ignited the lighter.

Count Wolfgang von Friedrich hears the click of his gold lighter. He feels the pain. He holds up his hands burning like Christmas candelabra.

It's very light. He's on the Brocken, crucified on the swastika from his own gold lighter. He's not alone. Through a fiery curtain he sees Colonel Kurt Schmidt dressed in his blue silk dressing gown, beating flames from his hands and hair, and Adolf Hitler in priestly brown robes, and Josef Goebbels in scarlet, and the double-headed black ram with the bloated features of Göring at the front end and the pinched ones of Himmler at the back. The Führer and Goebbels are throwing books and paintings onto the flames – Mann and Freud and van Gogh and Matisse and Einstein.

Wolf hears the snare drums more loudly than ever before, but he feels only elation. He seems to be rising. He's floating in a pair of inflatable silver wings higher than the Angel of Victory. A parade is coming through Bradenburger Tor and up Unter den Linden, lined with spectators. He can see almost to the end. Somebody's funeral but he doesn't know whose.

The first float has a maypole with colored streamers bearing historic dates. Dancing around it are red- and flaxen-haired Saxon warriors in animal skins, and Teutonic knights with whimpled chatelaines, and Charlemagne and Frederick the Great and Bismarck. Circling that is a ring of black forest where demons and kobolds and witches and the shadows of the maypolers dance in the opposite direction. A banner waves from pine boughs: ALL THIS YOU OWE TO WOTAN.

A battalion of lead solders escorts a gold coach with square wheels bearing his father in gold braid and his mother in frosty silver with a tiara of ice crystals. Wolf shouts and waves to attract their attention, but though they look impressive as they acknowledge the accolades of the crowd, he sees a key sticking in his father's back, which an aide must turn at discreet intervals while another oils his joints with a can of schnapps, and he knows they're only wind-up toys. They can't see or hear a thing, perhaps never could. A banner flies in the imperial colors: ALL THIS YOU OWE TO THE KAISER.

After this disappointment, Wolf is delighted to see Café des Westens, softly lit by gaslight, with his friends in their favorite corner laughing and drinking. On the table sits a brass chamber pot containing a single turd. His friends are arguing as to its artistic properties.

Leo Warner feels the decision depends on whose turd it is and for what purpose it was created. If, for example, it were routinely defecated into a toilet bowl, then it's no work of art. If, however, it were served to a capitalist under a silver salver by a disgruntled worker, then it would be a gut statement of its time and the issues. "Something I, for one, would be proud to call turdism."

As an actor, Christian Jürgens insists he would have to see the turd performed. "I'd also be influenced by how it was framed. The whole production, in short."

Raymon Arno argues passionately that whether the turd is a work of art depends on whether it was created by an artist. "No piece stands by itself, which is where most critics make their mistake. All are part of a single body of work and it's in that context it should be judged."

Professor Max Stein plumps for recognition of the artist in everyone. "Art springs out of play. The creative process is universal, whereas what is judged as art often has more to do with the eye of the beholder."

The novelist Renate Jürgens disagrees. "For me the only true test is that of time. What's universal lasts."

As a critic, Wolfgang von Friedrich also holds out for objective standards but rejects the test of time. "If something is good, it can be seen to be good by the critic who's properly schooled by the ages. To judge this turd as a masterwork I would merely have to examine it under my monocle to see if it has the proper classical proportions. Is it a perfect turd? Does it have essence of turd?" While insisting the art must be judged and not the artist, he finishes strongly: "I can state without fear of being disproved that the chances of an amateur producing the perfect turd are about as great as an infinite number of monkeys grunting into an infinite number of brass pots, producing the Parthenon."

The banner over this float charitably reads: ALL THIS YOU OWE TO YOUR YOUTH.

The next float is aglitter with copper sequins. Carmel Kohl, dressed like a mermaid, swims in a champagne glass, playing her musical saw. Nude guests slide down the tiers of a wedding cake, while Axel Berg tosses gold coins. On the top of the cake stand Wolf and Carmel, identically dressed in white tails, top hats and monocles. A neon banner flashes on and off: ALL THIS YOU OWE TO AMBITION.

Here come the clowns! A carnival with roller coasters
and Ferris wheels is sailing through Brandenburger Tor.
Everyone's having a jolly time, but a cheerful gray-haired
woman in flopping tennis shoes and wearing a crystal
headset is wrapping the carnival in black cloth. First to
disappear is the taffy apple booth, and then the merry-go-
round. Every time she hits a nail, her hammer bongs like
one stroke of Big Ben. All the loudspeakers on all the
lamp posts squawk and screech. . . . ULTIMATUM . . . WAR
. . . BRITISH . . . THEIR GUILT . . . WAR . . . DEMANDING
WITHDRAWAL. . . . FÜHRER REFUSED . . . HE SAYS IT'S NOT
OUR FAULT, MATTIE . . . WAR . . . IN STATE OF . . . GO WAR . . .

The carnival grinds down. The music stops. Blackout.
In the stillness, the roar of motorcycles is heard, and
tramping feet, truncheons on skulls, groans and screams
and breaking crystal. The sky rains glass. Many spectators
run for the exits while the orchestra plays "Stille Nacht,
Kristall Nacht." A float bursts into flame. Everyone can
see Max and Sara Stein waltzing inside barbed wire.
When they start to burn, some spectators protest. Others
shout back: "Fools! Those are just mannequins. Don't
you wish they *were* Jews." Across the blackened sky are
burnt the words: ALL THIS YOU OWE TO MARTIN LUTHER.
MARTIN LUTHER SLEPT HERE.

Sirens wail. You can hear tanks rumble and planes
drone in the finest cafés on Unter den Linden. Everyone is
scared silly as bombers sweep low to unleash their car-
goes. Down it comes. There's no escaping it: Danish hams
and Norwegian furs and French perfumes and Dutch
cheeses and Belgian lace. As squealing spectators scram-
ble for the loot, they notice each parcel stamped with a
swastika: ALL THIS YOU OWE TO YOUR FÜHRER.

Given the festive mood, the next float is a disappointment – a confessional, on wheels for easy accountability,
pushed by an arthritic priest twisted like a question mark.
A voice shouts: "Confess. Confess." The crowd hollers
back: "We haven't done anything yet." The voice
responds: "Precisely." An organ plays selections from

Bach's *The St. Matthew Passion:* ALL THIS YOU OWE TO
YOUR CONSCIENCE.

It begins to snow as the next float appears – a truck
pulled by blue-and-white striped figures attached with
barbed-wire harnesses around their foreheads and chests,
causing them to bleed and sweat even while they shiver.
Some are barefoot. Others slide in their clogs as dogs snap
at their heels. The lorry is heaped with old clothes marked
WINTER RELIEF, but that can't account for the millions of
buzzing flies, the pestilent odor, the sickening yellow cloud
that rains grease. Spectators rush the exits, but most have
their hands over their eyes and can't see. They hear
another band coming through Brandenburger Tor, and
gratefully return to their seats. But wait. The majorettes in
their brown party uniforms are twirling human femurs.
The xylophones are rib cages, the castanets jawbones, the
cymbals skulls, the bagpipes stomachs, the accordions
large intestines which can be pumped and unfolded, while
the woodwind section is too offensive to describe. Tattooed on the bass drum, made of human skin and beaten
by a thigh bone, is the name: SS SPARE PARTS BAND. They're
singing "Everything but the Squeal," to the tune of the
Horst Wessel anthem. A banner of butcher's paper is held
aloft by two yellow stars: ALL THIS YOU OWE TO HUMAN
NATURE INCLUDING YOUR OWN.

Such bad taste. Who's responsible? Whose funeral is
this? Whose world vision? It's impossible to leave. A bliz-
zard has developed, but not of snow. What's falling from
that treacherous sky is antimacassars. They're mucking
up the anti-aircraft guns and clogging the treads of tanks.
Planes can't take off because of the antimacassars stuck to
their wings. The lead soldiers, defending Berlin, are
chipped and bandaged. Who would have thought lead
soldiers could bleed? Enemy bombers strafe spectators in
the stands, none of your Danish hams this time. It isn't
fair. This wasn't supposed to happen. Herr Meyer, whose
name used to be Göring, promised it wouldn't. So did Dr.
Goebbels, whose name is Herr Mud. Unter den Linden is

a shambles. Severed arms and legs protrude from the ruins of cafés. When the crowd howls, the voice from the confessional taunts them: "They're just mannequins – dolls."

Everyone is so hysterical the next float seems comic – the skeletons of dinosaurs lying on their backs in the Tiergarten with signs around their necks: A WARNING TO HOMO SAPIENS. SPECIES DESTRUCTION. Charred trees are draped in tinsel that tinkles like moon chimes – Wotan's ash tree of life gone art nouveau. A tiger lies supine, tongue out, feet straight up, wearing the sign: THIS IS POSITIVELY THE LAST TIME I EAT CREAM CAKES AT KERN'S. Animals wait two by two at a phone booth, making love to pass the time – the elephants with their trunks entwined, giraffes ditto their necks, snakes ditto their everything. Do they think it's a comfort station? Nobody knows. The times are so crazy. At the prow of the float, shaped like Noah's Ark, rides Frau Fuchs, her peroxide hair in braids and wearing Brynhilde's horned helmet along with her feather boa. She salutes with her right hand. *THIS* IS HOW DEEP WE ARE INTO THE SHIT.

The best you can say about the next float is that it carries its banner at the front so everyone is forewarned: ALL THIS YOU OWE TO YOURSELF. Closing their eyes, the audience nod off. Just as well. This is the dullest part of the parade – no fanfare, no wit or originality, just a bunch of paintings and Jews and Bolsheviks and gypsies smuggled across one border or another. Heaps of forged passports and identity cards exchanged in alleys and seedy cafés, in churches and once or twice at Nazi rallies. Silverware, antiques and family heirlooms sold for financing. Boring stuff, without production values. Spoiled by snappier fare, the spectators awake only when they hear pistol shots. Two men, one in white, the other black, stalk through a maze of mirrors, shooting each other's reflections while a piano and a violin, unaided by human hand, play music by Mozart, Haydn and Brahms. Since each combatant is wearing the other's death mask, whenever a reflection spatters, no one knows who has killed whom. This revives speculation: Who owns this funeral? Suspense builds.

More snare drums parade through Brandenburger Tor. The hoofbeats of the riderless horse can be heard. Surely this will be followed by the gun-carriage bearing a flag-draped coffin with the honors and insignia that will identify this corpse. Everyone leans forward, refusing to rattle a program or to scratch a nose for fear of missing something.

Instead of a riderless horse with boots turned in the stirrups, a riderless ostrich trots through Brandenburger Tor, wearing a monocle and top hat, with coconut shells attached to its feet to simulate hoofbeats. Worse, it is trailed by a sign held by two white gloves: NOBODY "LIES" HERE. HE IS RISEN.

Now the audience are really mad, they're boiling. They've wasted a day expecting a nice little cry, only to find themselves taunted by this sacrilege. The funeral director slides by playing a barrel organ:

> "You *don't* have to dance to the tune
> That just happens to be on the roll."

They're ready for him with stones, slats torn from the bleachers, anything they can get their hands on. Nor is their wrath assuaged when he raises a white flag: WHAT DID YOU EXPECT FOR NOTHING? YOU WERE LUCKY TO GET ANYTHING WITH THE LOUSY BUDGET I HAD.

They rush for the exits. Neither rain, snow, sleet, hams, bombs nor antimacassars will hold them back now. Unter den Linden is soon deserted. A pity. For that's when the gayest, giddiest float of all slides through the arch – an enormous birthday cake with forty-two candles. Carmel Kohl, in simple white dress with hair of fire, scatters white rose petals while singing in her most thrilling voice:

> "It happens only once
> It will not come again.

It is too beautiful
To be true."

Afterward she calls to the figure floating over the Angel
of Victory in his inflatable silver wings: "They've gone.
You can come down now." When nothing happens, she
waves a pearl-handled revolver. "The last thing you'll see
before you go straight to heaven is Axel Berg's woman
who swore she'd get you." She shoots. A gold arrow pier-
ces the inflatable wings. Count Wolfgang von Friedrich
floats down beside her on his birthday cake. He tastes the
icing with his index finger before pronouncing: "A masterwork. Essence of birthday cake."

All his friends are there, wearing party hats and throwing silver streamers and singing "Auld Lang Syne" and
"Trink, Trink, Brüderlein, Trink."

Time to blow out the candles. Wolfgang makes a wish,
takes a deep breath and exhales. All forty-two snuff out at
the same time. The cake explodes. The party favors fly up
into a dark and infinite universe – the double helix and
golden spiral, the ring of fire and the snake biting its tail.
Even the Reinhard Heydrich Living-Well-is-the-Best-
REVENGE medal. What has been, can't be erased. Whatever was, is and will be forever: ALL THIS YOU OWE TO
ETERNITY

Last out of the cake are two white gloves. They turn
into a pair of doves, then fly off with the final sign: AMEN.

Kurt Schmidt had one more task. He centered the file on
his desk: BERG née KOHL, Carmel née Kara. No need to
open it. He knew it by heart. The choice was his. Power
lay in his hands.

Schmidt lit a Balkan cigarette with his gold lighter and
leaned back in his chair. If he chose, he could release a
report doctored with the "confessions" of Count Wolfgang von Friedrich that would ensure at least a trip to
Auschwitz. He imagined Carmel Kohl in one of the

interrogation rooms of The Labyrinth, humbled as the count had been. Alternately, he imagined her at his villa in Wannsee, receiving the guests they had met at the Berg, wearing the same white Grecian gown.

Kurt stubbed the Balkan cigarette, its sweet smoke bitter in his mouth, smelling on himself the stench of the slaughterhouse even through Graf's cologne, finding desire more difficult to retrieve than his satiated lust for revenge. Dropping Carmel Kohl's file into his wastebasket, he burned it with the gold lighter.

PART VII

"I am completely normal. Even while I was carrying out the task of extermination I led a normal family life and so on. From our entire training the thought of refusing an order just didn't enter one's head regardless of what kind of order it was. . . . Believe me, it wasn't always a pleasure to see those mountains of corpses and smell the perpetual burning."

– Rudolf Hoess, Commandant of Auschwitz

"I assure you we are all appalled by all these persecutions and atrocities. It is simply not typically German! Can you imagine that I could kill anyone? Tell me honestly, do any of us look like murderers?"
– Foreign Minister Joachim von Ribbentrop at Nuremberg

"No German is a Nazi until he has spat in the face of at least one Jew."

– Adolf Hitler

"Wecome to Germany, Herr Masur. It's time you Jews and we National Socialists buried the hatchet."
– Reichsführer Heinrich Himmler to a representative of the World Jewish Congress, April 21, 1945

Berlin

January 1945

A YEAR OF saturation bombing with raids of up to fifteen hundred planes had destroyed or badly damaged sixty-two percent of Berlin's housing and driven away half of the population of four and a half million. For many Berliners bombed out several times, underground living was a permanent condition.

Carmel Kohl's cellar group had been reduced by eight and increased by twelve. Since two of Herr Schnell's cots had collapsed, that meant eleven cots for twenty-seven people. The mathematics was further complicated by the fact that Fräulein Karnau's elderly parents had been assigned permanent cots. Though Herr Tafel's attempt to stake the same claim for himself on the grounds of "internal injuries" was derisively rejected, Carmel Kohl was unanimously granted permanent-cot status because she was eight months pregnant.

The pregnancy helped Carmel deal with Wolf's death, but Wolf had also done that by never allowing her to lean on him. She had been used to him disappearing for weeks and months. As she awaited the birth of their child, part of her accepted the fiction that he was off on another assignment.

In the sixth winter of war, death was all around her. One of the Boldt children – Claud, age eight – had investigated a "dud" while buying his grandfather a cigarette for his birthday and been blown up. Frau Giesseler had lost a

husband and two sons on the eastern front, as her astrological charts had predicted. Frau Stengel's daughter,
evacuated to the safety of the countryside, had been
struck by shrapnel while riding her bicycle. Carmel lived
in a city of widows and bereaved mothers. Everyone
shared in the larger tragedy. Everyone was numb with
shock. The sum of tears was constant: When life was
roughest, Herr Tafel's "internal injuries" gave him less
trouble, Herr Schnell's dentures didn't pain him and Frau
Giesseler's arthritis mysteriously disappeared. You
couldn't feel more than you could feel. The organism
became supersaturated with sorrow, and life went on.

Carmel became the group's pet project now that the
Vogel women had been spirited away by Herr Schnell and
herself from apartment No. 4 to St. Nicholas Church.
Frau Giesseler cast a horoscope for the child and pronounced "a male, comely in face and form, who will gain
international recognition in the arts." Frau Stengel
stopped knitting and reknitting the same sweater to use
the wool for a layette. Herr Schnell saved Carmel his milk
tickets.

In her third month, Carmel had visited Wolf's aunts in
Munich and received a loving reception. Aunt Mathilde
showed Carmel the family tree, going back to Charlemagne, and offered to teach the child court etiquette. Gertrude gave Carmel all Wolf's textbooks and papers. Both
had been full of anecdotes as they pored over the family
album. Carmel had never had so much family. She felt
blessed. Life was a series of tragic losses but you couldn't
lose something unless you had first had it, so the magni-
tude of each loss became the measure of life's gifts. Carmel felt comforted to read underlined in Wolf's copy of
Goethe's *Elective Affinities*, "Everything seems to be following its usual course because even in terrible moments
in which everything is at stake, people go on living as if
nothing were happening." She could imagine Wolf saying
that. It helped her understand the time Frau Giesseler had
vomited up fear and helplessness over her lap on hearing

her second son had been killed, then a day later greeted Carmel in the hall, "It looks like a pleasant day, Frau Berg. You won't need your umbrella." Perhaps that's how all families behaved, with these two faces – one minute birth or death, the next, "Pass the butter, please."

In Carmel's cellar, Goethe's "usual course" of events also meant Herr Tafel in his red nightshirt tirelessly proclaiming German victory. In the past year he had been joined by Herr Wirth, who had moved into the Vogels' flat with his wife. A seamstress, she was an anxious soul who looked as if she were holding a row of pins in her mouth, while Herr Wirth's patriotism outstripped even Herr Tafel's, earning them the nicknames Big Mouth and Supermouth. The two men argued constantly despite the fact they agreed on everything. Both touted the Führer's new eastern offensive, while disputing where it would be launched. Both made extravagant claims on behalf of Hitler's wonder weapons despite the fact that the V1s and 2s fired against London last June through September had not altered the progress of the war. Prevented from single-handedly manufacturing and launching them himself because of a bad back, Herr Wirth concluded all war talk with, "Trust A.H. He knows what he's doing."

Sometimes Fräulein Karnau, still in her hair curlers after a year, would taunt: "Oh, yes, we know all about Hitler's new wonder weapons – cripples to the front in wheelchairs! They've already called up the Hitler Youth." She waved Herr Tafel's copy of the *Völkischer Beobachter*. "Kids age fourteen receiving the Iron Cross. One day they'll be calling up internal injuries and bad backs."

Usually the pessimists didn't bother arguing their case. Each day's disasters did that for them.

Since the allied landing last June in Normandy, Paris had been liberated along with Belgium and most of Holland. In December Hitler's assault in the Ardennes had been painfully but inevitably beaten back. While British, American and Canadian forces under General Dwight D. Eisenhower advanced on the Rhine in a broad front, the

Soviets swept three hundred miles across the frozen Polish plains to line up on the Oder-Neisse rivers, forty miles from the capital, with three million refugees fleeing before them.

Though Frau Tafel dismissed everything else in her husband's *Völkischer Beobachter* as tripe, she accepted each word the paper said about Russians and rape as gospel. In a gloating voice, she translated the war into female terms: BLIND WOMAN OF NINETY-THREE RAVAGED. SCHOOLTEACHER VIOLATED BY THIRTY-SEVEN COSSACKS. RUSSIAN REGIMENT HAS ITS WAY WITH NUN. Having so terrified Frau Wirth that she dropped the pins from her mouth, Frau Tafel would read aloud the lascivious stories behind the headlines.

Of more general interest to the women were the Where-to-Get-It conversations: What butcher still had meat. Whose bread was edible. With the interruption of all public transportation, a trip across town had become an adventure for which Frau Giesseler's astrological charts were considered far more reliable than the newspapers or radio.

Carmel's group had one illicit ritual common to many cellars. They listened, riveted, to a mysterious radio personality known as The Fearless Phantom, who timed his broadcasts to correspond with the British raids. Changing frequencies and call signals, so far avoiding detection through the chaos of the bombings, he would encourage resisters in the jowly cadences of Churchill. Then, in devastating mimicry of Goebbels' metallic baritone, he would boast of the sex scandals long associated with the propaganda minister's name. As the corpulent Göring, The Phantom bragged about his stolen art collection, then described in tormenting detail a sumptuous meal he had just eaten while other Germans starved. As Himmler he confessed to the mass murder of Jews, gypsies, Slavs, Poles and the mentally retarded as matter-of-factly as if reciting the multiplication tables. Then, in imitation of the overblown homage the party had once paid to its martyrs of the unsuccessful 1923 Nazi putsch, The Phantom intoned The Gestapo Guest List, compiled of Berliners arrested that week.

In a comedy feature, *Berliner Blick*, named after the habit Berliners had of glancing nervously over their shoulders before making an unpatriotic remark, The Fearless Phantom told anti-Nazi jokes rated with one to three swastikas, depending on whether the penalty would be four years' hard labor, ten years' or death.

Today's offering was rated as one swastika:

"A British prisoner-of-war, who was eating bully beef from his Red Cross Parcel, called across the barbed wire to a guard: 'I understand things are so bad you fellows are eating rats.'

"The guard replied reminiscently: 'Gosh, and were those rats good, but now they're all gone, the government is feeding us ersatz rats!'"

As The Fearless Phantom signed off to the sound of Big Ben, Herr Tafel yawned. "We might as well pack up. That's as good as the all-clear."

"His timing – that's the giveaway," sniffed Herr Wirth. "It's the BBC. One of their acting groups that's got our accents down from prisoners-of-war. They're beaming their signal across the Rhine with some powerful radio equipment the Amis have developed. I got that straight from the Gestapo."

"Then why doesn't Goebbels say so?" demanded Herr Tafel.

"Because it would give the British too much prestige. Don't you get it? Better to pretend it's some of ours who have gone bad."

This was the same theory confided to Carmel by Willi Bliss, still sweating it out in the cellars of the Promi. She knew it was false. From the timbre of the voice, the intonation and pitch, she had guessed from the first broadcast who The Fearless Phantom was: Frau Fuchs.

"There goes the all-clear," announced Herr Tafel as if he were the only one with ears.

"Right on cue," confirmed Herr Wirth in triumph.

As everyone else in the cellar shook out cramped limbs and collected belongings, Carmel asked Herr Schnell: "Would you mind shining your flashlight under my bed? I think I've lost my opal brooch from my jewel case."

Wheezing, the old man got down on his knees at the foot of the bed, while Carmel searched through the covers. "Nothing here, Frau Berg."

"I can't understand it," fretted Carmel. "I'm sure I had it when I came down. It's one my late husband gave me."

Unexpectedly, Herr Tafel turned gallant. "Perhaps if I help move the bed."

With Herr Wirth offering instructions, he and Herr Schnell eased the iron cot out from the row.

"I don't see it," announced Carmel.

"I guess there's nothing for it but to move all the beds," offered Herr Schnell.

Herr Tafel lasted for two cots, huffing and puffing, while Herr Wirth muttered at intervals: "It must be somewhere."

"I'd assist further," claimed Herr Tafel, holding his red flannel belly like a beloved object. "But I'd have to be hospitalized. The rupture."

"Even to touch the iron frame would have me flat on my back," sympathized Herr Wirth.

"I'd feel dreadful if either one of you strained anything," assured Carmel. "It's not worth it. I'm going to search my apartment before bothering with anything more down here. Perhaps it fell out in one of my drawers." Putting her hand to her chest, she exclaimed: "I think I'm having an attack of heartburn myself. Perhaps I should lie down before trying the stairs. I'll knock on your door as I leave, so you can lock up, Herr Schnell."

"No, no, Frau Berg. I can wait."

As soon as the door closed behind Herr Tafel and Herr Wirth, the superintendent drew the bolt while Carmel sat up laughing. "I wasn't expecting so much attention. That's more acting than I've done in a year."

Turning out the contents of his pockets like a child at a treasure hunt, Herr Schnell announced: "Two police registration cards and three blank ration cards. All that for a box of cigarettes. This national identity card, I'm distressed to say, I stole from a corpse."

"That's quite a haul!" congratulated Carmel.

"Frankly, Frau Berg, it's getting easier. I don't have to listen to the BBC to know who's winning the war. People who've had doubts now feel freer to act, while others are anxious to build up a reputation for good deeds. If the war goes on much longer, helping 'U-boats' may become fashionable."

Opening her makeup kit, Carmel presented Herr Schnell with documents she had doctored. Though she didn't possess Wolf's high-class skills, growing up in a tough neighborhood had taught her a few homey tricks, such as steaming off photographs for replacement, then transferring the inked stamp by rolling a hard-boiled egg over the original. In these ways she was able to forge minor pieces of identification, such as postal cards and priority tickets, for U-boats, underground racial and political refugees without any papers. Lazier or more compassionate officials were inclined to give them the benefit of the doubt, while even the zealots had trouble checking, with all forms of communication becoming less reliable. Just as important, the possession of such a talisman bestowed on its owner the courage to bluff.

"Here's the list of names for Father Bauer's baptismal certificates," explained Carmel. "The postal cards have the addresses on them." She sighed. "I'm afraid they're all over town. I feel so sorry, Herr Schnell, that I can't help you."

"Don't forget I used to ride in the six-day bicycle races," boasted Herr Schnell. "My calf muscles are stronger than those of men half my age."

Carmel handed him two thousand marks. "This is for the Vogels." Enough to feed them for two months on the black market, where eggs cost twenty marks, or $1.50 a piece, while milk cost sixty marks.

Reluctantly Herr Schnell accepted the bills. Folding and refolding them, he murmured: "I know you don't have much."

"I don't have to live off the black market. Besides, it's ill-gotten gains – part of the advance for *Lola*. Goebbels is unlikely to send a studio car to get back the money for a movie he can't make, after creating such a fuss about it at Berchtesgaden. I can't think of a better use for it, can you?" She picked up one of Herr Schnell's ration-card blanks. "Let's see about making one of these into a ration card for Hilde Vogel. If it's beyond my skill, maybe someone from the Church of Sweden can put us in touch with a pro. I believe the going price is one thousand marks, but that's cheaper in the long run if Hilde can handle going into a store."

"I really think she can," enthused Herr Schnell. "With the clothes you sent her, she's gained a lot of confidence. It's as if her limp has improved. Certainly she's prettier, with more color in her cheeks."

"Well, the clothes are no use to me anymore."

"I wish I could persuade Frau Vogel to go out. She gets one cold after another in that drafty crypt, but she won't budge. Says the first person she meets is likely to be a catcher." Agents for the Gestapo's Jewish Bureau of Investigation, these were German fanatics or Jews, terrified they would be deported if they didn't turn in other Jews.

"Who can blame her?" sympathized Carmel. "It's so close to the end. Pastor Forell at the Church of Sweden told me about one male-female catcher team that turned in over two thousand Jews. The woman, a beautiful blond Jewess, used to be a cabaret singer. I knew her vaguely. First person she betrayed was her husband. She's working with a sporty young man who was caught selling forged papers – just a crook, scum."

Herr Schnell tucked Carmel's money into his pocket,

along with the documents for delivery, while Carmel slipped the newly acquired documents into her makeup kit.

"I don't think we should spend too long down here," she laughed. "Herr Tafel is spreading the rumor you're the father of my baby."

Blushing, Herr Schnell countered: "Just a godfather, I hope, Frau Berg."

As he waited with his keys to lock up, Carmel seized his hand. "May I ask one more favor?"

"Of course. But these things we do aren't favors."

"Will you help me get to the east end?" She burst into tears. "I want to go to The Red Fox. I want to go home."

TWO

Mullhorig, Bavaria

February 1945

ILSE SCHMIDT was twenty miles from the Lebensborn, driving an L-van along hard-packed country roads when she noticed the smoke – a dark smudge in the twilight. To the left she could make out the spire of the Catholic church of Mullhorig, marking the village. As she closed the gap, she saw fire bleed across the snowfields. Was the Lebensborn in flames?

Hunched over the wheel, Ilse pressed on the gas. So far as she knew no enemy planes had attacked this area, the cradle of National Socialism and the Alpine Redoubt, where popular wisdom claimed the Führer could hold out forever. Ilse had seen or heard nothing that alarmed her. Had a stray bomber missed Munich, then dropped its load to speed the race for home?

Ilse maneuvered the winding roads, skidding around corners in a panic as she pictured the overcrowded wards with mothers-to-be on stretchers in the labor rooms, the babies packed two to a cradle in the nursery. She prayed: "Mary, Mother of God. Save the Lebensborn and I'll do penance for the rest of my life. Don't punish me this way."

The winter of '44 had been a nightmare for Ilse. As the Third Reich became a dying star imploding inward to a dense black hole, the Lebensborn organization had evacuated its homes in occupied Europe, bringing an influx of pregnant women to Mullhorig along with orphaned and abandoned babies. Intended as a model home for fifty mothers, and one hundred maximum, Ilse's Lebensborn now accommodated three hundred with their offspring. Not only was she forced to jam six women into rooms intended for two, but she also had to officiate in quarrels between girls of pure German blood and the Norwegian, Belgian and French interlopers who had mated with German SS officers.

Last week, with mothers giving birth in corridors, the Munich administration had folded its headquarters, then fled to Mullhorig to escape the bombing. Ilse had thought this meant more helping hands. Instead she found she was expected to cater to the high-ranking newcomers while prisoners from Dachau worked around the clock putting up Quonset huts to accommodate them. Then they had helped themselves to the choicest furnishings.

Drastic solutions were needed to deal with the over-crowding. Two days ago Ilse had waylaid Dr. Zuckmayer, trembling with fatigue as he snatched a nap on his office sofa. "Let me take an L-van to persuade the heads of schools and churches and charitable organizations in this area to find homes for our orphans."

"How can we spare you, Nurse Schmidt?" Rubbing his red-rimmed eyes under his glasses, Dr. Zuckmayer asked plaintively: "Can't someone else go?"

"I know this area. In forty-eight hours I can do what it would take someone else a week to do. I also know what would happen if we had an outbreak of typhus or dysentery or influenza."

"Ja, ja," exclaimed Dr. Zuckmayer, waving his arms as if the words themselves might contaminate. "Go!"

With the efficiency of desperation, Ilse had managed to find permanent homes for thirty-seven babies and temporary accommodation for another forty-one. When she thought of the care with which she used to scrutinize each application to ensure the child and adopting home were of the highest Aryan standards, such haste made her sick, but what was the choice?

As Ilse sped back through the village of Mullhorig, she

could see the silhouette of the Lebensborn lit by flames. "Please let it be the Quonset huts," she prayed.

The village seemed unperturbed. No crowds of the sort that collect around disasters, and no firewheels. Were these people so vicious they would let mothers and babies burn rather than lend a helping hand?

Ilse shot through the Lebensborn gates, her eyes on the lick of flames against the sky. A bonfire was burning in the courtyard, but the Lebensborn was untouched except by reflection. Even from here she could see SS men with a water pump, just in case. But what were they burning? Renewed fear struck her: Were they destroying contaminated sheets and clothing?

Abandoning her van, Ilse ran toward the fire. Frau Heller Gross, second in command of the Lebensborn headquarters in Munich, was standing in the firelight, her mink coat over her shoulders. Wind blew flakes of charred paper in Ilse's face. The site was littered with filing cabinets, some overturned. Their contents were being fed into the flames by SS men under the instructions of Frau Gross.

Again Ilse experienced relief: The Munich group were burning their files. That was their business.

Wishing no contact, Ilse gave Frau Gross wide berth. Then she noticed one of the steel cabinets dumped in the snow was her own. Mistaking it was impossible. On the front was the picture of Bruno she had affixed to it to remind her of her sacrifice. It contained the records of babies she had sent away in L-vans, not only the secret Lebensborn files but personal jottings about them under the Christian names she had given them.

"Stop, that's mine," shouted Ilse.

Frau Gross scowled, then continued her work. Grabbing her arm, Ilse snatched a handful of folders.

"Let go," demanded Frau Gross, shoving her aside. "I have orders."

"These are my files."

"I have orders," repeated Frau Gross.

As Ilse again attacked, Frau Gross' fur coat fell into the snow.

"Now look what you've done, you clumsy cow."

"Give me my papers."

SS Major Hans Brüning, also from Munich headquarters, stepped into the circle of flame. "Return to your duties, Frau Schmidt, or I'll have you arrested."

Shaken, Ilse ran in the door of the Lebensborn, past three more SS men carrying cartons. Taking the stairs two at a time, she found the door of her office open and the light on. The lock on her desk drawer had been broken, the contents stolen. She sought Dr. Zuckmayer. His office too was unlocked. Though it seemed intact, it looked neater than usual. Opening files, she found them picked clean. Birth certificates, adoption records, Aryan qualification forms, even medical records had been seized.

Ilse hurried to the hospital wing in search of Dr. Zuckmayer. Chaos. Unbelievable. Children were crawling in the corridors, their diapers soiled. Snatching up one under each arm, Ilse headed for the nursery. The stench made her gag. Excrement had been smeared on the walls by babies left unattended on the chamber pots. A toddler had overturned one on his head. Several babies were screaming in a way that suggested hunger.

Ilse saw a student nurse and pounced. "Where's the nurse in charge here?"

"On the intensive ward."

"Where's Claudia? Where's Helga?"

"They've left."

"Where?"

The girl shrugged.

Grabbing her by the shoulders, Ilse shook her. "Don't shrug your shoulders at me. Where's Helga?"

The girl repeated: "She's gone. Everyone's gone. They left as soon as you did."

"Where's Ursula and Marlene?"

"Helga took them."

"But where?"

"Home to Dresden."

"Dresden doesn't exist anymore. It was bombed. Don't you read the papers?"

The girl broke into sobs. Impulsively Ilse put her arms around her. "I'm sorry, Irma. Just do your best. I'll help."

Together they fed babies, changed diapers, cleaned up the worst of the mess.

Fearfully, Ilse went on a tour of inspection. Half her staff had deserted. None of those left had slept more than three hours in the last twenty-four. Some mothers had gone into labor unattended. The corridor to the labor room was jammed with women awaiting their turn. Putting aside all thoughts of the outrage in the courtyard, Ilse scrubbed up to assist Dr. Zuckmayer.

It was after 3:00 a.m. when Ilse and Dr. Zuckmayer were relieved in surgery. As they stripped off soiled aprons and masks in a room the nurses called the decompression chamber, Ilse blurted: "They're burning our files."

Eyes bloodshot, face gray with stubble, Dr. Zuckmayer sighed. "I know."

Stirring the ashes of her indignation, Ilse protested: "They rifled our offices. Even my letters and photographs."

"I know." Taking off his glasses, he set them over the sink and rubbed his eyes. "I'm sorry about your personal papers. I gave the order."

"You? But you said it would take a hundred years to gather the genetic information we collected in ten."

"Destroying the record doesn't destroy the dream," intoned Dr. Zuckmayer, talking by rote.

"You insisted I record everything because the record was so important."

"Not unsorted, Frau Schmidt. No time for sorting."

"You said if people could read everything instead of bits and pieces, they'd understand our ideals instead of judging us."

"Everything?" growled Dr. Zuckmayer. "Even the frozen Polish sausages from Kalisz?" He was referring to the trainload of forty-three Polish children rerouted, lost in bombings, left at a siding then passed on to Mullhorig in subzero temperatures – forty-three frozen and emaciated corpses. "How would that look on the front page of the London *Times*?" Fumbling, Dr. Zuckmayer put on his glasses. "Many have fled. If you want to, that's up to you. When the Americans or the Russians come, I'll be at my desk in uniform. Heil Hitler!"

Stupid with fatigue, Ilse stumbled to the Lebensborn kitchen to get some milk to take with her angina pills. Her heart was fluttering, the way it did before an attack. She found the larder had been ransacked. A bag of potatoes had been used to prop open the door of the walk-in fridge, then abandoned so the remaining food had begun to spoil. A dozen eggs lay smashed on the floor. Hams had been carried out then dropped, bags of flour and sugar spilled. The linen closet had been rifled, the silverware stolen. Paintings had been stripped from the walls of the reception hall, the rugs yanked from the floor, several good antiques stolen.

Ilse found a Polish maid cowering in the broom closet. "Have the prisoners from Dachau broken free?"

The maid was shaking so hard she could barely speak. "Nein. Not the prisoners. The visitors. The visitors from Munich."

Ilse slapped her face. "You're lying!"

"No," she sobbed. "The visitors. They left in the L-vans."

Running to the door, Ilse saw the courtyard bonfire still smoldering. A couple of the doors of the Quonset huts were flapping in the wind. The L-van parking lot was empty. Not even one vehicle to deliver her babies!

Ilse went upstairs to her office, dragging herself by the banister. She turned on her light. Her sofa had been stolen. Slumping at her desk, she massaged her heart, feeling the rise of panic. At least they hadn't stolen her angina pills. Ilse dry-swallowed three, then tried to relax in her chair, staring at the Lebensborn poster of her, bare-breasted, feeding Bruno. It seemed to shimmer so her face melted into the face of the Virgin. The heart began to illuminate and pulse. Ilse's heart began to burn and pulse. Doubling over in pain, she gulped three more pink pills, then three more, chewing them like candy. Yanking the poster from the wall, Ilse felt a sharp pain as if her heart were splitting in two. She emptied the bottle.

THREE

Berlin

April 1945

AFTER MONTHS of saturation bombing, Berlin smoldered like a corpse. A green moon glowed malignantly through a cloud of pulverized limestone, its underside burnt crimson, while searchlights swept around like the hands of a broken clock – the sort of landscape Hitler had forbidden artists to paint because it was "unreal."

Camped in the Grünewald, Kurt Schmidt headed for the chancellery to join the Führer and a faith-hardened few for the Third Reich's last stand. That was what this war had come down to – one man and one city.

Kurt mounted guard over his possessions, packed into two shopping bags, his back against a pine tree, a rifle across his lap, watching refugees shuffle away from Berlin in the direction of safety and popular wisdom. This was what he called the nightcrawler, a ragged caterpillar, gray in the moonlight, made up of criminals and deserters. At dawn it would collapse into ditches, squirm under bushes, cover itself with leaves, and the daycrawler would take over, composed of women and children and a few old men, pulling everything they owned in anything with wheels.

The Battle for Berlin was about to begin. Like a reluctant bride in a Grimm fairy tale, the city had watched for months while her suitors in the east and the west ran lethal obstacle courses to determine which would claim her. Early in March, while the Red Army was stuck on the

Oder and Neisse rivers forty miles from the capital, the allies crossed the Rhine in three places so it seemed they might seize the prize. By mid-April they had ground to a halt on the Elbe River sixty miles away and were thrusting south toward Leipzig and Dresden, while the Russians had begun an encirclement. So it was to be the Red hordes after all, every German's nightmare.

Holed up in his fashionable villa in Wannsee, Kurt had tried to force himself to join the fleeing refugees. Every animal instinct urged him to it. Yet he held back. From his balcony casement he looked into the blank faces of these pilgrims of war, their minds fixed on their bellies, their center of emotional gravity fallen from their hearts to their feet, shadows of their former identities, neither living nor dead, and he felt contempt. Kurt had seen such stick people before, shuffling to the gas ovens. Subhumans, whether Jew or Aryan. The thought of casting his lot with them repelled him.

He clung to his bourgeois dream of wealth and status, the illusion of uniqueness. Already he had wrapped his property in barbed wire, padlocked the gates, posted signs: KEEP AWAY. DANGER OF PESTILENCE. Using the baron's gun collection, he booby-trapped the doors and windows. In the basement were bushels of potatoes and turnips, frozen hams and sides of beef, racks of fine wines, proving that the shady baron's high-minded zeal for saving the masses from the Führer's leadership had not included sharing his plenty with them.

On what was to prove Kurt's last evening in his villa, he lounged in Count Wolfgang von Friedrich's blue silk dressing gown, drinking a bottle of Rüdesheimer wine, looking toward Berlin, marked by a shimmering gray cloud stained acidy yellow, pink and green like a malignant rainbow by the setting sun.

Over Radio Berlin, the voice of Dr. Goebbels informed him: "Loyal Germans, the Führer is in Berlin and will die fighting in defense of the capital. Once again his yellow-and-white standard flies from the chancellery."

Across the Havel Kurt sees the Yanks are finishing a raid of six hundred planes. Mesmerized, he admires the red plumes of flame, the parachute flares Berliners call Christmas trees. He sees the explosion of a bomber in a green-yellow starburst destroying nine men.

A wounded American Liberator, its belly sprayed white in day-camouflage, bumbles over the Havel, pursued by two Messerschmitts flying high and closing in fast. The ME-109's dive on the bomber, machine guns spitting orange tracer streams as two Spitfires, almost invisible in the glare of the sun, slide downward. Doggedly the ME-109s torment the bomber at close range while the Spitfires attack them, sending it bucking, leaping and twisting like a harpooned whale the length of the lake. For forty-five seconds the sky above Kurt boils with planes leaving intersecting vapor trails. An ME-109 blows apart while the Liberator glides to earth, shedding its propeller, then a piece of tail. It stops, coughs, hovers, dips its nose and plunges, a dead weight accelerating.

Kurt feels a thud judder through him as the plane strikes, followed by an explosion, a heat blast and the stink of burning oil. As he grabs for something solid, he experiences one long bright moment in which he has the uncanny sense the air is falling apart and he's suspended in space, buffeted by waves as debris rains down. His sense of smell is acute – cinders, oil, plaster and the musty odor of loam. His body strikes ground while the universe spins.

When Kurt regains consciousness, the air is trembling with plaster dust, magnifying the moon into a sphere filling half the sky.

He hears voices. His villa has blown away like a top hat in a high wind. Two dozen cackling women scavenge through his belongings scattered over spacious lawns, reminding him of the crows that tore the flesh of cherries from the tree in his backyard in Dortmund while his

mother beat them off with a broom. Naked but for shreds
of blue silk, Kurt descends upon the flock, wielding the leg
of his Gründerzeit sofa like a club, sending the rapacious
crones back through the blasted wall.

Afterward he picks through the ruins, looking for small
items of value – silver, a bag of uncut gems stashed in a
bureau drawer. From that same bureau, he takes brown
slacks and shirt and windbreaker, along with his SS uniform decorated with a colonel's oakleaf.

Loyal Germans, the Führer is in Berlin and will die
fighting in defense of the capital. Once again his yellow-
and-white standard flies from the chancellery.

Even without his villa, Kurt doesn't feel low enough to
join the refugees in their rush to surrender. The uniform
is his identity, his one chance of again making contact
with privilege. In the belief that a fissure has developed
between Russia and her western allies, he knows that
Goebbels has been conniving, through discreet phone
calls, to take over the Reich. Rumor declares he has
drawn up a peace plan now secretly circulating among the
western allies. In competition to be the official representative of Germany, Himmler has been in touch with influential men in the British government and even world Jewry.
He is said to be compiling his cabinet list. Göring's illicit
negotiations are thought to involve generals in the western
camp. Kurt believes it's time for him to make firsthand
assessments and to stake his claim.

As he waited for dawn, camped in the Grünewald, Kurt
heard Soviet guns thundering from the west as well as the
east, tightening their armored noose around Berlin. He
played his flute:

>What is the Fatherland of the Germans?
>Is it Prussia? Is it Swabia?
>Is it where the grape ripens near the Rhine?
>Oh no, no, no!
>His Fatherland is larger still.

What is a German's Fatherland?
Name me then the great land.
As far as the German tongue is heard
And God in Heaven is singing songs,
So far shall it stretch.
So much, brave German, call your own.

Looking up through pines into the first pink streaks of day, Kurt smelled the moldy leaves and the spicy new ferns. He heard thrushes spill their cheerful songs as if the world were normal, and he thought of Ilse, the friend of his youth, shiny with her convictions; his Brynhilde, first glimpsed stirring soup through flames; his bride kneeling beside him in the alpine church. *This is the happiest day of your life. Take care of the children God gives you*; his wife, as radiant as a sunflower nursing their son. . . . Ilse Schultz Schmidt dead of a heart attack at age thirty-eight.

The silvery notes of Kurt's flute put him in touch with the raw, sad, lonely places he had almost forgotten. Tears ran down his cheeks. As he looked up into a dead elm and saw the silhouettes of half a dozen deserters twist with the wind while ravens plucked their eyes, it occurred to him that Ilse and his mother were the only people in the world who had ever liked him.

Kurt entered Berlin by Halensee bridge over a railroad cut with the tracks twisted into corkscrews. The city resembled a broken honeycomb blurred by brown drizzle. Streets began and ended in mountains of rubble through which only the rats could tunnel. Blocks of concrete had been cast like dice. Abandoned cars lay on their backs as if they were struggling beetles. The only trolley Kurt saw in use had riders hanging from the doors and lying on top as it jerked to a halt at nameless stops, then lurched forward like a mechanical Flying Dutchman sailing from nowhere to nowhere.

He smelled corpses. A garbage truck had been con-

verted into a public hearse, with three men sitting on
coffins, eating lunch. More usual were corteges carrying
bodies wrapped in newspaper, looking for a place to bury
them with the fear they would resurrect under the next
bombardment. Smoke, phosphorous fumes, gritty bits of
plaster and limestone thickened the air into something
tangible that made him choke. Tying a kerchief around his
nose and mouth, Kurt picked his way toward the centre of
the city.

The Kurfürstendamm was no longer a street of dreams
or even of illusions. As Kurt trudged along the wide
boulevard, carrying his shopping bags, he saw the display
cases had been smashed along with the windows of the few
remaining luxury stores. Bars, cafés and cabarets were
either bombed out or boarded – no more neon, no music,
no whores in gold boots, no dancing dogs or gypsy for-
tune-tellers. Some of the ruins were old enough to have
sprouted a fuzz of green. A calf on close tether was graz-
ing where an outdoor café had once been. Berliners were
as likely to be walking their goats as their dogs.

"Rubble rats" in clothes the color of mud poked
through the debris for anything edible, wearable, burn-
able, salable. Long lineups of hollow-eyed and emaciated
women waited at bakeries and groceries while others lined
at field kitchens offering coffee brewed from nettles.

A rheumy-eyed horse collapsed near a lineup of women
at a communal water pump. When the owner couldn't
whip it back onto its feet, he marched away infuriated.
The women stared expressionless at the quivering carcass
till he disappeared around a pile of rubble. Then producing knives from boots and cloaks like desert marauders,
they fell upon the twitching horse, filling their string bags
with hunks of red meat, bone, gristle and yellow fat,
reducing the poor beast to a skeleton.

Though Zoo station was intact, the Gloria Palast had
been pulverized, Kaiser Wilhelm Church reduced to a
single steeple, with its clock hands frozen at 7:30. Yet here
at least was activity beyond that needed for bare survival.

Paper flags celebrating Hitler's fifty-sixth birthday on April 20, six days ago, had been tucked in shop windows and even among the ruins. Lineups at phone booths indicated public switchboards were still operational and every wall had been requisitioned as a notice board.

"The family Dieder Kietel has moved to Hannover."

"Complete annotated texts of Goethe – foreign currency or barter."

"If anyone knows the whereabouts of Sergeant Otto Misch, please tell him his dear Marte has moved in with her parents."

"Has anyone seen our beloved Gretchen, age seven, missing since March 3?"

"Basic Russian in five days."

One-page newspapers, dated as late as April 25, threatened, cajoled, boasted with Dr. Goebbels' unmistakable flair for fantasy:

BERLIN: A MASS GRAVE FOR SOVIET TANKS!
WE WILL NOT LIVE LIKE NEGRO SLAVES – BERLINERS,
DO YOUR DUTY.
BERLIN WILL NEVER SURRENDER. THE FÜHRER LEADS US.

Across a story bragging about secret weapons as yet unleased, someone had scrawled: To the front with trolley cars!

Across another, gloating over the death of U.S. President Roosevelt on April 12, a cynic had written: To save myself from hanging, I suppose I'd better believe this will bring us final victory!

A still-wet war bulletin entitled "Armored Bear" informed Kurt that Bernau, twenty miles north, had been recaptured, providing him with the more reliable information that it had been taken in the first place.

Under the heading COWARDS WATCH YOUR CHICKEN NECKS! a correspondent named Willi Bliss ranted: "Our beloved Führer has vowed to fight to the last breath for victory. Would-be deserters, take a look at Soldier Stollen hanging at the Schoneberg station with a swastika carved on his chest. While you read this, vigilantes are searching cellars with ropes around their shoulders for flying court-martials. Also on the prowl looking for you is a six-foot-seven, one-eyed amateur we've nicknamed Der Henker. The Hanger likes to leave his disemboweled prey dangling from Albert Speer's bronze lamp posts!"

Judging by the discarded SS uniforms Kurt had seen clogging sewers or stuffed behind boulders, he concluded the cellars were indeed full of deserters. Except for the Home Guard and the Hitler Youth, who manned make-shift barricades with the self-assured invincibility of children playing at war, Berlin was now a city of women. Incredibly, in the capital of the Third Reich, German males had become the Jews – invisible, hunted and hanged.

Kurt felt a sharp tug on his sleeve. Looking down, he saw a spiky-haired kellerkind with a withered arm.

"Underground express!" bleated the kid. "Through subway and sewers, ten bucks American." Flashing his ragged cloak lined with papers he added: "Extra! Bust you to private for five bucks. Ten bucks made-to-order."

Before Kurt could cuff the boy, he ducked down a rathole into the earth.

"Lice!" fumed Kurt as he strode to the Tiergarten where he intended to spend the night.

April 27, 6:00 a.m. As Kurt crawled from his gray wool cocoon, it seemed as if spring had arrived all in one morn-ing. The sun had pecked like a fuzzy newborn chick through a crack in the sky, transforming a sepia world into a green and shining one. While Kurt washed and shaved in a blue pond between forsythia bushes like gold feather dusters, a black Russian rook and hooded Ger-man crow swooped and soared together, unmindful of their countries' hostilities. Yet something alerted Kurt's sixth sense as he donned his SS uniform. No planes had raided last night and now there was no Red Choir. No artillery. He could hear the birds sing.

Kurt picked his way like a combat soldier toward the southeast corner of the Tiergarten. Taking cover amidst bushes and boulders, he reconnoitered the wedge of land between Hermann Göring and Wilhelm Strasse known as the Zitadelle.

He heard a throaty growl.

An armored car turned the corner, followed by an olive jeep with two officers in olive dress, guarded by soldiers with machine guns perched on each fender. Foot soldiers displayed the Red hammer-and-sickle banner followed by more officers in jeeps, then a line of Russian flak, including those dubbed Stalin's organs. From a jeep mounted by four megaphones, a thickly accented voice spoke garbled German: "Comrades, Germans all. Your weapons lay down or face death. We have taken your city. No more Third Reich kaput ceases to exist. German people, we have liberated you from your evil oppressors. In welcome, come forward or death."

A metallic cough, then a repeat: "Comrades, Germans all . . ."

The smell of gasoline gave way to manure as jeeps and tanks were superseded by cavalry. Then came an olive-brown flood of raggedy combat troops, their broad faces carved out of potatoes with tiny brown eyes, dragging sacks of turnips and barrels of molasses, even herding cattle, laughing and singing, their veins flowing with vodka, exuding pungent animal spirits – the conquerors.

Kurt darted across Bellevue Strasse into the Zitadelle, containing the Reich ministries and the chancellery, joined by extensive gardens. Showing his papers three times, he traversed a maze of barricades dense with anti-aircraft batteries manned by Adolf Hitler's Honor Guard.

The old chancellery, where Adolf Hitler had a two-story apartment, had been extended in 1938 with a four-block yellow marble rectangle built by Albert Speer. Part of the roof had caved in. Many large windows set in gray limestone were shattered. The austere classical facade featuring monumental square columns was scorched and pocked with flak. Yet it was proving a sturdy fortress where a thousand elite troops might hold out till a decent peace pact could be signed.

Climbing the steep broad staircase through the portico mounted by a stylized German eagle, Kurt felt an upsurge of self-esteem. The Führer had not deserted his people or his post, and he would not desert his Führer. *I swear my loyalty and courage to you, Adolf Hitler. I vow obedience to the death to you and my superiors appointed by you. So help me God.*

He identified himself to a sergeant on desk duty. "Who's in charge here, sergeant?"

A blank stare.

Detecting the sour smell of beer, Colonel Schmidt demanded: "What's your name?" Barely controlling his rage, he stamped into the building.

Collapsed ceilings, charred beams, broken galleries, jagged hunks of marble had rendered the top floors uninhabitable, yet a thousand party members, their families, girlfriends and workers from the ministries jammed the ground floor and cellar. Everyone up and down the Parian halls of the chancellery seemed drunk. Though most of the men were in uniform, tunics were open, ties undone and nobody bothered to salute anymore. Cigarettes and cigars had been ground out in carpets, marble tables were littered with beer and wine bottles, moldy crusts and rat dung. Vases and umbrella stands overflowed with mess kits and Wehrmacht musette bags. Everyone was talking so loudly Kurt could have stood on a damask chair and shouted: "Fire!" without anyone noticing.

Outraged, he pushed his way into the garden, where he sat alone on a marble bench amidst pools and pavilions, fountains and hot-houses, classical sculptures and model tanks that the Führer displayed as artwork. What had he expected? A tautly controlled nerve center. Generals huddled around blowup maps. Stirring speeches. A sense of history. The Führer cheering on his troops, striking fire into his officers.

In the garden he could hear the guns again. Better than the uncanny silence or the carousing. Something normal like a heartbeat.

Kurt wondered why he had delivered himself to this madhouse. He could have been halfway to Paris as a refugee or safe in an American prisoner-of-war camp. How could he escape this marble tomb, ringed with German artillery and Russian T-34 tanks?

He remembered the kellerkind who advertised: "Underground express! Through subway and sewers, ten bucks American." Those little working-class buggers knew the tunnels and cellars under Berlin as well as the rats. A cooing Kurt thought to be birds turned out to be six women without bras sunning around an ornamental pool. Safe in their numbers, they gestured to him in mock seduction, sticking out their tongues and chests. "What's the matter, Colonel? Cat got yours?"

Feeling the fierce and inopportune return of sexual desire after being without it for almost a year, Kurt chose another bench. Opening a silver flask, he was gulping down schnapps when he heard grunts, giggles, belly growls from a nearby hothouse.

A plump blond in bra and panties ran squealing out one door, pursued by a hairy man, naked except for his SS tunic. Huffing, he waddled around the sculpture of a man taming a bull, then grabbed her by the scruff as she peeked between the bronze feet of Poseidon. Plunking down on a bench across from Kurt, he flung her over his lap, pulled down her panties and spanked her bottom hard enough to leave handprints. As she cuddled beside him on the bench, a nude brunette raced from the hothouse. Sitting on his other side, she patted his pendulous belly as if it aroused her maternal instincts.

As Kurt was about to relocate, the man stretched out a hairy arm. "Well, if it isn't the pretty engineer. A colonel now, d'ya know? 'Tis you under that shiny dome, isn't it?"

He shook Kurt's hand. "Hammel, here. Nibelheim. You've grown some skin on your head since I saw you last."

Offended, Kurt demanded: "Who the hell's in charge here?"

Captain Hammel laughed. "The Russkies." Pointing skyward, he added: "The Amis and Brits take turns too, d'ya know?"

"Where's the Führer?"

Hammel pointed down.

"With Satan," lisped his blond friend. "Where he belongs."

Ignoring her, Hammel expounded: "This here garden is honeycombed with bunkers and tunnels, d'ya know? Once the Führer went underground all the rats in the other ministries started digging toward him. They only come out at night to get drunk and grab a little action, d'ya see?" He pinched the blond so she yelped. "This here's Elisabeth." He patted the brunette. "And here's my friend Gita. But I'm a generous man, d'ya know?" He nudged Gita off the bench. A heavy-set girl with dark hair braided in coils and the shadow of a mustache, she offered a buck-toothed smile, then jiggled toward Kurt in a way intended to be seductive. Leaning so her heavy breasts grazed his chest, she took him by the ears then shoved her tongue into his mouth – a shocking pink intrusion. Kurt sucked on her lower lip. She bit through his top one. Electrified, Kurt yanked off his breeches, and minutes later they were rolling over the dewy grass while Hammel once more chased Elisabeth around the garden, sending peals of laughter from every bush.

As the day wore on, word seeped into the chancellery about the sack of Berlin.

Though a front had been formed on the Landwehr Kanal, the Red flag now flew from the Reichstag. Tempel-hof airport had been taken. A fierce battle was being fought at Potsdamer Platz three blocks away. Wedding, a working-class suburb with pre-war Bolshevik sympathies, was rumored to have welcomed the Russians with hand-made Red banners. Even in traditionally right-wing areas the resisters were meeting with local harassment. When the Home Guard attempted to blow up Halensee bridge, commuters begged them to spare it. Soldiers who set up a machine gun in front of an apartment had bricks tossed on them by the inhabitants who didn't want to attract a shelling.

Not only had the Russians arrived with their cows, horses and chickens, but they had bivouacked them in shops and dwellings in the city's core, turning the capital into an Augean stable of the sort Göring had pledged to clean up. Unable to understand toilets, they comman-deered them for everything from washing their feet to storing food, then became hostile when a pull of the cord caused a noisy swallow that finished off a pound of cheese. At the same time, they used every container in Berlin as a pisspot, and even relieved themselves like animals against posts.

No woman, no matter how sick or senile, was safe from the command, "Frau koom." Young girls were being hid-den in cupboards. Others were spotting their faces with lipstick to simulate scarlet fever or gouging their cheeks to create open sores.

While most of the chancellery women were terrified at the threat of rape, the stories motivated some to seduce German soldiers as if to inoculate themselves against vio-lations to come. As drunk as everyone else, Kurt entered into the frenzied mood, a byproduct of acute stress, even availing himself of Hitler's dentist's chair, which seemed to hold an erotic fascination for both Gita and Elisabeth who enjoyed being strapped in.

To sober up, he wandered the broad gravel paths of the chancellery garden, flanked at intervals with sculptures. Through the trees to his left he could see flashes of the yellow marble façade of the chancellery: columns, arcades, cornices and pilasters. Here was the grave of Bismarck's pet dog and his favorite horse. Centuries-old potting sheds, ponds and pavilions. A world hidden from the street, a world he was just beginning to know. Even now, when it was almost over, he could feel a sense of awe that he, a boy from the coal mines of the Ruhr, could have come so far.

A day and two nights without bombs had allowed much of the dust swirling around Berlin to settle. The three-quarter moon was silver instead of lime. Kurt sucked in the clear, cool air – Berliner Luft, the kind that was supposed to cure hangovers. Encountering the old city wall, with its sturdy watchtowers, he noticed a flash of light through what had seemed solid stone. Cautiously he approached. Where the fortification had been blasted by shells, the wall had been repaired by piling blocks rather than by cementing. The light on the other side revealed its chinks. Hearing a guttural murmur, Kurt crouched with his eye to the hole. In silhouette he saw what looked like a twenty-foot rectangular pillbox with a round tower. By the light of a lamp held by an SS officer, he watched a bent old man shuffle past. The hand on his walking stick was palsied, and he lurched with each step. Though the lamp cast a bright glow, he complained about the darkness. "Can't you brighten that a little so I can see my feet? Surely in all of the Third Reich there must be one lamp that will let me see my feet."

As the old man reached Kurt's hole in the wall, Kurt caught a clear view of his face in the lamplight: a wrinkled yellow mask with fleshy folds running from a putty nose to the pursed mouth under a square mustache. Bags hung below the droopy eyes, filmy like peeled grapes.

Kurt recognized the dog before the man. "Heel, Blondi. Heel, obey!"

April 30, 4 p.m. For two days Kurt had lived in the chancellery, sunk in lethargy, unable to mobilize his

energy for escape. Despair hung like a penance over everyone, and many bragged about purchasing cyanide cap-
sules, a hot item on the chancellery black market. To stay
or go, what did it matter? To go where? Kurt had a long
memory of the British and French after World War I.
Why should he regard them as his rescuers?

Once this war had been the story of countries lost and
won, then cities, then suburbs. Now they were down to
streets and plazas. Ninety percent of Berlin's core had
been demolished, with Bradenburger Tor and the Reichstag left as monuments. Germany, it was rumored, was to
be turned into a potato field.

While those in the chancellery reminisced lugubriously
about the good old days, half of Berlin's women had been
raped, many repeatedly. Some had developed coded
knocks and whistles so they knew whether to answer the
door or hide. Others had formed liaisons with Ivans who
would protect and feed them – a reversion to caveman
ethics.

Berlin was now on Moscow time. The Reichsmark had
been scrapped and the Russians were printing their own
money. Censorship and curfews had been imposed. A new
bureaucracy was issuing identity cards, ration books,
work slips. Berlin had another slogan: Ukas Stalinas, by
order of Stalin.

Against all this: Hitler Youth were still defending Frey
bridge over the Havel, and single kids whose Adam's
apples hadn't yet ripened were throwing themselves with
their bazookas into the paths of Soviet tanks and warning: "Halt, I've got you surrounded."

As Kurt and Hammel shared a cigarette, squatting on
the floor of an elegant salon where a perpetual party was
in progress, Hammel confided: "I don't intend leaving
here alive." He patted his Luger. "One bullet left. That's
not much for a few million Russians, but it's enough for
my little brain, d'ya hear?"

"You're a fool," protested Kurt. "We can escape
through the U-Bahn if we're lucky. A bunch broke out last

night. We should have gone with them. They were ducking down at the Tiergarten and coming out at the Havel river."

"But don't ya see? You've got engineer's papers. Prospects. D'ya think I could go back to bein' a pig farmer?"

"It's a lot better than being dead," insisted Kurt. "I've already used the chancellery black market to convert most of my loot into American bucks and cigarettes. We can buy false identity papers at the black market in Brandenburger Tor."

Shaking his head, Hammel whispered: "I hate to mention it, but I'm not sure I can live with what I done, ya know? I've already begun remembering too many things I don't want to. I'm a sensitive person. I really didn't like killin' even those little piggies. I hated their squeal and their trusting eyes, d'ya see?" He shuddered. "I'm spooked if I get out of here, even if they don't put me in a camp. I'm spooked and I know it."

Tensely Kurt struggled to counter and discredit the same morbid thoughts he found in himself. He had counted on Hammel's animal instincts to arouse his own, which was why he was willing to stake him. "Don't be an asshole! The Brits and Amis aren't going to be interested in our necks when they get their hands on the swine who gave us our orders. We only –"

Kurt stopped talking, his attention caught by a captain in the Adolf Hitler Honor Guard who had mounted a dais and was tolling a handbell. Soon everyone in the room was poised in silent expectation.

Clearing his throat, the captain announced: "At three o'clock this afternoon, our Führer, Adolf Hitler, fell for Germany, fighting to his last breath against Bolshevism."

A long hush blended into a low wail that rose and peaked as the women in the room wordlessly poured out their grief. Instinctively, Kurt took out his flute and played "Deutschland, Deutschland Uber Alles" while all stood at attention, tears streaming. As the sad triumphant notes swelled, he was not thinking of the palsied and quer-

ulous old man who stumbled about the broken chancellery garden calling for light. He was thinking of the
Führer on the night of the seizure of power twelve years
ago as he leaned from a casement window in this building,
hatless, radiating light, arms reached into the chilly night
as if to embrace the torch-bearing marchers as they
cheered and saluted him in their tens of thousands.

"Now someone is going to look after us!"

"Now the uncertainty and the rottenness will end!"

"Now there will be jobs and bread!"

"Now there is honor!"

*"Now he has come. Now we are safe. Now he will save
us. HE WILL SAVE US!"*

The room erupted. "Sieg Heil! Sieg Heil! Sieg Heil!"

The chancellery party moved into high gear. A loudspeaker attached to the sound system of the SS canteen
blared a never-ending concert of international hits – "In
the Mood," "Tipperary," "The Lambeth Walk," the German version of the "Beer Barrel Polka" which had origi-
nated as a Czech pop tune, and the hauntingly evocative
French melody:

> "Everything passes, everything has its day.
> After every December comes another May . . ."

In the midst of revelry, Kurt quietly prepared himself
for a post-midnight breakout. The spell binding him to
this place was broken. He was a free man.

May 1, 2:30 a.m. Kurt Schmidt crawls through a shell
hole blasted in the side of the chancellery, now listing to
starboard like a sinking ship of state. He is wearing a dress
once belonging to Gita, tennis shoes scrounged from a
potting shed and his gray blanket fashioned into a hooded
cloak. In his shopping bags he carries men's slacks and
shirt, U.S. money and cigarettes, water and a modest
cache of food, a few treasures from the baron's villa, a

flashlight, extra batteries, a knife, rope, his revolver and ammunition.

The air is cold and clammy with dust that clings to the nostrils like wet cement. An inversion has suffocated Berlin with a pale yellow cloud. Kurt doesn't mind. The foul mist inhibits visibility and may keep the Russkies inside raping women. It also provides a reason for covering his face.

He can hear shelling, perhaps five miles away, and notices the occasional crimson flash. Otherwise all's well as he peers, eyes watering, through the fog, looking for familiar landmarks as the moon glides in and out of clouds that stain it to blood red and then burnt orange. After sprinting along Wilhelm Strasse, he must cross Wilhelm Platz to seek cover at Kaiserhof station – about a hundred and fifty yards away. His first concern is not the Russians but Hitler's Honor Guard. Fanaticism in Berlin these days runs inverse to age. Will some beardless savage with a voice like a choir boy's take a pot shot at him?

Gripping his shopping bags under his armpits, Kurt dashes through the pre-dawn darkness. He hears guns being cocked all around him, but instead of fire is greeted with: "Good luck, brother."

Ducking into the Kaiserhof station, Kurt crouches against a wall and listens. Nothing but his own raspy breathing. As his eyes adjust, he sees a black hole where the stairs to the U-Bahn should be. Since turning on his flashlight is out of the question, he gropes his way around a jagged granite chute, the result of Russian dynamite. How deep is it? Would he break a leg if he jumped? Has the station been flooded? Was the lethal third rail still activated? Is the tube booby-trapped?

As a burrowing animal, Kurt is tempted to go to earth here, but he is faced with too many unknowns. The Tiergarten route is riskier, because it means showing himself to the Russians, but it heads due west and affords a chance to hire a cellar kid as a guide.

Vaulting from pillar to boulder to bush, Kurt sprints

west on Voss Strasse to the Tiergarten, then north toward Brandenburger Tor – a tall gray shadow in a city that is supposed to have only dumpy olive-brown ones. Despite the danger, he is thrilled to be on his way, to be faced with problems that can be solved by nerve, stealth and strength. Three times he sees Russian guards but none is so foolish as to dare the park after nightfall. Curling in his gray blanket, he snoozes like a cat, with ears turned on radar alert.

Kurt hears roosters crow as the sun slowly rises over charred hulks and dead ashes. Soon the Tiergarten teems with women headed toward Brandenburger Tor. In their mended sweaters and shoes tied with rope they are no better dressed than he. About a third have kerchiefs over their noses and mouths – especially the pretty young ones. At the edge of the park he sees Russians patrolling in their muddy uniforms, rifles slung over their shoulders, but none ventures into the park.

Kurt fixes his holster under his arm, concealed by his gray cloak: If a Russian wants to arrest him, he'll die for it. Tying his kerchief around his face, he feels stubble but knows that hardly matters. His plan depends on his not attracting attention. As soon as he hears the Russian word "stoy," meaning "stop," the masquerade is over.

Sliding from the bush, Kurt joins the rush of women, dropping his shoulders, lowering his head and cutting his stride. As he hoped, Pariser Platz beside Brandenburger Tor is crowded. What strikes him first is the number of animals these conquerors have brought – hens, roosters, goats, cows, even a pig or two. The horses are beautiful beasts, better groomed than their owners, but the stench of excrement is gagging. Berlin is a human and animal barnyard.

Women in rubble brigades pass buckets of debris to carts running on narrow-gauge tracks imported from the Ruhr. Other women and children line up for water, bread, soup, ration cards, registration. Fortunately for Kurt, most Russian soldiers are gleefully looting – not furtively but Ukas Stalinas. Anything that can be uprooted is being loaded into vans – office equipment, cars, safes, radios, bathtubs, appliances, even phone booths with the severed cords dangling.

Too late, Kurt notices a Russian soldier five yards ahead commandeering pedestrians to load.

"Stoy!"

Kurt freezes. He stares at the Russian with his rifle slung over his shoulder, wearing a copper Stalingrad medal with multi-colored ribbons. As their eyes lock, Kurt's hand moves to his revolver.

He knows the Russian has penetrated his disguise and he telegraphs the message: Arrest me and I'll kill you.

A second soldier joins the first. Sizing up the situation, he turns his back and strolls away. Another clear message: Don't bother me and I won't bother you.

This breaks the tension. "Schnell, schnell, hurry, hurry," orders the first soldier, gesturing for Kurt to be off.

Kurt slides back into the crowd, one drop of water in a stream. Why should they risk their lives tangling with an armed and desperate Nazi on the last day of war? They have more reason than Kurt to want to survive. Berlin is like Paris, with booty for the plucking.

Brandenburger Tor stands four-square, as reassuringly German as a plate of bratwurst and sauerkraut. With its broad artery turned into a market, this classical edifice is closer to its original function: a toll gate for a mercantile city. All goods still available can be purchased here, openly hawked and under the cloak.

Amidst hardware and secondhand clothes, Kurt finds Russian textbooks and Red flags crudely manufactured from Nazi banners with stars, hammer and sickle sewn from a yellow blouse or tablecloth. Some of Berlin's seamstresses, with fingers as versatile as their loyalties, have also created American flags with differing numbers of stars.

Kurt sidles up to a hawker whom he's watched slip British pounds from a book she's supposed to be sizing up for barter. While pretending to examine a dinted tea kettle, he whispers: "You, mother. I need a kellerkind."

Showing no surprise at his masculine voice, she responds: "None left. There's more of you down in them sewers than rats."

Kurt flashes a couple of American bills.

Her interest sharpens. "Want a gold star? One buck U.S."

He sneers. "Keep them for making your Russian flags."

Fanning her greed, he slips a Lucky Strike into the spout of the tea kettle. "Get me a kellerkind." Nastily, he adds: "Schnell, schnell! I'll be in this square for thirty minutes."

Milling with the crowd, Kurt checks notice boards. A Communist paper has appeared, entitled *Berliner Zeitung*. After a list of proclamations and ordinances, he reads: "The Commandant of the city has ordered nightclubs and cafés to be reopened. Bands may play on Sunday. The populace must realize the criminal Hitler war is over. Berliners, return to joyousness! The Red Army has liberated you from the horrors of war! After work, pursue your pleasure."

As Kurt absorbs this, he notices a crowd collect around Brandenburger Tor. Glimpsing a statuesque peroxide blond in red satin dress and feather boa, he comes to the startling conclusion that a theater troupe is taking the commandant at his word by using the Tor as a stage. Irresistibly he is drawn to the edge of the crowd.

"Hello, Berliners. Don't be bashful," calls the blond, gesturing for everyone to move in closer.

"It's been a long time. I tried to phone but the Russkies carried off the booth. I tried to write but my arm was too stiff from saluting. Remember that big black Mercedes I told you about driving through the streets of Berlin with Nazis in it? Well, I checked their papers. They weren't Nazis after all. They were Wehrmacht privates. Had been for weeks."

Fixing on a half-dozen Russian soldiers drawn by duty and curiosity, Frau Fuchs flexes her tattooed biceps. "Now don't drool, boys. I just look defenseless. I got these as a Bund deutscher Mädchen fighting off the advances of Hitler Youth. Now they want me to pose with my fist clenched for Communist posters. I said: 'If you don't mind, boys, I think I'll wait and see what the Amis will pay me to hold the torch for the Statue of Liberty.'"

She bangs one of the pillars of the Tor. "I advised Frederick the Great to build this thing three hundred miles farther west. If he'd listened to me, we'd all be smoking Camels instead of sleeping with donkeys."

Unable to follow the fast delivery, the Russians grin as the crowd laughs, convinced this must be part of Berlin's fabled night life, as it was.

"Do any of you Russians have the time?"

When the soldiers look puzzled, Frau Fuchs taps her wrist. "Watch. Time."

Catching on, one reveals his arm banded with half a dozen watches.

"Why does a Russian wear six watches at once?" Frau Fuchs asks. She answers: "Because he couldn't find seven."

She asks: "What's the difference between Berlin time and Moscow time?" She answers: "About five hundred years, but give these Ivans a thousand and I'm sure they'll catch up.

"Ahh, it's not so bad. Some things are even better: We women no longer have to look over our shoulders when we make dangerous remarks. . . . Just under our skirts.

"I'm sorry, I'm sorry. I shouldn't make jokes about a serious thing like rape. The other day my friend Gretchen came staggering out of the Tiergarten, bruised and naked. Her husband, in bed with a broken fingernail, demanded:

'Who did this to you? I'd beat him up if my fingernail weren't so sore.'

" 'It wasn't Ivan,' explained Gretchen. 'It was a pack of German seamstresses making Red flags. I was wearing a yellow blouse.'

"Did I tell you? I was in the part of the Adlon that's still standing when a big Red Russian staggered down the steps with a bathtub on his back. 'Where are you going with that?' demanded the clerk. Said Big Red: 'My German Fräulein told me I should take a bath.'

"But don't get depressed. All this is temporary. Just yesterday I saw the Hitler Youth erecting a blockade at Leipziger and Friedrich – a ton of alphabet blocks and about the same number of rattles. I said: 'That will last about two hours and two seconds – two hours while the Russkies roll on the ground laughing, and two seconds while they roll through it.'

"How do I know all these things? Where do I get my information? By keeping my ear to the ground." She bends, hand cupped. "I was talking to a guy down there – a Dr. G. Any of you know a Dr. G? Yeah, well he's down there like I said, looking through the flames, and he says: 'Don't worry. This next war's ours. We've got them outnumbered ten thousand to one. I've been here twenty-four hours and all I've seen are Nazis.'

"But tell me seriously, folks, why are we Germans always the last to know? I want the answer to that one because I think it's important. Why doesn't anyone ever tell us the truth? During the First War, I went to the post office to mail a letter and the caretaker said: 'You'll have to come back next week. It's a holiday. We're celebrating a big victory.' Next time I went back, he told me: 'I'm sorry, but we've closed the post office again. We're celebrating another great victory.' The third time, I could see the CLOSED sign, so I asked: 'Which victory are we celebrating today?' He replied: 'Oh, didn't you hear? We lost the war.'

"Meine Damen, I want you to be honest with me.

Didn't I warn you years ago this was going to happen?
Didn't I tell you: 'Don't vote for a man who hangs his
toothbrush under his nose'? You wouldn't listen, and now
what have you done?" Pointing to a picture of Stalin:
"You've got yourself a guy with a bigger toothbrush! Am
I being unfair? Before the Russians shelled us, they should
have taken a straw vote. Raise your hands now, how many
did *not* vote for Stalin in the last election?"

No one raises a hand.

"All right, how many *did* vote for the Bolsheviks in the
last election?"

A forest of hands, all but the Russians, who become
nervous thinking this may be the Nazi Sieg Heil.

Raising her hand with the Communist clenched fist
salute, Frau Fuchs shouts: "This is how deep we're in the
shit!"

As Frau Fuchs backs into the Doric columns of Brandenburger Tor, blowing kisses, a boy in a tuxedo several
sizes too large sets a red stool on the cobbles. Holding a
musical saw between his legs, he strokes it with a resined
bow, producing a weird and wailing vibrato that grows
deeper and more poignant the more he straightens the
saw.

Pushing to the front of the crowd, Kurt knows: not a
boy but a woman with cropped copper hair, wearing a
mustache smudge, now reclaimed for comedy. Accompanied on the bass drum by an old man in bits and pieces of
World War I uniforms, she captures the melancholy Kurt
and other Berliners carry deep in their souls:

> "Berlin, Berlin, I hardly recognize you.
> Where is your reckless light heart?
> Where are the good old songs?
> You seem desolate and lost."

And then:

> "When morning comes and God is willing,
> We shall awaken once again."

Without taking a bow, Carmel Kohl slips into the shadows of Brandenburger Tor. Frau Fuchs wraps a gray blanket around her, not unlike Kurt's own. Fritz the midget hands her an infant swaddled in white.

As Kurt stares, making his calculations, he feels a sharp tug on his cloak. It's a kellerkind – the one with the withered arm he saw at the Zoo. "Underground express!"

With one long look back at Brandenburger Tor, Kurt follows the urchin to the Tiergarten.

Halfway into the park, the kellerkind halts, falls to his knees, then rolls back a hunk of grass like the kind used to sod cemetery plots. Underneath is a wood circle a yard wide. Kurt sees a black hole that seems to go down forever. He smells the stink of polluted water.

Grinning, the kid explains: "We have to wade through slime for half a mile. Then I have a boat. It's two miles after that before we connect with the U-Bahn. All the subway entrances have been blasted and booby-trapped. This is the only way left."

Looking up into the sky, Kurt sees a wheel of birds, perhaps ten thousand – crows, kestrels, magpies, ravens, at last driven crazy by phosphorescent bombs that turn night into day, that inflame and denude their roosting and feeding sites. Enraged, they have begun to attack each other, breaking wings, pecking out eyes, spinning in a black pinwheel till they fall from their wounds or in exhaustion. Already the ground is littered with corpses.

That's the last sight Kurt Schmidt sees as he climbs down into the sewer, those crazy birds swirling around the sun.

Afterword

*B*ERLIN SOLSTICE is a work of the imagination in which the author has closely adhered to the historical record. Minor liberties have been taken in blending the factual with the fictional and in recasting events so as to avoid unintentional biography. Where real characters are introduced, the author has striven for accuracy, though it must be remembered that even eyewitnesses sometimes differ sharply in their recollections.

On only a few occasions has the author deliberately changed the known facts. According to most historians, the assassination of Reinhard Heydrich was conducted by two Czech agents trained by the British government, working with the Czech resistance and the Czech government-in-exile. On the day of the ambush, Heydrich was accompanied only by his chauffeur, who performed many of the actions here fictionally attributed to the invented character Kurt Schmidt. Similarly, Reinhard Heydrich was not known to have shot a National Socialist demonstrator early in his career, as described in Part II, though impulsive acts of bravado were consistent with his personality.

The loose network of Nazi resisters, depicted in *Berlin Solstice* under the name of White Rose, bears little resemblance to the real group of resisters centered on Munich University, who actually worked under that name. The fictional group is closer in concept to the conspiracy of aristocrats and officers who attempted to assassinate Hitler on July 20, 1944. In using the historic name White Rose, the author wishes to pay tribute to all Germans who struggled against the tide of their country's history.

No fictional characters are knowingly based on the lives and personalities of real people, and none are an amalgam of real persons, though actual biographical incidents have sometimes been used, in whole or in part, to authenticate the fictional characters. For example, the suicide of Christian Jürgens and his wife, Renate, both inventions of the author, was suggested by the tragic fate of German actor Joachim Gottschalk, married to a Jewish woman whom he refused to divorce despite Nazi pressure. When he learned his wife and their child were to be arrested for eastern transport, he killed them both, and then himself. Comedian Weiss Ferdl, star of the Platzl in Munich, was imprisoned for several months in Dachau for telling the joke about the Nazis in the black Mercedes, here attributed to the fictional character Frau Fuchs. When released, he made the same rejoinder as she. Frau Fuchs' slogan, "This is how deep we are in shit," was part of the repertoire of satirist Werner Finck, who worked at the Katakombe in Berlin. Yet in no way is the life or personality of Frau Fuchs based on Ferdl or Finck, or on any other real person.

The above illustrations should alert the reader to the fact that it is likely to be the seemingly most far-fetched incidents and dialogue in *Berlin Solstice* that are the most authentic.